BIL

11 JUL 2015

-9 NOV 2015

D0766071

Please return this book on or before the date shown above. To renew go to www.essex.gov.uk/libraries, ring 0845 603 7628 or go to any Essex library.

Essex County Council

Proudly Published by Snowbooks in 2014

Snowbooks Ltd.
email: info@snowbooks.com

www.snowbooks.com

British Library Cataloguing in Publication Data
A catalogue record for this book is available from the
British Library.

Paperback ISBN 978-1909679-97-9
Ebook ISBN 978-1909679-29-0

MORNINGSTAR

Sarah Bryant

To my angels, Nuala and Finn.

Between two worlds life hovers like a star...
— *Lord Byron*

PROLOGUE

11 JUNE

*She stood on the ramparts of the castle under a black sky –
not a night sky, but a vast, terrible void from which every vestige
of light had been erased. Beneath it the city was a jumble of
broken buildings, glowing intermittently with sickly light. Dark
shapes crawled among the ruins like ants; doing what, she
couldn't tell. She didn't want to know.*

"It's time."

*The voice was calm, melodious and utterly, horrifyingly
inhuman. Instinctively, she cringed away from it, though she
knew just as certainly that there was no escape from the doom
embodied in its perfect timbre. She clutched at the stone wall
on which her hands rested, as if clinging to it could subvert that
doom.*

*"Turn around, Sophia," he said, this time with a flicker of
impatience.*

*She wanted to refuse, to defy him, but she couldn't make her
voice work. All she knew was that she couldn't turn around; that
if she did, she would be faced with a horror that would break her.
Her fingers scrabbled at the dry stone, seeking purchase, but it
crumbled away every time she got a decent grip.*

Then his hand fell on her shoulder, and she froze, her skin crawling, because it wasn't a human hand; no construct of blood and bone, but something as cold and alien as his voice. Metal and leather, cogs and pistons. He didn't quite grip hard enough to hurt her, but it was hard enough to assure her that she couldn't resist him.

He turned her around. Her eyes skittered over the forms of his brethren, who formed a semi-circle around them, and then up at her captor. His eyes met hers, devoid of colour or compassion.

"It's time to choose," he said.

"No," she answered, finding her voice at last.

"If you don't choose, I'll kill them both."

At last, she looked down, and there they were, looking back at her, as she'd known they would be: skin and bone, pale and beaten, their clothes worn to rags and their hands bound behind them. Lucas was bad, his hunger-sharp cheekbones and pleading dark eyes dredging memories of witches and misery. But the other one – the one she couldn't name – was worse. His June-blue eyes were too bright in his battered face and fixed on her in an accusation of a betrayal she couldn't remember.

It should have been easy. Lucas was her beloved; no one meant more to her, and a world without him in it was unimaginable. And yet, those blue eyes haunted her, nipping at her heels with a guilt she couldn't name.

"How can I choose between them?"

She didn't realize that she'd spoken the words out loud until her captor answered, "Then they both die."

"No!"

"Then choose."

"I can't...I can't..."

Quicker than she could see, a blade shot out of his mechanical arm, and he slit the prisoners' throats. They fell together into a pool of mingled blood. She cried out, lunged for them, but they were already gone, their eyes empty and staring. She lifted her hands, dripping with blood, and began to scream and then his arms were around her, warm and living, his lips to her cheek as he whispered reassurances.

"Lucas," she sobbed, "they killed you. They killed you and…and…"

"No one killed me, Sophie," he said, stroking her hair. "It was just a dream."

"A dream," she repeated. Slowly, the terrible images faded, and she was back in their bed, in their room with its ladders of books climbing the walls, and there were no monsters, no demons with metal arms and mechanical knives. There was only Lucas, who she loved, and who would never let a white-faced demon make her choose. And so she let him sooth her, though she was aware, as she slipped back into sleep, that the blue eyes still watched her.

CHAPTER 1

11 JUNE
DUBLIN, IRELAND

Esther woke screaming, her cries drowning out the bells ringing the call to Lauds. The eyes of the demon blazed in her mind like sun through ice. He hadn't said a word. He hadn't needed to. In his eyes, Esther could see every city he'd raze, every sea he'd set to boiling and the rivers of blood that would flow from the clenched fist of his leather-and-metal arm, while the girl in the tattered white dress and gossamer wings danced gleefully on the margins.

"Stop it!" Sister Agnes roared, slamming through the door with her pet goblin, Gasz, on her heels. It was a horrible, squat, green, slit-eyed thing that always made faces and lewd gestures at Esther from behind the nun's back, though it was the model of decorum whenever she was looking.

Faced with the nun's florid, furious countenance and the goblin's knowing grin, Esther's screams faded to whimpers. Sister Agnes took Esther's shoulders in a vice-like grip and shook her until she was silent, but Esther couldn't suppress the shudders that ran through her body at the nun's touch. Sister Agnes was peering closely into her face, looking, no doubt, for some sign of the evil she was certain Esther harboured.

"More dreams of murderous angels, I suppose?" she asked. Esther didn't answer, but she was sure that Sister Agnes read the truth in her eyes. *Eyes like an open book*, her father used to say, in a time so distant, a world so different from the one in which Esther now lived that sometimes she almost believed that it had never been.

Don't, she told herself. *You'll go mad that way.*

"I don't think they're angels, Sister," she answered softly.

"White robes?" Sister Agnes sneered. "Wings on their backs?" She shook her head. "No, Esther Madden: you are a wicked girl with a wicked soul, and your dreams are sacrilege."

Esther knew that there was no answer to that. She'd tried and failed to explain the dreams, the doom they portended and whose path everyone she knew was blindly treading. It wasn't particularly surprising that her mother hadn't believed her: she saw only what suited her, and if she could tune out the six children who went hungry while she drank, it was hardly surprising that she'd ignore the imminent end of the world.

But the nuns' disbelief had been a bitter blow. Esther had been certain that an order that called itself the Sisters of Charity would at least hear her out, and possibly help her make sense of what was happening. Three months on, though, it was hard to believe she'd ever had such naïve certainty. Telling the truth had got her nowhere but the cell where she was now locked; prayers and pleas had earned her nothing but beatings.

So, now, she kept her mouth shut, looking down at her hands clenched in her lap, thin and white except for the purplish threadwork of veins brought out by the room's sepulchral chill. The bells had fallen silent. Sister Agnes looked at her for another long moment, and then she said, "Get up, get dressed, or you'll be late for mass. And don't dawdle – Gasz will be waiting." She turned to go and shut the door behind her, the goblin on her heels.

Esther got out of bed. She pulled the flimsy nightgown over

her head and shoved it under her pillow, quickly tidying the bedclothes afterward. Then she pulled on the knitted, one-piece undergarment that still felt like a form of torture, even after so many months, and dropped the ugly grey dress over her head. She couldn't have come up with a less attractive design if she'd tried: shapeless bodice, straight, short sleeves, wide, high waist and a hemline that hit just under the knee. She pulled on greying white knee socks and black, lace-up shoes, a black cardigan that did little against the chill. Last, she picked up the comb from its place next to the battered Bible on the table beside the bed. They'd forbidden her a mirror (though whether to discourage vanity or some occult experiment, she had no idea) so she combed her hair by the faint reflection in the window.

In the glass, her long, light-brown hair and pale grey eyes were as colourless as the sky beyond, and as insubstantial as she felt. Esther set the comb on the windowsill and looked down at the street below. It was grey and slicked with the past night's rain. As she watched, an ancient, rusty car – the only kind that still existed – grumbled around the corner, blaring its horn at the horse-drawn carts and pedestrians crowding the street. A horse spooked and reared, upsetting its cart and spilling potatoes everywhere. The car's driver, a spikey-headed spriggan in a top hat, who had no doubt stolen both hat and car, laughed at the chaos as it blasted past. More of its kind hung out the windows, grinning and gabbling at the flustered humans they left in their wake. Sighing, Esther turned away. Though unpleasant, the scene was nothing out of the ordinary since the Change.

The Change. Esther wished she had a better name for it. She wished she had even an inkling of an explanation. All she had, though, was the memory of a life very different from the one she was now living, and the certainty that this strange new reality was the precursor to something horrific.

A hard rapping on the door made her jump. Esther's heart fluttered in response. She opened the brown glass bottle resting on the bedside table, tipped out two tablets and swallowed them. Then she picked up her black bakelite rosary, dropped it over her head, and opened the door. Gasz had rearranged his features into a grotesque jumble, no doubt in an attempt to provoke an outburst. Esther turned down the corridor toward the chapel, refusing to look at the creature scuttling beside her.

Esther lived in the nuns' wing. Each of the sisters had her own small cell of a room, like the one where Esther slept, except that Esther's cell was part of her punishment. At first she'd been put in one of the dormitories with the other girls, but her screams had awakened them night after night, and they were too curious about the cause of them for the nuns' liking. Bad enough to have one girl spouting blasphemy; the Sisters couldn't risk an epidemic.

When they reached the chapel, Gasz disappeared up the stairs to the organ loft – his kind weren't allowed into the main body of the church. As usual, Esther turned away from the pews where the other girls were assembled, toward the row of narrow wooden benches along the left wall where the nuns sat, each separated from the next by a carved partition. Esther sat down, focusing again on the hands in her lap so that she wouldn't have to look at the altar's painted saints. Their hard, crystalline beauty was too much like the demons' for her comfort.

When the priest began to speak, Esther relaxed slightly. The familiarity of the ritual was soothing, though she no longer believed in the words. The masses were one of a handful of things that hadn't changed from the world she remembered, and they made reality feel a little less awful, her task a little less hopeless. Because Esther was in no doubt that she had been tasked. She had to make the others see what was happening, make them stop it before the demons came and destroyed them all.

How, though, remained beyond her. She thought about it as she went through the motions of the service, mouthing the words of the hymn and letting her mind drift during the readings of the psalms and the canticle. Part of the problem was that there had been no warning, no time to prepare. The day before the Change had been an ordinary one, beginning with waking her mother from her fractious alcoholic doze, ending with trying to soothe the baby, who was teething, to sleep.

In the end, Esther had taken him into her own bed in her tiny, windowless box-room. She'd fallen asleep to the rhythm of the baby's gentle breathing, underscored by a tower-estate chorus of traffic and sirens and drunken men shouting on the stairs. She'd awakened to a world gone mad. The baby was no longer beside her, but wailing in a funereal black perambulator with large, spindly wheels, parked just outside the door of her room. The digital clock-radio on her bedside table had become an old wind-up alarm clock with two metal bells, and her cheap fibreboard bed had turned to chipped wrought iron.

She'd picked up the baby, rushed to the next room to find her little sisters buttoning each other into drab, smock-like dresses as if they'd worn them all their lives, and brushing their short bobs, which had been long plaits when they went to sleep the evening before. For a time Esther just stared at them, wondering if she was dreaming, or insane, or if she'd died in the night and awakened in some kind of purgatory. She went back to her room, sat down, shut her eyes tightly and prayed, but when she opened them again nothing had changed. Whatever had happened to the world she knew, this new one was apparently here to stay.

Her first mistake had been assuming that everyone else would remember the other one, as she did. When she went back to her sisters' room and asked them what had happened in the night, they looked at her with varying degrees of puzzlement. Nine-year-old Martha, always the most practical, finally said, "Well, Dad brought bacon for tea – but you ate it, too."

Esther blinked at her in shock for a moment before blurting, "Dad is dead!"

Martha's shock was just as apparent. "That isn't funny, Esther," she said.

Esther handed her the baby and ran into the kitchen, where her mother stood at the stove frying bread and humming a hymn. For once she appeared sober, though she was wearing an odd, dumpy dress, high-heeled Victorian buttoned boots and a spotted headscarf that reminded Esther of posters from the Second World War. But that wasn't what stopped her in her tracks, and had her reaching for the worktop for support as the room tipped and wheeled around her. It was her father, sitting at the table with a mug of black tea in one hand and a newspaper in the other, as he'd done every morning from the time she was aware of it until the day he died.

"Daddy?" she choked out, her throat tight with tears.

"Esther, *mo chroí,*" he said, looking up at her with warm blue eyes and the smile she'd almost forgotten. "Why are you crying, my girl?"

"I thought…I thought…" She couldn't speak the words, couldn't tell him that as far as she knew, he'd been dead three years, killed when a section of scaffolding collapsed on a building project where he worked as a foreman. "I had a terrible dream," she answered at last.

"Well, that's no excuse to be standing there in your underclothes!" her mother said, frowning at her as she put a plate of breakfast in front of her father.

Esther looked down at herself, and found that the t-shirt and tracksuit bottoms she'd gone to sleep in had been replaced by a scratchy woollen vest top and shorts. The sight of the strange clothes jolted her back to the present. "Mam…Dad… has something happened?"

Her father looked at her, surprised and puzzled. Her mother muttered, "Not unless you mean the bloody king putting up the price of tea again."

"What king?" Esther said, the world reeling again.

"Charles," her father said, his smile gone and his eyes worried. "Unless you know something I don't?"

"No…I just…" Except she had no idea what to say next.

"What's wrong with you, girl?" her mother asked.

"Are you ill?" her father said, pushing his plate aside and coming to feel her forehead.

"I…" Esther began, knowing she had to make a difficult decision, and quickly: tell the truth and hope it jogged her parents' memories, or play along until she figured out what was going on and how, hopefully, to reverse it.

She'd chosen wrong. Attempting to explain what had happened since she'd gone to bed the night before had done nothing but convince her parents that she was delusional. Later, when Esther went out to school and then came immediately back, hysterical at having discovered mythical creatures walking quite naturally among humans in broad daylight, her parents quietly agreed that she'd lost her reason. After that, she wasn't allowed out much, and never on her own.

Even then, her father had held onto the belief that her madness was temporary. But her mother had become convinced that her problem was more sinister than that. As soon as she heard about the dream demon with the clockwork arm and the eyes full of ruin, she had called in the local priest. He had examined Esther and then spoken to her parents in low tones about possession and a soul compromised by evil, and the danger it posed to the other children. In the end, even her father's love couldn't save her. Under her mother's pressure, he'd broken down and signed the papers releasing her into the care of the Sisters of Charity and their School for the Rehabilitation of Wayward Young Women.

The title still made Esther smile, if bitterly. She had always been a good girl. The things her classmates had done to earn their places at the school horrified her. And yet she was the one who was kept under lock and key, as a danger to the others. She had a nun to guard her every moment of the day – from chapel to classes to the hard hours of "remedial" labour in the laundry – to make sure she didn't so much as look askance at the other students.

Someone jabbed an elbow into her ribs, interrupting her reverie. Esther flinched, glancing up at the hard eyes of the nun beside her. The woman shook a prayer book in her face, letting Esther know that she was aware her attention had lapsed. They'd moved on to the responsory. Hastily Esther fumbled for the correct page in the book, and then mumbled the responses to the priest along with the others. She managed to pay attention through the rest of the service, breathing a sigh of relief at the final "Amen".

"Not you, Esther," Sister Agnes said sharply, grabbing her arm as she turned to leave the chapel.

"What is it, Sister?"

"Father Xavier has asked that you make confession this morning."

"But it was Father Paul who said the mass."

"Don't contradict me, girl! Father Xavier came along specially, to hear you confess." Sister Agnes spoke with a tone of satisfaction and a glint in her eye that told Esther she'd been behind this exception.

Inwardly, Esther shuddered. She had hated confession even before the Change, but now she despised it. Part of the problem was Father Xavier himself. He was the oldest of the priests who served the convent, but he wasn't beyond looking at the girls with an appraising eye, and he had a particular fondness for hearing confession. It always seemed to Esther that she could feel the priest's eagerness through the screen, as if for all his canting about sin, he secretly wanted her to be acting out the will of a demon. He certainly found it easy enough to twist her simple words into something sinister, and make penitence into a misery.

"I already confessed to him last night, after Vespers – " she began desperately.

"Aye, and you woke screaming blasphemy. I don't even like to think what you were dreaming about. Go." The nun pointed toward the confessional booths at the other side of the chapel.

Reluctantly, Esther opened the dark wooden door of the confessional and sat down on the hard, narrow bench. She could hear the priest breathing on the other side. She could feel him waiting. With a trembling hand, she crossed herself, and then, taking a deep breath, she said, "In the name of the Father, and of the Son, and of the Holy Spirit. My last confession was last night."

There was a long silence on the other side of the screen. She could still hear the priest breathing, but the sound had become stilted, erratic. There was a knock against the wall that separated them, hard enough to make the booth shudder. Alarmed, Esther stood up. Her hand was on the door when a strangled whisper came from the other side of the screen: "Wait!"

The priest still gasped and wheezed alarmingly. And yet, something in the choked word made Esther pause. Something that sounded like a plea, rather than an order. Reluctantly she sat back down, poised on the edge of the bench to run if her instinct proved false.

"Father?" she asked apprehensively.

The priest pressed his hands against the dividing screen. "Sophia?" It was the priest's voice, but it was so low, so close to both hope and despair that she couldn't believe she was speaking to the same crotchety man who doled out her daily penance.

"No, Father," she answered. "It's Esther."

"Esther?" he repeated. "What's your surname?" He spoke with an accent she couldn't place.

"Madden, Father," Esther answered reluctantly.

"No relation of a family named Creedon?"

"Not that I know of."

The priest let out a jagged sigh and lowered his hands from the screen. Esther knew that she should leave, that the priest had had some kind of turn and perhaps needed help. Yet a part of herself – the part she had tried so hard to suppress over her months with the Sisters of Charity – was whispering to her: *What if he isn't mad at all? What if this is the chance you've been waiting for?*

His next words seemed to confirm her thoughts. "Well, Esther Madden, can you tell me where I am?"

"You're in Northside."

"The north side of what?"

"Dublin," she answered, settling a little further back onto the bench. "At the convent of the Sisters of Charity." And then, because he seemed to be waiting for her to say more, "Ah... specifically, you're in a confessional booth in the chapel."

To her surprise, the priest let out a low, acid laugh. "Of course I am."

"Father?" Esther asked, poised again to go for help.

But she sat down again abruptly when the priest said, "I'm not your 'Father', Esther. My name is Theletos. I'm an aeon – "

"A what?"

"Kind of like an angel. I'm trying to save the world. But I'm finding it a bit difficult, as I'm currently incarcerated in the Deep, at the mercy of the daevas."

Most of what he'd said made no sense to Esther, but one phrase stood out, gleaming like a beacon on a night-shrouded sea: "Save the world?" she whispered. "From what?"

"From Hell, Esther," he said with bitter irony. "Because that's where it's headed, though no one appears to have noticed."

She swallowed, shut her eyes, and willed her voice to be steady. "*I've* noticed."

There was a pause, and then another jagged breath. "You mean...you know that everything's changed?"

"Yes."

"You remember the time before?"

"As clearly as I remember yesterday."

The priest – or Theletos – let out the breath he'd drawn. "What is the date, Esther?"

"The eleventh of June, I think."

"Ten days," he muttered. "It might just be long enough…"

"Father – I mean, Theletos – I have no idea what you're talking about."

"It doesn't matter," he answered, suddenly all grim efficiency. "You have to do something for me. You have to find a girl called Sophie Creedon, and tell her that unless she goes back to the Garden immediately, the world as you know it will end, and the human race will be enslaved to the daevas. And you have to do it before Midsummer."

"Why Midsummer?"

He sighed. "Because it's her birthday."

"Funny. Mine too…"

"Figures," the priest muttered.

"But I don't know any Sophie Creedon."

"I suppose she could go by a different name, now…" He paused, and then said, "Am I right in assuming that you have psychic talents?"

"I…I don't know. Sure, sometimes I dream things, or know them before they happen, like. But you'd be the first to call it a talent."

"Good enough," Theletos answered. "Put your hand on mine, Esther." He laid his hand on the screen again.

"Why?"

"Because it's the easiest way to explain."

Tentatively, Esther placed her hand against his, and then she gasped as a surge of energy flowed through her, along with a string of images. They moved so quickly that she only caught a few of them: a woman with green hair and silver eyes, a hole in the ground with a curved stairway leading into it, the face of the metal-armed demon and the one in the wings and wedding dress, and then a girl of about her own age, standing on a rocky sea-shore.

Here the flow stopped, giving her a clear view of the girl's face. It was heart-shaped and sweet, with a soft, sensitive mouth and wide, grey eyes very like her own, framed by thick dark hair. But there was something about her more striking than her beauty. A light surrounded her, a faint wash of pure, clear blue which Esther recognized as the light she saw sometimes around her own face in the mirror. Her aura – she knew that's what they were called, having once seen a man at a street fair who claimed to be able to photograph them.

She also knew that good Catholic girls weren't supposed to believe in them, let alone admit to seeing them, and so she never had. But despite that, she'd seen enough of them to know that they were as individual as the people they belonged to. No two were ever quite the same colour – except, apparently, hers and the one belonging to the girl on the beach.

"That's Sophie Creedon?" she said.

"Yes," Theletos answered.

"I've never seen her before. I'm sure she doesn't go to this school. Does she live in Dublin?"

"I don't know for certain, but I think she's more likely to be in Scotland – a village called Ardnasheen."

"Scotland! How am I meant to get to Scotland when the nuns don't even let me out the front door?"

A few moments passed in silence. Then, abruptly, the rosary that hung around Esther's neck dropped to the floor. When she bent to pick it up, the cross was gone, replaced by a key of the type that fit a Yale lock.

"That will open the front door," Theletos said. "The rest, I'm afraid, you'll have to sort out for yourself."

"But how did you – "

"There isn't time to explain. Just find Sophie and tell her what I said."

"And she'll believe me?"

Theletos sighed. "I hope so. If she doesn't, you'll have to make her."

"I haven't had much luck with that, so far."

"You have to try. I'm sorry, Esther. I can't keep the connection any longer – "

Abruptly, the man slumped against the screen. His face was clearly the priest's, and it was grey and lifeless, with dark patches round the eyes. He didn't seem to be breathing. Slipping the rosary back over her head and into the bodice of her dress, Esther opened the door. The chapel was empty, except for Sister Agnes, snoring in one of the back pews, and Gasz, who was drinking the communion wine, his back turned to her. Esther was tempted to make a run for the front door there and then, but she couldn't quite bring herself to abandon the priest in that state.

Her heart beginning to skip erratically, she opened the door to the other half of the confessional. Gingerly, she shook the man's still form. When he didn't respond, she took his wrist. It was still and cold, without a pulse. She thought about calling Sister Agnes, but she knew that the priest was past saving, and that if she sounded the alarm now, she would be blamed for whatever had happened to him. She would have no chance at all of escaping. So she closed the door again and then, composing herself, she shook Sister Agnes's shoulder.

The nun started awake. "You were long enough about it," she grumbled, heaving herself to her feet. Gasz returned to her side, swaying slightly.

"I suppose I had more to confess than I thought," Esther answered.

"I don't doubt it."

If only you knew, Esther thought as she followed her out of the chapel. And despite what Theletos had told her – despite the fact that she had no idea who he really was, or if he could even be trusted – for the first time in months, she felt hope.

THE DEEP
THE DEMON DOMINIONS

Inside the ring of frigid flames, Rive sank to his knees, shaking uncontrollably. Though once it would have been an easy task, making the key for the girl, Esther, had sapped him completely. He hadn't even been certain that he'd be able to do it. The staves the daevas had set around him were stronger than anything he'd ever come across, never mind the ones they'd set up around Earth. They'd also found a way to weaken him, dulling his aeon's abilities almost to nothing. Apparently, though, they weren't gone altogether: he'd heard the key clatter onto the confessional's floor with metallic clarity before he lost the connection.

Still, he knew that small victory wouldn't help him much. He wasn't likely to escape his prison anytime soon. He'd tried enough times to be certain he couldn't cross the staves, and he had the scars and bruises to prove it. As if in response, the flames leapt higher around him, towering over his head, blue as arctic ice. They'd been there for a while now, replacing the hedge of poison thorn bushes that had been there before, as the thorns had replaced the wall of piercing, maddening sound, and so on, back through countless variations on prison walls to the moment he'd first awakened here.

Now, though, thanks to Esther, he knew how long it had been. It was almost six months since the night he'd leapt into the Deep to save Sophie from the daevas; eleven days before her eighteenth birthday. On Midsummer's Day, if the two of them didn't re-form their syzygy and return to their dominion in the

Garden, she would die, and take with her any hope of saving Creation from its impending doom.

Stop it, he told himself angrily. Eleven days was better than nothing, even if Sophie was brainwashed, he was in prison, and their only ally was an Irish schoolgirl he knew nothing about.

Or do I? Absurd as it was even to consider it, he couldn't help feeling that Esther wasn't entirely a surprise. He hadn't been able to see her, but there had been a rush of energy when she'd laid her hand against his, an effervescent jolt of recognition, very like what he felt when he touched Sophie, but also very different.

Stop, he told himself again. He was making something out of nothing – or rather, out of the deep-seated longing he could never quite subdue, for a partner who would complete him in the way that the other syzygies were complete, in the way that Sophie never could. But he'd long since accepted that he'd never experience the other aeon pairs' fundamental love, and he couldn't afford to waste his time daydreaming about it. The only thing that mattered now was helping Esther get to Sophie. That would be difficult enough, never mind convincing her to go back to the Garden. But the Keeper itself had charged him with the task of re-claiming Sophie and thereby restoring the Balance – the first time the Keeper had spoken at all in thousands of years. Rive had no choice but to keep trying to find a way out of the daevas' prison.

As if in response to the thought, the flames died down until they were only a couple of feet high, revealing Abaddon's black-clad figure just beyond the circle. His pale face was bluish in the light of the fire, spectral against the surrounding darkness. Lilith slouched behind him in her white dress and gauzy wings like a depraved angel. Her hands, clad in black leather gloves, were busy with something, but in the shadows, Rive couldn't tell what it was.

"How does this morning find you, Theletos?" Abaddon asked, his tone cool and pleasant.

"Much as you'd expect, Abaddon," Rive answered, with perfect nonchalance.

"You're comfortable? Not too chilly? I told Lilith that the flames were too much. After all, it isn't our intention to torture you, simply to keep you out of trouble until we're ready to proceed – "

"Can you please cut to the chase?" Rive interrupted.

"Very well," Abaddon answered, crossing his clockwork arm over his ordinary one. "Lilith heard you talking to someone. I need to know who it was."

"Myself," Rive said. "Isolation's getting to me."

Abaddon smiled fractionally. "You're far too self-possessed to talk to yourself. Besides, Lilith is certain that she heard a conversation. Your side of one, at any rate."

Rive couldn't help glancing at Lilith. She gave him a voluptuous smile over Abaddon's shoulder, its effect ruined somewhat by the flash of her pointed teeth. "That's a bit vague, as evidence goes."

"She also felt you shift matter."

"Your consort is talented, as well as beautiful," Rive said, careful not to show that he was rattled by this information. He'd known Lilith had some psychic ability, but not that she could tune into the rhythms of Creation.

Abaddon waved the words aside. "What did you make, Theletos? Some kind of weapon, I suppose?"

Rive fixed dispassionate eyes on Abaddon and spread his arms wide, revealing his torso, unadorned except for the intricate, vinelike tattoos he'd given himself over countless years. His tattered black jeans were the only clothing they'd allowed him to keep when they'd put him in his prison, probably because they were too thin to hide much of anything, let alone a weapon.

With a flicker of movement so quick it barely registered,

Abaddon crossed the flames and twisted Rive's arms up behind his back, high enough to make him gasp with pain despite himself. "I asked you once nicely. I won't be nice if I have to ask again."

"I didn't make anything," Rive answered with steely defiance. "And if you damage me, I won't be much use to you as a bartering piece."

That made Abaddon pause. "What makes you think we plan to barter you?"

Rive laughed grimly. "How else would you get your hands on Sophia? No doubt it's the only reason you're keeping me here."

"I knew you had a martyr complex, but I didn't realize that you had quite such a low opinion of yourself."

"So you don't want to trade me for Sophia?"

Abaddon held onto him for another moment, and then, abruptly, he released him. Rive whirled to face him, ready to fight, but Abaddon was smiling serenely. "Lilith," he said, never taking his eyes off of Rive, "would you please provide chairs for myself and our guest?"

"But the dollies!" she protested, her high voice petulant. She'd come closer, and now Rive could see her gloved hands clearly, as well as the spider-silk lines running from her fingers to something nearer the floor. Despite himself, he was curious. He moved as near to the flames as he could without touching them, and then, when he realized what he was looking at, he recoiled. The lines from Lilith's fingers connected to two puppets – exquisitely detailed marionettes, a girl and a boy, both with dark hair. Lilith watched the understanding dawn on him, and then she flicked her fingers in an intricate dance, so that the figures moved together, into an embrace. Rive shuddered.

"Put them to bed," Abaddon said with a touch of impatience.

Lilith gave him a petulant look, and Rive thought that she might challenge him, but then she crouched down, hooked a finger into the shadows, and pulled them aside to reveal a miniature bed. Dark wood, white covers, and towering piles of books dissolving into the shadows surrounding it. Rive couldn't deny anymore what he was seeing. He looked away in disgust as Lilith tucked the two puppets lovingly into the bed – and then, with another flick of her delicate finger, it was all gone.

"Lilith," Abaddon said, a trace of menace in his voice, and then she was standing by the wall of flames, swirling a finger in it thoughtfully. After a moment she hooked out a spindly chair of the same, changeable blue. Once more, and she pulled out another just like it. She offered them to Abaddon with a triumphant smile.

"Beautiful, my darling, as always," he said, accepting the chairs. He set them down and seated himself on one of them, then indicated to Rive to sit in the other one.

Rive looked down at it dubiously. He didn't trust the chair any further than he did its maker. "I'll stand," he said.

Abaddon shrugged, and then said, "You were speaking to your consort."

"Wrong," Rive said, without pause.

"There's no one else you could have reached across our staves – and frankly, I'm astounded that you could reach her."

Rive tried not to think about the sensation of Esther's small hand against his, pulsing with strange energy – a disconcerting mixture of determination and doom. He held the daeva's colourless eyes with his own brilliant blue ones. "I was not talking to Sophia," he repeated, slowly and clearly.

"There really isn't any point in denying it," Abaddon said. "It won't change the outcome either way."

"What outcome?"

Abaddon answered smoothly, "We make her ours."

"And what do you mean to do with her once she's yours?"

"All in good time."

Inwardly, Rive seethed at the daeva's blasé assurance that

he'd get what he wanted. He was angrier still at the knowledge that it might well be justified. But he was careful not to betray it to his adversary when he said, "It'll be quite a task, with Sophia on Earth, and you forbidden to go there."

"Things on Earth have changed."

"Not enough that you can bypass the Keeper's moratorium."

"And yet you found a way to circumvent that problem."

"As I've told you, I had a dispensation from the Keeper." Abaddon gave him a faint, supercilious smile that made him wonder what was behind it, but not enough to ask. "Somehow," he continued, "I don't think you're going to find that so easy to come by."

Abaddon shrugged. "All going to plan, I won't need any kind of dispensation."

"What, you'll leave the job to your demon agents? They'll never get past Lucifer. He may not remember who he is, but he's still an angel, and he'd fight to the death to protect Sophia."

"No doubt he would. But I don't intend to use demon agents."

All at once, Rive understood: the staves, the isolation, the fact that they'd bothered to keep him here at all, when he wasn't the one they wanted. "You think you're going to use me to get to her," he said incredulously.

"No. I know we are."

"I'd die, too, to protect her."

Abaddon smiled and stood to face Rive. "Touching. Especially when she doesn't feel the same way about you." He put his hands on Rive's shoulders. "But this is Hell," he continued, "and you're my prisoner." The hands were heavy as boulders, and Rive felt himself sinking to his knees, desperately as he fought it, until he was on the floor, looking up at the daeva in mute fury. "I'm willing to bet that even an aeon can be broken."

DUBLIN

Esther could barely concentrate on her classes that day. She tried to listen – or at least to appear to be listening – to the teachers droning on about the history and literature and theology of a world that shouldn't exist. But the key hanging inside her dress kept calling to her, dragging her attention back to the plan that had been forming in her mind since she left the chapel that morning.

It hinged on the laundry. Esther knew that such places had once been common: convent-run workhouses where single mothers and prostitutes and girls who were simply considered too bold were forced into long hours of "remedial" work. In the world before the Change, these places had all been shut down, but the Sisters of Charity followed the model to the letter (aside from the addition of some faery drudges.) So, though the girls were given a rudimentary education, the true focus of the reform school was the laundry. It was located in the basement of the building, the washtubs, rinse sinks and wringers, drying racks and ironing boards laid out in long lines. After classes, all of the girls went to work, their specific tasks rotating on a weekly basis.

Esther was on ironing duty that week. It wouldn't be easy to steal and hide a set of clothes, but it would at least be possible. The money would be more difficult. She knew that it was kept in a strong box in the office in the corner of the room, guarded by a dour dwarf. Its key – the only one, as far as Esther knew – would be on a chain around his neck.

One thing at a time, Esther told herself as the bell sounded, signalling the end of lessons. She put her books and papers away in her desk and then followed the other girls, who were lining up behind Sister Bridget in the doorway, ready to follow her down to the basement. An unnatural silence hung over them. The girls weren't allowed to speak to each other in between classes or at mealtimes, and a host of nuns patrolled the floor of the laundry to stop any attempt at a conversation.

The laundry was already thick with steam from the washtubs the brownies – the little household goblins whose loyalty to the nuns Esther could never decipher – had earlier set boiling. Esther made her way to her ironing station, dodging the tiny faeries as they hurried to and fro. Cliona, the girl she shared the station with, was there already. She had long, black hair and a thin, dark-complexioned face, which would have been pretty if her expression hadn't always been one of mild disdain. Esther hoped that she was as uninterested as she looked.

Esther took a flat iron from the range where they sat heating, licked a finger to test it, and then reached for the first damp item in the basket. Her heart sank when she found herself holding a pillowcase. If they were on linens that day, she'd be unlikely to find anything to wear. Still, it was only the first basket. She'd get through a dozen before she was finished.

As she worked, she tried to find the mindless trance she usually fell into in the laundry, and she'd almost succeeded when one of the girls from the drying racks came for her empty basket and dumped another in its place. It was full of clothes, the dull greens and greys and blues of utilitarian fabric harshly washed and often worn. She tried not to be too obvious as she examined each piece of clothing. Most of them were men's, aside from a few that belonged to a boy smaller than she was. And then, at the bottom of the basket, she struck gold: a dress made of blue sprigged cotton with mother-of-pearl buttons down the front, which looked about her size.

As she laid it out on the ironing board, she was certain that Cliona must see her hands shaking. But a glance showed her that the other girl was struggling to fold a heavy linen sheet. Esther looked around quickly. None of the patrolling nuns or scurrying brownies were anywhere nearby, and the other girls were all engaged in their work. Heart pounding so erratically that she wished she had her medication with her, Esther took off her cardigan. There was nothing inherently suspicious about this – most of the other girls had already removed theirs in the steamy heat. With one more glance to make sure no one was watching, she crumpled the dress into a ball and shoved it into the sleeve of the cardigan, then set the lot down at the foot of the ironing board.

The rest was easier. In subsequent baskets, she found a pair of dark blue woollen tights and a set of underwear made of silk so fine it fit into her closed hand. Her own black cardigan and boots were ugly, but plain. They would pass in the outside world as ordinary apparel, without her uniform dress.

As she started on her last basket of the evening, Esther began to relax, as she hadn't since that morning in the confessional. When the bell rang for Vespers, she hauled her basket to the receiving door and set it down by the others with a sigh of relief. She made her way back to the folding table and crouched to pick up her cardigan and its precious contents, and then stopped cold. Cliona's face was six inches from hers, set in a knowing smile.

"Running away, Mad Girl?" she asked in a low voice.

Esther was too stunned to speak. She had made certain that Cliona was turned away from her when she'd hidden her selections. But there was no doubt that Cliona knew exactly what she'd done.

"Don't look at me like that," Cliona said, when Esther said nothing. "I'll not turn you in – as long as you give me the goods."

"W-what?" Esther stammered at last.

Cliona rolled her eyes. "Give me the clothes you stole."

"But I need them!" Esther pleaded.

"Aye, and how do you mean to get past the battle-axe with them?" She jutted her chin toward the door that led upstairs. Sister Agnes was standing guard as Gasz prodded the girls into line, her heavy-jowled face set and arms crossed over her breast, just waiting for anyone to act up. "Give them to me, Mad Girl, or I'll call her over."

Furious, Esther pushed the cardigan toward Cliona, certain that she would never see it again. Cliona grinned at her and said, "That's the way. Now run and queue up. I'll find you after mass."

"What?" Esther asked. "Why?"

But Cliona was already gone, walking off toward the receiving door without a backward glance, the cardigan and its cargo hidden who-knew-where. Esther felt her hope fade with every step the other girl took. It wasn't the loss of the clothes, or even the cardigan – though she would no doubt be punished for losing it – that upset her. It was the fact that now, Cliona would be watching her, making it harder than ever to escape. Perhaps, given her last words, she even meant to blackmail her into stealing on a regular basis.

Sure enough, Cliona touched her arm as they were leaving chapel later that evening. Esther flinched, but then she saw that Cliona was holding out her cardigan, empty of the stolen clothes. "You left this in the laundry," Cliona said, handing it to Esther. "Wouldn't want your hands to get cold."

She was gone before Sister Agnes had time to tell her off for speaking. Esther pulled the cardigan on, wondering what Cliona had meant about her hands. She slipped them into the pockets of the cardigan, and sure enough, in the right-hand one, hard as a pebble, was a wadded bit of paper.

It was bedtime before Esther dared to read Cliona's note. Once the light in the corridor went off, she slipped the paper out of the pocket, glad for once of the dingy light that came into her room from the street below. She unfolded the paper and held it toward the window, her heart beating hard in dread, which turned to mystification as she read:

"Mad Girl,

"The sisters say you're touched, but I don't put too much stock in what they think, and touched or no, I know you mean to give em the slip, and I want to know how you plan to do it. Put the details in your maths book and swap with me tomorrow. If you don't, I'll make it known how that dress disappeared.

- Cliona"

Esther lay looking at the note for a long time before she let it drop with a sigh. She couldn't help respecting Cliona for her quick evaluation of the meaning of the stolen dress, and how succinctly she'd turned it to her advantage. However, it did little to convince Esther that the other girl was trustworthy. If she learned about the key, what was to stop her blackmailing Esther for it and leaving her behind?

Yet Esther was well aware that she had little choice other than to do what Cliona asked. If it came down to her word against Cliona's, she had little doubt whom the sisters would believe, and she didn't like to consider what the result of that would be. She would have to tell Cliona the truth, or something like it.

Thinking about it was making her heart beat too quickly again. She fumbled on the bedside table for the tablets, and swallowed one. Then, turning over and smoothing the scrap of paper on which Cliona had delivered her ultimatum, she picked up a pencil and began to write.

HEAVEN
THE DOMINION OF SURIEL

The image of Esther's face, wan in the faint streetlight, hovered for a moment within the small, scrolled silver frame. Then it faded, leaving an apparently ordinary mirror, reflecting two sets of eyes – one black, the other bottle-green, but identical in their anxious concentration.

Suri dropped the scrying-glass into her lap. "And so the plot thickens."

"Hm," Michael said, running a hand over his short, coppery

hair. It was the first time he'd moved in days. It made his exhaustion show all at once, as if, until then, he'd been holding it back by force of will.

"'Hm'? Is that all you have to say?"

"What do you want me to say?"

Suri rolled her eyes in exasperation. "I don't know; you could venture some opinion about who the hell this girl is? And why she knows what happened, when as far as we can tell, none of the other humans do? And why Theletos can communicate with her, a total stranger, when we can't even show up as nightmares to our closest friends? And – "

"*All right*, fine, I get it – you're frustrated."

"You think?"

"Don't take this out on me, Suriel. I'm just as frustrated as you are."

Suri flopped back into the long grass, staring up through the trailing, silvery branches of the willow tree to the butter-yellow sky beyond. Her long, platinum dreadlocks spread around her like a spikey halo. "Okay," she said. "Esther. Any idea who she is?"

Michael shook his head, picking three strands of grass and beginning to plait them together. "I've never seen her before... though she had a look of Sophie about her. It's the eyes, I think."

"But she told Theletos she didn't know Sophie. Maybe you've ministered to her?"

"I always remember the faces of my supplicants."

"Maybe it was someone close to her, and you saw her when you helped them?"

"In that case, she's out of my jurisdiction. Are you sure *you* don't know her?"

Suri rolled her eyes. "Angel of Death, here, remember? She seems distinctly alive to me." She frowned. "Though I don't much like the look of those pills she takes."

"I didn't mean to suggest she'd passed through the

34

cemetery," Michael said. "I thought you might have run into her in Edinburgh, or maybe in Ardnasheen?"

Suri gave a derisive snort. "A sweet little convent schoolgirl, downing pints with the deadbeats at World's End? I don't think so."

"Well, she might not have been a convent schoolgirl, before."

"Oh, she was – or near enough."

"How do you know?"

"They have a look. Kind of endearing, kind of clueless. Like lambs to the slaughter."

Michael laughed, though without much humour. "How did you ever get to be Angel of Death with so little compassion for humans' earthly plight?"

"I've got compassion," Suri answered. "But if I listened to it all the time, I'd drown in my own tears."

"Charming image," Michael said, throwing away the plaited grass. "But back to the matter at hand: we don't know Esther. And Theletos didn't seem to know her either."

"Still, did you see his face when they touched hands?"

"Yes. He looked apoplectic. But what does that prove? That priest was clearly on his last legs anyway."

"Well then, did you see her face?"

Michael half-smiled. "You said it yourself: convent schoolgirl. It's probably the first time she's ever touched a man who wasn't a blood relation."

Suri chuckled, then sobered, saying, "Still, it's hard to believe that in all the time Theletos has lived – I mean, given he isn't in love with Sophie – that he never thought of anyone else."

Michael smiled wryly. "You must be joking."

"Why?" Suri asked, irritated.

"You think Theletos has a crush on Esther?"

"Why not?"

"Because she's human, and she's a child – sixteen, maybe

seventeen at most? How would he even have known about her? Besides, he seemed confused to have contacted her."

"And yet he did contact her."

"I'll bet my sword that has everything to do with her and nothing to do with him. Or else, why did he trust her with possibly the most important message since the beginning of time?"

Suri shrugged, looking speculatively at the fronded branches of the overarching tree. "He didn't have much choice, did he? I mean, it didn't sound like he's had any more luck communicating with the Earthbound than we have. I guess he just saw a chance and grabbed it."

"I wonder why she remembers," Michael said thoughtfully. "In all this time, she's the only human we've come across who does." After a moment's consideration, he said, "You don't think..."

"What?"

Michael's eyes flickered away from hers, almost as if he were embarrassed by what he was about to say. "Well, humans have been chosen for higher purposes before, in times of great need."

"Chosen? Like, by God? Seriously, Michael?"

"It's possible," he said defensively.

Suri's smile was as close to bitter as it ever came. "The Keeper gave up caring what happens to the human experiment a long time ago. Or us, for that matter."

"That's one opinion."

"Well, until the Keeper shows up to challenge it, I think it's got to be the accepted one."

There was another long silence. Then Michael said, "So what are we going to do? I mean, besides sit here watching the End of Days through a witch's mirror?"

Suri said doubtfully, "I suppose we could try to contact Esther..."

Michael shook his head. "What could we say to her that Theletos hasn't already said?"

"Well then maybe we should try to figure out how he got through to her," Suri said, winding a dreadlock around one slender finger.

"You have a theory?"

She shrugged. "Not so much a theory – I just wonder, what if he's got some kind of connection to her that bypasses whatever staves the daevas have put up around Earth to keep us out?"

"He's an aeon. She's a human."

"And so is Sophie – well, mostly. You said there was a resemblance. If Esther's related to Sophie, then in a way, Theletos is related to Esther…"

"But Esther was clear that she doesn't know Sophie."

"She didn't think she did. But humans are clueless in the grand scheme. They could be long lost cousins, and not know it – especially since Sophie was adopted."

"That sounds like the plot of a bad romance novel," Michael said.

"Well, we have to hope for something! If we don't, we might as well just throw ourselves off of the nearest mausoleum and be done with it."

Michael cracked a smile. "Glad to see impending doom hasn't dampened your flair for melodrama." His smile died then, and he sighed. "Look, Suriel – even if there is some connection between Theletos and Esther, what good does it do us if no one knows what it is?"

Suri thought for a long time. At last, she said, "The Change passed over Esther and, as far as we know, no one else. Theletos and Esther, and no one else, can circumvent the staves. The two things have to be connected, and they have to mean something."

He shrugged. "Yes, but to even begin to guess what, we'd have to find out more about Esther. And at the moment, that's impossible."

"Jeez, you're a buzz kill."

"We have to face the facts."

"Face the facts," Suri repeated thoughtfully, pulling a catkin from a trailing branch and rolling it between her fingers.

Michael watched her for a moment, and then said, "You're scheming, Suriel."

"Not yet," Suri answered. "At the moment, I'm only thinking. Ruminating, considering, pondering – "

"About?"

She gave him a measuring look. "If Esther and Sophie are linked, then the aeons must know about it."

"The aeons don't answer our calls. Or won't…" He trailed off, frowning. The angels had heard nothing from the aeons since the daevas had shaken up Earth, but they didn't know whether it was by chance or choice.

"Right," Suri said. "So maybe it's time we looked into that."

"How? We can't make them come here. Short of going to the Garden ourselves – " He stopped when he saw Suri's smile. "You can't mean to go to the Garden?"

"See, Mike?" Suri smiled. "You do get it."

"But angels can't enter the Garden!"

Suri stood up with a purposeful expression. "Couldn't. Key distinction. Everything else has changed – why not that, too?"

"You can't be serious," Michael said.

"I can," Suri said with a brilliant smile, "if absolutely necessary. Luckily, it usually isn't. Coming?"

CHAPTER 2

12 JUNE
DUBLIN

Esther woke to darkness and the sound of bells – not the familiar call to morning mass, but a crashing cacophony, as if someone were hitting them all over and over again with a sledgehammer. Her disorientation was worse for the fact that she'd been dreaming, and for once, it hadn't been of the demons. She'd lost all but a few threads of it when the bells wakened her, but she remembered blue eyes and a white hand that seemed to be covered in black vines, curled around hers; an enveloping sense of peace and safety, the like of which she hadn't felt since her father died.

She shook her head, trying to clear it, and reached for the alarm clock. It was twenty past three in the morning. Something was very wrong, and she had a good idea what it was. She pulled her cardigan on over her nightgown and hurriedly filled the pockets with the few things she had that meant anything to her. A photo booth snapshot of herself and her father, which had miraculously survived the Change; a five pound note that she'd found stuck in the leaves of her prayer book two days after she was brought to the school, and whose provenance she'd never discovered; her bottle of tablets; and, of course, Theletos's key.

She'd only just secured this last one when the door burst open and the lights came on. Sister Agnes stood heaving in the doorway, her face drained of colour. Her eyes, however, were as furious as Esther had ever seen them, and Gasz, for once, was serious.

"Up already, are you?" she demanded accusingly, grabbing Esther's arm and dragging her toward the door.

"The bells woke me, Sister," Esther said. "What's happened?"

"Do you really have the nerve to ask! Come on." She pulled Esther into the hallway.

"But I'm not even dressed!"

"It hardly matters, where you're going."

"Where am I going? What is this about?" But though Esther entreated, Sister Agnes wouldn't say another word to her, only hauled her through the half-lit corridors where the nuns and the other girls were stumbling from darkened doorways, looking as perplexed as Esther felt herself.

At last they arrived at their destination: the chapel. The door was open, with light blazing from within. Esther only realized that the bells had fallen silent when she became aware of the sound of voices speaking in hushed panic, drifting from within.

Sister Agnes shoved Esther into the unnatural brightness. There, she saw, the nuns hovered in clusters: the source of the anxious murmuring. They fell silent, though, as Esther passed, watching her with a mixture of horror and curiosity. Sister Agnes didn't stop until they reached the confessional, the grim, dark, closet gaping now like a gutted fish.

The Mother Superior, Mother Helena, was standing by the booth from which Esther had fled the previous morning, flanked by her black cat. The cat was as large as a dog, making Mother Helen's diminutive form seem even tinier. The nun was just past middle age, with inscrutable blue eyes and a quality of unshakable will. She nodded at Sister Agnes, who let go of Esther's arm and retreated into the string of nuns who had followed them up the aisle.

"Esther Madden," Mother Helena said, "what do you have to say about this?"

It took a concerted effort for Esther to make herself look up, and follow the Mother Superior's pointing finger into the shadows of the confessional booth. Father Xavier sprawled against the bench as he had when she'd left him, but his lips were now a vivid purple, his eyes sunken into bruised-looking sockets, his hands clenched like claws.

"Esther Madden," Mother Helena repeated, "as far as we have been able to deduce, you were the last person to see Father Xavier alive. I'd rather hoped you might shed some light on what happened to him."

Esther shrugged listlessly. "Sure, I don't know."

The nun's eyes bored into her, along with the unblinking yellow eyes of her cat, but the look in them was more speculative than accusatory. "Was there nothing unusual about your conversation with him?"

Esther struggled to think clearly. Obviously, she couldn't tell Mother Helena what had really happened. But to deny any knowledge of something amiss didn't seem the right tack, either. After all, didn't the guilty always deny everything? She remembered something that she'd heard or read once: that if you are going to lie believably, you have to stick as close to the truth as possible.

So she answered, "Well…when I came into the confessional, he seemed out of breath."

"Out of breath?" the nun repeated, as the others inched closer, eager for details.

"As if he'd been running. I thought…I thought perhaps he'd been late. That he'd been hurrying to get here on time."

The nun studied her. At last she said, "Was there anything

in the nature of your confession that might have caused him a shock?"

"I had nothing to confess at all, Mother," Esther said softly.

The woman's eyebrows drew together. "How is that possible?"

"I'd only confessed the evening before."

"Then why did you choose to visit the Father again so soon?"

Esther glanced up briefly at Sister Agnes, whose face was growing dangerously mottled. She didn't want to provoke her, but it seemed more important to tell the Mother Superior the truth. "Sister Agnes told me I must."

Mother Helena glanced at Sister Agnes, while Esther kept her eyes carefully trained on the floor. Then the nun seemed to come to a decision. "Please come with me, Miss Madden."

Hesitantly, Esther stepped toward her, clutching her cardigan around her.

"You can't take her away!" Sister Agnes cried as they turned toward the chapel door.

"And why not, Sister?" Mother Helena answered, with raised eyebrows and a steely look.

"The police will be here any moment," Sister Agnes faltered.

"The police can question Miss Madden perfectly well in my office," Mother Helena answered. "Better, in fact, than here, where anyone might be listening. Sister, I'll leave you to restore order among the other girls. Miss Madden, come with me."

Esther felt every set of eyes that followed her out of the chapel burning into her back, but she tried not to think about them, or the dead priest, or what part Theletos's possession of him might have had to play in his death. She knew that if she did, she would panic, and right now she needed her wits about her more than she ever had before.

Mother Helena led her through the gathering crowd of girls, the cat padding after them, silent as a shadow. They turned down a dim corridor, climbed a flight of steps, and finally passed through a dark wooden doorway into a surprisingly cosy office. It had dark panelling and walls lined with bookcases, a few tasteful paintings – landscapes rather than religious scenes – and a thick Persian carpet. The nun sat down behind a mahogany desk, indicating to Esther to sit in one of the two armchairs pulled up in front of it. The cat, rather alarmingly, lay down in front of the door and began purring with a sound reminiscent of an electric drill.

Mother Helena looked at Esther for a long moment over her folded hands. Esther tried not to fidget under the direct gaze. Finally, Mother Helena broke the silence: "You do seem to have a talent for attracting the wrong kind of attention, Esther Madden."

"Yes, Mother," Esther answered, uncertain what else to say.

"I don't suppose you want to change your story, now we're on our own?"

"My story?"

The nun shrugged. There seemed to be a faint glint of humour in her eyes, which disconcerted Esther more than anything that had yet happened that night. "About what happened to Father Xavier."

"No, I don't," Esther said, trying to hold the nun's gaze steadily. Innocently.

"That's unfortunate," Mother Helena answered, settling back into her chair, "because something tells me you've more of it to tell, and you're going to be hard pressed to keep it from the police. At least if I knew the truth…well, forewarned is forearmed, as they say."

Esther blinked at her, trying to digest the words, wondering if it was truly possible that the head of the Sisters of Charity was suggesting she might help her. "I don't understand," she said bluntly.

The nun smiled humourlessly. "No – I don't suppose you

do. How could you, in this sheltered place, and forbidden to speak with the other girls?" She sighed, shook her head. "What is it, three months you've been with us now?"

"Four," Esther answered.

"Four," the nun repeated with another glint of humour, "not that you're counting." Esther only shrugged. "At any rate, it's safe to assume that you don't know about the murders."

"Who's been murdered?" Esther asked anxiously, thinking of her family.

Mother Helena opened one of the drawers of the desk and took out a manila envelope. She reached into the envelope and removed a sheaf of black-and-white photographs, set them down in front of Esther, then folded her hands beneath her chin once more, and watched her as she took them in.

Many images had come to Esther's mind when Mother Helena said "murder," none of them pleasant; still, none of them came close to the horror of the one she was now looking at. A young woman with short, blonde hair lay sprawled on damp cobbles at the foot of a set of steps. She lay on her front, so that the dipped back of her evening gown revealed a dark tattoo that followed the sweep of her shoulder blades. Her face was delicate, perhaps once had been beautiful, but where her eyes and mouth should have been, there were only charred black holes. At the bottom corner of the picture, someone had scrawled, "St. Augustine's, 7/2."

"Sweet Jesus," Esther said.

The Mother Superior met her eyes as Esther looked up, her own frankly unapologetic. "Look at the next one, Esther. Look at them all."

With a trembling hand, Esther pushed the photograph away to reveal the one beneath, and so on through the pile. There were six in all, each one showing the body of a young man or woman, each body with burned out eyes and mouth. Each had a saint's name and date in the bottom corner, all of the dates within the past few months. By the time she reached the last one, Esther felt physically sick.

"Who...who killed them?" she asked, pushing the pictures toward the nun.

"There are those who'd say that you know the answer to that already."

The room swam around Esther. "But how could I know such a thing?"

"Well, if, for instance, you'd been party to those killings..." She trailed off, eyebrows raised.

"You mean people think that – that I knew they were going to happen?"

Mother Helena shrugged. "Perhaps you even had a hand in the planning."

"The planning! I would never kill anybody! I couldn't!"

Mother Helena studied her for a moment, and then she said, "I know that."

Esther paused, taken aback. "You do?" she said at last.

A near-smile showed again on the lined face. "Is it such a surprise that I don't believe you're a murderer?"

"Yes...I mean no...it's only, no one here ever believes what I say."

"I saw your face when you looked at them," Mother Helena said, touching the pile of photographs. "You were horrified."

"Of course I was!"

Mother Helena looked at her and then sighed and said, "I've been watching you these last months, Esther, and I've revised my initial opinion of you. To an extent, I should say. I still believe that you're delusional, and that the nature of those delusions is disturbing at best. But I don't think that you're possessed by the devil or that yours is an evil heart."

"I'm glad of that."

Mother Helena shrugged. "I'm afraid it won't help you

much. The others are all too willing to believe you capable of any atrocity, including killing Father Xavier."

"But I didn't kill him!" Esther pleaded. "You believe me, so – "

Mother Helena shook her head. "Even my word won't be good enough. In fact, it won't matter at all. His death is too similar to these," she tapped the pictures.

"But those people are…I mean their eyes, and their mouths…" Esther shuddered.

Mother Helena sighed. "I know. But the similarity of the discoloration on Father Xavier's face is near enough. Near enough for the Sword of Justice, at any rate."

Esther shook her head. "Sword of Justice?"

The nun sighed again. "A religious group, made up of clerics and lay people of different Christian orders, which formed after the first couple of murders. It's fairly taken hold – fairly spread out too, as these bodies have been found worldwide. And with every new death, they gain momentum." She indicated the pictures again. "You see, Esther, aside from the obvious similarities, each of the bodies was found on church grounds. The Sword of Justice believes the murders are a direct attack on the Christian religion by anti-Christian terrorists."

"I don't mean to contradict you, Mother," Esther said after taking a moment to absorb this, "but that seems a stretch. And the way these people died – it seems more like something a serial killer would do."

"Perhaps, but as I said, the bodies have been found in various locations all around the world – some of them so near the same time that a single person couldn't have been responsible. Plus, these killings have been perfectly coordinated, leaving no evidence. Whatever the truth of it is, there's no doubt that this is the work of a group, not an individual – and a group of diabolical ingenuity."

"But to decide that it's a group of religious terrorists…well, it seems quick to come to that."

Mother Helena said wearily, "And so it would be, if it weren't for the Prophet. Ah, of course – you won't have heard of her, either. She's a nun – showed up several months ago at a small convent near Galway, talking of being visited by an angel."

"And they believed her?" Esther asked.

Mother Helena offered a small smile that suggested she saw through Esther's question to the real one. "Of course they did," she answered. "She's a nun. But also, by all accounts, there is an aura of great holiness about her. Some are even suggesting that she's one of the saints, reincarnated."

"Which one?" Esther asked, instinct telling her to find out as much as she could about this so-called prophet.

"That, Esther, is the prize question. She's told no one her name. Her accent, apparently, is impossible to trace. No one has even seen her face – she goes veiled at all times, touches no one – she even wears gloves, to avoid contact with anyone else. She insists on seclusion, except right after the angel speaks to her. Then, she'll hold audiences to deliver his message."

"What does he say?" Esther asked.

"Many things," Mother Helena answered. "But one is rather pertinent to our present situation. You see, she claims that the angel has interpreted the murders for her. He says that the dead are all people of God: would-be saints, destroyed and defaced by agents of Hell."

"Demons?" Esther couldn't help asking.

"No. Humans. Vulnerable humans, who have fallen prey to the influence of Satan. And according to the Prophet, they aren't just murdering the holy – they're forming an army."

"What for?" Esther asked.

Mother Helena shrugged. "For every army's purpose, I suppose: to take power from one and hand it to another." She paused, looking questioningly at Esther. "Do you understand what this means for you?"

"They might think that I'm one of those agents," she said slowly, trying to digest it. "That I killed Father Xavier because I'm possessed by evil."

"Esther," the nun said wearily, "they already do. Father Xavier'd not been discovered ten minutes before Sister Agnes connected you to his death, and from there, linking you to this army of killers was easy enough. Your strange dreams and visions, your ranting about the world being changed…" She trailed off, shaking her head. "You've made yourself an easy target."

Esther sat for a moment, absorbing this new information. "But you don't believe it," she said at last. "That I'm evil."

Mother Helena smiled ruefully. "I don't, as I've said. But it'll do you little good, when the story gets out."

"What will happen to me?" Esther asked after a moment.

The nun was looking at her speculatively again. "I believe I'm going to leave that up to you."

"What?" Esther asked sharply.

"It won't be long now before the police arrive. But it will be a while before they come to any conclusions, and longer, I hope, before the Sword of Justice is organized enough to come after you." She sighed. "There's precious little I can do for you, Esther. Even if it didn't mean risking the safety of the nuns and the other girls, the Sword of Justice has too firm a grip now on people's minds for me to stand against it. But I can give you a little bit of time. In a moment I'm going to walk out of this room. I will not lock the door. What you do beyond that is your own decision."

"But I have nowhere to go!"

The Mother Superior smiled again, and this time there was sympathy in it. "Anywhere will be better than here for you, child."

Esther took a deep breath, and then let it out, wishing that it weren't so shaky. "*All right*. And thank you."

The nun nodded, and stood up. The cat stood too and stretched. "I wish you luck, Esther Madden." Mother Helena was half way through the door when she turned back. "And Esther – God go with you."

*

It was only after Mother Helena had left that Esther realized the enormity of what lay ahead of her. True, she had been planning to run away, but she'd counted on having more time to work out how best to do it. Now she had minutes to run, with nothing but her flimsy convent nightgown and cardigan and the few things she'd shoved into her pockets.

Moreover, she had assumed that when she left, everyone would be glad enough to forget about her. She'd thought that if she found her father, told him about the school, he would take pity on her, at least long enough for her to pack properly and get away. Now, clearly, this wouldn't be the case. She couldn't go back to Ballymun. She couldn't go anywhere where anyone might think to look for her.

With an effort, she shook herself from the inertia of these thoughts. Mother Helena had made it clear that she didn't have much time. She got up and peered out the door, into the corridor. It was empty. She'd been to the Mother Superior's office only once before – on the day the parish priest brought her to the school. She couldn't quite remember the route to the front door, but she thought that she remembered turning left into the office, and so now she turned right.

Somewhere in the building she could hear voices, but they didn't sound too close. After a few turns she found herself in a hallway she recognized. She darted past darkened classrooms, hoping that nothing was watching from the shadows, and was nearing the front of the building when she heard men's voices up ahead. She backtracked and dipped into one of the classrooms, crouched behind the teacher's desk. Peering around the corner, she watched as Mother Helena went past, at the head of a knot of Garda constables and two ominous, gliding figures in black cloaks.

As soon as the voices faded, Esther ran back to the door and down the corridor, carrying her boots so as to make as little noise as possible. She crept carefully along as she neared the front door, but when she finally reached the entry hall, it was empty and silent. The door was firmly locked, but Theletos's key went into it easily, and the bolt slid back. Esther was half way through the door when a cold, spindly hand came down on her shoulder.

Stifling a shriek, she whirled around to find Gasz grinning at her, his slit-eyes shining like dingy lamps in the darkness. "Caught you!" he hissed, grinning. "Bring you to Mistress…"

Esther tried to pull away, but his bony fingers clamped her wrists like vices. His pockmarked head was only as high as her shoulder, but he was wiry, and he began dragging her back toward the corridor she'd come from. "Let me go," Esther pleaded. "Just let me go!"

"Never, never, never – " he muttered, until a soft voice interrupted him.

"Gasz – Gasz, is that you?"

He stopped, looking up and around. Cliona stood at the entrance to the other corridor, holding a bottle in front of her. "I've brought something for you," she said, her voice still low and wheedling. She proffered the bottle.

Gasz's grip on Esther loosened. "What be it?" he asked suspiciously.

"Wine," Cliona said. "Your favourite."

Gasz let go of Esther and ran to snatch the bottle from Cliona. He sniffed it, and then upended it into his wide, snaggle-toothed mouth. A moment later, abruptly, he stopped. Eyes widening in horror, he looked at the empty bottle, and then at Cliona. "There be iron in the wine! Poison!" he rasped, and then he collapsed on the floor, convulsing, the bottle rolling away into the shadows.

"Come on," Cliona said to Esther, stepping over the twitching goblin, her voice suddenly brisk. Esther saw then that there were three other girls behind her. All of them were dressed in street clothes – the mish-mash of styles from Victorian through the 1950s which she'd slowly grown to think of as "normal" – and carrying small bundles bound with knotted kerchiefs.

"Where?" Esther asked.

"As far from here as we can get," Cliona answered, taking her arm and leading her toward the door, "before Sister Agnes realizes that someone's poisoned her goblin."

"You can't come with me," Esther said, pulling free.

"I thought we had a bargain," Cliona answered with infuriating calm.

"That was before – you've no idea what's happened – "

"You mean that you've murdered the priest?"

"I didn't!"

Cliona shrugged. "Well done, I was going to say."

"What?" Esther choked.

"Come on," Cliona said, shoving something into one of Esther's hands and dragging her through the door by the elbow. "You've got to get out of here, unless you want to be blamed for killing the goblin, too!"

Esther knew that she had no choice but to follow Cliona and the other girls. Once outside, Cliona produced a length of rope from her coat pocket and deftly tied the knobs of the double doors together.

"It won't stop them, but it'll slow them down," Cliona said. Then, taking Esther's hand firmly in hers, she said, "And now we run!"

They left the main road behind in favour of the smaller thoroughfares that wound like a web among the tenements of the working-class neighbourhood. Esther wanted to ask where they were going, and why they were taking her along with them, but it was all she could do to draw breath enough to keep up. Her heart beat so hard she thought it would burst, and she knew she needed a tablet, but even that request was beyond her.

Finally, the other girls ran out of breath too. They stopped in the shadowy doorway of a joiner's shop. Without a word, Cliona reached into the pocket of her coat – a threadbare hounds-tooth riding jacket that looked Edwardian, and at least a size too big for her – and produced a dented metal flask. She took a swig of whatever was in it, then handed it around, naming the other girls as she did so. Dervla was a short, plump girl with curly ginger hair and amber eyes in a round, good-natured face. Rose was thin and fragile-looking with long, straight, platinum hair. Una was tall and stately and beautiful, with ivory skin and blue eyes and thick black hair cut in the bob that had become the prevailing fashion since the Change.

Esther nodded to them all, but shook her head when the flask came to her. Having recovered enough to find her voice, she demanded, "Where are we going?"

"Somewhere safe," Cliona told her.

"Why? I mean, why bring me along?"

Cliona looked around at the other girls. Apparently picking up on some unspoken assent from them, she answered, "Because we think you know something that would make it worth our while."

"I don't. Believe me."

"Aye, well, the thing is," Cliona said, taking another pull at the flask, "I don't."

"Why not?"

"Because you killed the priest."

"I didn't kill the priest," Esther protested.

"Maybe not, but you had some hand in it. I'd bet my freedom on it."

Esther looked at Cliona's dark, clever eyes, and then

52

around at the other girls. They all looked back at her with equal expectation. She sighed, suddenly more exhausted than she'd ever been. "I was there when it happened," she conceded. "But it had nothing to do with me."

"Let us be the judge of that. And change while you talk, or you'll have us all behind bars inside the hour." Cliona poked the cloth bundle that she'd given to Esther.

Esther unknotted the corners. Inside the scarf were the clothes she'd taken from the laundry the day before, as well as a tweed coat, as threadbare as Cliona's, and a pair of high-heeled, lace-up boots. They even looked like her size.

"Fine," Esther said, "but turn around."

The girls obliged, and she began to shed her old clothes, pulling on the new ones in their place. "Yesterday morning," she began, "after mass, Sister Agnes asked me to make confession. I went into the booth, and Father Xavier was acting strange."

"He tried to grope you through the screen?" Una muttered.

"No," Dervla answered, "strange would be if he didn't." They all giggled.

"He didn't try anything…like that," Esther said, flushing. "He only sounded strange. Out of breath. Like he'd been running." For some reason, this set the other girls off laughing again. "Then," she interrupted firmly, "he said a lot of funny things."

"Like what?" Cliona asked with sudden interest.

"I can't recall," Esther said, hoping the other girls wouldn't push her. The last thing she wanted was to tell them about Theletos and her promise to him. "It didn't make much sense."

"Did he talk about the murders?" Rose asked in a voice as faint as her colouring.

"Murders?" Esther asked.

"Them with their eyes burned out," Dervla explained.

Esther froze for a moment, and then she answered, "He didn't say anything about any murders."

"Aye, but you know about them," Cliona said, with a probing look at Esther. "Oh, don't bother to deny it. Your face is like an open book." Esther shuddered at the similarity of Cliona's observation to her father's old endearment. "Come on, if you're done dressing. We aren't out of the woods yet."

Esther rolled up her nightgown and cardigan and tied them into the scarf that had held the clothes she was now wearing. Then Cliona linked arms with her, and they set off again down the dark street. "Well? So what do you know about the murders?"

"Only what Mother Helena told me before I…left."

"The Mother Superior told you about them?" Dervla asked incredulously.

"Aye. She thought that Father Xavier's death would be linked to them, and then I'd be blamed, since I was the last one to see him alive."

"Jesus! That's some bad luck."

"Were his eyes burned out?" Rose asked.

"No," Esther said. "Just kind of…bruised looking."

"So why would they connect his death to the others?" Cliona asked.

"And why blame you?" Una added.

Esther was silent for a moment, considering how much to tell them. There seemed little point in keeping from them what Mother Helena had told her. Telling them was even the decent thing to do, given that if they kept company with her, they, too, would be implicated. So she explained about the Sword of Justice, and the Prophet, the people allegedly doing the work of Hell – and the fact that the Sisters of Charity thought that she belonged to them.

When she was finished, Cliona gave her a level look and said, "So, are you?"

"Am I what?" Esther asked.

"Possessed by the devil."

"Of course I'm not!" Esther snapped.

"Are you mad?" Una asked, the bluntness of the question tempered by her serene beauty such that it almost sounded reasonable.

"No," Esther sighed.

"Then why would the Sisters think you were doing a demon's grunt-work?" Dervla asked.

"Because…" Esther paused, wondering how to explain it. "I have nightmares," she said at last, figuring that it wasn't quite false, but not too much of the truth either. "I dream of bad things, and the nuns think it means I'm evil."

The other girls' looks were sceptical, but they didn't press the point. They walked on in silence for a little while longer, until Dervla turned down a narrow alley between two tenements, then stopped and knocked softly at what must have been a cellar door. When there was no answer, she knocked louder. This time, there was the sound of footfalls beyond the door, and then it slid open a couple of inches. An amber eye showed in the crack. The eye widened as it took in the girls, and then the door flew open.

Dervla flung herself into the arms of the boy on the other side. He looked so much like her that they could only be brother and sister. Esther guessed that he was a couple of years older than Dervla was. He was dressed in ragged trousers held up by braces and a white undershirt. By his rumpled hair and glassy eyes, Esther knew that they'd awakened him.

"Hello, Sis," he said genially, as if it were entirely normal for her to show up in the middle of the night with a bunch of girls.

He shut and chained the door as Dervla explained, "This is my brother, Declan. Declan, Cliona, Una, Rose and Esther." The girls nodded to him in turn. "Fellow inmates. Or should I say, former inmates."

"Make yourselves comfortable," he said, "if you can." He gestured to the sparsely furnished cellar room. Walls and floor were made of stained concrete, while a webwork of pipes covered the ceiling and far wall. Against another wall was an army cot, its tumbled blankets making it clear that it was the bed Declan had recently vacated. There was little else in the room besides a few articles of clothing hanging on a line, three overturned fruit crates, and a camp stove with a battered tin kettle on top.

The girls sat down on the crates. "Tea?" Declan asked.

"If you've nothing stronger," Dervla answered dryly.

Declan smiled and filled the pot from a tap in the wall of pipes. Then he lit the stove and set the water on to boil. "Well, then," he said, leaning against the wall and surveying his guests, "to what do I owe the honour?"

"To her," Dervla said, pointing at Esther. "Sneaky wench had a key to the front door."

"And provided distraction," Cliona added, "by way of a dead priest."

Declan raised his eyebrows. "Aye?"

Dervla nodded. "She says she didn't do it, but we've our doubts."

"Sweet Jesus, I never – " Esther began, but Cliona interrupted, smiling.

"Ah, pipe down! She's only winding you up. It's clear enough you couldn't kill a flea...or run away to save your life. Good thing we caught up with you, eh?"

Esther's smile was lukewarm at best, but Cliona had already turned away from her, focusing on Declan. "They're saying he was killed by minions of Hell, or suchlike."

"Who's 'they?'" Declan asked.

"What were they called, Mad Girl? The Slayers of Truth?"

"Sword of Justice," Esther answered, accepting the soup can of hot black tea that Declan handed her. Though she normally didn't like tea without milk, she was glad of it now after the chill of the street.

"Have you heard of 'em?" Dervla asked her brother.

"Oh, aye," he said, handing around the rest of the cups –

a collection of aluminium cans like the one he'd given Esther. "They're in all the papers these days, blaming this and that and the other on some army of devil-worshippers."

"It's a new thing, then?" Rose asked, sipping her tea more daintily than Esther would have thought anybody could out of an old bean tin.

"Aye, well," Declan answered, "new since Dervla was last taken in."

Last? Esther wondered. She hadn't realized that the girls incarcerated with the Sisters of Charity were ever allowed out. Nor could she imagine how, having escaped, any of them would let themselves be caught again. But none of the others appeared to think there was anything off about what he'd said.

Declan continued, "I guess if you've all been in the lock-up as long, you'll none of you've heard of them. It's all coming from some nun in the west, calls herself the Prophet. Sure, she claims she's been visited by angels, and it's up to her to save the world from this army of evil."

He rolled his eyes and pretended to strangle himself, eliciting giggles from the other girls, but Esther was lost in thought. The Mother Superior's story had apparently been accurate. Esther felt lower than she had since Cliona had caught her stealing clothes from the laundry.

"So there really is a band of murderers possessed by the devil?" Cliona asked.

Declan shrugged, then sat down on the cot and sipped his tea. "That all depends on who you ask. But the numbers that believe it are growing."

"Why?" Una asked.

"Fear, I suppose," he answered, turning from Una's clear blue gaze with a flush. "With every new killing, people get more frightened and keener for an explanation, so." He shrugged. "And then there's the Sword of Justice, saying that those who join their ranks will be safe. I guess that convinces a lot of folks who are wavering."

"And how do they figure that, then?" Dervla asked. "I mean, that joining will keep them safe?"

"Spiritual protection, I expect," Rose suggested from over the rim of her tin-can teacup. "Or strength in numbers. Perhaps both."

"Aye," Declan agreed, "and then there's the fact that none of them that join the group have been killed."

"Honestly?" Una asked.

"Not yet, anyway."

As the others talked, Esther became aware that Cliona was looking at her with an unblinking intensity that she had learned, during their brief acquaintance, preceded an acute observation. A moment later, she said, "This is all well and good, but none of it explains how Esther got a key to the convent door."

Caught off guard, Esther stared at her for a moment, her mind blank. As near to the truth as possible, she reminded herself, and answered, "I found it."

"You just found a key to the front door?" Una asked.

"Yes," Esther answered firmly.

"Where did you find it?" Cliona asked, her dark eyes probing.

Once again, Esther drew a blank. Wondering why Theletos couldn't have chosen to speak to a girl who was half-way decent at lying, she said, "In the confessional. It was…on the floor."

To her surprise, the others seemed to accept this. "Aye," Dervla said, "one of the Sisters must have dropped it."

"Perhaps after finishing off the communion wine," Rose added, making the others laugh.

"It's clear enough why you'd want to run," Cliona said, still looking inquiringly at Esther, "but where did you mean to go? You can't go back to your family. They'll be watching for that, you know. The Sisters – and the others."

Esther did know, though hearing Cliona say it aloud was still depressing. "I'll think of something," she said. "But now, I can't keep my eyes open." Before anyone could push her further, she retreated to a corner, wrapped her coat around herself, and lay down to at least pretend to sleep.

*

They stood on the ramparts of a castle, a charcoal sky above them and a barren park below. Beyond the park was a street lined with shops in pretty antique buildings, but it was deserted, drifts of paper blowing along the empty pavements in a bitter wind.

The demon with the clockwork arm was standing on one side of Esther, the one in the white dress on the other. He swept the arm wide at the view and smiled. "Behold," he said, though his lips never shifted from their smooth curve. The voice seemed to bore right into her, between her eyes, like an icy needle. "All of Creation, yours for the taking."

She was so intent on him that she didn't notice the one in the white dress had moved, until a frigid, leather-clad hand slipped into hers. Instinctively she jerked away, but the demon girl held on, her smile an echo of the pale man's but too full of teeth, her eyes like pools in a bog, opaque and voracious.

"I don't want it," Esther protested.

"You all want it," the demon girl answered, tightening her grip on Esther's hand until she could feel the bones grinding together.

"Let me go!"

But the demon didn't let go. Instead, she took Esther's shoulders in her hands and shook her as black clouds rolled across the sky, and the grass of the park split open, and an army of monsters came pouring from the rift. They swarmed into the empty park, weapons glowing with eerie light.

"They're here to give it to you," the demon said. "Take it, take it, TAKE IT –"

Esther screamed, but the grip on her shoulders didn't relax. It tightened and tightened until

her eyes flew open, and instead of the demon's terrible, beautiful face she saw a ring of human ones, cast in expressions ranging from bemusement to horror. Esther stopped screaming abruptly, and Cliona let go of her shoulders, sitting back on her heels.

"*Now* I see why they think you're possessed," she said.

"And you think she isn't?" Rose asked, her face paper-white and her eyes round.

"It was a nightmare, is all," Esther said, but her shaking voice and erratically pounding heart belied it. She fumbled for the knotted scarf she'd used as a pillow, untied it and dug the bottle of tablets out of the cardigan pocket. She swallowed two of them.

"And what are those, then?" Dervla asked.

"Medication," Esther said. "I've a heart condition."

"No bleedin' wonder," Una muttered, "screamin' like that."

"What is it that you dream about?" Cliona asked, watching her closely.

Esther was too shaken to try to lie. "Bad things," she said. "A ruined city with all the people dead. And…and those that caused it."

"Other people?"

"No…I don't think so. They look like a man and a woman, but all wrong. He has an arm made of cogs and gears…and she has wings." The other girls looked at each other, and Esther could all but hear them regretting having brought her along.

When she turned back, though, Cliona seemed more interested than ever. "Are there ever other ones? Those creatures, I mean – in your dreams?"

Esther thought confusedly of Theletos, but she didn't want to tell the others about him. "No. Just the two," she said. "And, well, some kind of army. Their army, I suppose. But it's made up of monsters, and they're far away…"

Cliona scrutinized her for another moment, then she stood up, brushed her hands together briskly and said, "Well I'm starving. Where do you suppose Declan's got to?"

Dervla shook her head. "He went out for bread, but that boy knows everyone in this neighbourhood. No doubt he's stopped to speak to every single one of them along the way."

"Do you suppose he'll forget about us?" Rose asked.

"Nah," Dervla said. "Especially not when we've Una with us." She poked Una in the side with her elbow. "Have you seen how he looks at her?"

"He doesn't," Una said, flushing.

"Sure, he does. They all do."

"Aye," Una sighed, her face suddenly grim. "Which is how I landed in the bleedin' convent."

"What do you mean?" Esther asked, intrigued. Ever since they ran from the school, she'd been wondering how the others had ended up with the Sisters, but hadn't known how to ask.

Una smiled bitterly. "My father didn't like the way the boys looked at me. He said it was my fault – that I was bold." She shrugged. "After Mam died, he said he couldn't be bothered with it. So he brought me to the convent, and the Sisters took me in to save my soul."

Dervla laughed. "I never met a soul could be saved by slave labour in a laundry – and I should know."

"Why?" Esther asked.

"Because I've been at it since I was ten – excepting a little holiday here and there, when I could find a way out."

"So you've escaped from the convent before."

"Oh, aye," Dervla said, getting up to fill the teakettle and set it on the stove. "Twice before this."

"But – how did you end up back there?"

Dervla shrugged, her yellow-brown eyes frank, and even

slightly humorous. "Same way I landed there in the first place. The fingers weren't quick enough." She wiggled the fingers of one hand at Esther, and then, seeing her incomprehension, she rolled her eyes and said, "I was caught stealin'."

"Oh," Esther said faintly.

Dervla frowned. "Don't give me that look, Mad Girl," she said. "We weren't born with silver spoons in our mouths – well, except Miss Rose."

"Little good it did me in the end," Rose muttered.

"Sure," Dervla said, her expression softening as she looked at the pale, thin girl, "it was bad luck your dad dyin', and worse your aunt couldn't be bothered with you. I know well enough how that goes."

"At least I remember my dad," Rose said in a small voice.

Dervla handed her a can of tea. "True enough. I wish I did. But I've Declan." Rose's lip trembled at this, and Dervla rushed to put an arm around her. "Now don't you cry, Miss Rose. We're going to be all right. We're old enough now to work, there's no need to steal – all we need to do is keep out of sight of the Sisters, and in Northside that should be easy enough."

Rose nodded, wiped her eyes on her sleeve and then sipped her tea. Esther watched her, full of pity. She knew what it was like to lose a father and be left to the mercy of the world, too young to take it on. But she'd never lived an easy life, as Rose clearly had. At least she'd been used to hard work when her father died – and it had happened before the Change, when there were still such things as Child Welfare laws and benefits cheques, and workhouses were only a memory. Hearing these girls' stories made her wonder how many others in the care of the Sisters of Charity weren't bad at all, only victims of the new world order the demons had manufactured. It made her sick to think about it, and to remember the dream she'd awakened from. How far away, she wondered, could that empty city really be, when people were as helpless against the demons' machinations as these girls were?

"What about you?" Cliona's voice cut into the mire of Esther's thoughts.

"Pardon?" Esther said.

"How did you end up with the good Sisters?"

Esther wondered how to answer her. It seemed wrong to let these girls who had helped her remain ignorant of their impending doom, and yet she knew too well what happened when she told people the truth. So she said, "The dreams. They…well, they came out of nowhere, really. When I first started having them I – I thought they were a kind of warning."

"What, like heavenly visions?" Cliona asked.

"Or like that nun in Galway," Rose suggested.

Esther shrugged. "I suppose – but not heavenly. I kept dreaming of that man and woman, and I knew that they were evil. That they caused the bad things they showed me. So I tried to tell my parents."

"And they brought in the parish priest," Cliona said, the intensity of her eyes belying her deadpan tone, "and he pronounced you possessed, and gave you to the Sisters for the sake of your soul."

Esther looked up at her. "Aye," she said. "How did you guess?"

Cliona shrugged. "It's what always happens to girls who know things they shouldn't, and won't keep their mouths shut about it."

The word "know" wasn't lost on Esther. She scrutinized the other girl. Cliona looked back, her dark eyes unyielding – perhaps even challenging. "You haven't said how *you* ended up with the Sisters."

"No," Cliona said with a defiant smile, "I haven't."

Before Esther could ask any more, the locks rattled and then the door opened, and Declan came in. The girls' delight at the two loaves of bread and the tin of jam he carried dried up when they saw his grim expression.

"What's happened?" Dervla asked anxiously.

In response, Declan pulled a newspaper from inside his jacket and dropped it on one of the fruit crates. The girls gathered around, their faces registering horror when they saw the headline: "Schoolgirl Murderer at Large," printed above a head-shot of Esther looking wan and sullen. It was the identification photograph the nuns had taken of her the day she was brought to the school. Esther snatched up the paper with shaking hands, and began to read:

"The search is on for seventeen-year-old Esther Madden of Ballymun, North Dublin. The schoolgirl is accused of killing an elderly priest connected with the Northside convent of the Sisters of Charity and its School for the Rehabilitation of Wayward Young Women. The priest's name is being withheld until his family have been informed. Miss Madden was consigned to the convent by her parents in February, after developing a severe religious paranoia.

"'We had no choice,' an emotional Mrs. Madden told our reporters after being given the news about her daughter early this morning. 'It were clear she were a danger to the other children. We thought that the nuns could give us back our Esther – and now it's come to this!' The accused's father, James Madden, declined to comment.

"The cause of the priest's death will not be confirmed until completion of an autopsy, expected within the next couple of days. Investigators have said, however, that many details closely resemble those of other victims of the so-called Hell's Army, an anti-church splinter group said to be dabbling in the dark arts. It is suspected that Miss Madden has been under the group's influence for some time.

"'It was clear enough to me from the start there was something off about that girl,' said Sister Agnes, a member of the convent who acted as Esther's overseer. Sister Agnes is also integral to the Dublin chapter of the Sword of Justice, a well-respected religious group that has formed in response to the Hell's Army killings. 'Something right sinister. We did our best to keep her from corrupting the others, but whatever power she answers to was too much for us. She even killed my poor little goblin on her way out! Now all we can do is pray that she's found and dealt with properly before she can do any more harm.'

"Miss Madden is thought to have escaped the convent during the confusion resulting from the discovery of the priest's body late last night. Four other girls are also missing from the school: Cliona McCaffrey, 18, of Bray; Rose Kinsella, 17, of Dun Laoghaire; Dervla Brennan and Una Boyle, both 16, of Dublin. All four are considered to be in great danger from Miss Madden. Any information on their whereabouts should be directed to Dublin Police Headquarters."

Pictures of Esther's companions were printed below the article. Esther dropped the newspaper and sank onto one of the fruit crates as the others snatched it up. "Well, well," Cliona said when she'd finished reading, "the good Sisters haven't wasted any time washing their hands of Father Xavier."

"You can't exactly blame them," Declan argued, giving Esther a leery look. "It's not good publicity to have been harbouring a murderer."

"How many times do I have to tell you, I didn't kill that priest!" Esther cried.

"We know," Cliona said, deflating her indignation. The other girl even laid a hand on her shoulder.

"Do we?" Declan asked, with a sceptical look. "How well do any of you really know each other?"

"I don't much like what you're suggesting, Declan Brennan," Cliona said quietly, her hand tightening on Esther's shoulder.

The boy shook his head, sighed, and poured a tin of tea. "And *I* don't much care whether you're the general of Hell's

Army or my long lost guardian angel – I can't keep you here if the likes of the Sword of Justice are after you. I can't keep any of you," he said with a wistful glance at Una, "saving of course my sister. I need my job and I need this room, and I'll lose both if I get involved in the likes of that." He gestured to the newspaper.

Cliona folded her arms across her chest and, fixing him with a steely look, she said, "Fine. But you can't put us out on the street in broad daylight. We'd be caught in an instant."

He sighed. "You can have until tonight, then. I'll not be back until nine or ten. But I expect you all to have cleared out by then."

Cliona shrugged, her lips tight and her eyes never leaving Declan's, until he looked away. Taking his tea with him, he went out the door.

"Well," Cliona said, "that's an unfortunate turn of events." She broke a heel off one of the loaves, opened the jam and dipped it in. "I thought you said he was all right," she said to Dervla before she bit into it.

"Sure, he didn't turn you in, did he?" Dervla answered defensively.

"Only because it would mean turning you in, too," Rose said. Dervla shrugged and reached for the bread.

"What time is it?" Una asked.

"Half two," Cliona answered, looking at the battered clock beside the bed. "Which doesn't give us long, but still long enough…"

"Long enough for what?" Esther asked dejectedly.

"To disappear," Cliona said, and smiled.

*

Dervla volunteered to do the shopping, saying that she knew the neighbourhood better than the rest of them, but Esther suspected it was because she felt guilty about her brother chucking them out. Una and Rose opted to go with her. Cliona took a cloth purse from her bundle of clothes and fished some bills out of it. When Esther saw how many more were left, her jaw dropped.

"Where did you get all of that?" she asked.

"From the laundry, of course," she answered calmly as Dervla took the money, and the three girls slipped out the door. "I liberated it when I took down my last basket yesterday."

"But how?"

Cliona shrugged. "Sister Marie had the cash box open to pay one of the delivery men. I got Una to distract the dwarf and took it while his back was turned."

Despite the gravity of their situation, Cliona's nonchalant audacity made Esther feel slightly better. Her spirits fell again, though, when Dervla returned some time later with a rattling bag and without the other girls.

"Where are Una and Rose?" she asked.

"They decided it was as easy to keep going as come back."

Esther swallowed hard, feeling still worse – no doubt the girls had seized on the opportunity to get away from her. Cliona didn't question Dervla, other than to say, "Did you give them money?"

"Everything I had left."

Cliona nodded. "That's good."

"I'm sorry," Esther said.

"Why should you be?" Cliona answered, rummaging in the shopping bag. "We tagged along with you, remember."

"I know, but still…" She trailed off as Cliona took out a pair of sewing shears and a brown bottle of liquid. "What are those for?" she asked dubiously.

"You'll see," Cliona said. "Sit." She indicated one of the fruit crates. Reluctantly, Esther sat. Cliona produced a brush, and began to pull it through Esther's hair. "Your mug shot shows all of this quite clearly." She ran a hand down the length of Esther's hair. "So, it has to go."

Cliona took a firm grip on her hair and cut it at the nape

of her neck. Esther yelped, but Cliona only smiled and stuffed the cut hair into the shopping bag. "I told you, you've got to disappear. Murderer-Esther had long hair. You can't."

"But it must look awful!" Esther said, feeling the ragged ends of her now-bobbed hair.

"Just now you look like a scarecrow," Cliona agreed. "But sure, I don't mean to leave you that way."

"Trust her," Devla said as Esther drew back. "She's good with hair. Besides, it can't look worse than it does right now."

"Fine, then," Esther said through gritted teeth.

After studying her intently for a moment, Cliona began to snip carefully, first one side, and then the other. After a quarter hour of miniscule adjustments, she said, "*All right*. Now you can look."

Dervla took Declan's shaving mirror from its nail on the wall and handed it to Esther. Esther raised it with trepidation, but when she looked at herself, it turned to bemusement. She'd had long hair as far back as she could remember, and without it she looked like somebody completely different. But the effect wasn't a bad one. The chin-length bob made her eyes look wider and accentuated her cheekbones. She looked older, but more than that, the face in the mirror reminded her of someone. After a moment it came to her: she looked more than a little like the girl, Sophie Creedon, whom Theletos had shown her.

"Thank you," she said to Cliona, handing the mirror back. "You've made a good job of it."

"I'm not done." She was holding the bottle of liquid, appraising it. "Were there no instructions with this stuff, Derv?"

Dervla sipped from the can of tea she'd just made and shook her head. "Only the woman said to put it on neat."

"And leave it for how long?" Dervla shrugged. "Ah well, we'll just have to keep an eye on it."

"An eye on what?" Esther asked apprehensively.

Cliona rolled her eyes. "Your hair. We're going to bleach it."

68

"Oh, no!" Esther said, backing away.

"You still look too much like Murderer-Esther. Blonde, though, you'll be someone different. Now, come lean over this."

Sighing, Esther leaned over the basin that Dervla produced and let Cliona work the clear liquid into her hair. "Ouch, that stings!"

"That means it's working," Cliona said, patting her shoulder consolingly. Then she wrapped a threadbare towel around Esther's head and turned to Dervla, brandishing the bottle, which was still half-full. "Want to try life as a blonde?" she asked.

Dervla made a face. "Never! I've a ginger complexion – I'd just look daft."

Cliona sighed "And I'd look dafter. I guess Declan gets the rest of this." She put the bottle aside, then picked up the shears and nonchalantly hacked off her own blue-black hair.

"Why did you do that?" Dervla cried. "Your hair was lovely!"

Cliona shrugged. "Because I can't dye it. Now here, make it look presentable." She handed the scissors to Dervla, who took them reluctantly, and started trying to even out the ends of Cliona's bob. When they were finished, she filled the basin and rinsed Esther's hair over the floor drain. Then she held up the mirror so she could view the results. Esther blinked at her face, framed now by wet, yellow-white strands of hair.

"Well?" Cliona asked.

"I do indeed look like someone else."

"You look like that film star," Dervla said, "what's her name?" she asked Cliona.

"I don't know," Cliona said, "I've never been to a film. Anyhow," she said briskly, before the others could question this, "it's time we were going."

"We?" Esther asked confusedly.

"Aye," Cliona said with an even look, "unless you've somewhere to stay tonight I don't know about."

"Do you?" Esther asked her.

"I will."

"How can you know that?" Esther argued, desperate to get away from these girls and begin her real journey.

"I'm resourceful," she answered, a hint of challenge in her voice. In the ensuing silence, Cliona gave her that probing look. "Unless you'd rather I not know where you're going. If, say, you have an appointment to keep with an army of demon worshippers…"

Esther smarted with frustration, wondering why Cliona seemed so intent on attaching herself to her – because there could be no doubt anymore that this was what she was doing. "I'm going to Scotland," she said, hoping to shake Cliona off without revealing too much of her actual plan.

But the other girl's eyes only brightened. "Are you, now? I'm not going far from there. And you'll need money for the crossing, so."

"I suppose I will," Esther agreed sullenly. She doubted her five pounds would cover it – especially if she wanted to eat between here and Ardnasheen.

"Then it's lucky I have lots, isn't it?"

Resignedly, Esther nodded.

CHAPTER 3

13 JUNE
ARDNASHEEN, SCOTLAND

"Sophie, will you hold still!" Anna Creedon entreated around a mouthful of pins.

"Sorry," Sophie said, straightening and planting her feet firmly on the chair on which she was standing. "It's itchy."

"Well, *I* wasn't the one who chose the antique lace," her mother chided, pinning an expert tuck into the bodice of the dress, so that it fitted Sophie more closely.

Sophie had got the idea for the dress from a picture of a ball-gown in a Victorian lady's magazine she'd found in one of Madainneag's disused rooms. Her mother had redesigned it, scouring the Edinburgh antique shops to find the perfect, delicate ivory lace to make it from. It had a sweetheart neckline and tiny sleeves that left her shoulders bare, a graceful skirt less bell-like and more sweeping than the original, and a sash of cornflower blue silk ribbon.

"Who knew that lace was so scratchy?" Sophie asked.

"Who cares, when it looks that lovely?" her friend Ailsa answered from the curtained bed, where she was stretched out in her bridesmaid's dress, the same colour as Sophie's sash, eating bourbon creams.

"Either way, it's too late to change your mind," Sophie's mother said briskly, but Sophie could hear in her voice that she wasn't really annoyed. She was happier about the upcoming wedding than she had been about anything in years. "Now, have a look," Anna said as she stuck the remaining pins back into the pincushion.

Sophie turned to face the old oval dressing-table mirror and her breath caught.

"Well?" Anna asked. "What do you think?"

"I think it's the most beautiful dress I've ever seen," Sophie said softly, and then she stepped carefully off the chair to hug her mother. "Thank you, Mum."

"Sophie?" someone called from the corridor outside of her room.

Sophie's face lit up, and despite her mother's protests she ran to open the door. "Lucas?" she said, her face falling as her fiancé stopped, stunned, in the doorway. "What's wrong?"

Lucas pushed his unruly black hair out of his eyes. "Nothing," he answered. "It's just...I mean, you're...you're – "

"Out!" Ailsa said sharply, inserting herself between Sophie and Lucas and pushing him back into the hallway. "Don't you know that you're not meant to see her in her dress before the wedding?"

"But – " he began to protest.

"No buts!" Anna snapped, throwing a dressing gown over her daughter. "Ailsa's right – it's bad luck. You can speak to her when she's changed."

"Sorry," Ailsa said and shut the door in Lucas's still-stunned face.

"Mum!" Sophie protested.

"Well, it's true! He's not meant to see you."

"He didn't mean to see me..."

"She's right," Lucas said from beyond the door. "I didn't."

"Doesn't matter," Ailsa said, handing Sophie a biscuit. "It's still bad luck."

Sophie rolled her eyes, but her mother said, "Let's get you out of the dress, before he tries again."

"Don't worry yourself, Mrs. Creedon," he said. "I wouldn't want to tempt fate. I'm going to meet the afternoon boat, Sophie. Meet me at the pub when you're done?"

"All right," Sophie said, with the pang of loss she always felt when they parted. It had been like that from the day they met. As soon as Sophie had set eyes on Lucas, she'd known that she would never again feel complete without him. Even now, nine months on, it amazed and terrified her how much she loved him. The idea that he loved her back as fiercely was almost unbelievable.

Of course, Lucas's irritation with the wedding-inspired influx of people into his house had brought things down to earth a bit. Normally, he made do with a part-time housekeeper. He didn't even keep faery servants, of which most other villagers had at least one. "I don't feel like it's mine anymore," he'd complained to her after a long argument with a decorator Sophie's mother had hired to make the public rooms "presentable."

"I know it's annoying," Sophie had said, "but it's only a couple of weeks. Then it will be all yours again."

"Ours, you mean," he'd said, then he'd smiled and kissed her, and she'd known that he didn't really mind.

Still, Sophie thought as her mother and Ailsa helped her out of the dress, she would be as glad as he was when the chaos was finished. She looked forward to her wedding, and she knew that it would be a rare treat for the people of their tiny village, but the truth was, she would have been as happy to marry Lucas at the registry office on the mainland. The big wedding had been her mother's idea, and Sophie had humoured her partly out of only-child guilt, partly because she knew that her mother regretted her own registry-office wedding.

The Creedons had married quickly, like so many of their generation, on the eve of the Irish War. There'd been no time or money for anything elaborate; Anna hadn't even managed a white dress. So it was really no surprise that she had gone into overdrive as soon as Lucas and Sophie announced their engagement the past Christmas. She'd been up and down from Edinburgh to Ardnasheen at regular intervals since then, each time bringing with her another expert on some esoteric aspect of wedding planning.

"Lucas is gentry," Anna had answered when Sophie had complained that it was too much.

"But he's never gone in for any of that," Sophie had countered. "Nobody here even thinks of him as the laird."

"Aye, well, he *is* the laird, however he might feel about it. There'll be expectations."

"Not from the village."

"*Especially* from the village. Wait and see."

And Sophie had to admit that her mother had been right. She'd come to Ardnasheen as a temporary music teacher at its primary school, and the villagers had treated her as one of them even after she began spending time with Lucas. But as soon as their engagement became public, everything changed. It was as if their imminent wedding turned them from children to adults in the eyes of the village and gave sudden gravity to their roles as laird and future lady of the estate.

"Sophie?" Ailsa said. She had changed back into her printed cotton work dress and was twisting her long, auburn hair into a knot at the nape of her neck.

"Sorry – what?"

"I said I have to get back to the pub, or Ruadhri will have my head. I've already been gone longer than I said I would."

"Right. I'll walk with you – I mean, if I'm done, Mum?"

"Aye, you're done…for now."

Sophie pulled her own clothes on quickly, as Ailsa said, "Thanks ever so much, Mrs. Creedon. The dress is lovely."

"It's a pleasure, Ailsa." Sophie's mother smiled at Ailsa as she threaded a needle.

"Bye, Mum," Sophie said. Her mother smiled distractedly, already absorbed in her work.

Sophie followed Ailsa out of her bedroom, into the corridor. The room was located next to Ailsa's in one of the newer wings of the house, but it was still old enough for the decorative plaster moulding to be raining paint-chips onto the faded, rose-patterned carpet. Lucas's house, Madainneag, had begun as a peel tower in the Middle Ages, and every subsequent generation of Belials had added onto it. The result was a vast, sprawling mishmash of architectural and decorating styles that Sophie adored almost as much as she adored Lucas. Which was lucky, as Lucas had confided to her early on in their relationship that he could never have loved someone who didn't love Madainneag.

The two girls made their way to the grand staircase and then down, dodging cleaners and decorators as they went. In the entrance hall, two women in dusty smocks were arguing in Gaelic over the chandelier, an elaborate construction of deer antlers, which had been lowered from the ceiling, apparently for cleaning.

"If you ask me," Ailsa said, "they should just throw the horrible thing out and begin again."

"I don't know," Sophie said, examining it. "I think it fits the room."

"It did," Ailsa agreed, "before your mum set her minions loose."

Ailsa had a point. The antlers had blended into the old, murky colour scheme, but now the plaster walls had a fresh coat of whitewash, while the dark wainscoting and the parquet floor had been waxed to a mirror shine. The oil paintings had all been dusted, the rugs beaten, and the vast fireplace divested of centuries' encrustation of soot. Any part of the house where guests were expected to be present had undergone similar treatment.

"I suppose she's airing years of frustration," Sophie said as they maneuvered to the front door and down the stone steps to the porte-cochere.

"About what?"

"She wanted to be an artist," Sophie said, shutting the inner door behind them.

"Wouldn't your dad let her?"

"I'm sure he'd have done anything to make her happy, at least at the beginning…" She trailed off, thinking about her parents' current strained relationship, then shook her head. "But Dad was still at university himself when they got married. There was no extra money and not much time left for her to do anything else after keeping house." Sophie shrugged uncomfortably. It always made her sad to think about her mother's unfulfilled dreams, embodied in the sketchbooks she brought out less and less often with every year that passed.

Ailsa's hazel eyes were keen on her friend's face. "Well, at least you'll never have to worry about that."

"What do you mean?" Sophie asked, as they entered the wood that shadowed the road to the village.

"You'll have other people to do all the boring things; you can do whatever you like. And besides, I can't imagine Lucas ever letting you give up music. Not with the way he looks at you when you play."

"Does he?" Sophie said distractedly, peering off into the shadows beneath the trees. The woods always made her uneasy, and this patch in particular. She felt as if something were watching her from its shadows.

"Does he!" Ailsa cried. "You'd have to be blind not to notice! He was smitten the first time he saw you play."

Sophie forgot the forest's menace, smiling at the memory

of that night. It had only been her second night in Ardnasheen. Angus Forsythe, the schoolteacher who had hired her, had talked her into playing a short recital in the pub, to introduce her to the village. She hadn't taken much stock of her audience before she played – she was always too full of nerves at the beginning of a recital, and looking at the crowd made it worse. But when she'd looked up at the end, still half-lost in the music, Lucas Belial's black eyes had been fixed on her. In that moment, that one look, she'd seen her life change completely, and forever.

"*All right*," she conceded, "maybe he does. But to be honest, there isn't much that I want to do, except be with Lucas... and maybe, someday – well, I would quite like children." She flushed, glancing away.

Ailsa rolled her eyes, but smiled. "And no doubt you'll have them, and every one of them will be clever and beautiful and talented, and you'll be the picture-perfect family. Lord, if I didn't love you so much, I'd hate you!"

"Ailsa!"

"Honestly, though – your life is just so absurdly perfect."

Sophie didn't know what to say. It *was* perfect – so perfect that sometimes she didn't quite believe that it was real. Maybe, she thought, that was the reason for her nightmares: the dreams from which she woke shaking and weeping and unable to remember why, except for the feeling that something precious had been lost. Maybe, she thought, the price of happiness was the fear that something would take it away.

Don't think of that, she told herself immediately, looking further down the road at the small, stone church where, in little over a week, on her eighteenth birthday, she and Lucas would be married. It sat just up from the shore, the old lime tree in its yard marking the limit of the forest and the beginning of the village. From there, the road curved around the bay, with rocky beach on one side and low, white buildings on the other.

The mood of Ardnasheen's sea-loch was always changing:

part of what Sophie loved about it. Right now it was calm, glowing turquoise and soft green where the sun shone through chinks in the clouds. The mountains ringing the bay were a deep, brooding blue, their tops swirled with cloud. The ferry from Mallaig, the nearest town to Ardnasheen's remote peninsula, was tied up at the pier. It looked distinctly abandoned, however. Sophie guessed that captain and passengers alike had retreated to the pub, aptly named World's End.

Sophie and Ailsa followed them, pushing through the cloakroom's jungle of oilskins and into the room beyond. Sophie loved the pub's warm atmosphere of ale and peat smoke, and the low murmur of people chatting in Gaelic over their pints of ale or cups of tea. If a village could have a beating heart, World's End was Ardnasheen's.

Ruadhri looked up from behind the bar as the girls came in. "You're late, missy!" he grumbled at Ailsa. "Will you never learn that time is money?" Ailsa just rolled her eyes, took her apron from its hook behind the bar, and begin chatting genially to the group of taciturn dwarves leaning on it with their pints.

Sophie looked for Lucas and spotted him sitting at a table by the far window with another group of men. As she approached, she saw that they weren't just talking, but studying something laid out on the table in front of them. A newspaper, she thought. But when they saw her coming, one of them picked it up and put it into his coat pocket, as the others began to disperse.

"Please don't go on my account," Sophie said. "It looked like you were in the middle of something." A couple of the men exchanged uneasy glances. Lucas, too, looked strangely serious, his eyes distant. A cold needle of fear pushed into her. "What is it?" she asked. "What's happened?"

Lucas came back to himself then. He smiled and put an arm around her waist and drew her down onto the bench beside him. "Nothing that concerns us," he said, running a hand down her back, leaving a trail of tingling warmth that made her want to bury herself in his arms.

But she was well aware of the others watching them, and of the current of unease that had not dissipated. "Lucas," she said, "please tell me what's going on."

With a sigh, he gestured to the man who had taken the newspaper. He looked doubtfully from Lucas to Sophie and back again, saying, "Begging your pardon, Sir, but it doesn't seem fit reading for a young lady."

"Sophie knows her own mind," Lucas said, tightening his arm around her waist.

The man shrugged and took the paper from his coat pocket, placed it in front of Sophie, then quickly retreated. She looked down at a grainy image of a girl with pale, soulful eyes. The girl looked miserably unhappy, but the chord she struck with Sophie was far deeper than that. Looking at the girl's picture gave her a flicker of that feeling she had when waking from her nightmares: a grief so profound she could hardly bear it, but for the clawing sense of urgency that accompanied it.

Finally, she looked at the headline above the girl's photo. "The New Face of Evil" it announced in stark black capitals, each one like a blow. Feeling sick, she began to read through the accompanying article. The girl in the picture, Esther Madden, was from a reform school in Dublin. She was accused of murdering a priest on behalf of a terror group called Hell's Army. The name was familiar to Sophie, though she couldn't remember whether she'd read about them or someone had told her. She knew that they were being blamed for a slew of ritualistic killings all over the world, but she'd been so wrapped up in plans for the wedding that she hadn't given it much thought.

Now she wished she'd paid attention, and not just because of the photograph's plangent effect on her. At the beginning, the killings had been few and far between. But according to the article, the Irish priest's murder was the third in a week, and the other two had also been in Britain. The timing and proximity of the murders had fanned the flames of a vigilante group called the Sword of Justice.

"Every sign indicates that Hell's Army is zeroing in on the United Kingdom," an Edinburgh-based spokesman for the group had told the paper, "but where will they strike next? And what could these appalling murders possibly mean?"

Sophie had reached the end of the page. She went to turn it over. "Sophie, wait – " Lucas began, but it was too late. On the flip side of the page were three more pictures, police photographs of the murder victims. The priest, frozen apparently in a rictus of fear within a confessional booth, was awful enough. But the other two were horrific. One was a young man, found on the steps of Rosslyn Chapel near Edinburgh. The other, a young woman, had been left in a mausoleum in a London cemetery. Both bodies had singed holes where their eyes had been, and the skin around their mouths was also blackened and cracked, as if they'd breathed fire.

As Sophie looked at them, a whirl of images flashed through her mind. A young woman with dead eyes and a red parka and a knife protruding from her breast. A fiend with tattered skin and clothes, reaching a supplicating hand. A skull in the golden helmet of a Viking warlord, gold torques clattering around the bones that were all that remained of his arm. And a woman in a torn wedding dress and gossamer wings, her wine-coloured lips curved into a knowing smirk, her black eyes like a scourge.

The room reeled around Sophie; she felt faint now as well as sick, and the bright confetti that presaged a migraine was dancing at the corners of her vision. She looked up at Lucas, wanting to ask him what it all meant and unable to put any of it into words.

"Sophie, I'm sorry," he said. "I should never have let you look at this – "

"No!" she cried as he reached to fold the paper away, putting out a hand to stop him. She flicked back to the first page, to Esther Madden's pleading eyes. "I…" she said to Lucas's questioning look, then she stopped, and thought, and began again. "She… this girl…she didn't do it. She didn't kill the priest."

Lucas's brow furrowed; now he looked more than concerned. "Sophie, what are you talking about? Do you know her?"

"No; I mean, I don't think so. But these people, the Sword of Justice, they have it wrong. It's not her…it's…it's…" She trailed off, seeing the confusion in his eyes, knowing that she sounded like a madwoman. She tried to collect her thoughts, to steady herself. At last, shaking her head, she said, "I'm sorry. She just…she doesn't look like someone who could have done those things."

Lucas looked from Sophie to the picture and back again. "I suppose not…" But he was clearly unconvinced. "Sophie, I'm worried about you. Those nightmares you keep having, and now this…is the wedding putting too much strain on you? Because we don't have to do it, you know. If it's too much, too soon – "

"No!" she cried again, earning curious looks from the people at the tables around them. She flushed, lowered her voice and clutched his hands in hers. "No – never think that! There's nothing in the world that I want more than to marry you."

Despite what he'd said, Lucas was visibly relieved at this. "I'm glad! But we don't have to do it like this. We could forget the big ceremony, go to the registry office in Fort William, just you and me and two witnesses – "

"No, Lucas," she interrupted. "Everybody's expecting it now, it would kill Mum – and anyway, honestly, this isn't about the wedding."

Though even as she said the words, she wondered if they were true. Her disturbing dreams accorded with her acceptance of Lucas's proposal almost exactly, and now, after reading the newspaper article, she realized that the Hell's Army murders did too. And yet, it had to be coincidence. To imagine it was anything more was beyond absurd – it was insane. With an effort, she shoved the dark thoughts aside, and with them the newspaper.

She smiled at Lucas, loosened her death-grip on his hands. "Or maybe it is about the wedding – but not in the way you think. It's still hard to imagine that in a week's time I'll be Lady Belial, when six months ago, I was nobody."

"You were never nobody."

"You know what I mean – nobody of any significance. And now all of these people will look at me, and expect me to be… well, Lady Belial. It's daunting, but it doesn't change the way I feel about you. Or my wanting to marry you, and for everyone to witness it."

He looked into her eyes, his own serious and probing. "Honestly?"

"Honestly," she said.

She watched his face relax into a smile. "Good. Because I'd really hate to miss seeing you in that dress."

"You already saw me in it," she smiled back, "and Mum is distinctly less than pleased about it. Bad luck and all that."

He laughed and took her face in his hands. "I don't believe in luck."

"Then what do you believe in?" she murmured as he lowered his face to hers.

"This," he said and kissed her, and she forgot the questions and the shadows and the sad girl in the paper.

"Hello!" an overly cheery voice called. Lucas and Sophie abruptly broke apart. Sophie looked up, blushing, as Angus Forsythe sat down across the table from them. He wore muddy work-clothes and carried a canvas knapsack and miner's helmet, which he set down under the bench he sat on. He pushed the sun-streaked brown hair out of his eyes, which settled on Lucas with a distinct challenge.

"Hello, Angus," Lucas greeted him with a clear lack of enthusiasm.

"Hope I'm not interrupting anything," Angus said.

"Actually – " Lucas began, but Sophie interrupted.

"Of course not," she said quickly, with an inward sigh. She had known Angus since she was at music college in Edinburgh. At the time, he was doing his teacher training at the university. He'd introduced himself to her after a recital, and they'd become friends. After a while, Sophie had realized that he hoped they could be more than that. But though she liked Angus a great deal, she didn't return his feelings and had known she never would, even before she met Lucas. Since then, their relationship had become increasingly strained, especially as she suspected that he'd offered her the job in Ardnasheen in hopes of finally winning her over.

"How is the investigation going?" she asked, hoping to steer the conversation into neutral waters.

Angus brightened. He had an interest in archaeology, and he'd been investigating a sea cave on the peninsula that had a wall of ancient drawings. It was called Uamh-an-Aingeal, the Angel Cave, because one of the images was of a winged figure. Angus was hoping to discern its origin and meaning.

"Actually, there's been a development," he said.

"Really? Have you found more drawings?"

He shook his head, pulling his pack up onto the table. He rummaged inside it and then pulled out another, smaller bag made of black canvas. It was damp and sandy, wrinkled and faded as if exposed to the elements for some time, but Angus beamed at it as if it were a treasure trove.

"It looks like an old postman's satchel," Lucas said.

"Aye," Angus agreed, "but it isn't."

He opened the flap of the bag and tipped the contents onto the table. Some were recognizable – a hair brush, a change purse, and various bits of paper now sodden and illegible. Others were more intriguing, like the palm-sized plastic oblong whose tiny numbered buttons produced no effect when pushed, or the smaller turquoise one with a blank screen and a cord snaking from it, tipped with what looked like miniscule speakers. There was also a small, hexagonal jar made of deep blue glass. It had a cork stopper sealed with gold wax, and the wax had an imprint of what looked like a jug with two handles.

"What are these things?" Sophie asked, weighing the blue jar in her palm. There was something familiar about it, even more so about the symbol in the sealing wax.

"I have no idea," Angus said. "But look at this." He took a cloth-wrapped object from his pack and handed it to Sophie. It was heavier than it looked. Carefully, she peeled back the wrapping, until she was looking down at a silver dagger with a hilt carved with intricate Celtic knotwork. Though the metal had a cold blue tinge, almost a glow, the hilt was warm when she curled her fingers around it. Like the symbol on the jar's lid, the weight of it in her hand was oddly familiar, though she couldn't recall ever having held a dagger before.

Sophie looked at Lucas. He was gazing at the dagger perplexedly. "Where did this come from?" he asked Angus.

"The same trench as the bag. It was right beside it – it could well have fallen out of it." Sophie heard the barely-contained excitement in Angus's voice.

"And that's significant?" Lucas asked.

"I think it is," Angus answered. "As far as I can tell, the bag and its other contents can't have been in the cave more than a few months. But by every indication, the knife is early medieval, perhaps even older."

"Couldn't it be a replica?" Lucas asked. "It looks in too good condition to be so old."

"I suppose it's possible," Angus conceded, "after all, I'm no expert. But the irregularities of the design and the quality of the metal suggest something older. Besides, judging by the nicks in the blade, it's been used for it's intended purpose – most recently on something solid."

"Solid?" Sophie asked. "Like what?"

"Like bone," Lucas said.

Both Sophie and Angus looked at him in surprise. "Well – yes," Angus said after a moment. "But what makes you say that? Do you know something about this knife?"

Lucas's thoughtful look turned to one of confusion. "No – not at all. I don't know why I said that." He shook his head, frowned at the silver blade. "Perhaps there's a record of it somewhere in the library? Something I read once? I could have a look."

"Well, let me know if you find anything," Angus said, taking the dagger and wrapping it back up. "Meanwhile, I'll research it too, as well as these other things. I believe the symbol on the jar is Egyptian. Peculiar thing to find all the way out here…" He shook his head. "Sorry. I must be boring you."

"Not at all," Sophie said. "I think what you've found is fascinating. Will you be sure to let us know if you learn anything?"

"Of course," Angus said, smiling at her in a way that made her feel obscurely guilty. "Now I'd best be going – essays to mark, you know." Angus piled everything back into the pack and then said his good-byes.

"Well, that was odd," Lucas said once he'd gone.

"It's been an odd day all around."

"I could do with a walk before tea." He held out a hand to her. "Coming?"

Gratefully, Sophie took it.

THE DEMON DOMINIONS

Rive watched Lilith from the far side of a fence of buzzing, angry wasps as her hands danced, making the boy puppet circle the waist of the girl puppet. He dipped her backward, and their wooden lips met in a kiss. Set against the miniature village and mountains and forest, it was a parody of a little girl playing with her puppet theatre – except that when Lilith let the strings go, the figures didn't topple lifelessly to the ground. Instead, they joined hands and walked off into the dim blur at the edges of the scene, while Lilith smiled after them like an indulgent mother.

"They're sweet, don't you think?" she sighed, sitting back on the heels of her knee-high boots. Without waiting for Rive to answer, she said, "I love happy romances. I've been thinking that Ardnasheen needs more couples. What do you think about Angus and Ailsa? Too obvious?"

"I think you're depraved," Rive muttered, hating to watch her but not quite able to look away. Lilith was far from the most beautiful female that Rive had seen, but she had the kind of charisma that's more powerful than beauty.

Lilith pouted. "That's not very nice, Theletos."

Rive laughed incredulously. "Not nice is holding me prisoner and abusing my consort for entertainment."

Lilith looked at him for a moment with black-glass eyes. Then she swept a gloved hand across the shimmering image of the Scottish village, erasing it with a darkness blacker than the shadows outside of the prison. She stood up, and pushed through the wall of wasps as if they were mist. The wasps didn't even seem to notice, closing ranks behind her once she was through. Rive looked on in despair, knowing that if he tried to do the same thing, they would sting him into paralysis. Never death, though. Even if it was possible for him to die here – and he didn't know whether or not it was – Abaddon would never allow it. He didn't yet know why, but he knew that they needed him. They would never have kept him otherwise.

Lilith sat down facing him where he knelt on the floor. Her eyes were inquisitive and remorseless. "I don't understand," she said at last, her high, dreamy, childlike voice making his flesh creep.

"You don't understand what?"

"Why you care what happens to Sophia."

Rive smiled bitterly. "I wouldn't expect you to."

"She doesn't love you," Lilith persisted.

"It doesn't matter," he said, deathly tired of having to confirm that melancholy truth.

"What *does* matter to you, Theletos?" she asked, with a shrewd look that belied the little-girl tone.

An image of a girl's hand, her palm pressed to a wicker screen that obscured her face. Rive fought to subsume it, even as he felt Lilith's frigid creepers trying to penetrate his mind.

"A girl?" she asked curiously. "Who is she?"

Panicking, his head full of her name and the shadow of her fragile hand, he forced himself to think of something else. Iterations of the name sped through his mind – Esther from Ishtar, Ishtar from Setara, the ancient Persian word for star – and became a poem. Lord Byron, he thought, though he couldn't quite remember. He let it fill his consciousness, until it blotted out everything else:

Between two worlds life hovers like a star,
'Twixt night and morn, upon the horizon's verge
How little do we know that which we are!
Of time and tide rolls on and bears afar –

Abruptly, Lilith was furious. "You're hiding something! No one hides anything from me!"

"And no one takes an aeon prisoner. Get used to disappointment, Lilith."

Lilith's eyes narrowed. "If that's how you want to play," she said, and she cupped her hands together, then drew them apart. In the space between them was a bubble of light, on which an image slowly took form. Ardnasheen again, the road that led out to the peninsula with the Angel Cave. Sophie and Lucas walked along it, hand in hand, deep in conversation.

Lilith reached out a finger and poked the image of Sophie. She stumbled, and Lucas caught her. She righted herself, looking around, confused about what had tripped her. Lilith stared at Rive, waiting for his reaction, and Rive had to fight hard not to show one. He knew that he would only make it worse for Sophie if he did. But at least he'd got a handle on Esther, pushing her into a small, dark capsule in his mind that he knew Lilith couldn't penetrate.

"I could make her walk into the sea if I wanted to," Lilith taunted, the words grotesque in her chiming, child's voice. "Make her walk until she drowned. I could drop a stone on her, push her over the bannister in Lucifer's silly house – "

"But you won't. You need her."

Her pause told Rive that he'd hit on a truth. After a moment, though, she rallied: "I can hurt her. There are so many ways that I can hurt her and still leave her fit for our purpose."

Rive fought the rage that blossomed at these words. "What do you want from me, Lilith?"

"I want to know what you hid behind that poem," she answered, leaning close to him, her eyes wide and voracious. "I want to know who the girl is."

Rive remained silent.

"You shifted matter!" she fumed. "You thought of a girl's hand, and it wasn't Sophia's! I want to know why. What could be more important to you than your consort?"

Still he said nothing. After a moment, Lilith smiled.

"*All right*, Theletos," she said. "Play your game. But before we're done, I'll have you playing mine. And there's no way that you can win."

Rive lay down, turning his back to her and pulling his knees up to his chest. Because, for all his good intentions, he suspected that she was right.

THE DOMINION OF ARITHIEL

"You don't even have any idea where you're going," Michael said as he caught up to Suri. She was striding purposefully through a meadow full of pure white sunflowers, their velvety golden centres clocked toward the flawless sky. As the angels brushed against them they let out faint, tonal sighs, filling the air with whispery music.

This was the Dominion of Arithiel, Angel of the Sun, but at the moment she was nowhere to be seen. This wasn't unusual. The lower orders of angels were confined to their own dominions unless called out by a higher power. The higher ones – like Michael and Suri and Arithiel – could travel around Heaven as they pleased.

"Of course I do," Suri answered, drawing a finger across a ruffle of white petals, sending out an arpeggio of breathy notes. "I'm going to the Announcing Rock."

"That's only a platform, Suriel. A stage for Logos to make his proclamations, not an actual door to the Garden."

"How do you know?" she retorted.

"Because the Garden is sacrosanct! The aeons would never make it so easy to get in."

"But there is a door, somewhere. There has to be, or Logos couldn't have come to us."

"Very well – but it could be anywhere," Michael argued. "For all we know, it could be invisible to angels. In fact, it probably is."

"It might be invisible, but that doesn't mean we can't find it. All of the universal realms are made of the same basic material. Somewhere, there'll be a trace."

"Even if you find it," Michael said in exasperation, "it'll be staved against us."

Suri turned to him, quizzical but unperturbed by his argument. "How many times will I have to point out to you that

89

the Grand Scheme is in a million little pieces? Why not its old rules, too?"

"So we're going to just go to the Announcing Rock and start looking for a secret passage to forbidden territory?"

"More or less. Glad you're on board."

"I never said I was on board."

"You said 'we'."

Michael sighed in exasperation. "All right, I will come with you to the Announcing Rock – but only to make sure you don't get yourself in trouble."

Suri smiled archly. "If I don't get myself in trouble, I'll consider the trip a failure."

"You're infuriating," Michael muttered, but he followed her nonetheless.

Arithiel's field of sunflowers bled gradually into another of shimmering, deep-blue grass, which sloped upward until it became the hill where once Sophia had sat and wept for the world she'd made and lost. It was actually a corner of the Dominion of Dumah, the Angel of Dreams.

Dumah sat at the foot of the hill, pewter hair falling around him in long waves, deft fingers working the loom in his lap. "Greetings, Suriel, Michael," he said as they approached, looking up at them with silver eyes, though his hands never stopped moving among the countless gossamer fibres on the loom. Despite the colour of his hair, his face was ageless and serene.

"Greetings, Dumah," Michael answered. "I'm glad to see that the changes on Earth haven't stopped your industry."

Dumah frowned, then sighed, looking down at the fabric unfolding away from him. It was as fine as if it had been woven from spider webs, drifting and turning in the breeze that eventually lifted it, bearing it into the bright sky and away towards the distant Earth.

"Humans haven't stopped dreaming," he said sadly, "but the

fabric is all wrong. Full of flaws." He stopped weaving, tilted the loom so that Suri and Michael could see it. Dumah's fabric was normally as smooth and fine as mist, but the bit stretched across the frame was full of tiny pulls and puckers and holes, and odd threads that looked like coarse, black hairs.

"What are the holes and weird threads?" Suri asked, putting a finger to a rent.

Dumah put his own finger underneath, so that it met Suri's. "Human dreams are unbridled truth," he said. "But the daevas can't allow them to dream truthfully, or else they would recall what they have been made to forget. And so they twist and divert them." He touched other imperfections with a delicate finger and then indicated the dark fibres. "These...well, I can't say for certain, but I think they're what the daevas put in truth's place, when a gap would otherwise be too big."

Disturbing as this thought was, it gave Suri an idea. "If the daevas can add things to human dreams, why couldn't we do the same? Give them back some of the knowledge they've lost?"

Dumah shook his head sadly. "I've tried it. It doesn't work. It only warps the fabric further."

"Why?" Michael asked.

Dumah shrugged, and resumed weaving. "It's another question without an answer."

Suri straightened up. "It has an answer. They all do. It's only a matter of finding them."

Dumah smiled, still sad. "And that's where you're off to, isn't it."

"We hope so."

"I wish you luck and give you my faith."

"Thank you, Dumah," Michael said.

Dumah nodded, already lost again in his weaving. Suri and Michael continued onward, skirting the thickly wooded Dominion of Arael, the Angel of Birds. He nodded to them from his perch high in a tree, barely visible for the hundreds of winged creatures flitting around him. After that they crossed the foggy boundary of the Dominion of Seraph, the Angel of Fire, and then the cloud-ridden realm of Ridya, Angel of Rain.

At last they arrived in a birch wood just woken from winter, sweet with the smell of new leaves and dewy grass. They made their way to a glade at its centre, carpeted with wildflowers. An angel sat in the middle of the glade, the skirts of her white dress spread around her. She looked like a human child of about eight. Her skin was the colour of milky coffee, her gold-brown cornrows plaited with tiny silver bells, her golden eyes warm as the month of May that was her dominion. She was making a daisy chain, sunlight flashing off of the silver bells and the matching bands on her wrists – the staves that bound her to her dominion.

When she saw Suri and Michael enter the clearing, she put the daisy chain aside and leapt up. "Suriel!" she cried, running to hug her and sending the bells tinkling. "And Michael too. It's been so long."

"Too long, Ambriel," Suri said. "Things have been... difficult."

Ambriel nodded. "I heard about Lucifer and Sophia, and how you were trying to help them again before..." She trailed off, her sweet face troubled.

"Yes, well, that's actually why we're here," Michael said.

"We need to go to the Announcing Rock," Suri added.

Ambriel said, "But the aeons haven't been there in – actually, I don't even remember how long it's been."

"I know. That's why we have to go."

"I don't get it."

"She wants to find a way into the Garden," Michael explained.

Ambriel cocked her head. "Is that even possible?"

"Want to find out?"

"Of course!"

Suri smiled and held out her hand. "Then lead the way."

*

The Announcing Rock was a vast slab of glittering, pale grey granite in the midst of a meadow beyond Ambriel's glade. The last time Suri had been there, the meadow had been packed with thousands upon thousands of angels, come to hear Logos' latest proclamation. Now it was empty, but for the azure poppies swaying in the breeze among the long grass.

"So obviously, the rock is still here," Ambriel said, "but I don't see how that's going to help you find the Garden."

"Exactly what I keep telling her," Michael muttered.

"It's logic," Suri said to Ambriel, ignoring him. "Why would the aeons make things hard for themselves by putting the passage to the Garden somewhere far away? It must be near here, only hidden."

"Well," Ambriel said doubtfully, "have you got any idea how to find it?"

"Nothing's ever truly invisible, right?" Suri said, beginning to poke around in the grass hemming the stone platform. "Like our armour when we go to Earth – it's only invisible if you don't know how to look at it right."

"I see what you mean. But we aren't humans. I think if the aeons were hiding a door from us, they'd make it harder to find than that."

"We can at least try," Suriel argued. "Let's spread out. We'll cover more ground that way."

Michael wandered gloomily off to scan the edges of the meadow. Suri and Ambriel worked outward from the Announcing Rock, searching for anything anomalous while Suri filled Ambriel in on what they'd seen in the scrying glass. But after hours of examining every odd-looking twig or beetle, none of them had turned up anything that remotely suggested a door into another realm. They gathered again at the rock, and sat down on it.

"Are you ready to let this go yet?" Michael asked Suri.

"Absolutely not!" she snapped. "If we give up now, we're as good as damning ourselves, never mind the poor suckers stuck on Earth."

"Maybe not," Michael said speculatively. "I mean, we've heard the daevas' threats, but we don't actually know that Heaven would fall if Earth does – "

"I can't believe you would say that! We're supposed to guide and help humans, not deliver them to Hell on a platter!"

"I never said anything about Hell or platters – "

"Stop fighting," Ambriel broke in, her voice soft but firm. "It won't help."

They fell silent. Ambriel squinted off into the forest-rimmed boundaries of the meadow, and said, "Have you considered asking Sartael?"

"Sartael!" Michael scoffed. "That skinny, squinty packrat?"

"Well, he is the Angel of Hidden Things," Ambriel countered.

"He should be the Angel of the Bad Attitude," Suri said with an expression of distaste.

"And he's of the lowest order besides," Michael added. "I very much doubt that his jurisdiction includes hidden aeon doors."

"You're grumpier than you used to be," Ambriel observed mildly.

Michael threw up his hands in exasperation, but Suri smiled at her. "You're right. We're all a little stressed right now…but actually, Sartael's not a bad suggestion. Better than anything we've come up with anyway – right, Michael?"

"Oh, sure – if you enjoy beating your head against brick walls." He stomped off in the direction of the forest on the horizon.

"Coming?" Suri asked Ambriel.

Ambriel looked after Michael and then smiled regretfully at Suri. "No thanks. But good luck."

"With Sartael?"

Ambriel shook her head. "With Michael."

THE DOMINION OF SARTAEL

The Dominion of Sartael was on the far side of the Dominion of Saranyu, Angel of Clouds. Suri and Michael stumbled among the billowing drifts of white and grey until Michael lost patience and drew his sword. The flaming blade burned a path through the mist with a hiss of steam. Suri was glad that Saranyu was nowhere to be seen, as he was well known to be volatile, and no doubt he'd have objected violently to Michael's destruction of his element.

At last the cloud began to thin. At the same time, it took on a darker tone and a gauzy quality, so that it didn't look like condensed water anymore, but rather like lint or cobweb. The angels could make out murky shapes within it, but it was too dense to tell what they were.

"Saranyu's dominion is bigger than I thought," Suri observed.

"We aren't in Saranyu's dominion anymore," Michael said, tossing his sword back into the ether with flick of the wrist. "This is Sartael's. I thought you'd been here before."

"There are thousands and thousands of dominions, Michael. Even you can't have visited them all."

"I made a regular point of it," Michael answered.

Suri rolled her eyes behind Michael's back. "Fine. I get it. It's cloudy in Sartael's dominion because he's the Angel of Hidden Things. That's sort of almost cute."

"It's nothing of the sort," Michael contradicted. "Sartael has neither a sense of humour nor a sense of irony. It's misty because he doesn't like visitors. He thinks that if he makes himself difficult enough to find, no one will bother looking." Michael dodged one of the dark shapes swimming out of the fog, which, when Suri got a better look at it, turned out to be a vast pile of treasure-chests.

"So how do we find him?" she asked.

Michael shrugged. "We follow the trail of detritus, I suppose. It'll lead to him eventually."

Gradually, as they walked, the mist began to clear, while the junk piles grew more frequent. They contained everything from maps to coins to soiled children's clothing to jewellery. One hulking pile seemed to be composed entirely of odd socks. Beside it was a vertiginous tower of well-thumbed diaries, and beside that, a mound of mouldering Easter-eggs.

"Where does he get all this stuff?" Suri asked, picking up one of the diaries, which promptly disintegrated.

"They're counterparts of all of the things that humans hide and fail to recover," Michael explained.

"What does he do with it all?"

"Hoards it, as far as I can tell."

"I heard that!" a reedy voice snapped from somewhere up ahead.

"Bingo," Suri said, turning in the direction of the speaker. They found him hunched over a rococo mahogany desk, peering down through a pair of surgeon's spectacles at a tray of rusting keys as he sorted through them with a mismatched pair of lacquered chopsticks.

"Sartael," Michael said, "how wonderful to see you. It's been too long."

Sartael looked up at him, frowning. His form was hunched, his white face pinched inside its frame of messy black hair, his green eyes made enormous by the magnifying lenses. "I'm not the one's who's free to move about at will," he answered testily.

"True," Suri answered, trying to sound conciliatory. "We should visit more often."

Sartael peered at her for a moment as if she had spoken a foreign language and then went back to his keys. "What do you want?" he asked, his tone making it clear that he didn't particularly care to know the answer.

"We need your help," Suri said.

"No."

"But you haven't even heard what it is we need help with!"

"Answer's still no."

"Why?"

"Because you'll be the one who benefits from it, not me."

"How can you say that, when you don't even know what we want?"

"Because that's how it always is." Sartael looked up again, adopting an exaggerated pout. "Oh no, I was certain I buried my jar of pennies here, how will I ever find it?" His expression changed to one of pleading anxiety. "I'm sure my husband is dallying with his secretary, now where can he have hidden the evidence?" His face shifted again, this time showing agitated distraction. "The treasure map said that the chest should be right here, but there's nothing!" Sartael shook his head. "They never even bother to call me by name!"

"To be fair," Michael answered, "they don't usually call any of us by name. They just supplicate."

"Easy for you to say," Sartael grumbled. "At least they've heard of you. You get hymns, prayers, paintings, the adoration of good Catholic girls the world over. Who ever gives thanks to the Angel of Hidden Things? I'll tell you: no one! They just want, and want, and want."

"This is beyond wanting and thanking," Michael said, his exasperation finally showing. "The Balance is at stake."

"Right, I've heard that one before."

"Don't you know what's happened?" Suri asked incredulously.

"Again: can't leave my dominion."

Suri looked at Michael, who only shrugged. "Okay," she said, "well, the daevas have made a bid for Earth, and they've

97

already got the humans partially under their control. If someone doesn't stop them, the Deep will subsume all of Creation. I guess you could say this is the End of Days."

Sartael gave a languid, infuriating shrug. "Well there's not much a third-rate angel's going to be able to do about that, is there?" He gave Suri a cold once-over. "Or a first rate one, for that matter. Sorry. Goodbye."

"This is hopeless," Michael muttered.

But Suri had a glint in her eye. She studied Sartael for a moment and then said, "What if you could have what you want most? Then would you help us?"

"What I want most?" Sartael repeated, giving her a speculative look in return. "In that case, I might be inclined to reconsider. But first, you have to promise you'll give it to me, whatever it is."

"I really don't think – " Michael began, but Suri interrupted: "Done," and held out her hand to shake on it.

For the first time since they'd encountered him, Sartael smiled. "Very well. It just so happens that I know how to find your door."

"We never told you that we were looking for a door."

"You didn't have to," he smirked. "You should learn to keep your voices down, if you mean to keep secrets."

"You heard us talking about this?" Michael asked. "How is that possible?"

"I have an extensive collection of ear-horns."

"Who would hide an ear-horn?" Suri asked sceptically.

"Any number of young women married off to rich old men despite a weakness for penniless day-labourers. Now, do you want my help or not?"

"We want it," Suri said, before Michael could respond.

Sartael removed his spectacles and stood up. Surprisingly, he was taller than Michael by several inches. "I require payment in advance."

"Right," Michael said without enthusiasm. "What is it that you want?"

Sartael smiled his smug smile and held up his wrists with their bronze cuffs. "Freedom from my staves."

"Absolutely not!" Michael spluttered. "Only angels of the highest order are given that privilege! It's been the same since the day we were made, you can't just – "

Sartael shrugged. "Find the door on your own, then."

"This is blackmail!"

"No, it's the barter system," Sartael argued. "You shook on it, remember?"

"I don't think it's even in my power to do it."

"Then let her do it," he answered, jabbing a finger toward Suri.

"If Michael can't free you, I definitely can't," she said.

"Then it looks like the deal is off."

"Michael," Suri said.

"But – "

"We're running out of time! Please, just try!"

"Fine," Michael growled. "Give me your hands."

Sartael extended his wrists. Michael clasped his hands around the bands. For a few moments, nothing happened except that Michael's face flushed red. Then the bands began to glow, their light increasing until it was blinding. Abruptly, both the light and the bands were gone. Sartael looked at his bare forearms in disbelief for a few moments. Then he let out a whoop and took off at a run.

"Crap!" Suri said. "We never should have agreed to payment in advance."

"Is there any point in saying I told you so?"

"Just run, Michael."

They set off in the direction that Sartael had taken. As they ran, the mist began to thin, exposing more and more of Sartael's piles of hidden things. The occasional footprint in the damp soil told them which direction he was moving. They found him at last on the shore of a small, silver lake. In the middle of the lake there was a pagoda decorated in red and green and gold. A female angel was seated in the middle of the pagoda, apparently deep in meditation. She wore white, flowing robes and a white hood over her black hair. What was visible of her face beneath the hood was exquisitely beautiful.

Clearly Sartael thought so, too. He stepped purposefully into the lake, heading toward the pagoda until Michael caught his arm and dragged him back. "Don't disturb her!" he hissed.

"Why not?" Sartael asked, gazing at the meditating angel longingly.

"That's Quan Yin," Suri told him, "Angel of Mercy. Suffering humans are kind of her raison d'etre. She's taken it hard, being barred from Earth. If she's found some peace, we'd better leave her to it."

"If you say so…" Sartael said, still gazing at Quan Yin.

"The door, Sartael," Michael reminded him.

"What door?"

"The one you promised to show us in exchange for your freedom!" Michael snapped.

"Oh, that," Sartael said. "It's wherever you want it to be."

"What?" Suri asked.

Sartael rolled his eyes in exasperation. "It manifests wherever you decide to put it."

"It can't be that easy!"

"I never said it would be easy. Just because you can find it, doesn't mean you can get through it."

"How do you know all of this?" Michael asked doubtfully.

Sartael shrugged. "It's a Hidden Thing. I have a list of all known Hidden Things, and where they're hidden."

"I don't believe this," Michael muttered. "We didn't even need you!"

Sartael shrugged, smirking.

"But how do you manifest something when you don't know what it looks like?" Suri asked.

"It looks like whatever you want it to look like," Sartael told her.

"Seriously?"

"Watch and learn," Sartael said. He focused his eyes on a tree a little way into the forest. At first, nothing happened. But then the surface of the tree began to shimmer, then to glow, and suddenly it burst into flames. In the middle of the flames was a double door made of spiked iron bars, with a sign over it that read: "Abandon all hope, ye who enter here."

"Seriously?" Suri said. "You can choose anything in Creation, and you manifest the Gates of Hell?"

Sartael grinned.

"Tasteless, even for you," Michael told him.

"How can Dante be tasteless? Anyway, I was going with the End of Days theme."

Michael just shook his head, gave the flaming gateway a quick, intense look, and abruptly it turned to an ordinary wooden door. He approached it, and turned the knob. None of them were expecting what happened next, though: the door opened entirely without event. A flood of incandescent light poured through from the other side.

"*All right*…that was too easy," Sartael said, looking at the light in dubious wonder.

"Something's not right about this," Michael said, frowning.

"Michael," Suri said wearily, "nothing is right at the moment. Let's just go with it."

"What if we go with it and it turns out to be a trap?" he asked. "There's nothing to say that's actually a door to the Garden, and not some kind of daeva trick. They could have infiltrated the Garden already. In fact that's quite likely, given that – wait! What are you doing?"

Sartael had stepped part way through the door. He turned back to say, "Going to the Garden."

"You can't! You're only a – "

"Third-rate angel, conveniently divested of his staves," Sartael answered, holding up his bare wrists and wiggling his fingers. Then he stepped the rest of the way through the door and was swallowed by the light.

Suri looked at Michael. "Well, we can't exactly leave him to rampage through the Garden alone, can we?" Without waiting for Michael to answer, Suri stepped through the door, too. And with the absolute certainty that he'd live to regret it, Michael followed her.

CHAPTER 4

MID-IRELAND

A starless night sky hung over the city. She wasn't on the castle walls this time, but on a street somewhat beyond and below them. From there, she could see that the city had an ancient kind of skyline, all pitched roofs and steeples and turrets, the castle rising up above the rest. It might have been beautiful, if it hadn't been so bleak. The city was deserted. No light shone, no people walked the pavements, cars and wagons sat abandoned every which way on the streets, and rubbish blew along the dry gutters, chased by a bitter wind.

Yet Esther had the feeling that the city's people hadn't left, only retreated, hiding as deep within its buildings as they could get, huddling in the darkness, in terror of – what? Despite the emptiness, there was nothing obvious to be terrified of.

On the heels of the thought, the sky exploded, torn by vast, bright shapes that seared through the darkness like falling stars, except that they didn't fade as they fell. Instead, as she watched them, they became clearer, larger, until they resolved into human-shaped figures with vast, white wings. But they weren't angels. Their wings were the jagged shape of terror, trailing darkness behind them – a perfect, impenetrable blackness that greyed the cloudy night by comparison. The creatures plummeted toward the patchwork city, erasing the sky with every wingbeat.

Esther felt, rather than heard, the people's screams. She sensed their terrified despair as they realized that they could not hide from what was coming for them. And then she forgot about the people, because one of the winged creatures was coming for her. It swept down on her, smiling with eyes and lips as dark as the erasure unfolding in its wake. A tangle of black hair and white train streamed behind her, and Esther knew her. She turned and ran, with no idea where she was going, only that it was away from the black-eyed demon.

"Wait!" the demon called after her in a chiming, child's voice. Esther didn't dare turn to look. She ran faster, feeling her heart begin to skip in protest. "You can't outrun me, with a body coming to pieces," the demon mocked. Esther looked down, and sure enough, the edges of her body seemed to be disintegrating, blowing away like ash.

"Oh, God," she whispered, stilled by terror.

"And you can't pray for salvation, with only a piece of a soul. Come to me, and I can fix it all."

Esther knew that she could never go to her, that the demon might mend her body, but there would be a price to pay, and it would be far too high. She looked around. There was a flight of stone steps ahead of her, impossibly long and steep, their top lost in the sweeping darkness. She would never make it to the top, but still she began to climb, as the downdrafts of the demon's wings, soft and subtle as kisses, eroded her slowly but surely. She could feel her heart begin to fail, as she slipped toward oblivion –

And then someone caught her. The bad light and her pounding dizziness made it hard to see him clearly, but what she could make out was arresting. Slanted blue eyes above sharp cheekbones. Long, straight, dark hair. A beautiful mouth set in a terrible line. White skin patterned with intricate black. Long, sinewy arms that looked fragile but felt as strong and sure as steel, circling her like redemption, filling her with a warmth and peace she'd felt only once before – through a screen in a confessional. A guardian angel, she thought, as her body became whole again, and her heart resumed its proper rhythm. Esther watched with calm detachment as the demon landed a few steps above them, darkness cracking out around her where her feet touched the old stone. But it couldn't cross the circle of the angel's arms.

The demon screamed in outrage, bearing sharklike teeth, but Esther's angel didn't let go of her. If anything, he held her more tightly. "Don't be afraid," he whispered to her. "You're as strong as she is."

"No," Esther answered, wishing that she didn't have to tell him that he was mistaking her for someone else. "I'm nothing."

"You are everything. You can be our salvation, if you choose it."

That voice, soft and musical. She knew it. She knew his name; she knew him. Struck with the wonder of it, and tottering on the edge of a deeper realization, she forgot the city crumbling around her. She forgot everything but his blue eyes, looking down into hers.

"Theletos?" she said, and he smiled like every dawn there'd ever been.

THE DEMON DOMINIONS

The first time he'd seen Lilith cup an Earthly scene in her hands, Rive had known that he would have to try it, too. He had no idea whether it was even possible. He'd never seen anyone else do it: not the other aeons, not even Abaddon. But the fact that he'd managed to reach Esther in the confessional gave him hope, and with nothing else to do but try, he watched Lilith carefully whenever she came to torment him with scenes from Sophie's life. He provoked her to it – pretending that it hurt him, begging her to stop – and she acquiesced so easily that it was almost laughable, opening window after window on Sophie's oblivious happiness with vicious glee.

When Lilith left, he worked tirelessly to replicate her movements. It was easier said than done. A human mind is an ever-shifting paint-spatter of thoughts. An aeon's is a galaxy: as close to omniscience as any being comes. It is constantly aware of every single human and angel consciousness. To Rive, they sounded like a vast choir in constant song, and even in his prison in the Deep, he could hear them. Picking out a single one, however, was almost impossible. The only reason he'd even attempted it was that he thought his connection to Sophie might make her stand out.

Instead, he'd stumbled onto Esther Madden. And so he wasn't especially surprised that his window, when he finally managed to open one, opened on her. The first images were so blurry and tenuous, he could barely tell that he was looking at a human, let alone work out who it might be. But as he got better at conjuring the window, the figure became clearer: a girl who wasn't Sophie, though she bore a definite resemblance to his consort. But her hair was white-blonde instead of mahogany brown, her features softer, her eyes a hazier shade of grey. Her manner was quieter, her smile more reticent, and yet there was a light to her face that was just like Sophie's. He'd known that this was Esther Madden even before he heard the girl she travelled with call her by name.

Rive watched her every minute that he could, trying to figure out what it was that connected them all. But gradually, as he watched, the wondering faded. It wasn't so much that he stopped wanting to know what it all meant, as the fact that Esther's own story captivated him in and of itself. He was amazed and appalled at the tenacity with which she was pursuing the task he'd set her, particularly when he realized how ill she was. He had hoped that she would look for Sophie. He had never expected her to risk her life to do it.

Likewise, he was never sure when his admiration for her calm determination turned into something more, but he wondered if it was when he began to view her dreams. They were clearer to him even than the scenes of her daily life – maybe because they came from Abaddon and Lilith. That worried him; it would have worried him just to know that the daevas were aware of her, never mind that they were tampering with her subconscious. But it wasn't why he finally stepped into them. He did it because he could no longer resist it. He couldn't resist her, facing down Lilith with nothing but her unassuming courage, as the world crumbled around her and her own body dissolved.

He slipped into the folds of her dream as easily as a swimmer slips into the current of a river, and when he took her in his arms – when she looked up, and knew him, and spoke his name – he felt that he belonged somewhere for the first time in his long, lonely existence.

Later, he realized that that was when he should have known. But they were too struck with the wonder of each other to see Lilith smile.

14 JUNE
BELFAST, IRELAND

Esther jerked awake, the ground beneath her juddering. It was very dark, and for a panicked moment she thought that the dream had been real, that she'd awakened in the lightless emptiness the demons had made of that city. But the darkness she'd woken to was incomplete, cracked with dingy light, and someone was speaking out of it.

"Morning, Sunshine. Dreaming of clockwork demons again?"

At the sound of the sarcastic voice, everything came rushing back: the night-time flight from the school, the miserable day at Declan's place, and then the gruelling walk from the city centre to the port. Cliona had hoped to find them a way onto a ferry crossing to Holyhead, the quickest route to Britain. But after standing for three hours in a queue that seemed to Esther to contain an inordinate number of faeries, they learned that all the boats were sold out for the next two days.

Esther and Cliona had hung around the docks for a while, hoping that something else would turn up. But they were wary of lingering in the open too long. "Belfast it is," Cliona had said at last, sighing. And then with more resolution: "Anyway, the crossing's shorter there. It might be easier to find a boatman who won't ask questions."

So they'd made their way to the port's railway station and jumped an empty ore car on a train going north to Tara Mines. It was market day in the nearby town of Navan when they arrived, and they scoped out the market until they found a morose Bean Nighe selling second-hand shirts out of the bed of a dilapidated lorry. Its number plate was from Belfast.

"There's our ride," Cliona said.

"But isn't that one of those washer-woman faeries?"

"Aye."

"So those shirts came off of dead people?"

Cliona shrugged. "She's a washer-woman. They'll be clean."

Esther couldn't really argue with that. And more to the point, she couldn't suggest a better option. So, at the end of the day, when the Bean Nighe finished re-packing her unsold wares, the girls sneaked under the tarp covering them. Corpse's shirts or not, they made the softest bed Esther had lain on in days, and in minutes she'd fallen asleep.

"I don't know," Esther said now, still bleary with sleep, still partly lost in that crumbling city, and the arms of the dream angel. Because clearly, she'd been dreaming...yet the feeling of those arms around her had been so real, so familiar, that she couldn't quite attribute them to her imagination. "I suppose so," she said at last, doubtfully.

"Hm," Cliona said, and though she couldn't see it, Esther could imagine the speculative glint in her eyes. "So who's Theletos, then?"

Esther cringed. If she'd spoken in her sleep, what else had Cliona heard? "I don't know," she repeated, glad that she mostly told the truth. Though she still had no idea who he was, it felt wrong to deny Theletos. At the same time, she didn't want to talk about him to anyone, least of all Cliona, with her probing, knowing eyes.

Cliona studied her for a moment longer, and then she sighed. "Ah, well, I'd hoped for a better story than that. But we don't have time for it, really. We'll have to get off this lorry before it stops, or face the washer-woman's friends. "

"Are we in Belfast?" Esther asked.

Cliona lifted an edge of the tarp. All that Esther could make out were dark shop fronts and the occasional pool of murky light from one of the gas street lamps. But Cliona said, "I think so."

"You think so?"

"That's the best I can do," Cliona answered with a half-smile, picking up her kerchief-wrapped bundle. "Get ready to jump!"

Esther didn't like the thought of jumping from the truck while it was still moving, but she knew that Cliona was right: they couldn't afford to be caught here. She picked up her own bundle and crouched by Cliona at the tailgate. Cliona shimmied out until her legs were dangling over the edge. Then she slipped off, landing almost gracefully.

Esther panicked. The thought of being in this strange place, alone, was more than she could bear. Taking a deep breath, she shut her eyes and dropped onto the tarmac. She landed sprawled out on her backside, her shins jarred by the fall, but otherwise unharmed. The lorry disappeared around a corner, leaving them alone on the deserted road. Esther stood up and brushed herself off.

"All right?" Cliona asked.

"Sure," Esther answered, though she was cold and aching and now winded in the bargain. "Any idea what to do now?"

"Well," Cliona answered, considering the still, dark shop fronts and blind windows of the flats above, "we'll have to get to the port. But first we need to find something to eat."

"I'm hungry, too," Esther admitted. "But it doesn't look like anything's open. And besides, do you think it's safe to go into a shop?"

Cliona shrugged nonchalantly, her half-smile back again. "I don't think anywhere's safe for us, now. But this is a damn sight safer than Dublin." She began to walk in the direction the truck had taken, so confidently that if Esther hadn't known better, she would have believed that Cliona knew the city well.

"How do you know where you're going?" Esther asked, running to catch up to her.

"The sea is to the east," Cliona answered. Then she pointed up to the sky, where the stars were just visible through the hazy streetlight. "That's Polaris – it tells you where true north is. You know that, you'll never get lost again."

"Where did you learn about stars?" Esther asked, impressed.

"The library."

"At the convent?"

"Where else?"

Esther walked beside Cliona for a few moments in silence, wondering about this. Cliona didn't seem the type of girl to read in her spare time, let alone about ancient navigational practises. But then, she really knew very little about her. To that end, she asked her the question that had been bothering her since they ran from the convent: "Cliona, why are you doing this?"

"Looking for food or walking east?"

110

"Staying with me," Esther said, not trying to hide her exasperation. "I mean, if you get caught on your own, I suppose you'll be sent back to the convent. But if you're caught with me, it'll be something a whole lot worse. Why take the risk? Why not just leave me to it?"

Cliona turned back to the road ahead of her, and for a moment Esther thought that she wasn't going to answer. Then, finally, she said, "Because I can't."

"Sure you can! You've got money, you look different, and no one thinks you murdered a priest. You could do anything you like." Esther hadn't realized how much she resented that fact until she said it and heard the bitterness in her own tone.

"No, I can't," Cliona said quietly, not looking at Esther.

"Why not?"

There was another long silence. Then Cliona spoke in the same soft tone, all of the irony and bravado gone: "How do you think I knew your story?"

"What?"

"About your parents turning you in to the parish priest and him handing you over to the Sisters?"

"You said that's always what happens to girls like me. I thought you must have known others like that at the school, or else…" Esther looked at Cliona; Cliona couldn't quite meet her eyes. "Or else that's what happened to you."

Cliona smiled bitterly. "Not me. My mam. But it all came to the same thing in the end."

"I don't understand."

Cliona shook her head. "Of course you don't. I'll bet you grew up in a nice house, with a nice family. You never got called a Paki, and you didn't even know places like the Sisters' school existed, before they brought you there."

Esther was taken aback by the venom in Cliona's voice. More to the point, she didn't know how to answer her. What Cliona had said about her ignorance was true, after all, but not

111

for the reasons Cliona thought it was. Stick as close as you can to the truth, she reminded herself.

"You're right," she said. "I didn't know about the school before they brought me there. But the nice family...well, my mam had me when she was only seventeen, and I don't think she ever forgave me for it. She never told me who my real dad was. Maybe she didn't know. My stepdad loved me like I was really his, but then he died, and Mam started drinking and left the other five kids for me to deal with. And if you think I ever lived in a nice house, then you've never been to Ballymun."

Cliona was clearly surprised by her challenging tone. Then she smiled. "Nice to know you have a backbone. And sorry if I accused you of being middle class. You're right, I've never been to Ballymun. Is it horrible?"

"Unless you like high-rise estates."

"I wouldn't know," Cliona said. "I've never been to one."

"Why? Did you live in a nice house, before?"

Cliona laughed humourlessly. "Esther, until we ran the other night, I'd never been out of the convent in my life."

Esther stared at her, stunned. Finally she said, "But – how is that possible?"

Cliona shrugged, but Esther could tell from the way she turned her face to the shadows that she was far from nonchalant about what she was going to say. "I was born there."

"So your mam..."

Cliona nodded. "Looks like you and I have something else in common: Mam was a 'wayward woman'. I was...well, living proof, I guess."

"They put her in the school because she had you?" Esther asked. It didn't make sense. She knew that many of the girls in the convent school were there on account of promiscuity, but if any of them had had children, those children had never been visible.

"No," Cliona answered. "She didn't have me till several

months after she went to the school, and she managed to keep her condition hidden until it was almost her time. Otherwise, she'd never have been let in with the other girls."

"So if she wasn't taken in for being pregnant, then why?"

Cliona's dark eyes locked with Esther's, heavy with an unspoken plea. All at once, Esther wished she hadn't asked the question, but it was far too late to take it back. "My mother was committed to the Sisters because she had visions of demons. She said they were coming to take over the world, and she was their prophet."

She waited a moment for Esther's reaction, but Esther said nothing. She couldn't. The word "prophet" had taken her back to the night in the Mother Superior's office and the terrible photographs of the murder victims.

After a moment, Cliona continued, "Of course, no one believed her. Her parents thought she was mad and kicked her out. She lived on the streets for a few months before some nun in a soup kitchen handed her over to the Sisters."

Esther considered Cliona's story for a few long moments, and then she said, "How do you know all of this? I mean, look how hard the Sisters worked to keep me from talking with any of you. They can't have let your mam just tell you these things."

"Of course not. They never even meant for me to know who she was. But news travels, in a convent. People can be bribed to pass messages, or the like."

"Even the nuns?"

Cliona laughed. "They're the worst! It was one of them first told me who my mother was. For a while she passed notes between us..." She trailed off, shook her head.

Esther didn't want to push her on the topic. Instead, she asked, "Did your mother tell you anything about these demons, aside from them meaning to take over the world?"

Once again, Cliona gave her a look that was half scornful, half supplicating. "She tried to get me to join them – whatever that meant. She said that anyone who sided with them would be saved from the coming apocalypse." Cliona glanced at Esther, then said, "She also told me that one of them was my father."

Esther swallowed around the growing lump in her throat. "That's just mad."

"Like you?" Cliona demanded.

"I…" Esther began, and then had no idea how to continue. At last she said, "It's not the same." Then, after a pause during which Cliona was markedly silent, she asked, "Where is your mother now?"

Cliona shook her head. "She was too much for the nuns, in the end. She was sent to an asylum in Yorkshire."

"So that's why you came with me," Esther said, as the pieces fell into place. "You want to see her."

But Cliona said fiercely, "No. I came with you because I would have thrown myself from the roof rather than stay in that place another minute. As for Mam…well I guess I just want to know if I should bother."

"Pardon?" Esther said, suddenly on her guard.

"I want to know whether or not my mother was telling the truth. Whether or not the demons are real. If she's sane or…not."

At last, Esther understood Cliona's interest in her and the supplication in her eyes. Her head swam with the weight of what the other girl wanted from her. "Cliona," she said at last, "I don't know your mam, and even if I did, it still wouldn't be my place to judge her."

"I don't want you to judge her!" Cliona snapped. "I just want to know what you dream about. What these demons look like. What they say to you. Whether they're what Mam saw or not."

"I've told you about them already," Esther answered.

"Tell me again."

Esther sighed. "Well…the man is very pale, his eyes and skin and hair all kind of colourless. And he has that weird clockwork arm. The woman has dark hair and white skin."

"Is she pretty?"

"Cliona, she's a monster. She's terrifying."

Cliona considered this. Then she said, "And those are the only ones you've seen?"

"Why? What did your mam's one look like?"

"He was dark. I guess I take that from him."

"Don't say that!"

"Why not? I sure didn't get my looks from my mam. She's pure Irish ginger."

Esther sighed. "Even if your mam really did see a demon, there's no reason to think he's your dad. Ireland has plenty of people with dark skin." But she knew that her words lacked conviction. A human-demon hybrid would hardly be the strangest thing she'd encountered since the Change.

"In your dreams," Cliona continued, as if Esther hadn't spoken, "they talk about the end of the world, aye?"

"Aye," Esther answered slowly.

"Do they ask you to join them?"

Esther paused. *Come to me, and I can fix it all*... It wasn't precisely an invitation to join their ranks, but it was an invitation nonetheless. She said, "Not in so many words."

"But they do offer you something."

"I suppose they do."

"What else do you see? What do they show you?"

Esther shook her head, tired and beginning to be irritated by Cliona's grilling. "They show me destruction. Ruin. The world coming to pieces."

"But why?"

Esther paused again. Until her most recent dream, she'd have said she didn't know, and meant it. But she couldn't forget the other presence in that dream, the one who had protected her from the demon girl, and whose touch had reminded her

115

so powerfully of Theletos. Nor could she forget about Theletos pleading with her to find Sophie Creedon. And then there was the fact that whatever had made the rest of the human race forget what had happened to them had somehow passed her by. Clearly, she was an anomaly. Now it seemed that she might be valuable, too, to these demons who were pursuing her. Also, perhaps, to whomever was fighting against them. But still, she had no idea how or why.

"I'm not sure," she said slowly. "But I think it's either because they want me to help them – or they're afraid that I might help whoever is working against them."

Cliona walked in silence for a time. At last, she said, "So you believe it. You believe that what you're dreaming is real."

Esther didn't know how to answer. It seemed wrong to get Cliona's hopes up about her mother when there was nothing to prove that she wasn't insane. But in the end, she knew that Cliona had trusted her with a secret both precious and painful, and she couldn't offer less in return.

"I know that it's real," she said.

"How?"

At that point Esther wanted nothing more than to tell her the whole truth. Given her history, Cliona might even believe her. But she couldn't do it – not because Cliona might not believe her, rather because she might. Esther couldn't burden Cliona with a painful knowledge that wouldn't help her, when she carried so many burdens already.

So, thinking of the arms that had circled her, keeping her safe in the crumbling city, she said, "Because I've also dreamed of an angel."

Cliona's ironic smile was back. "Doesn't every good Catholic girl dream of angels?"

Esther shook her head. "He's real."

"A male angel?" Cliona smirked. "Now I know it's a dream."

"He's not a dream!"

"How do you know?"

"Because I also spoke to him once. I mean, once when I wasn't dreaming."

Cliona looked at Esther closely. "You're serious, aren't you?" she asked. Esther nodded. "When did this happen? You talking to him, I mean?"

Esther took a deep breath, then said, "He spoke to me through Father Xavier. In the confessional, just before he died."

Cliona stopped. "Are you bloody kidding me?"

Esther turned to her, held her eyes. "No, I'm not. I went to confession, but when the priest spoke, it wasn't him. It was someone else – someone who called himself Theletos."

"Okay," Cliona said after a moment, beginning to walk again, "but what makes you think you were talking to an angel and not another demon or even just a delusional, dying priest?"

"The things that he knew…the way that he said them. And then, the feeling when I touched him…"

"You touched the dead priest?"

"No! I mean, he wasn't dead then. And it was only our hands that touched – barely even that, since it was through the screen. But still, I knew he was something else. And then when I dreamed of him – well, he looked like an angel."

The smirk was back. "A winged man in a loin cloth?"

Esther couldn't help laughing. "Hardly! He didn't have wings, and he was wearing…um…clothes. But his eyes and his face…" She trailed off, realizing she had no idea how to describe him. "He was beautiful and terrible at the same time. But he protected me from the demon. He must be an angel."

Cliona shook her head, but the small smile remained on her face. "And let me guess – he's the one who told you to go to Scotland."

"Yes…"

"Well, that settles it."

"What settles what?"

"Your story sounds mad. But you don't. In fact, you seem like the sanest person I've met in a long time. So, if you're sure enough of all of this to go to Scotland, then I'm sure enough to try to help my mam. But first, we've got to eat. Look, there's a bakery."

"It's not open yet."

"No, but there's a light on in back. They'll be in working already. If they've burnt the muffins, they might even give them to us for free."

Without waiting for an answer, Cliona was off across the street. Someone had let her in before Esther caught up to her. She peered in the window of the bakery. The front was dark, the trays and shelves empty, but the back was indeed lit, and she could see Cliona talking with a young man. Esther left her to it, crouching down with her back against the cold stone wall of the building to wait.

She'd sat there a few minutes when something caught her eye. A block down, a woman stooped with age stood in a street lamp's hazy pool of light. She seemed to be washing a window, dipping a brush into a bucket and then reaching up to scrub. Without quite knowing why, Esther stood up and made her way toward the woman. Still distrustful of strangers, she kept to the shadows, but when she was a few meters away the woman gave her a calm, direct glance, as if she'd been expecting her.

"Good mornin' to you, lass," she said in a low, lilting voice.

"You're Scottish!" Esther cried, forgetting herself in her surprise at the coincidence.

The woman smiled slightly. Esther saw that her eyes were milky with cataracts. "Aye, I am. Is it a trouble tae you?"

"No. It's only that I – " Esther stopped, wondering why she had the sudden urge to tell this woman her plans. Instead, she said, "I couldn't help noticing that you were washing windows. It's a strange time of day for it, and I thought…well…"

"That I'd mislaid my reason?" the woman finished for her, her look and tone still amused.

"Well, it is the middle of the night," Esther said, wondering how to extricate herself from this increasingly embarrassing situation.

"It's nearer tae mornin', truth be told, though I take your meanin'. But I heard them puttin' this up, and I couldnae let it rest. I cannae bear tae see the things, never mind on my ain front windae."

Esther looked at the window the woman was washing, and a shiver went up her spine. Half of the poster was scrubbed away, but there was enough of it left to make out her own face looking back at her, under the heavy black capitals, Have You Seen This Girl? It was the same picture that had run in the newspaper. Most of the message underneath it was obliterated, but it was easy enough to guess what it had said.

Though she knew that she should brass it out, Esther found herself backing away, as if the poster could reach out and grab her. She nearly screamed when the old woman's hand shot out and did just that – until she realized that the milky eyes were looking at her sympathetically. The woman's grip was strong but gentle, clearly meant to steady and comfort rather than accuse.

"Why don't you come inside, lass," the woman said then. "I'll make you a cup o' tea. Calm your nerves." Esther looked back the way she'd come, thinking of Cliona. "Dinnae worry, hen. She'll be occupied a while, yet." The woman gave her a knowing smile, and for a moment it seemed that her eyes flashed green.

Esther looked at her sharply. "Who are you?" she asked, wondering whether she could be some type of faery. Yet none that she knew of seemed to fit. The woman was too jovial to be a Banshee, too old to be a nymph or dryad or any of the more seductive female faeries, and too human-looking to be any of the rest.

"Call me Morag," the woman said, sounding like nothing more than an old woman. She opened a door beside the window she'd been washing, took up a walking stick carved with intricate symbols, and beckoned Esther inside. Seeing Esther hesitate, she said, "I dinnae bite," and winked at her.

Relenting, Esther stepped through the door. There was a shingle hanging beside it, gold leaf letters spelling "Books, New & Used" curved around a design – a triangle formed of three interconnected spirals. Once inside, Esther looked around with interest. Aside from a tiny counter with an elaborate Victorian cash register, the entire shop was full of shelves, and the shelves were full of books. It had a comforting atmosphere of leather and old paper, and a hint of something else – something wild and growing, though she couldn't name it or even find its source.

Morag turned on a couple of green-shaded reading lamps, then led Esther to an armchair upholstered in cracked maroon leather. "Rest yourself here," she said. "I'll be but a moment." Then she disappeared through a narrow door behind the counter.

Esther looked around her at the dizzying array of book spines, which reached up into the ceiling's shadows and lost themselves there. She had a strange thought then that there was no ceiling; that the shelves continued up and up forever, containing every book that ever had or ever would be written.

What's wrong with me? she wondered at the same moment that Morag returned with a tea tray and set it on the counter. She lifted the willow teapot and poured the tea through a strainer into a matching cup. Esther caught a quick glimpse of twigs and berries and blossoms in the strainer's basket before Morag set it aside and handed Esther the tea. It was mellow and sweet and soothing. She felt herself relax with each swallow.

Morag watched her silently until she'd drained the cup. "There now," she said. "Feelin' better?"

"Aye, thanks," Esther said dreamily, putting the empty cup into Morag's outstretched hand. "What was in that?"

Morag re-filled the cup and handed it back to her. "A bit o' this, a bit o' that," she said, and pouring a cup for herself, she sat down behind the counter. "Now tell me: how can I help you?"

Esther sighed. "I don't think you can."

Morag regarded her for a moment, and then said, "The Sword of Justice is strong. But you're strong too, Esther Madden."

Esther looked at her in horror. Her hands went to her face. But Morag smiled, shook her head. "Dinnae fret, hen. Your disguise is a fair one and will fool most."

"Who are you?" Esther asked again, torn now between the deep, inadvertent trust she felt for this woman and the instinct to run that had been driving her since the awful night she fled the convent.

Morag smiled enigmatically. "A friend."

"How do I know that?"

"You ken it, Esther Madden."

Esther studied her, and Morag met her eyes unflinchingly. At last, Esther said, "You know about the Change, don't you."

"Aye," Morag said, with a look that suggested she'd like to say a good deal more.

"Do you know why it happened?"

"Aye," Morag repeated, "I ken, and it's still happenin'. But it's where it's leadin' you should mind."

"Where is it leading?" Esther asked.

Morag seemed to be weighing and discarding words. At last she said, "To Hell." The word rang in Esther's head with cold finality, echoing Theletos's warning in the confessional. She opened her mouth to question Morag, but nothing would come out. "We're livin' in the End of Days, Esther," the old woman continued. "The prelude tae the Apocalypse. If nowt stops it, the world we ken'll be gone by Midsummer, leavin' one more awful than you can imagine."

"But I have imagined it," Esther said, thinking of empty city streets, of jagged white wings in a blackening sky. "I've been dreaming of it ever since the Change. Dreaming of them."

"Who?"

"The demons. The ones who destroy everything."

Morag narrowed her eyes. "And wha' do these demons look like, then?"

So Esther described them as best she could, watching Morag's frown deepen as she spoke. When she was finished, Morag sighed. "Those arenae demons, lass. They're called daevas, and demons are only their lapdogs."

"Daevas," Esther repeated, wondering why the word sounded familiar. Racking her brain, she finally remembered: in the confessional, Theletos had told her he was at the mercy of the daevas. She couldn't believe that she hadn't made the connection before. The word precisely fitted the spectres that haunted her dreams, and it made sense that they and Theletos and all of the rest of the current strangeness would be connected.

"What do they want?" Esther asked at last.

"Power."

"Over what?"

"O'er everything."

"Then what do they want with me?"

Morag studied her, her eyes taking on a green cast once again. "Are you sure it's you they want? Could you nae be pickin' up someone else's messages, like?"

"Sure, it wouldn't be the first time."

Morag's eyes sparked with interest. "Meanin'?"

Too tired and despondent to lie, Esther shook her head. "It's happened before. Someone gave me a message meant for someone else. It's how I ended up here."

"Who gave you this message?"

"He said his name is Theletos," Esther answered.

"Theletos?" Morag asked, leaning forward eagerly. "Are you certain?"

"Yes," Esther said. She doubted she would forget the name as long as she lived.

"You've seen him?" Morag demanded, with such hope in her face that Esther hated to quench it.

"Not quite," she answered regretfully. Then she explained about the priest in the confessional, the message he'd given her, and the dream she'd recently awakened from, where Theletos had saved her from the daeva.

"Interestin'."

"He told me he's an aeon," Esther said. "Is that some kind of angel?"

Morag shook her head. "An aeon's to an angel what a daeva is to a demon."

"But he's good, right?"

"You dinnae need me to tell you that," Morag answered with a knowing smile.

"I don't put much faith in my guesses, anymore."

"Frae wha' you've told me, you've done well so far."

"If so, it's mostly luck. Please, Morag, if you know what's happening, and why all of these — whatever they are — are talking to me, you've got to tell me."

Morag sighed. "I cannae."

"Because the daevas won't let you?"

"Nae: because I dinnae ken."

"Oh," Esther said, even more dejected.

"And it's that wha' gives me hope," Morag continued. Esther looked up at her in surprise. "It's rare I dinnae have answers, Esther Madden. Nae often that I cannae read a soul easy as I can read these books." She gestured at the burgeoning shelves. "But you are an enigma."

"What do you mean?"

"Just that. There's nowt about you tae say that you're nae an ordinary lass. Yet the daevas' madness passed over you. You foresee their plans. Creation's most powerful beings speak tae you, and Theletos, at least, had tae breach the walls of Hell tae do it."

"Hell?" Esther repeated with a shiver. "He said he was in the Deep."

Morag nodded. "Aye. In the demon dominions on the outskirts of Pandæmonium."

"Right…you've lost me."

"The Deep is the proper name for Hell: the broad name for the realm o' the daevas and demons, like Heaven is to the angels and aeons. Pandæmonium is the part of the Deep where the daevas live. It's the capitol, like. The dominions spread out around it."

"Hell has a capitol?"

"Aye – and Heaven too. The Garden, where the aeons live."

"So the daevas and aeons and all of this – it's basically good versus evil?"

Morag shook her head. "Forget your catechism. There's nae original sin, nae good and evil, nowt that's nae connected. All of Creation is paired off into polar opposites, and that's the way it's meant tae be. How it has tae be, tae exist: two of everything, both absolutes, equally weighted, tae keep the Balance."

Esther began to understand. "So those demons – sorry, daevas – I've been dreaming of, they're a pair?"

Morag nodded. "Abaddon and Lilith. The first daeva pair tae be created, and the most powerful. They balance the first aeon pair, Zoe and Logos."

Esther felt like the air was being crushed out of her lungs. Though she'd known Theletos only as a borrowed voice and a dream, she realized now that in some visceral way, she'd come to depend on him. "And Theletos is in their dominion. I guess that means he's their prisoner."

"Aye – since Midwinter."

"What did he do?" she asked. "I mean, for them to want to take him prisoner?"

"Nowt," Morag shrugged. "It was Sophia they wanted, but he went in her place."

"Sophia? Is that the Sophie he was talking about?"

"Aye."

"Why would he do that?" Esther asked, feeling an unexpected pang of anger and jealousy.

Morag sighed. "Because he loves her."

"He loves her?" Esther repeated, the jealousy redoubling.

Morag looked at her with pity. "Of course. She's the other half of his syzygy."

"What?"

"His pair. Theletos and Sophia were created together, like Abaddon and Lilith, Logos and Zoe, and all the others. They are consorts on the most fundamental level."

Esther felt gutted. She managed to choke out, "Then what is she doing in a remote village in Scotland?"

"That's a very long story, half o' which I couldnae tell you if I wanted tae."

"But he – Theletos – he sent me to find her because he's in love with her."

Morag looked at Esther sadly. "It's nae so simple. Nothing ever is, wi' those two. So many confused loyalties and criss-crossed intentions..." She trailed off, shaking her head. "But tae answer your question: nae. He wanted you tae find her because he believes she can save us. Stop what the daevas hae started."

"Can she?" Esther asked bluntly.

"That's beyond me, lass."

Esther shook her head incredulously. "So all I've done, all I'm trying to do, might be for nothing."

"Does it feel like it's for nowt, Esther?" Morag asked softly.

Esther thought of her nightmares, of the falling city; she thought of the fleeting peace she'd felt in Theletos's arms. "I suppose not," she conceded grudgingly. "But I don't have any way to get to Scotland, and in the meantime I've got the Sword

125

of Justice after me and my face in all the papers, and even if I get through all of that and find Sophie, she's as clueless as everyone else, so how am I meant to convince her that what she thinks is real life is all lies, and instead she has to go to some garden in Heaven and save the world – "

Morag reached out and touched Esther's shoulder, stopping her. "I ken, it seems impossible. But Theletos wouldnae hae asked this o' you if there wasnae a way tae do it."

"That's not especially encouraging," Esther said.

"I'm nae through yet. Ye need tae cross the sea, aye?" Esther nodded. "Go tae the docks when you leave here. You arenae far now, and I can tell you the way. Find a boat called Wave Sweeper. You'll ken it when you see it. It will take you across the sea."

"That would be a good start, sure," Esther said doubtfully, wondering whether the captain of this boat was aware of Morag's magnanimity.

Morag took a folded square of paper from the counter, and handed it to Esther. She opened it. It was a map. "And this will guide you once you're there. Remember it if you're ever in need of direction."

"Thank you," Esther said, re-folding the map and putting it in her bundle.

"As for the Sword o' Justice, I'd say you're doing a fine job on your own keeping out of their way. But if you find yourself in a tight spot, use this." Morag reached into her pocket and drew out a scrap of grey fabric, and handed it to Esther.

"Ah – thank you," Esther said. "What is it?"

"Llen Arthyr," Morag answered. "Arthur's mantle."

"As in King Arthur?"

"Aye. If you wear it, you'll nae be seen."

Esther considered the fabric doubtfully. It was no bigger than a handkerchief, never mind the dubious plausibility of

126

invisibility cloaks. Still, there was no point in offending Morag over a scrap of fabric.

"But choose wisely when tae use it," Morag warned as Esther tucked the fabric into her bundle. "It only works in a time o' great need, and the effect doesnae last long."

"All right," Esther said, trying not to show her scepticism.

"As for Sophia," Morag continued, "if she willnae believe you about the daevas, give her this." She reached into one of the shadowy shelves and brought out a book. It was a slim volume bound in leather, the cover blank. Esther opened it. It was a notebook, full of ruled pages. On the first, someone had written in beautiful script: The *Book of Sorrows*.

Esther observed the title doubtfully. "That doesn't sound especially helpful."

Morag shrugged. "Maybe no, but it should jog her memory."

"Why?"

"She wrote it."

"Before the Change?" Esther asked.

"Oh, aye. A few thousand years before, give or take."

Esther eyed the modern-looking notebook thoughtfully, and Morag smiled. "Not this copy, o' course. I wrote this one out myself. Translated it from the Aramaic. She wouldnae be able tae read the original in her current state." She shook her head sadly, then said, "You gie it tae her. Tell her tae heed the prophecy."

"What prophecy?"

Morag flipped toward the back of the book, and pointed out a passage to Esther. She read: "When the Morningstar regains the Heavens, the Balance will be restored." She looked up at Morag. "What does that mean?"

"That's what Sophia needs to winkle out." Morag pushed the book toward Esther, who was beginning to revise her opinion of Morag's sanity.

She stood up. "I'd best be going, then. Thank you for the tea."

"Wait," Morag said, taking her gently but firmly by the hand as she turned to go. "Choose a book," she said.

"What?"

"Any o' them," Morag said, encompassing the shop in a sweeping gesture. "Take one. I always find a book a comfort on a difficult journey."

Esther wanted nothing more now than to be away from the strange woman and her shop, but at the same time she didn't want to upset her. She reached for a shelf at random and pulled out a book. It slipped from her hand and landed on the floor, falling open in the middle. She bent to pick it up, and found that a passage on the right-hand page had been underlined.

"Between two worlds life hovers like a star,
'Twixt night and morn, upon the horizon's verge
How little do we know that which we are!
Of time and tide rolls on and bears afar
Our bubbles; as the old burst, new emerge,
Lash'd from the foam of ages; while the graves
Of empires heave but like some passing waves."

The words made her shiver, echoing in her head with a ring of purpose she couldn't quite decipher. "Thank you," Esther said again. "For everything."

Morag's look was one of sudden sadness. "You're welcome, Esther. *Turas math dhut*."

Esther nodded at the old woman and then stepped through the door.

THE DEMON DOMINIONS

Rive let the window collapse into a skim of light, staring, unseeing, at the wall of furious black water encircling him.

Understanding crashed over him, clear and terrible. Star – Setera – Ishtar – Esther. Morning – Matins – Maidin – Madden.

Sophie had had it wrong all along.

THE GARDEN

The light drove into Suri's skull like a spike, so intense that it was visceral, as much a shriek or a bodily blow as it was something seen. She fell to her knees, her eyes squeezed shut and her arms around her head. She was aware that she was screaming, but she couldn't hear herself, only feel the reverberation somewhere deep inside her.

And then someone was shoving something into her hand. She couldn't make her fingers work to understand what it was, and after a moment it was taken back, re-placed on her face, and the light and noise and pain abruptly fell away. She reached up and touched the thing on her face: sunglasses.

"All right now?" Michael asked. He crouched beside her, also wearing sunglasses. They were thicker and darker than any Suri had seen before. He reached down and put a third pair on Sartael, who was stretched out on the ground in front of them, unconscious.

"What's wrong with him?" Suri asked.

"Same as what was wrong with us," he snapped. "We aren't meant to be here."

"But why did he pass out, and we didn't?"

"He may have got rid of his staves, but he's still a third-rate angel. Perhaps it's slightly less toxic to us than it is to him."

"Is he going to be all right?"

"I have no idea. I don't even know if we're going to be all right. I mean, look at this place!"

Suri turned away from the stricken angel and looked around. Though the light was bearable now, she was still stunned speechless with what she saw. It was a garden, but nothing like any she'd seen before. Even Eden paled in comparison to this place. The world seemed made of growing things, trees and plants and vines and flowers that curled and climbed and tumbled every which way. They were larger than any she'd ever seen, their leaves and flowers blooming in colours that she never could have conceived of before that moment. The grass was somehow green and violet at once, the edges of every blade pulsing with indescribable light. Likewise the sky was blue and yellow and silver at the same time, and Suri couldn't look at it long without feeling like she was going to topple next to Sartael.

Gradually, as she looked, she became aware of structures, too: columned grottoes that were vaguely Greek, carved from opalescent stone; pagodas like Quan Yin's, but palatial in scale; flights of stone steps that could have come from medieval castles but instead spiralled up into the sky and were lost in some realm too distant to see.

"Wow," she said in a voice that sounded strangely plangent, "this place is really..." But she couldn't continue. It wasn't simply that she couldn't find the word to describe it; her throat and tongue were paralyzed at the very attempt.

"I see now why they never wanted us to come here," Michael said.

"I don't know," Suri answered. "I'm not sure they thought about it that way at all. It feels more like...like we just aren't meant to be here. We're not made to be able to bear it."

Michael gave her a wry smile. "Suriel waxes poetic. I never thought I'd see the day."

"I'm not poetic!" Suri argued. "I just feel all..." Again, she couldn't make her visceral body produce the word that would describe the ethereal quality she felt. Or perhaps there simply wasn't one. She shook her head. "Anyway, we're here now. What happens next?"

"Honestly," Michael said, looking around at the brilliant,

burgeoning foliage, "I have no idea. I expected a gang of irate aeons to be waiting to drive us away, but…"

"I don't see any aeons at all."

"Exactly. Which is strange, at best."

"And at worst?"

Michael gave her a distracted look. "Let's leave that until we're sure they really aren't here."

"But where do we even begin to look for them?"

"I don't know," he answered. "I suppose we should assume that this place works much like Heaven does – as a series of dominions. I mean, Heaven must be a direct offshoot of the Garden, right? Like we're a direct offshoot of the aeons."

"I guess that makes sense."

"And if I'm right, then we're in luck, because there are only fifteen pairs of aeons. It can't take too long to search fifteen dominions."

Suri wasn't at all convinced that this was good logic, but she was glad enough to have Michael on board that she didn't argue. "What about Sartael?" she asked.

"What about him?"

"We can't just leave him here. What if he wakes up and goes wandering around and, I don't know, breaks something?"

"We could shove him back through the door before he wakes up."

Suri grinned. "Wow, Michael, that was almost catty!" Michael shrugged. "I meant it as a compliment. But I don't think it would work. I mean, he'd just come back."

"Do you have a better idea?"

"We could tie him up and strip him."

"Suriel!"

"Well, he probably wouldn't go anywhere without his clothes." Seeing Michael's look, she said, "Okay, fine. How about we lock him in one of the buildings? With a note, of course, telling him we'll be back for him. That way he might stay out of trouble."

"Very well," Michael said. "That pagoda is nearest. You get his feet."

They dragged Sartael to the building, wrote him a quick note explaining that they'd incarcerated him for his own safety, and then Michael reached for a tendril of a vine that sprawled over the roof of the house, planning to use it to tie the door shut. But when he wound the vine around his hand and pulled to break it, the vine wrenched free, emitting a hiss as it gathered all of its tendrils together into a shape that looked not unlike a fist.

Michael leapt back, but Suri stepped forward, reaching out a tentative hand. At first the ball of vines reared further back, out of her reach. But she stood waiting patiently, her hand open and extended, and at last, it sent a few creepers toward her. She touched one of them, and when it didn't pull back, she took it gently in her hand.

She held it for a moment, and then she said to Michael, "This plant has a human soul."

"Are you certain?" he asked, still looking at it dubiously.

"Positive." Suri let it go and touched a bush nearby that was flowering in every colour of the rainbow. "This one does too. Feel it."

Michael reached out and put a tentative hand around a bloom, and his eyes widened. "So it does."

Suri had moved away from him, touching plants and trees and blossoms. "They all do," she said, and turned back to Michael. "This is their hereafter? Their eternal life?"

"Some of them, at least." He shook his head. "I never would have guessed."

Suri looked at the lily-like flower nodding beside her for another moment, and then she turned back to the pagoda. "Well anyway, we still need to look for the aeons. And first we need to lock the door – " Except that when she looked at it, the vine that Michael had tried to break had grown down over the door, weaving around the handle so that it looked like a hand holding it shut.

"Okay, well…thank you?" Suri said to it, uncertain whether it could hear and understand, but figuring that it was better to be safe than sorry. "Which way should we go first?" she asked Michael.

"I don't imagine it much matters. You choose."

Suri turned in a slow circle. Her gaze settled on a copse of trees that were shaped like birches, but had golden trunks and ultraviolet leaves that shimmered in and out of visibility, in a breeze she couldn't feel. She walked a little way into the glade, Michael following her. She wasn't particularly surprised when a door appeared in front of them. It was a full-blown Art Nouveau fantasy, adorning 29 Avenue Rapp in Paris – one of her favourite doors. It made her wonder something.

"Michael, what do you see there?"

"A door."

"Yes, but what does it look like?"

"Actually…I believe it's the main door to St. Michael's Cathedral. Kiev, not Toronto. Why? What do you see?"

Suri smiled to herself. "Something like that." She winked at the saucy stone Eve and reluctant Adam presiding over the corners of the door, reached out for the lizard-shaped handle, and pushed the door open.

CHAPTER 5

BELFAST

The sky was a wash of pinkish grey when Esther came out onto the street. She was sure that Cliona would have given her up long since and made her own way to the port, but instead she found her outside the bakery where she'd last seen her, drinking tea from a chipped china cup along with a young man of about their age, who was wearing a flour-stained apron that set off his ethereal beauty. By that, the slight point to the tops of his ears and the gem-like brilliance of his blue eyes, Esther knew that he was a faery.

"There you are!" Cliona cried when she saw her coming. "Another five minutes, and I was going without you."

"Sorry. I met the old woman with the bookstore," she said, glancing at Cliona's companion. "Morag."

"Is that what she called herself," he said with a knowing smile.

Esther didn't much want to know what else Morag might call herself. "Come on, Cliona – we'd better be going."

"Thanks for the tea," Cliona said, rather wistfully, handing the cup back to the faery man.

"It was a pleasure. *Go gcuire Dia an t-ádh ort.*" Cliona smiled back at him, as Esther pulled her down the street.

"You should know better than to flirt with faery men," Esther said when they were out of earshot.

Cliona waved a hand dismissively. "He was nice. Gave me a half dozen scones for nothing."

"Did you eat them?" Esther asked, horrified.

"Not all of them. I saved some for you." She handed her a warm paper bag.

"Faery food will bewitch you!"

"They're just scones, Esther. It's an ordinary bakery. Besides, I walked away from him, didn't I?"

"I suppose," Esther relented.

"He gave me directions to the port in the bargain. He said there's a ferry going at nine that's never too crowded."

"You shouldn't have told him so much," Esther said worriedly. But the smell of the scones was making her realize how hungry she was. She took one out. It was spread with jam and butter and was delicious as it smelled.

"See?" Cliona said. "Not everyone is out to get us. Besides, what about you with your old lady in the bookshop?"

"That was different," Esther said, chewing. "I met her scrubbing a Sword of Justice poster off a window."

Cliona shrugged. "We'll never get to Scotland if we don't trust anyone. We're going to have to get on that ferry."

"Maybe not," Esther said, and she told Cliona about the boat that Morag had suggested.

"Well, I suppose we can take a look at it," Cliona said doubtfully. "But how do we know that it's not dodgy? Or that the captain won't take our money and chuck us overboard when we're half way across?"

"We don't, I guess."

"We're well away from Dublin now."

"Aye, and that poster Morag was scrubbing off her window? It had my face on it, big as life."

135

Immediately, Cliona was serious. "Jesus. *All right* – we'll look for Morag's boat first."

They walked in silence, keeping to the street margins as the city awakened around them. Shopkeepers rolled back their blinds, mothers shoed children on their way to school as the streets filled with carts pulled by feather-legged draft ponies, and the odd, rusting automobile. When they reached the port, it was teeming with activity. Cliona stopped on a dockside, looking out across the harbour at the opposite docks lined with steamboats and smaller sailing vessels, the brick warehouses rising up behind them and the low grey-green hills of Antrim behind that.

"So," she said after a moment, "did the old lady tell you where we'd find this boat?"

"No," Esther admitted, wondering now why she hadn't thought to ask.

"Or what it looks like? Or the name of the captain, say?"

"She said it's called Wave Sweeper, and I'd know it when I saw it."

Cliona raised her eyebrows, but all she said was, "We've an hour before the ferry leaves."

They walked along the quays, in the direction of the sea. They passed boats of all shapes and sizes, coming and going or tied up to the docks while passengers or goods were loaded on or off, but none was named Wave Sweeper. Though Cliona said nothing, her doubt was almost tangible, and after a while, with Wave Sweeper nowhere in sight, even Esther began to doubt Morag's words. What reason, after all, was there to trust her? Some of what she'd said had been frighteningly accurate, but other parts of it had sounded just plain mad.

In the end, though she'd told Cliona that she didn't want to ask anyone for directions and risk the scrutiny, she decided that it couldn't be any worse than taking the ferry. Casting around for someone who looked likely to know the boats in the harbour, she finally settled on an old man with a curling grey beard, human except for his webbed hands and feet. He was sitting alone on the quay by a rickety fishing boat, mending a net.

"I'll ask," Cliona volunteered. "You stay out of sight."

"Thank you," Esther said, dipping back into the shadow of a pile of packing crates as Cliona approached the man. They talked for longer than Esther thought it should have taken to answer a simple question, but she was too far away to hear any of what they said. She saw the man gesture a few times, and Cliona shook her head. Then Cliona nodded, and the man set down his net and moved off down the quay.

Cliona looked back, caught Esther's eye and gave her a tiny nod. Then she turned and followed the man down the quay. Esther trailed behind, keeping her head low. Cliona and the man walked past the bigger boats, then the smaller fishing boats, and Esther began to wonder whether following him further was a bad idea.

At last, the faery man turned onto a smaller, wooden dock that jutted off the main one. A few rowing dinghies bobbed alongside it, as well as a longer, open boat. It appeared to be made of wood and woven reeds, covered with tough white leather. There were oarlocks, but no oars in sight. At the stern of the boat, someone had painted a Celtic spiral and the name *Scuabtuinne* – "Wave Sweeper."

Esther's heart sank. She couldn't imagine crossing the Liffey in that fragile boat, let alone the Irish Sea. Clearly, Cliona agreed. She was arguing with the faery again, but he kept gesturing to the boat and nodding, and finally he threw up his fan-like hands and walked away. When he was out of sight, Esther came out from behind the pile of fishnets where she'd been watching the exchange and approached Cliona, who was sitting on the dock with her legs dangling over the water.

"So," she said when Esther sat down beside her, "do you still think this is a better idea than the ferry?"

137

Esther looked down at the white boat. "Maybe it's the wrong one."

"The codger swore to me this was the only boat in the port called Wave Sweeper."

"Maybe it's stronger than it looks," Esther said doubtfully. "It reminds me of those boats in old drawings of saints. Curraghs, I think they were called."

"Right," Cliona scoffed, "and we'd need a saint as captain to have any hope of making it to Scotland in that." She toed the boat, which bobbed gracefully, sending out rings into the still water. They seemed to Esther to shimmer for a moment before they faded.

"Did the faery tell you who it belongs to?" Esther asked.

Cliona shook her head. "He said he'd never seen anyone with this boat."

"But someone must look after it. It's spotless."

"There's a box down there," Cliona said, nodding to a small wooden chest set in the centre of the boat, where it was widest. "Maybe there's information in it."

"I'm not really sure we should – " Esther began, but Cliona had already leapt down into the boat. Reluctantly, she followed.

"It's stuck," Cliona said, frowning as she tried to pry the lid off of the wooden chest. "Give me a hand?"

Sighing, Esther set down her kerchief bundle and went to help Cliona with the lid. But hard as they pulled, it didn't move. It was as if the entire box were carved from a single piece of wood. She was about to suggest to Cliona that they give up and go for the ferry, when Cliona let out a shriek.

Imagining the Sword of Justice descending on them, Esther clutched Cliona's hand as she looked up. It took her a moment to make sense of what she saw. No angry horde surrounded them. Nothing surrounded them but brownish-green water, ruffling in the slight breeze. Somehow, while they had been trying to open the box, the boat's painter had slipped, and they had washed out into the harbour. Cliona dropped to her knees, huddling by the wooden chest, as low down in the boat as she could get. But after the initial shock, Esther pulled herself together.

"Don't worry," she told Cliona. "A current or something must have taken us. I'm sure it'll carry us back to shore, or in sight of a bigger boat – "

"Aye – that'll run us down and drown us!"

"I'm not sure what else we can do."

"The box," Cliona said, turning to face it. "Maybe there are instructions in it."

"Instructions?" Esther repeated incredulously.

"Or something. Come on, let's try again."

Esther put her hands on the edges of the box lid. She pulled as hard as she could, and landed on her back on the bottom of the boat as the lid came away easily.

"We must have loosened it before," Cliona said.

Esther had her doubts, but she kept them to herself.

"Jesus, look at this!" Cliona cried. Inside the chest was an array of food, a couple of bottles of dark liquid, and several woollen blankets. Cliona picked up two perfect apples with golden-green skin.

"It's like someone packed for a journey," she said.

"I'm not sure you should – " Esther began, but Cliona had already bitten into it.

"It's good," she said. "Perfect, in fact. Try it."

She handed the other one to Esther. And though Esther knew every admonition against eating faery food, she couldn't resist the golden sheen of the fruit. She bit into it, even as half of her was loudly protesting. Once begun, she couldn't stop – she chewed the apple down to the core, as if she hadn't eaten in days.

When she finished and looked up, she found that the little boat came out of the harbour and into the open sea, its prow turning northeast. She had a feeling that she should be alarmed, but everything had grown hazy and uncertain. She turned to

Cliona, whose face had taken on a dreamy look, her movements a languidness that Esther was beginning to feel herself. She wondered if the apples had been drugged, but found she didn't much care either way.

Cliona took two of the blankets out of the box, handed one to Esther and wrapped the other around herself as the wind freshened and the small waves sent up a fine spray. "This reminds me of a story I read once," she said, her tone as vague as her expression. "An old myth about the god of the sea. He had magical things, like they always do in those stories. A sword that won him every battle, a horse that was faster than the wind, and the like. But he also had a boat, which could travel without sails or oars, by obeying his own thoughts."

Esther felt now as if she drifted somewhere outside of herself. "You think this is that boat?" she asked, her voice also sounding as if it came from somewhere else.

Cliona lay back on the rocking deck, her eyes on the lemon-white sky. "I think that if demons are real, then anything else might be, too." And with that, she curled up, shut her eyes, and fell asleep.

For a little while, Esther fought the drowsiness that was overtaking her. But at last, there seemed no point. Either the boat was a magical one or it wasn't, and either way, they were at its mercy. So she wrapped herself in her blanket, laid her head on her kerchief bundle, and fell asleep.

THE DEMON DOMINIONS

The image of the sleeping girls wavered and collapsed. The slant of light that had held them fell to the stone floor and dispersed like mist, leaving only a faint, lemony dusting on Rive's fingers to show that it had ever been.

But it was enough. "See? I told you he was spying!"

Rive's heart pounded at the sound of the bell-like voice he'd come to loath. Abaddon and Lilith stepped through the ring of hissing, intertwined snakes that was the latest incarnation of his prison walls. Lilith's arms were folded across her chest, her dark lips sulky. But Abaddon's cold expressionlessness was infinitely more disturbing.

"What?" Rive asked, his voice low and trembling with shock. He had been so certain that he was alone when he opened the window – but then, how long had he been watching Esther? He realized that he didn't know. Since he'd learned what she was, who she could be to him, watching her had become an addiction. This last time he had been utterly absorbed – careless, to be honest – and he knew that he was about to pay for it. He only hoped that Esther wouldn't be made to pay, too.

"How could you think we wouldn't find out?" Abaddon shook his head, his translucent eyes full of contempt. "Lilith sensed it. She's been watching you ever since she felt you shift matter."

"My windows were breaking," Lilith said, her eyes accusatory, "whenever I tried to open them. I knew someone was stealing energy from them. I don't like it when someone steals my toys."

Rive looked down at his hands, hoping he appeared contrite, and took a gamble. "I'm sorry," he said. "I know I shouldn't have done it. But it's so hard not knowing what's happening on Earth…"

Abaddon studied him with emotionless, unblinking surmise, while the snakes hissed and slithered, twining over and under each other in their unending, monstrous plait. Finally, he said, "We want to show you something."

Rive turned to Lilith, expecting her to spool out some torturous scene from Ardnasheen. Instead, Abaddon reached forward and touched the ring of snakes. He let his hand rest for a moment on their sinuous bodies, and then, abruptly, the ring fell apart, the snakes slipping rapidly away into the shadows. Rive stared at his captor in disbelief. This time, Abaddon afforded him a small, chilly smile.

"You've been here a while now," he said. "I think it's time you stretched your legs. Come."

There was nothing Rive wanted to do less. There was also no choice. Lilith slipped her hand into his. Its leather-bound chill felt like despair, and he had to fight not to snatch his hand back. She seemed to know this, and twined her fingers with his. Her dark lips split into a smile, showing rows of pointed, pearly teeth. Then she pulled him after Abaddon, whose long strides had already taken him almost out of sight.

For all the time he'd spent in the Deep, Rive knew almost nothing about its geography. He vaguely remembered landing on dark cobblestones after he dove into the pit that had opened in front of the sea-witch's throne, but he'd immediately been surrounded by thirty daevas, armed to the teeth. He recalled looking up from their midst, catching a glimpse of intricate stonework rising above, and beyond that, a scatter of cold, alien stars, for a few brief moments before Abaddon put a hand on his head, and darkness closed in.

When he'd awakened, he'd been inside a ring of fire, in the hall with the broken pillars. The hall he hadn't left until now. It was already behind them, and they were walking on a street paved with the cobbles he remembered from the night of his fall. There was a strange, smooth, familiar roundness to them. When he realized that they were human skulls, he turned his eyes toward the sky. It was dark with the Deep's permanent night, flecked with those stars he remembered, so different from the ones visible from Heaven or Earth. On either side of the road there were stone buildings, but they were all crumbling ruins, in places reduced to powder, as if bombs had blasted them sometime in the past. A distant past, as time had overtaken them, encrusting some with a viscous-looking, lichen-like growth, binding others with dark vines that let off a peculiar, ultraviolet glow and a sickly-sweet smell.

"What is this place?" he ventured after they'd walked a while through the desolate cityscape.

Lilith looked at him in surprise, as if she'd forgotten he was there, although she was still holding his hand. "A demon dominion. I forget whose."

"What happened to it?"

"One of their wars."

"The demons are at war?"

"Usually," Lilith said, with a dismissive flick of her hand, as if this ought to have been obvious. "It's one of their favourite pastimes."

Rive lapsed back into silence until a purplish glow began to show above the buildings ahead, silhouetting Abaddon's striding figure. It grew brighter as they walked, until Rive could see into the empty windows and doorways of the abandoned buildings. He was watching them so intently that he almost ran into Abaddon, who had stopped at a street corner. In the cloying light, Rive saw that his expression, for once, was neither cold nor blank nor supercilious. Instead, there was an anticipatory pride in his smile as he met Rive's eyes, like a child about to display his prized possession.

"Ready?" he asked.

"For what?" Rive asked dubiously.

"Pandæmonium," he answered and turned the corner, Lilith dragging Rive behind, her face lit with gleeful anticipation.

Though Rive had imagined the daevas' city many ways, it had never occurred to him that Pandæmonium might be beautiful. But it was. The skull-cobbles had given way to gleaming obsidian bricks, spreading into a vast plaza ringed with buildings. They rose like a mountain range, the dark stones they were built from carved and stacked and moulded into arched doorways and turrets, multi-story windows, spiralling stairways leading up to a network of soaring bridges that wove a fractious pattern across the sky. Facades were heavy with mosaics of coloured glass and bone, upper storeys adorned with gargoyles and grotesques that peered down on the scene below. Window boxes spilled moonflowers and Indian Pipes, night-blooming vines climbed the walls, their fruits and blossoms feeding flocks of moon-white bats.

The crowd filling this courtyard was equally surprising to Rive. Heaven and the Garden had their dominions, and even on Earth, he found humanity kept a certain unconscious, hierarchical order. In Pandæmonium, though, all lines seemed to be blurred. Daevas and demons intermingled with no hint of Heaven's strict divisions. To his right, a brilliantly coloured Rakshasa demon played cards at a green baize gaming table with two daevas Rive remembered from the fight in the sea-witch's palace. As the Rakshasa leaned forward to scoop up his winnings – a pile of human teeth – one of the gargoyles from a nearby rooftop spread its stone wings and swooped down, screeching, to steal them. On a doorstep with elaborately carved rococo balustrades, a black-skinned daeva with tree roots splayed across her face poured tea into toadstool cups for three waiting trolls, from a silver-chased pot made of a distinctly inhuman skull. In an open spot on the cobbles, a troupe of beautiful dancers with writhing snakes for hair performed for an audience of pallid incubi.

And then Rive's roving gaze stopped cold. On the far side of the plaza, a daeva with black hair and a steel-and-cobalt monocle stood on a stairway before a cluster of willowy, long-haired figures dressed in varying shades of green.

"Those are dryads!" he said in disbelief.

Abaddon followed his eyes. "They are."

"But what are they doing here?"

"Waiting for payment."

Rive's eyes snapped to his captor's face. "Payment for what?"

"Services rendered," Abaddon answered with infuriating, offhanded calm.

"Since when are the Seelie fae in your service?" Rive demanded.

Abaddon turned to him with pale, inscrutable eyes. "Since we offered them what they want most."

"You aren't in a position to offer them anything," Rive said with more certainty than he felt.

Abaddon only smiled again. "And you, Theletos, have no idea what you're talking about." Rive's only answer was to glare at him, and so Abaddon continued, slipping his arm through Rive's as he began to walk again. "Six months isn't long, perhaps – not even by human standards. But it's long enough for a lot to change. For the tables, so to speak, to turn."

He guided Rive up the steps of one of the buildings, a cone-shaped structure of telescoping storeys that ended in a widow's walk so remote Rive could only just make out. "You see, while the humans have lost their senses, the other denizens of Earth are rapidly coming to their own. They know there's a war brewing, and they know who's going to win it. The clever ones sided with us as soon as we shook things up on Earth. The others are learning quickly."

He stopped before the great double-doors of the house. They were so skilfully crafted that it took Rive a few moments to realize that they weren't made of studded oak, as they appeared, but the same stone as the rest of the city. The grain of the wood had been meticulously carved into it.

"Wonderful craftsmanship, isn't it?" Abaddon said, running a loving hand down the smooth surface. "It was a fairly recent addition. The man who made it was a master sarcophagus builder in ancient Egypt. It took him five hundred years to complete."

"He wasn't human?" Rive asked.

Abaddon shrugged. "He was, more or less. Somewhat less by the time he was finished. He's still around here somewhere…"

He gestured offhandedly, and then opened the doors. "Come in," he said.

"What is this place?" Rive asked.

Abaddon gave him a look that said the answer should have been obvious. "It's Lilith's and my dominion, of course." Then he took Rive by the shoulder and steered him inside, Lilith trailing behind. The doors shut noiselessly after they'd passed through.

Once again, Rive was caught completely off guard. He had envisioned an interior that matched the Gothic fantasy of the outside of the house, complete with cobwebs, a suit of armour, and a staircase spiralling up into the shadows. Instead he found that they were standing in a plain corridor that stretched away from them in a straight line, until it was lost in the distance. It had a floor of stone the infinite, matte black of a starless sky, and blank white walls intercut with arched stone doorways. Lilith wandered ahead and then turned, disappearing into one of them. As the door opened briefly to admit her, Rive heard blood-curdling screams; then the door clicked shut, and they were standing in silence again.

"Why am I here, Abaddon?" Rive asked, his patience exhausted.

"I told you, I wanted to show you something."

"If this is some kind of punishment for looking at Earth, can't we just get on with it?"

"Trust me, we are. Walk." He strode off down the corridor, and reluctantly, Rive followed. Each door they passed was shut; each was exactly like the last. It seemed to take minutes to cross from one to the next, but when Rive paused once to look back, he could no longer see the beginning of the corridor.

Finally, Abaddon stopped at one of the doors and pushed it open. There was little light inside, but as Rive stood in the doorway, his eyes slowly adjusted. Horror dawned on him as slowly, and as inexorably. The room beyond the door was so vast he couldn't see its margins, and it was packed with demons of every shape and size. Some of them were species Rive recognized, but many more weren't. They stood inert, unbreathing, in neat regiments of their own kind. All of them were armed.

Rive approached one of them, a thing with a human-like body in heavy plate armour and the head of a wild boar, with huge, curving tusks. He reached out tentatively, touched its bristled face. The skin beneath was pliant, but cold.

"What is this?" he asked, pulling his hand back in disgust.

"It's our army, of course."

"Where did you get them?"

"We made them."

"The Keeper allowed that?"

"When was the last time the Keeper disallowed anything?"

"How would I know?" Rive snapped. "I've been locked up down here. And by the way, if you're showing me this to try to blackmail me, don't bother."

Abaddon leaned back against the doorframe, his eyes unblinking. "I have no need to blackmail you. Not now that you see the utter folly of trying to stop us."

Rive smiled wryly. "You're going to have to do better than an inanimate army if you want to scare me."

At last, a shade of exasperation crossed the daeva's face. "Oh, we'll animate them. With your help."

Rive gave Abaddon a narrow-eyed look, and then, abruptly, he began to laugh. "That's why you want Sophie? That's your plan?" He shook his head. "Sophie may be able to create something from nothing, but I'm willing to bet the spark of life is beyond even her."

"You have no idea what you're talking about."

"I know Sophie better than anyone in Creation."

"Maybe. But you don't know her as well as you think you do."

"Keep it coming, Abaddon. I'll never believe you."

"Which is why I intend to show you, beyond the shadow of a doubt, who your consort really is."

"I can't wait," Rive said. But he was uneasy as Abaddon cupped his hands, generating the now-familiar light, expertly stretching it into a window. Rive expected to see Sophie, most likely blissful in Lucas's embrace, but the scene that grew in the window was something quite different. He knew the place he was looking at, and he knew the two figures standing in it, as well as he knew that they should never have been there. That if anything was as it should be, they couldn't have been there. Yet there they were: Suri and Michael, in his own dominion.

For the first time since Abaddon had taken him prisoner, Rive felt the spectral chill of doubt.

THE GARDEN

At first, the very beauty and novelty of the aeon's realm had kept Suri and Michael's minds off of the increasingly worrying fact that every dominion they explored was deserted. They'd crossed brilliant rivers to shadowy forests full of glittering lights that were always just out of reach. They'd walked the halls of vast castles carved from ice that never melted, towns made entirely of cobalt glass. They'd crossed plains of magenta grass where golden horses ran and silvery, bison-like beasts grazed. There were caves with walls like glittering geodes, lakes black as ink whose water turned clear when they scooped it up, orchards of fruit trees that sang like choirs as they filled with wind. But they never saw an aeon, or any sign that such creatures had ever walked these dominions.

At last, in the purple shadow of a vermillion mountain, Michael stopped and said: "Enough. They're gone."

Suri shivered, her eyes on the beautiful, barren distance. Though she'd known it for some time, Michael's acknowledgement made it not just real, but frightening. "Did the daevas do this?" she asked softly, hugging her arms around herself.

Michael looked at her in surprise. "I very much doubt it. For one thing, I don't think they've been here…at least not recently."

"Why not? We got in easily enough."

"I don't mean that they couldn't; only that if they'd been here recently, they'd have claimed it, and we wouldn't be standing here talking about them. We'd be polishing their boots, or stretched out on racks, or whatever they plan to do with angels if they win the war for the Balance."

The War for the Balance. Suri had never thought of it that way, but she knew that he was right. The daevas had declared war, and all of Creation was fighting it, whether they wanted to or not. Whether they realized it or not. She said, "That still doesn't explain why there are no aeons here."

Michael's eyes were steely. "Doesn't it?" Suri waited. Michael sighed and said, "I think they fled."

That thought was even more disturbing than the admission that they were at war. "Why would they do that?"

"Maybe because they know what's coming, and that they aren't strong enough to fight it."

"But where could they go to that would be safe?"

"Not where," Michael answered. "To whom."

Suri shook her head, not so much in negation as disbelief. "You mean the Keeper? Is that even possible?"

Michael sighed. "I don't like to speculate anymore on what is or isn't possible. But one thing is certain: the Keeper made the aeons, and I have no doubt that if it wanted to, it could take them back."

Suri was silent for a moment, trying to process this. Then she said, "So what about us?"

Michael's voice was tired but not bitter when he said, "I guess we don't matter as much as we thought we did."

149

"But they made us, and we've served them faithfully!"

Michael only shrugged. The two of them stood in silence at the foot of the blood-coloured mountain for a few long minutes. And then Michael spoke again. "There is one thing that doesn't quite make sense."

"Only one?" Suri asked acerbically.

"The Well of Souls. If the aeons *have* abandoned the Garden, then they've abandoned that, too."

"You always said it was Sophia who abandoned the Well of Souls," Suri said, not quite able to keep the accusation out of her tone. "That that was why everything started going wrong."

Michael's mouth set in a stern line. "That's also true, and a completely different matter. It was her own selfish choice."

"We are *not* having this argument again."

"Fine. Just don't ask me to believe that getting Lucifer back to Heaven is going to fix all of this."

"Okay – as long as you don't ask *me* to believe that everything that's gone wrong is Sophia's fault."

"Suriel," he sighed, "whatever else you think, you can't ignore the fact that humanity started to lean toward the Deep when Sophia left her place at the Well to go after Lucifer."

"Not according to the *Book of Sorrows*," she argued. "We've both read it, Michael: Sophia left the Garden because she believed that the Well was already tainted, the Balance was tipping, and that restoring Lucifer to Heaven was the only way to fix it."

"Right – she believed. She made a decision that wasn't hers to make, at least not alone."

"Yeah, well, now the other aeons have done the same thing. So maybe she was right after all."

The two angels stood glaring at each other for a moment. Then Michael shook his head, ran a hand across his hair. "Okay, let's just deal with what we *do* know."

"Which is?"

"Aeons, angels, daevas, demons – we all need the energy of human souls in order to survive. And those souls have to be equally divided between our two camps in order for the Balance to govern Creation. At some point, around the time Sophia left it, something happened to allow the daevas access to the Well. But they couldn't just come in and take the souls. The aeons would never have let them. So things didn't swing too far toward the Deep."

"But now the aeons have abandoned the Well," Suri said.

"Right. Which either means that they found a way to protect it before they left, or…" He trailed off, biting his lip. Their eyes met in a moment of mutual surmise.

"Or it's no longer worth guarding," Suri finished softly.

Michael said, "Let's go."

The Dominion of Sophia and Theletos

In all the thousands of years that she and Sophia had been friends, Suri had never once heard her talk about the home she'd left to live in Heaven. Suri had assumed that was because she hadn't liked it, and having chosen something different, she wanted to forget it. But as soon as she crossed the border into Sophia's dominion, she wondered if she'd had it wrong all along; if Sophia's silence hadn't come out of disregard, but the simple fact that speaking of her old home was too painful.

Because Sophia's dominion was beautiful, but more to the point, it was an exact reflection of her. Everywhere she looked, Suri saw her friend's hand, from the subtle cornflower shade of the sky to the beds of cottage-garden flowers, the ones she must have loved best on Earth. Channels ran among the flowerbeds like bright threads, spanned by delicate bridges. There was a

Victorian summerhouse with gingerbread arches and a swing hanging from the centre; trees full of birds from every earthly continent; horses grazing in distant, verdant meadows. It was difficult for Suri to tear her eyes away from all of the beautiful things her friend had made in homage to her favourite of her creations: the human world.

But Michael strode on purposefully, almost wilfully disregarding the beauty around them. And deep down, Suri knew that he was right. They had no time to be distracted by it, or by anything else. So she followed him.

She had thought that the Well of Souls would fit somehow into the dominion's décor, but when they finally found it, the only remarkable thing about it was how unremarkable it was. It was a circular pool of still, slate-grey water, perhaps twelve feet in diameter. There was no sign to mark it, no bench or even a rock to sit on beside it, but still, Suri had no doubt that they had found the right place. The human energy radiating from it was so strong it was palpable. She stopped several meters away, too dizzied by it to get closer.

Michael stopped too. "Strange – it doesn't *feel* violated."

"We have no idea how it's supposed to feel."

"Of course we do. We know what a human soul feels like, and these feel – "

"Healthy," Suri finished for him.

"I was going to say 'neutral' – but I suppose it comes to the same thing." His brow furrowed. "Somehow I'd have expected the daeva's influence to be more pronounced."

As Suri acclimated to the powerful energy coming off of the water, she eased closer, until she was looking directly down into it. She was so used to seeing them at the other end of their existence, that at first she couldn't make out the souls beneath the surface. But gradually, as she watched, she began to see movement, and then forms. They were vaguely human, but tiny and diffuse, unfinished, like they'd been drawn in mist, each a subtly different colour – the colour that their auras would take when they incarnated, their own unique energy. When they moved, their shapes drifted apart before slowly coming back together again. But there was no doubt that they were human souls, and they were neither good nor evil – exactly as embryonic souls were supposed to be.

"It's not just unpronounced," she said, tearing her eyes away from them at last. "I don't feel the daevas' influence here at all." She paused in partial disbelief of what she was about to say, and then she spoke again: "Whatever they were doing here, I think they've stopped."

"It does appear that way," Michael said grimly.

"Can't you crack even half a smile? I mean, this is a good thing, right?"

"How can the Angel of Death be so naïve?" he muttered.

"Why is it naïve to think the daevas have given up messing with the Well of Souls?" she snapped. "I mean, they never had direct access, so it wasn't exactly a surefire way to gain power over humans."

"That's my point," Michael said, as if it explained everything.

"What's your point?"

Michael gestured to the pool. "It might have been slow, but whatever the daevas were doing to turn humans to their side, it was working. So why would they suddenly stop?"

"Maybe they didn't need any more. Maybe they had enough power."

"They don't have enough power. I mean, they upset things on Earth, but they still can't set foot on it. If they're ignoring the unguarded Well of Souls, I'll bet it's because they've found a better source."

"Like what?" Suri asked, exasperated. "The rest of the human souls are either already in the Deep with them, or they're here in the Garden."

Michael's green eyes were troubled. "You're forgetting the ones on Earth."

"But you just said, the daevas can't get to Earth!"

"No – but their demons can."

"If you've got a theory," Suri said resignedly, sitting down beside the pool and gazing into its flickering depths, "just spill it."

"It really is just a theory," he said, sitting down beside her, "but such as it is – what if there's a connection between this, and all of those fallen who've started slipping their staves and turning up dead?"

Suri turned to him in surprise. "You think the daevas are behind that?"

"All I know is that they have the power to disarm the staves, and if there's one thing the fallen have in abundance, it's human souls. The ones who've turned to stealing them, anyway."

"But to compare those souls to these," Suri gestured to the pool, "is a stretch at best. I mean, these are pure, whereas a soul that's been sucked out and stored in a fallen angel? I don't even want to speculate what that looks like."

"I'll bet it looks good enough, when it means scoring hundreds, even thousands of them in one shot. Plus, they're adult souls: theoretically more powerful than these. And if they've been corrupted in the process, who knows? Maybe that makes them better fit for the daevas' purposes."

Suri combed the long grass with her fingers. "So let me get this straight: you think the daevas have got demons stealing stolen human souls, and then handing them over to them?"

"I said it's only a theory."

"And not a bad one – except, what's in it for the demons?"

"Who knows? They're easy enough to bribe – the lower orders anyway."

"Hm," Suri said, squinting off toward the violet horizon.

"Hm, what?"

"Hm, where does Sophia fit into it all?"

Michael shrugged. "Maybe she doesn't, anymore. Maybe erasing her memory and getting her off their backs was enough for the daevas – especially since she's likely to be dead in a week anyway."

Suri shuddered. "Don't say that. And anyway, I don't buy it. Not after all they went through with Lucas and Dahud to get hold of her – and how mad they were when they lost her. I mean, hell literally broke loose when Theletos jumped into the Deep in her place, if you haven't forgotten."

"It doesn't matter. They *didn't* get her."

"And you think they've stopped trying?"

Michael shook his head. "I'm just hoping that they're having trouble coming up with a new strategy."

"So what about Esther and Theletos and all that weirdness back in Dublin? That has to be about Sophia."

"What do you want me to say? I don't know any more than you do – and now there are no aeons to help us."

"Then we'll look for answers somewhere else."

"Where?"

"The source," Suri said, her eyes on the dark pool.

"We've scoured the *Book of Sorrows*. There's nothing in it about what's happening now, and you know what I think about the prophecy."

"I don't mean a book, or a prophecy, or anything like that. To get to the bottom of what's going on, we need to go to the *actual* source. The moment Sophia decided to leave. We need to know exactly how she did it." She looked him in the eye. "We need to witness it."

"Last I checked, Suriel, time travel is still impossible," Michael said dryly.

"Physically, yes," Suri said, her eyes still fixed unblinkingly on his. "But we can tear time."

"Yes – in Heaven, and occasionally on Earth. But we can't tear time in the Garden."

"How do you know?"

"We'd be mad to try! We don't know anything about this place. We might make it all come tumbling down around us. We might upset the Balance irreparably – "

"Or, we might find out how to save our sorry asses," Suri interrupted. "Desperate times, and all that."

Exasperation and tiredness and hope competed in Michael's expression. At last, he threw up his hands. "Fine…but I know I'm going to regret this."

"Think positive, Michael. Now, do you want to do it or should I?"

"You have more experience. And probably a steadier hand."

"Clearly! But I didn't want to say so."

Michael just rolled his eyes and then sat back to watch while Suri closed hers. Tearing time wasn't as easy as it sounded, even in a place where one had experience with it. It took intense meditation to be able to clear the mind enough to feel the different layers, fine and brittle as onionskins and too numerous to count. Finding the right one was another process altogether, involving an angelic sense that combined all of the earthly senses with a kind of reaching faith, a feel for the essence of the specific scene's energy.

Michael watched as Suri retreated deeper into herself. At the same time, she raised her hands and her fingers began to move subtly in the air, like a weaver plying different skeins, or the player of some intricate musical instrument. When her hands finally stilled, she pinched thumb and forefinger together, then pulled upward, as if she were tearing a piece of wallpaper from a wall.

The change was so subtle that it would have been undetectable to someone who had never seen this done before. But Michael could make out the precise margins of the window into the past.

Within it, the grass and the grey pond looked almost the same, but their colours were slightly less intense in tone and saturation, like a photograph that's bleached out in the sun.

At first, there was nothing else in the window. But then a figure came into the picture. Michael knew her immediately, though he hadn't seen her aeon form for millennia. She wore a flowing, twilight-blue dress that floated around her like cloud. Her dark hair swept down to her knees, and her grey eyes shone like jewels. A pale blue light radiated from her, leaving faint trails when she moved. In her hands she held a beaten silver bowl.

Sophia knelt by the pool, and gazed into it for a long time. Then, slowly, she lowered the bowl into the water and scooped some up, as if she meant to drink. Instead, she set the bowl in her lap and stared into it with rapt intensity.

"What is she doing?" Michael asked, when, after several minutes, Sophia hadn't moved.

"She's captured a soul," Suri said softly, "and as far as I can tell, she's reading it."

Michael's brow furrowed. "Why would she do that?"

Suri pulled her eyes away from the window into the past, troubled. "Sophie Creedon has a human soul."

Michael felt queasy. "You think Sophia stole it from the pool?"

"I'm not sure, but if she did, it wasn't that one." She pointed, and Michael turned back to the window in time to see Sophia gently lower the soul back into the water, and then turn dejectedly and walk away. "This is the wrong window," Suri said. "Too far back."

Once again, Suri went into her meditative state. Once again, she reached into the air and plucked, apparently, at nothing. Rather than a peeling away a layer, though, this time she seemed to be drawing a shade over the window. The hue of the torn patch changed subtly again. Sophia was centred within it, once

157

again holding the bowl of water on her lap as she peered into it, but this time her dress was a pale, cloudy blue. After a moment, disappointment crossed her face, and she tipped the contents of the bowl back into the pool.

Suri tried again, and they watched another variation of the scene play out. And so it went: Suri painstakingly sifting through the rice-paper layers, while Michael watched in increasingly grim silence. After a while, Suri began pulling back inches, then handfuls of layers. It didn't change anything. Sophia still came to the pool hopeful, and left disappointed.

And then, finally, they found it. The window opened on a Sophia visibly diminished by her long and fruitless quest. Her hair was lank and lifeless, her eyes dull, her clothing carelessly arranged. Her blue aura had weakened to the faintest wash of light. But this time, when she looked down at the soul she'd captured in the silver bowl, her eyes widened. For a few long moments she just stared into the vessel. And then, with trembling hands, she reached down into the water and lifted the soul out.

Out of the water, condensed in form, the soul fit easily into the palm of her hand. It flickered and fluttered like a tiny, bright bird, glowing blue – a blue almost identical to the colour of Sophia's own aura. She studied it reverently for a time, and then she cupped her other hand around it, shut her eyes, and brought her hands to her breast.

As Sophia sat holding the soul, her appearance began to change. She lost her tired and haunted look; her aura strengthened again, until it was as bright as it had been in the first window. Finally, Sophia opened her eyes and her hands. Where there had been one flickering blue light, there were now two, and as far as Suri could tell, they were indistinguishable.

Slowly, gently, Sophia lowered her hand into the water, releasing one of the souls back to its rightful place. She looked for a moment at the one remaining on her palm. Then she cupped her hands around it again, stood up, and hurried away.

Suri turned to Michael, her eyes wide. "She copied a soul! That's how she made herself human!"

Michael frowned. "It's only a part of it. She needed a body, too. A human infant to put that soul into – one without a soul of her own."

"One who wasn't born yet?"

"Or one whose soul had just left her."

"That's creepy." She considered it, then added, "But Sophie did say that she'd been found abandoned as a baby. And she and Esther share a birthday…"

They looked at each other, deducing the same thing, but neither wanting to speak it out loud. At last, Michael shook his head. "There are so many levels of sacrilege here, I don't even know where to begin."

Suri's horrified fascination turned to annoyance. "Do you always have to be such a sanctimonious buzz-kill?"

"Suriel, Sophia cloned a soul and co-opted a body! Do I really need to explain to you what's wrong with that?"

"She did it to save us all!"

"So she says."

"What does that mean?"

"It means, it's highly convenient that saving us all also meant saving her lover."

"We've both seen the prophecy."

"Yes – the prophecy that Sophia herself supplied."

Suri was ready with a sharp retort, but then she swallowed it. "Okay, fine," she said. "We can agree to disagree about her motivations. But there's no getting around the fact that Sophie Creedon has the same soul as another human being. So logic says that human being must be Esther Madden."

Michael frowned. "On the face of it, it would seem so."

"What do you mean, 'on the face of it?' It would explain the whole weird Theletos priest thing if Esther shares a soul with

Sophie. It would even explain those pills she takes. I mean, she's probably destined not to live past eighteen, either."

"Maybe," he said. "But what about all the things it doesn't explain? Like how they happen to look so much alike?"

"Assigning souls isn't our jurisdiction. For all we know, what a human looks like has as much to do with his or her soul as anything else." She thought about this, then added, "Or maybe copying the soul copied the body, too."

"They're similar," Michael said, "but they aren't identical."

"But still, I mean it's possible, it just – "

"Suriel."

"What? It's a good theory! I mean – "

"Suriel, shut up and look!"

Michael's eyes were fixed on the still-open window, where something else was moving. Distractedly, Suri looked back at it. And then she, too, was riveted. The moving figure was Theletos, but he was barely recognizable as the aeon he had been, or even the human they'd known as Rive. He was crawling toward the pool, his aura barely visible, his face pinched with pain.

"Sophia!" he called weakly, and then he collapsed into a fit of coughing. When it finally stilled, he looked ragged, beaten. "Sophia," he cried, or tried to cry, "I can't feel you anymore... are you here?" But there was no answer.

"What's wrong with him?" Suri asked.

"His consort has left him," Michael said dryly.

Suri looked at him in irritation. "It's more than that, obviously. She left him before, and it didn't make him sick."

Michael watched for another long moment, as Theletos dropped his head dejectedly on the grass by the pool. "Of course it didn't," he said bitterly, "because she didn't change her nature, those other times. This time she did, and they were separated completely – or nearly so."

"Riven," Suri repeated softly, looking at Theletos with pity. "She can't have meant to hurt him."

"How could she have thought she wouldn't," Michael snapped, "when she knew that her own lifespan would be cut to eighteen years?" His eyes were jewel-bright, seething. "The damage she's done…"

Both of them were silent for a long time, watching Theletos, who seemed to have fallen asleep. At last, Suri drew the layers of time back over the window, smoothing the edges until there was no sign that it had ever been disturbed.

"You know, Michael, being mad at her isn't going to help anything, least of all stopping the daevas."

"And what will, in your opinion?"

Suri sighed. "Fulfilling Sophia's prophecy."

"Do you honestly still think Lucifer is the answer to this mess?"

"I don't know," Suri admitted. "But I do know that we need to tell Sophie what we've found out, and see if it means anything to her."

"How, when we can't get to Earth?"

Suri was looking off into the middle distance, a sign that she was on the brink of an idea. Michael braced himself, and sure enough, she said, "Yeah, about that. There is one thing we haven't tried."

Michael's look turned leery. "What's that?"

"Sorcery."

"Sorcery is forbidden!"

Suri smiled joylessly. "By whom? Everyone who ever had any authority over us is gone."

"Even if you're brazen enough to try it," he said, "you don't know how. Even *I* don't know how. It was Azazel and the other fallen who learned those secrets – "

"Exactly."

Michael stared at her. "I truly hope you aren't suggesting what I think you're suggesting."

Suri only smiled, stood up, and summoned the door back to Heaven.

CHAPTER 6

15 JUNE
TROON, SCOTLAND

Esther woke with a start as the gentle rocking that had lulled her to sleep came to an abrupt, juddering halt. She sat up, rubbing her eyes to clear them and trying to recall where she was. She remembered a lorry full of shirts, but now she had a tartan blanket wrapped around her, and she sat in the V of a boat's hull. The boat had run aground on a sandy beach, but the thick white fog that swirled around it made it impossible to tell anything more than that about her location.

Cliona was still asleep in her own blanket. Esther shook her gently. Cliona's eyes snapped open and she sat up abruptly, saying, "Where are we?"

Esther gestured to the fog. "I have no idea. But at least it's dry land."

Cliona stood up, bracing herself as the boat lurched with her weight. Grabbing her bundle, she leapt onto the sand. She stood for a moment peering into the fog, as if she might part it by force of will. Then she turned back to Esther. "We'd better see if we can find a road."

Esther nodded. "We should probably take some food with

us, too." She gathered some of the items from the wooden chest, handing them to Cliona.

Then, in the bottom corner of the chest, she saw a small metal box. Esther picked it up and opened it. Inside were a piece of stone, a D-shaped bit of metal, and what looked like a square of burnt cloth. "What is this?" she asked, showing it to Cliona.

Cliona gave her a strange look. "Do you mean to say you've never seen a tinder-box before?"

"Ah…I…"

"Never mind," Cliona said, seeing her confusion. "Best take it with us, all the same. You never know when it might come in handy."

So Esther closed up the box and added it to the pile on her kerchief. Then she tied it up and followed Cliona onto the strand. As soon as her foot left the deck, the boat slipped back into the water. She saw the flash of iridescent scales, white arms, long hair: mermaids, carrying the boat away.

"Wait!" Esther cried after them.

Cliona put a hand on her arm. "It's okay," she said. "We were done with it anyway. Or more to the point, it was done with us."

A moment later, it was lost in the fog. Esther sighed and opened one of the bottles she'd taken from the chest of food. She took a sip from it. It was some kind of berry cordial, sweet and tart at the same time. As she swallowed it, she felt calmer. She took another sip, then handed the bottle to Cliona as they made their way up the beach.

Neither of them spoke as they climbed the low dunes, emerging onto close-cropped grass. They saw no sign of fences or animals as they walked along, and Esther was trying to work out where they could be when they reached a circle of velvety-smooth grass with a hole in the centre, marked by a small flag.

"It's a golf course," Cliona said.

"Then there must be a sign somewhere," Esther answered. "We can find out where we are."

They continued to walk inland until a dark, hulking shape loomed out of the fog. It resolved into a grand stone house as they came closer. There were lights in most of the windows, so the girls hung back as they walked around the perimeter. At last they found what they were looking for: a sign that read "Royal Troon Golf Course".

"Where is Troon?" Cliona asked.

"I don't know," Esther answered. Remembering the map that Morag had given her, she rummaged in her bundle and pulled it out. It was a large map, showing both Ireland and Britain.

"What are these lines?" Cliona asked, indicating one of a number of straight blue lines that ran across the map.

"Roads, maybe?" Esther said.

Cliona shook her head. "They're too straight for roads, and anyway they run right over things like mountain ranges and forests."

"I don't know, then," Esther said. "But look, a lot of the lines intersect here: Troon." She pointed to the town marked on the southwest coast of Scotland, and felt a flood of hope.

Cliona smiled, speaking something very close to Esther's own thoughts: "The boat *did* know what we were thinking!" *Or something did,* Esther thought, looking at the convergence of lines. "Are we anywhere near where you're going?"

"I don't know," Esther answered, following her finger up the west coast. At last she located the Ardnasheen peninsula, just across the water from the Isle of Skye. Several more of the blue lines ran through it, converging on the village. She pointed it out to Cliona.

"It's a long way from here," Cliona commented.

"And the opposite direction from Yorkshire," Esther added. Cliona didn't answer that. Esther said, "We'd better find the town. Then we can figure out how to get to where we're going."

Cliona nodded, and they set off along the Club House drive, which led to a road running past several more large buildings. Before long, they found a sign pointing the way to the town centre. As they walked, the early sun began to burn through the fog. By the time they reached the town, they could see the buildings, though their lines were still softened by mist. The shops weren't yet open and there were few other people on the streets.

Abruptly, Cliona stopped by the window of a corner shop. There was a train schedule taped up in it. "Look," she said.

"I'm not sure about a train…" Esther answered.

"Esther, you can't walk to Ardnasheen, and I don't see any more magical vehicles waiting to spirit you there."

Esther sighed. "Do the trains even go anywhere near there?"

"It looks like Kilmarnock is the end of the local line."

Esther consulted her map again and found the town some ways inland, but hardly any farther north. "That doesn't help at all," she said dismally.

"How do you know? If it's a bigger town, there might be a connection there that gets you closer to where you're going."

"And you," Esther reminded her.

Cliona's eyes flickered away.

"All right. I guess we'd better find the train station."

In the end, they had to ask directions, which Esther left to Cliona, who did a remarkably good Scottish accent. Within half an hour, they had reached the whitewashed station. There was a train to Kilmarnock at half eight – they had an hour left to wait.

The two girls sat down on one of the benches on the deserted platform. The rest of the fog had burned off, leaving the sky a clear, translucent blue. The sun even had a hint of warmth in it. Esther took off her coat and opened the bottle of cordial. She drank some and then handed it to Cliona, who gave her a scone in return, taking the last one for herself.

They sat in silence as they ate, but when Cliona finished her scone she turned to Esther and said, "Are you still sure?"

"Sure of what?" Esther asked.

"This plan to go to Ardnasheen. What if you get there and find out the angel was wrong? What if he was never real in the first place?"

Cliona's eyes were strange and glittery and furtive as she spoke, as if she were waiting for Esther to be angry with her. And Esther *was* angry, but at the same time, she couldn't quite blame Cliona for doubting her. Most likely she would have been wondering the same thing in Cliona's place. And because Cliona might also be doubting herself, she said with all the conviction she could muster, "He's real. And in any case, where else would I go?"

Still not meeting her eyes, Cliona said, "You could come with me."

Esther was silent for a long time, wondering how to answer this. At last, she said, "You need to go to Yorkshire the same as I need to go to Ardnasheen." Cliona finally met her eye. "But you've been a good friend, Cliona, and I'm grateful to you. Without you, I'd never have got this far."

Cliona blinked, and then she turned away. "I'm afraid," she said softly.

"Of course you are," Esther answered. "But you're strong. Look how far you've got us. You can do the last bit – I'm sure of it."

Cliona nodded, but she looked miserable. Once again, Esther had the urge to throw caution to the wind and tell her everything. But once again, she pushed it back, knowing that it would be for her own sake rather than Cliona's. Cliona didn't need any more burdens.

Still, it seemed wrong to leave her with no idea of what was coming. So she said, "You know, my dreams…the ones I've told you about, with the demons…well, I think they may come true."

Cliona studied her for a moment, and then she said the last thing that Esther had imagined: "I think you're right."

"You do?"

Cliona nodded. "Between you and Mam – well, there must be something in it." She paused, and then she said, "Do you think the world is ending?"

They were the words Esther hadn't allowed herself to think. And yet, spoken in Cliona's pragmatic voice, she couldn't deny them. What else could it mean, that she dreamed of monsters erasing cities and her own body disintegrating?

"I don't know," she said at last. "But whatever is coming, it won't be pretty. Cliona – promise me you'll be careful. And if it doesn't work out with your mam, come find me. You know where I'm going."

Cliona smiled a joyless smile. "Oh, aye. And yes, I'll be careful."

"I'm glad," Esther said. But she still felt guilty.

*

The train to Kilmarnock had a number of unsavoury-looking faeries on board, as well as a good many creatures the girls couldn't identify, making it impossible for them to talk about anything substantial. Once in Kilmarnock, they found a bigger rail map, which told them that they both needed to get to Glasgow. From there, Esther could pick up a direct train to Mallaig, which was as close as she could get to Ardnasheen by land. Cliona, meanwhile, had to head toward Edinburgh and then Newcastle. After another silent ride on a train carrying even more suspicious-looking creatures than the last one, they emerged onto Glasgow's Queen Street, which was full of mid-afternoon crowds. In Queen Street Station, they easily found a train headed to Edinburgh. But Esther had missed the only train going to Mallaig that day; she would have to spend the night in the city.

"I can stay with you," Cliona offered. "There are plenty of trains to Edinburgh. I can go in the morning."

Tempted as she was to take Cliona up on the offer, Esther shook her head. "You need to get to your mam."

"Are you sure?" Cliona asked, pinning Esther with her intent, dark eyes.

Esther sighed. "To be honest, I don't know how much time we have before things…" She shook her head, still unable to say it. "Anyway, I think you better get to your mam as soon as you can."

"Okay," Cliona said. Then she reached into her bundle, took out the purse with the laundry money, and divided it, handing half to Esther.

"I can't take that," Esther said.

"Too good to take stolen money?" Cliona taunted.

"Of course not, it's just – oh. You're kidding."

Cliona smiled her ironic smile. "Whatever happens to you, Esther, please don't change."

"What do you mean?"

"The world needs more innocents," she said, and then, as Esther was about to protest, she shoved the money into her hand. "I meant that as a compliment. Now take this. Sure, it's as much yours as anyone's."

"Thank you."

"You're welcome." This time, Cliona's smile was genuine. "I hope we meet again."

"Me too," Esther said. Cliona hugged her once, fiercely, as the steam engine let out a whistle, and then she ran for her train, which was already moving.

Esther watched as it rumbled off into the approaching evening. She didn't want to turn and face the city that suddenly seemed vast and hostile. Although it wasn't the city from her nightmares, it had the same grey hue and sinister feel in the gathering twilight. She had planned to find some doorway or outbuilding in which to spend the night, but as the evening deepened, the faeries that thrived on darkness began to roam, and she lost her conviction. She counted the money Cliona had given her, and then remembered the five pounds from her prayer book. That gave her enough to buy her train ticket tomorrow with some to spare; enough, she hoped, for a room for the night.

She walked across George Square and on into the web of smaller streets around it. She passed several bed-and-breakfasts that looked too expensive, and then she turned down a smaller street, lined with tenements and lit only by a single gaslight. The spire of a large church rose up into the slate-blue sky beyond the rooftops, and Esther couldn't shake the feeling that it was watching her.

Half way down the street she found a boarding house with a vacancy sign. The place looked shabby and disused, not the type to attract a lot of customers – perfect for Esther's purposes. She climbed the cracked steps to the front door and rang the bell. After what seemed an eternity, she heard approaching footsteps. A shadow loomed behind the frosted glass of the door, and then it opened, revealing a dour, middle-aged woman with her hair in curlers and a scarf tied over them, holding a paraffin lamp. Another one on the table provided the foyer's dim light.

"Aye?" she said, looking Esther up and down.

"I'd like to take a room for the night."

"I dinnae let rooms for less than two."

"But I'm leaving town in the morning. And besides," she added, wondering where the boldness was coming from, "it's not likely you'll have another customer at this time of night."

The woman raised her eyebrows and then narrowed her eyes. Finally, she said, "I'll take an extra pound for the trouble."

"Fine," Esther sighed, though she'd been hoping to use the extra money for something hot to eat.

"I'll have to make the room up," the woman said. "Come back in a half hour."

"But I've nowhere to go!"

"Go along and look at the cathedral." She pointed at the steeple Esther had seen rising above the tenements. "It'll still be open." With that, she shut the door in her face.

For a moment Esther stared at the door, fighting back tears. She hadn't realized how much she'd looked forward to locking a door behind her and lying on a real bed until it was denied her. *Don't be a baby*, she told herself and turned toward the cathedral's steeple, nearly swallowed now by the gathering darkness. Given her recent experience of churches, it was the last place she wanted to go. But it was still better than sitting alone on the stoop of the seedy boarding house. Wearily, she set off down the street.

The cathedral wasn't as big as St. Patrick's in Dublin, but it was more arresting: an austere Gothic structure, its grey stone marked in dark waves by centuries' worth of rain and soot. Though the surrounding grounds were now completely dark, the entrance was lit, and coloured light showed through the stained glass windows. The light brushed Esther with the ghost of her lost faith. Longing for even a scrap of that old comfort, she crossed the street and climbed the steps to the great double doors. One was ajar, and she heard organ music coming from within – something intricate, with a resonant, repetitive bass line. She slipped inside, thinking that an evening mass was as good a way as any to pass a half hour.

But the church was empty. Vast pillars reached up, curving toward each other into arches that met in the shadowed vaults of the ceiling, like the canopy of a petrified forest. At the base of the pillars were altars dedicated to various saints, the figurines or painted panels bearing their likenesses banked with flickering candles.

Half way up the nave was a rood-screen carved of stone, the pipes of the organ rising above it on either side. Esther made her way toward the screen, and then climbed the steps and passed through its arched door, into the quire. In front of her were two rows of pews, beyond them the choir stalls and the altar. The red carpet on the floor had an image of a tree in gold, its vast branches curling outward into Celtic symbols. Esther was about to sit down on one of the pews when, abruptly, the organ fell silent.

She turned to look behind her, but the organ loft was hidden from view. She strained against the sudden, resounding silence for any sound that might tell her that she wasn't alone. What she heard made her wish she hadn't: it was a gasp, and then a sharp cry that was stifled a moment later.

Heart skipping, Esther slipped behind a pillar, looking for any exit that wouldn't involve passing back under the rood screen and organ loft. The only door she saw led to a flight of steps running downward. She looked at it, and then, once again, at the organ loft. Now there was a faint light coming from it, like an aura, but greyish-blue and crackling with unearthly energy. She dove into the stairwell.

Esther had hoped to hide just inside the doorway until whatever was in the organ loft left. But she heard movement above her – the scuffling sound of a struggle – and the next moment, something was falling from the loft. She watched with horror as the figure hit the floor, certain that whoever it was would now be seriously injured or dead. But the young, olive-skinned woman landed in an improbable crouch, catlike and unharmed.

The aura wasn't hers – in fact, she seemed to have no aura at all. She looked up at the flickering glow above her, her face a mask of terror, and then she whirled and ran toward the door where Esther was hiding. Esther's heartbeat was so irregular by now that she thought she would faint. But she held on against the darkness at the edges of her vision, flying down the stone steps before the woman and whatever was following her could see her.

At the bottom of the stairs she passed through a wrought iron gate, and then stopped in confusion as she found herself in another church. It didn't have the great vaulted ceiling of the space above, but it had similarly huge pillars, which met in webs of arches on the ceiling. In the centre of this under-church was an altar covered in a blue patchwork cloth that spread out around it on the floor. Esther crawled underneath it a moment before the woman reached the bottom of the stairs.

Esther peeked out beneath the bottom of the altar cloth. Slowly but surely, the weird aura was filling the stairwell, and now Esther could see the figure it was attached to. The creature was more or less human in form, but if it had ever been a living man, it hadn't been for quite some time. Yet though its spectral aura suggested a ghost, Esther knew that this label wasn't right either. It was too solid, even if that solid form seemed to be disintegrating, corpselike, as it moved.

She wanted nothing so much as to scream: to close her eyes, cover her ears and drown out any possibility that the thing she was now looking at was real. But terror compelled her to keep her eyes open, locked her arms by her sides and paralyzed her tongue as the glowing figure made its slow, inexorable way toward the pillar where the woman was hiding.

Reaching it, the creature fumbled behind it with fleshless hands. The woman ran again, narrowly escaping the wraithlike fingers. The thing didn't cry out or growl or express any kind of irritation that its prey had escaped. It only shifted its trajectory and continued to pursue her. Esther was beginning to wonder how long such a chase could go on, when she realized that the stairwell was glowing again.

This time two figures descended, both of them recognizably female, though in similar states of decay as the man. One wore the remains of a Victorian ball-gown, the other what might once have been a medieval smock. With the same inexorable slowness, they positioned themselves in a triangle around the woman they were pursuing and began to close in on her. Realizing that she wasn't going to be able to escape them, she began to plead.

"Don't do this!" she cried in a voice rough with fear. "I'm not the one who made you!"

Made you? Esther had a moment to think, before one of the creatures – the man – was answering in a strange, wispy voice, which stretched the words like a sigh on a breeze: "Doesn't matter…you've made others."

The woman sank to the ground, tears in her eyes, flaying Esther with guilt for watching and doing nothing. But she had no idea what to do, no inkling of how to fight a creature she couldn't even name.

"I'm sorry! I was desperate!"

"So…are…we," whispered the creature in the Victorian dress, reaching out a gnarled finger to touch the woman's cheek.

She shrank back, shuddering. "You have no power over me. You have no strength." But she didn't sound convinced of her own words, and she didn't seem surprised when the creatures laughed: a weird, papery sound like dry leaves brushing together.

"We have been given dominion over the fallen," the man said.

"By whom?" the woman asked.

"The one…who dismantled…your staves."

"Dismantled?" she asked, obviously confused.

"Keeper's…staves…don't…fail…"

The creature in the medieval dress added, "Your kind…are dying."

"You can't mean…you can't – "

But the three creatures had linked arms now, locking her in, and though she pushed against them they were immovable as stone. Esther saw confusion and disbelief along with the fear on her face as the medieval creature reached out and took that face in her hands. The woman whimpered, trying to pull away, but the creature hung on, its lips twisting into what might have been a smile, had its face been whole.

"See how you like it," she whispered, and then she bent her head to the woman's, as if she meant to kiss her. But when their lips met there was a searing light. Esther watched long enough to see that it was coming from the woman's eyes, and then she shut her own against it.

She didn't know how long she'd huddled beneath the altar with her eyes closed, but slowly, she became aware that the light had faded, and a sound was filling the room. Through her shock, it took her a few moments to recognize it as laughter. Nor was it the weird, dry laughter of the glowing creatures, but the resonant sound that comes from a whole body. A human body.

"It worked!" the laughing woman's voice said. Gingerly, Esther lifted a tiny corner of the altar cloth. Two of the creatures, the male and the Victorian female, were exactly as they had been when she shut her eyes. The other one, though, had transformed into what looked like an ordinary woman, though she was dressed in strange, archaic clothing. She kept looking at her hands, white and perfect, as if she couldn't believe that they were real. Beyond them, a crumpled figure lay in the shadows.

"You…have…them?" the male figure asked the medieval woman.

"I have them all!" she answered gleefully, putting her hands to her chest.

"You'll…deliver…to Abaddon?" the Victorian figure asked.

Esther was arrested by the name of the daeva, so shocked to hear it that she had to force her attention back to the conversation.

"That was the bargain we made," the medieval woman answered, suddenly on her guard.

Esther willed the woman to say what the bargain had been – to say anything that would explain what she had just witnessed. But the woman was speaking briskly now, saying, "I must go. We promised to deliver them immediately." She paused, her eyes on the other two. At last, regretfully, she said, "Good luck to you," and then she said a good many more words that Esther couldn't make sense of. As she spoke, a darkness welled up out of the floor around her, climbing like smoke until it engulfed her figure. Then, abruptly, both the woman and the darkness were gone.

The two glowing creatures hovered for a moment, watching the place where she had been. Then they drifted back up the stairs. Esther watched them go, still shaking, her heartbeat still wild. After a few minutes, though, she was confident enough that the creatures weren't coming back that she risked the noise of untying her bundle and shaking a couple of tablets into her hand. Her mouth was so dry that she could barely swallow them.

As her heart steadied, she began to feel better, and to consider her predicament. She was going to have to come out from under the altar sooner or later. It was long past time for her to have returned to the boarding house, and she had no doubt that the owner would lock the doors against her if she were too late. But she couldn't stop thinking that the grey creatures were lurking just beyond the doorway, waiting to do to her whatever they had done to the woman in black.

They're gone, Esther told herself, trying her best to believe it. They got what they came for – whatever it was. Slowly, she began to re-tie the kerchief, but as she lifted it, something dropped out. It was the scrap of fabric that Morag had called Arthur's Mantle.

Except that now, it was more than a scrap. As she held it in her hands it began to unfold in layers light as mist, until it was easily big enough to fit around a man's shoulders. Where the fabric draped over her arm, it took on the colour and texture of the altar cloth behind it, making her arm almost invisible. With shaking hands, Esther pulled the cloak over herself. It had a hood deep enough to hang down over her face, concealing all of it.

Tucking her bundle beneath the cloak, she edged out from under the altar. The weightless fabric shifted, now mimicking the stone of the floor and pillars. Emboldened by this, Esther approached the still figure of the woman the creatures had attacked. As the figure took shape amidst the shadows, though, Esther saw something that made her pause. The woman's wide-necked top had fallen away from her shoulder on one side, revealing an intricate black tattoo spreading across her shoulder blade. Though it wasn't the same as the tattoo on the dead woman in the photograph that Mother Helena had showed her, it was close enough to make Esther's heart begin skipping again.

The woman had fallen face down when the creature let her go. It took every ounce of courage Esther had to reach out and put her hand on the tattooed shoulder, and turn the woman over. Yet when she saw her ravaged face, though she was disgusted, she wasn't surprised. Like those in the nun's photographs, it had burned black holes where the eyes should be, and scorched skin around the mouth, fixing it in a silent scream.

Esther didn't bother to check for breath. She let the figure fall and backed away. She knew that what she had witnessed here was important, but she also understood that there was nothing she could do about it. No one would believe her story if she told it. No one would believe that she hadn't killed the woman herself. And so she left her for someone else to find and moved toward the stairway.

Climbing out of the under-church, she saw no sign of the ghostly auras. The church above was hushed and still, but its very silence and emptiness seemed full of menace. As she walked back up the aisle, Esther kept her eyes fixed firmly ahead of her, not wanting to see what might be hiding in the shadows. She ran the last few feet to the door, and all the way back to the boarding house, finally letting out a breath of relief when she saw that the faint light in the entryway. She ducked into the shrubs by the steps and removed the mantle, which immediately shrank back to the size of a pocket handkerchief. She stuffed it into her bundle, and then she went up to the boarding-house door.

"You're late," the landlady said irritably when she finally answered Esther's knock. "I was about to lock up."

"Sorry," Esther muttered.

"All of the best rooms are gone. It's only the loft left now."

"If it has a bed and a blanket, it's enough for me."

"Hm," the landlady said, giving her a suspicious once-over. Then she picked up the lamp, and without bothering to see whether Esther followed, she started up the stairway.

They climbed three flights and came out onto a narrow landing under the eaves with unfinished wooden walls. The landlady indicated one of two doors opening off the landing, which had a number 6 painted on it. "That's your room. Here's the key, mind you don't lose it. And a candle." She lit a stub of candle in the lamp flame, and handed it to Esther. "Breakfast is at eight, if you want it."

"Is it included in the price?" Esther asked.

The woman just laughed.

"Then no, thank you."

"Suit yourself," the landlady said and retreated back down the stairs.

Esther stood for a moment in the weak light and then she unlocked the door. The room was tiny. Both walls slanted up toward the roof, the same unfinished wood as the walls bordering the landing. Looking through the cracks in the wood, Esther could see the slates of the roof above, which explained the draughty chill. There was a cot under one eave with a thin mattress and a threadbare blanket, and a side table under the other, with a vase of black, desiccated flowers on it. An old sink projected from one wall, its single tap promising that it would offer nothing but cold water. Esther saw a chamber pot under the end of the bed, and hoped that she wouldn't need the toilet before morning.

Still, the door had a lock, which she wasted no time in setting. The tiny window on the gable wall wasn't made to be opened, for which she was grateful. She pulled the coarse, feed-sack curtain over it, stuck the candle to the bedside table, and then pulled off her boots and sat down on the bed. She had some food left from the chest on the boat, but she wasn't hungry. Instead, she took out the books that Morag had given her.

Esther held them beside each other, resting on her knees. They were very much alike, both bound in deep green leather, except that the cover of the *Book of Sorrows* was blank, while the poetry book was stamped in gold. On the spine of each book, where a publisher would put its insignia, there were identical gold-leaf symbols: three interconnected spirals, forming a triangle. Esther remembered that the same symbol had been painted on the door of Morag's shop, but it seemed familiar beyond that – something she had seen, perhaps, in the world before the Change.

Ever since Morag had given it to her, she had wondered what was in the book she was meant to deliver to Sophie Creedon. It had seemed a kind of trespass to read it, but after the events in the Cathedral, she felt more than justified in looking for information. She opened the book to the first page and began to read. When she finally slept that night, she dreamed of a star, bright as music on a pre-dawn horizon, and her own fingers trying to reach it.

CHAPTER 7

16 JUNE
GLASGOW, SCOTLAND

Esther awakened early. She washed as best she could in the tiny sink and then packed her things and crept down the stairs. No one was awake yet, not even the landlady, which was exactly what she'd been hoping for. She left her payment on the front desk, then opened the door and let herself out into the grey morning.

It was warmer than it had been the previous few days, but damp, the air full of a dense mist that wasn't quite heavy enough to qualify as rain. It deadened sound, fuzzed the tops of the tenements and obliterated the cathedral's steeple completely. She was wondering whether the dead woman had been discovered yet when a wailing rent the early-morning silence, and an antiquated black police wagon raced past, in the direction of the church. Shaking, Esther ducked into a stairwell as another one followed it, and then, when she was certain that no more were coming, she hurried down the street in the opposite direction, toward the city centre.

George Square was already busy, but still, she couldn't shake the feeling that she stood out among the crowds as clearly as she would have if it had been empty. She clung to the margins of the pavement, keeping her head down and trying not to look agitated. But her heart was beating erratically again, the darkness creeping along the edges of her vision. She paused at the mouth of an alley to shake two tablets into her palm. When she saw that there were only six left, though, she put them back. She could do this without them. She had to.

Esther leaned against the stone wall behind her, trying to steady her breathing, and her heart-rate along with it. When she felt a bit calmer, she came back out onto the pavement and made her way toward Queen Street station. She bought her ticket and then located the train. It was older than the ones she'd taken the day before. Through the windows she could see that the first-class cars were richly decorated and furnished in deep colours and heavy fabrics.

The second class carriages were as stark as the first class ones were opulent, with slatted wooden floors and straight-backed wooden benches that reminded Esther of the stalls where she'd been made to sit at mass in the convent. She walked along the line of carriages until she found an empty one. She got on, took a bench in the middle and slid over beside the window. The train blew its warning whistle.

Esther was just about to breathe a sigh of relief that no one had joined her in the carriage, when an elderly man boarded. He stood wheezing for a moment, as if he'd run to catch the train. He was dressed like a farmer in a well-worn waxed jacket zipped right up to his weather-beaten face, his white hair covered by a flat tweed cap. He carried no luggage or packages. His eyes settled on Esther, a peculiar golden-brown colour, like dark honey. Esther looked quickly out the window, but he was already approaching.

"Off north, lass?" he said, stopping by her seat.

Esther nodded without glancing up, praying that he would get the message and leave her alone. Instead, the man collapsed onto the bench opposite her, saying with a sigh, "Aye, me too.

Can't wait to be home. I never could stand the city. Too noisy and dirty. Ach, where are my manners? Would you like me to help you lift your bundle?"

Esther looked from the bundle in her arms to the luggage rack overhead, where the man was pointing. She hadn't even noticed it until then, and wouldn't have wanted to use it if she had. She shook her head and looked away again.

But the man was determined. "Cat got your tongue, lass?"

Esther wanted nothing less than to reveal her Irish accent even to someone as harmless-seeming as he was. "No, sorry," she said, trying to mimic the intonations of his accent and wishing she had Cliona's skills. "I'm just very tired."

"Ah – you're Irish!" Inwardly, she sighed. "And what takes you to Fort William, then – if it's Fort William where you're stopping?"

"Aye," Esther said, though she had no intention of stopping before Mallaig. "I...I've family there."

"Do you, now? What is the name? I might well know them – I've lived there all my life, and it's not yet that big a town."

The train had begun to move. Smarting with frustration, Esther watched as the platform slid past, trying to think of a common Scots name. The best she could do was, "Burns."

"Burns?" the man repeated, frowning. "Now that's not a common one in the Highlands."

"Isn't it?" Esther said, trying to sound disinterested. Beyond the window, the station had been replaced by the backs of tenements, laundry waving in their yards like flags, looking brighter than they really were against the drab stone and grey sky. Then the tenements gave way to the sprawling, miserable shanty-towns that had sprung up around the cities since the Change.

"No, it isn't. Nor in Ireland, eh?"

"They're from Edinburgh, and they haven't lived there long."

"Ah," he said, and then, at last, lapsed into silence. Esther's head was beginning to ache, and she rested it against the cool glass of the window. It wasn't long before the city was behind them, giving way to fields hazed with green, the colour rich and alive. There was something comforting in the fact that for all the damage they'd done, the daevas hadn't been able to quell the rhythms of nature.

"No!" the old man cried suddenly. "You cannae do it!"

Esther jumped, barely suppressing a cry of her own, and looked around at him. But her horror subsided when she saw that he had fallen asleep, and had apparently been speaking from a dream. He mumbled something, let out a loud snore, and then settled back into silence. Once again, Esther began to relax.

The landscape had changed again by the time the train made its first stop. The station was at a place called Ardlui, near the shore of a somnolent swath of water that Esther thought might be Loch Lomond. The landscape continued to change as they headed north, the green of cultivated fields giving way to forests and hills that grew continually steeper and starker. Just past a tiny village called Crianlarich, Esther took out her map. She followed the line of villages they'd passed through, measuring the distance she'd travelled against the distance she still had to go.

"Not too long now," spoke a cheerful voice at her elbow.

Esther whirled to find the old man had awakened, and was leaning across the aisle to look at her map. "Good to know," she said warily, and went to fold the map away, but he put a hand on her arm to stop her.

"Where did you get this?" he asked.

"I brought it from home," Esther said, hoping that it would shut him down, but instead his eyes lit with interest.

"This is no ordinary map, you know."

"Isn't it?" Esther replied.

"These blue lines, you know what they are?"

182

"No," Esther said, pulling the map firmly away from him and folding it back into her bundle.

"They're leylines."

Though Esther wanted to know what that meant, she didn't want to encourage him. "I really don't know anything about it."

"It's an odd thing to have if you don't know anything about it," he said mildly, but pointedly. He held her eye for what seemed a moment too long. They really were a peculiar colour, she thought – more tawny than brown, like an owl's.

"It was a gift from a friend."

"Was it, now?" he asked, his eyes lit suddenly with interest.

"Sure, it was her type of thing."

He watched her a moment longer, and then smiled. "Aye, well, you look after that map. You might find yourself needin' it before you're through."

Esther nodded, hoping that the man would go back to sleep. However, he seemed refreshed by his nap, once again in a mood to talk. "The line splits here, you know," he said, indicating a stretch of railroad track running away from the station they'd just left behind. "That bit's off to Oban, on the coast. After that, it's not long to Rannoch Moor."

Esther looked out the window. The mountains reared up all around them, dim and hostile, some still streaked with winter's snow. "Ah," she said, though she knew nothing about Rannoch Moor.

"Aye. Some would say there's no lonelier place in all of Scotland."

Brilliant, Esther thought, watching as the train rounded the base of a vast, conical mountain rising from the plain, deep grooves cut into its surface by centuries of melt water. The train negotiated the wide bend around the edge of the glen, and then began to climb. As the ground rose, the grey sky seemed to hang lower and lower, the clouds on the horizon darkening until it was difficult to distinguish between them and the brooding black mountain peaks.

When they finally gained the high ground the terrain flattened into a bleak piece of country intercut by pewter pools of water. Scattered amongst them were scarred and lichened boulders that seemed to have been flung there in some distant age. If this was Rannoch Moor, she thought, then the man had been right. The eerie landscape gave Esther a creeping sense of isolation. The further they moved across its sepia expanse, the more she felt cut off from the world. Though the mountains behind them receded, those on the horizon never seemed to come any closer. She saw no living creature except once, far off, a herd of deer, running as if they were pursued, and behind them, what looked like a flock of crows.

Abruptly, the train's brakes slammed on and it screeched to a halt, letting out a cloud of steam that hung around them, as if the damp atmosphere and low clouds were too thick to let it disperse. Esther swallowed around the sudden lump in her throat, her fingers whitening as she gripped her little cloth bundle. She looked around at the man across the aisle, hoping that her alarm didn't show. He gave her what was clearly meant to be a comforting smile, though in the murky light it looked grim.

"No need to worry, lass," he said. "No doubt it's only sheep on the tracks. I expect they'll have it all cleared up in a few minutes."

Esther tried to believe this, although she hadn't seen any sheep at all since they began to cross the boggy moor. Minutes came and went without any sign that the delay was about to end. Outside it grew darker still, and something clattered against the window. Esther's heart skipped, but it was only rain, though the heaviest rain she'd ever seen, almost opaque as it moved across the moor in charcoal sheets.

As Esther watched the rain, a group of dark figures emerged

from the gloom, moving slowly up the line of train carriages. The ones behind seemed to glide, as if their feet didn't touch the ground, but the woman in the lead was clearly walking. She was dressed in a grey, voluminous coat that could have belonged to the same era as the train. The coat's hood was pulled up, and a white veil hung down from it, concealing the face within. In her hand she held a staff. Where it touched the ground, it left circles of frost.

As she approached Esther's carriage, the woman paused, turning one way and then another. The dark, floating shapes hovered around her, as if awaiting instruction. Esther began to shake.

"Esther," someone said softly, and she'd turned before she realized the folly of it. The old man was looking intently at her, his amber eyes as steady and unblinking as those of the owl she'd imagined. She froze, horrified that he knew her name, ready for him to seize her. But instead, he said, "You're soon to be tried. Stay true to yourself."

"Ah…all right…"

"Esther?"

"Aye?"

"Run, lass."

"What?" she whispered.

"Run!" he repeated, and this time it was a roar that shuddered right to the core of her, though oddly, the figures outside didn't seem to hear it.

The man's image flickered, becoming for a moment a strange, terrifying creature, which looked like a cross between a man and a stag. The frock-coated woman had reached the front door of the carriage, and put one gloved hand up to open it. Esther crouched low and crept to the back. When the woman stepped inside, she jumped down from the train, landing silently on the waterlogged peat and springy heather. Esther knew that she couldn't outrun the woman, let alone the hovering figures –

not in such treacherous terrain, and with her heart tripping as it was.

Instead she reached into her bundle, pulled out the scrap of shadow-grey fabric, and permitted herself a brief sigh of relief as it unfolded again into a long, fine cloak. She pulled it on and watched herself fade into the brush and water. Then she set off at a right angle to the train tracks. She had no idea where she was going, only that she had to get as far away from the grey figure as she could. She took one last glance at the dim lights of the train. They already looked remote, like those of a ship adrift in a dark, rainy sea. Esther turned her back on them and ran.

When she couldn't run anymore, she walked, until, tripping and falling for what felt like the hundredth time on a grassy hummock that dissolved into a muddy pool of water, she didn't have the will to go on. As if in response, the mantle reverted to a scrap of grey fabric. She stuffed it into her bundle and then she sat on the oozing ground, looking around. The scene hadn't changed since she ran from the train. Even the light hadn't changed, hovering somewhere between day and darkness.

Esther began to shiver. She knew that this was bad, that she could as easily succumb to hypothermia in these wet, tepid conditions as she could in winter snow. She had to find some kind of shelter. First, though, she opened her bundle and took out the bottle of pills. The rhythm of her heart had been irregular since she fled the train, and even now, sitting, it fluctuated between too fast and too slow. She put two tablets in her mouth, held out her cupped hands until the rain filled them, and used it to swallow them. Then, slowly and painfully, she pulled herself to her feet and began to walk again.

She made her way to a rocky outcropping at the edge of a black pool full of yellow reeds, and then climbed up to the top, turning in a slow circle. It was hard to see much of anything through the rain and mist, but on one side of her the landscape grew abruptly darker: a forest. Thinking that it might be drier underneath the trees, Esther set out in that direction.

The sky had finally begun to darken by the time she reached the edge of the woods. She had expected an orderly patch of forestry service firs, but the trees she faced were huge and ancient, strewn with moss like ghosts' garments. Esther peered into the shadows beneath them, and then, taking a deep breath, she entered the woods.

It wasn't as dry as she'd hoped under the pine canopy, but the wide old branches kept off the worst of the pelting rain. Esther stood for a few minutes, allowing her eyes to adjust to the deeper gloom, and then she pushed further into the woods, hoping to find some kind of shelter. She walked slowly, carefully, her hands out to feel for broken branches. Instead, she stepped on one. It let out a report like a gunshot, and something black hurtled in front of her, croaking and squawking. She cried out, putting her hands up to shield her face, but it was gone already, fleeing on wide black wings, leaving only its strange, croaking call trailing behind in the gathering dark.

A raven. As her eyes followed the path it had taken, Esther saw something pale and luminous amongst the murky shapes of the trees. She made her way toward it, pushing back moss and branches impatiently until the tangle of forest opened out into a small clearing. There was a tiny white cottage at the centre. Its two windows had broken panes, the roof was missing slates, and the faded green door hung from a single hinge. Esther pulled the door open. The air that greeted her wasn't damp and musty smelling, as she'd expected; in fact it smelled much like the air on the moor, of rock and heather and water. Still, she hovered in the doorway, not much liking the idea of bedding down on a floor she couldn't see.

Then she remembered the tinderbox. Opening her bundle, she took it out. She picked up the stone and the D of metal and banged them together over the charred cloth. Sparks flew and landed on the cloth, lighting a tiny flame. She held up the dim light, peering into the deep shadows. The hearth appeared intact, and on the mantle-piece she found a glass jar with a stub of candle stuck to the bottom.

Esther took it out and lit it, chasing back the shadows. She looked around the cottage. The whole thing couldn't have been more than twice the size of her cell at the convent, yet it managed to incorporate a wooden cupboard, a small table, and an old-fashioned dresser of the type that displayed china. Now the dresser contained nothing but cobwebs, its shelves warped by years of damp. The table looked ready to collapse at the first touch. But the walls of the cupboard still looked straight and true.

Esther approached it. Up close, she could see that the door had a motif of Celtic knotwork cut into it. She put her fingers into the hole and pulled, and the door swung back to reveal a space that looked like it had once housed a bed. There was no bedding there anymore, though, only a mound of dry bracken.

Esther took some of it out and spread it in the hearth, along with a bundle of twigs already lying there. The dry matter caught the candle flame easily. Esther gave the rickety table a shove, and it collapsed. She broke the wood into smaller pieces, and added them to the fire until it was roaring.

With the warmth, the entire fraught day seemed to catch up to her at once. She felt as if a hundred years had passed since she'd run from the train; leaving Glasgow seemed to belong to another lifetime. Thinking of the veiled figure in the grey coat, she began to shiver. It didn't help that she was still soaking wet. Esther pulled off her sodden coat and laid it on the floor by the fire to dry. The rest of her clothes were equally soaked, and so she stripped the layers one by one, hanging them wherever she could find a spot, until she huddled by the fire in her underclothes. Slowly, she began to feel warm again.

She took an apple and some bread and the bottle of juice

from her bundle. She wasn't particularly hungry, but she knew that she had to eat if she was going to stay warm that night, never mind carry on the next day. Despite their rough treatment, the bread was still fresh and the apple un-bruised. As she ate, Esther studied the map that Morag had given her. She found Rannoch Moor easily enough, an area marked by cross-hatching, intercut by water. On the shores of a small loch there was a darker area mapped out, marked "Blackwood." This must be the forest where she now found herself. In the midst of the forest, the map's strange lines – leylines? – intersected. She wished she knew what they meant.

Esther folded the map again and put it away. She piled more wood onto the fire, and then she curled up in front of it, resting her head on her arm and pulling her coat over her. But though she was exhausted, she couldn't fall asleep. Her front was too warm, her back too cold, and a clammy chill seeped upward through the dirt floor. The wind moaning through the broken windowpanes and the gaps in the roof made her feel watched.

She got up, opened the cupboard. The feathery leaves of the bracken inside looked less dry than they had when she'd first seen them, and they smelled sweet. Esther climbed into the nest of leaves, covered herself with her coat, and then pulled the doors of the box bed shut.

PANDAEMONIUM

Rive lay curled on the floor, his knees to his chest and arms wrapped around them. In the few lucid moments since he'd learned the truth of what Sophia had done, he'd wondered why it should affect him so. After all, he'd known for as long as she'd been his consort that she didn't love him. He'd stood by in silence as she abandoned him more than once. And yet the knowledge that she had deliberately tampered with their shared spirit without asking him – without even telling him – was one betrayal too far. Hopelessness and fury twined, battering him.

He didn't know how long he'd lain there when the door opened and a wedge of harsh light fell across him. A figure stepped forward, indistinct except for long, dark hair and pale skin. He was on his feet in a second, uttering a snarl as he grabbed her by the shoulders – a snarl that choked to silence as he realized it wasn't Sophia he held.

"Lilith," he said, abruptly letting her go.

"You didn't need to stop. In fact I could get to like that side of you – "

"Enough!"

Lilith smiled. "You're angry about your consort." He glared at her. "Abaddon told me all of it. I'd be furious, too, if I found out he'd done such a thing – "

"Go to hell, Lilith," Rive muttered, turning away from her, toward the static ranks of demon bodies.

"Cute," she smiled. "Unfortunately, I can't leave you alone with our army. It's too much of a liability. That's why Abaddon sent me to get you."

"And now you've got me," he said, pushing himself to sitting. "Lucky me."

"I've come to reason with you."

"That would be a novelty," he said, but he followed her out of the room, glad enough to be away from the staring monsters. She shut the door behind them, then threaded her arm through his and began to walk down the corridor. Rive was too dispirited to fight her. Besides, he'd lost track of which way led back to the street.

"Now really, Theletos, you have to stop this. Melodrama doesn't become you."

"What do you want?"

"I thought Abaddon had told you?"

"I'm not going to bring you Sophia," he said.

190

Lilith appeared genuinely surprised. "But she betrayed you!"

"She did," he agreed. "And if I ever did love her, it's officially dead. But I won't condemn the rest of Creation to take revenge on her."

"What do you mean, condemn the rest of Creation?" Lilith's eyes were innocent, but Rive could hear the sly, hidden smile in her voice.

"Don't bother prevaricating," he said. "I get it, now: you want her because she copied a soul, which your army appears to be lacking. So she brings them to life for you, and then what? She mass-produces human souls to feed your power?"

"Possibly," Lilith said. "If we don't have enough by then."

"Do you really think I'd help you do that?"

Lilith's smile flattened. She stopped walking and regarded Rive with probing eyes. "You can't stop us. We *will* have dominion over Earth, and we *will* use Sophia to do it, even if you refuse."

"I refuse."

Lilith rolled her eyes, resumed walking. "Of course you do. You know, your basic decency is going to be your undoing."

"Very probably. You still can't force me to help you."

Lilith smiled slightly. "I wouldn't be so certain. But of course, we're hoping that you'll come to the decision on your own."

"I'm done, Lilith," he said dully. "Take me back to my prison."

"I don't think so," she answered. "We know everything, Theletos: about Esther, and what you've asked her to do, and your sad little infatuation with her."

"Leave her out of this!" Rive said fiercely, but thankful, deep down, that they didn't seem to have guessed Esther's true importance.

"You're the one who brought her into it."

Rive shut his eyes, cursing himself. "So what: if I bring you Sophia, you'll leave Esther alone?"

Lilith smiled at him curiously. "You really don't know anything, do you?" He stared her down, and at last she elaborated: "Those pills she's always swallowing? How often she has to rest or sit down?"

Rive went cold. "What do you mean?"

"Her heart is failing. She won't last past Midsummer...not without help, anyway."

Rive took a moment to digest this, carefully masking his emotions before he said, "I didn't know that daevas were in the business of repairing human bodies."

"We aren't, unless it happens to be mutually beneficial." Rive shut his eyes, as if he could block out what Lilith was saying by blocking out her image. "It goes like this: we let you out, you bring us Sophie, we fix Esther. Then the two of you can go on your merry way."

"And you think Esther will want to go anywhere with me, after watching me betray Sophia?" he asked, fixing her with ironic eyes.

"Esther won't know. In fact, she can't know. That's the caveat to the plan: if you try to tell anybody about it beforehand, then our offer is nullified. You'll be our prisoner forever and Esther will die, rather less than peacefully. Those are our terms. Take them or leave them."

He smiled sourly, looking up at the blank ceiling, trying to find a loophole. But whichever way he turned it, it came down to the same single, desolate choice: Sophie or Esther. Trick Sophie into coming with him to the daevas, and the war was as good as won for them. Let Esther die, and the prophecy would never be fulfilled – the daevas won again.

"I can't. I can't choose."

Lilith looked at him a moment longer, and then she smiled –

a gleeful, terrifying smile. "Abi thought you would say that. He said if you did, then I could play with you."

"Play with me?"

She nodded, her eyes child-bright. "It's a new game. I'll show it to you."

"No, thank you."

Lilith's smile widened, showing her predator's teeth. "The thing is, you're still our prisoner, so you don't actually have a choice."

She was right. And so, when she opened a door and gestured to him to follow her through it, he went.

Inside was a nightmare museum, its shelves and surfaces crammed with various collections that spilled over the edges, spreading across the floor. One table was entirely covered with bones. Another held a display of children's toys that Lilith seemed to have taken apart and re-constructed into horrific parodies of themselves. There was a case of moth-eaten stuffed birds, a pile of candle ends, bowls of rotting fruit, a corner filled with armour and weapons, and any number of apparently demonic devices that Rive couldn't begin to imagine a use for. The whole place was lit by a violet tinged fire in a grate so large, he could easily have stood upright in it.

"What is this place?" he asked.

"My room," Lilith answered, as if it should have been obvious. She beckoned, and he followed her to a table holding what looked like a doll's house. It was a simple whitewashed cottage, with two windows on either side of a central door – the type found all over rural Britain. Lilith lifted the roof off of it, and peered inside. Rive looked over her shoulder.

There wasn't much in the doll's house – some broken furniture, a small hearth with a real, tiny fire burning in it, and some clothing hanging in front of it, apparently drying. Then he looked into the shadows of the box-bed, and his breath caught.

Esther was sleeping there, curled up on what looked like a pile of leaves, beautiful and fragile as a damselfly.

"What is this?" he demanded.

"This," Lilith answered, her eyes steady and cold on his, "is how you choose."

"What are you going to do to her?" he asked warily.

Lilith smiled. "It's your game, so the question is what will *you* do to her?"

Lilith walked over to the table of toys, picked something up, and brought it back. She opened her hands. Within them lay three small dolls with waxy white faces, tattered clothing, and features that were subtly and disturbingly out of proportion. Their parted, smiling lips revealed rows of tiny, perfect, pointed teeth, reminiscent of Lilith's own. As Rive watched, one of them twitched. Lilith smiled and set them down by the cottage. Slowly they rose to their feet and began to move toward it with weird, lurching steps.

"What are you doing?" Rive demanded.

"Rolling the dice," Lilith answered as the dolls approached the cottage window. "It shouldn't be hard to break her. She's already run ragged, poor thing. A good scare should be enough to do it." She smiled fondly at the dolls, then her eyes flicked back to Rive. "Of course, as soon as you promise to bring us Sophia, I'll give you your dolly back. I'll even fix her for you."

"And what good would that do either of us, in a world gone to Hell?"

The irony was lost on Lilith. "We'd give you a Dominion. Somewhere you could take her, far away from everything else…"

Rive shut his eyes against the ghost-dolls, which were now scrabbling at the windows of the cottage. "I can't choose between them!" he grated out.

"Well then," Lilith smiled, "let the games begin."

BLACKWOOD

Esther!

A sweet voice, perhaps a child's.

Esther! it called again, this time joined by several more.

"Cliona?" Esther muttered, opening heavy eyelids. But Cliona wasn't there. She was alone in the dark on a rustling mattress, a Celtic symbol on the wall above her, glowing with the deep russet light of a dying fire. Watching it, Esther remembered where she was. She had only dreamed that she heard Cliona calling to her, and the flickering symbol was the decorative cutwork in the door of the box bed, with the firelight showing through. She turned over in her bed of ferns, shut her eyes and tipped back toward sleep.

"Esther, come to us!"

Esther sat bolt upright. There was no way she had imagined the voices that time. They sounded like a group of children, though there was something off about the timbre: something oddly plangent, but also insubstantial, as if they came from very far away. Esther sat up on her knees and peered out cautiously through the knot-work hole in the door. The room beyond was still, washed in the glow of the hearth's embers. At first she could see nothing that might account for the voices. But as she watched, a pale form materialized in the broken window, surfacing as if from dark water. It was a little girl's face, white and distorted, her eyes overly large and mouth far too small.

She put a hand to the glass and called, "Come to us, Esther! Only you can help us!"

More faces appeared then, clustering at the window, smeary with the rain running down the glass. Esther felt as cold as if she'd stood in the deluge with them. Shaking, she sank back down, huddling away from the door. She pressed herself into a corner of the bed, pulling her coat around her, wishing that she'd brought the rest of her things with her as well – wishing for Arthur's Mantle. But her bundle was still on the floor by the hearth, the magical mantle inside.

The ghostly children continued to call to her for a time, but at last their wistful voices faded into the wash of the rain. Esther breathed a cautious sigh of relief, and lay back down. But she'd only just settled into the ferns when something scratched at the box-bed's door, scrabbling like bare twigs over the wood. Esther curled into herself, watching as a shadow slipped across the chinks in the boards, blocking out the red seams of light. The scrabbling moved upward, and then she saw them: five spindly fingers, poised just beyond the knot-work circle.

Esther watched, petrified, as the wasted hand fed its fingers through the holes. But when it tried to clasp them together, she heard a howl of pain. Esther smelled smoke, and the fingers fell away, leaving a patch charred and blackened around the knot-work circle. She heard the screeching thing retreat, its cries swelling for a moment into a chorus of other, similar voices. And then they faded, falling back into the hush of the rain until they were gone.

Curled into the corner of the box-bed, Esther didn't think she would sleep that night. At some point, though, exhaustion overtook her, and she fell into a fitful doze full of spectres and voices which, half-waking, she couldn't distinguish as real or imaginary. Then, during one of these periods of half-sleep, she thought she heard a dog pacing somewhere beyond the box-bed's walls. At first it sounded like an ordinary dog, but its footfalls grew heavier and heavier until the ground shook with them.

Esther! the dog growled, and she could see it in her mind's eye, as detailed as if it stood before her. It was as big as a horse, and instead of fur it was covered in thick, shaggy, green-black moss, which formed a lion-like ruff around its neck, and twisted into complex plaits at its tail. Its eyes were golden, yet cold, with a black hyphen of pupil like a goat's.

Come with me, it growled.

"You're not real," Esther told it, praying that this was true.

I am as real as the stone and water and twisted roots of this place.

"What are you?"

I am death's minion.

"Stay away from me!"

I offer you peace.

In Esther's mind it leaned down, opened its mouth to show cruel teeth and a tongue of golden fire. It licked her forehead, and though the first touch seared, the pain faded quickly, turning to a warm numbness. Esther's thoughts turned dreamy; when she looked at the dog's face again it didn't seem terrible – in fact, it seemed almost kindly, its yellow eyes solicitous.

Come with me, it said again, its voice this time like a cat's purr.

Esther reached up, burying her hand in the green ruff. Though it looked like the moss that grows on trees that never see the light, it felt warm and smooth as silk. "Yes," she said, though she couldn't quite remember what it was she was agreeing to.

No! another voice cried, sharp as a whip-crack, shattering her reverie. She knew that voice, but its significance was lost on her as she looked up to find that she'd left the box bed, and knelt now on the cold floor, with the beast she'd dreamed crouching over her, jaws gaping, greedy and solid. She shut her eyes and screamed, "Theletos!"

There was a roaring, and then a flash of brightness, as if the fire had flared and engulfed the cottage. Then it all fell away again. She opened her eyes and the room was empty, except for her own things, the last fading embers of the fire and the first, milky light of dawn.

"Theletos?" she wavered. There was nothing but silence in response. "Theletos, please, don't leave me alone!"

But the silence didn't shift. Overcome at last by the long,

horrifying day and longer night, Esther sank to the floor and wept.

17 June
Rannoch Moor

Once it was light, Esther left the cottage. With the help of Morag's map, she managed to find a road – a single-track dirt road that ran between the edge of the forest and the shore of the loch she'd seen on the map the day before. She started walking. At first she felt ill and tired after the long, fraught night. But the air was sweet with damp pine and bracken and heather, and as the sun rose, it burned through the cloud cover, promising a fine day.

Slowly, Esther began to feel better, though she also felt her solitude sharply. Every time a tree rustled or a bird flapped out of the undergrowth, she froze, expecting to see a shadowy dog or a veiled woman bearing down on her with silent intent. A splay of bare twigs would turn for a moment to a ghost child's reaching hand. When these horrors failed to materialize, though, a more insidious thought struck her: maybe reality had been upturned again, and she really was alone. Maybe she was doomed to walk this road eternally, and never see another living soul…

Stop it, she told herself firmly. A narrow road through a highland moor was bound to be less than well used, but it had to lead somewhere. It has to.

After a while the forest thinned and then gave way to moorland. The road continued to follow the stony shore of the loch, serene in the summer sun, and gradually, the loch began to narrow. Sometime after that, Esther spotted the roof of a stone house rising above the trees. She picked up her pace. When she reached the house and heard voices coming from the yard, she was tempted to stop there, if only long enough to convince herself that they were real, and human. But then she thought of the past day, the stalled train and the veiled figure, and walked quickly past.

Not long after that, the road widened and entered a tiny village, no more than a few buildings clustered on the banks of the loch. She passed a schoolhouse with a handful of children playing in the yard and then a tearoom with a hand-painted sign reading "Moira's". Esther stopped in front of it, looking through the window. It was just a tiny room with a few tables, decorated in a jangle of conflicting floral patterns. But it looked warm and homely, and more to the point, it was empty, and she was hungry. Before she could lose her nerve, Esther pushed the door open.

"Be there in a tick!" someone – presumably Moira – called from an open doorway that Esther guessed led to a kitchen. "Sit anywhere you like."

Esther picked a table in the corner and sat facing the window. A moment later, a middle-aged woman with a bulky figure and a magenta smile came out of the kitchen. "Sorry you had to wait, lass," she said. "What can I get you?"

It hadn't even occurred to Esther to look at a menu. She doubted she had enough money left for more than a cup of tea, anyway, so that was what she ordered.

"Irish, are you?" Moira asked, looking at her curiously.

"Aye," Esther said, and then, before the woman could ask, "I'm here to visit family."

"Are you, then?" Moira asked, her speculative look deepening. "I'd no idea someone in the village had Irish family."

"Not right here," Esther said quickly. "They're in Fort William."

The woman cocked her head. "Then what on earth are you doin' in Bridge of Gaur?"

"I…" Esther began, and then drew a blank. "My ride… didn't work out," she said when the silence grew too long.

"Well," the woman said, "you can't be meanin' to walk to Fort William from here." She poured boiling water from a kettle into a china teapot and began loading tea things onto a tray. "It's all mountains, and the road's barely fit for motor cars, let alone a girl on foot. Can your people not come for you?"

"They haven't got a car," Esther answered.

"Hmm," Moira said with a speculative look, putting the tray down in front of Esther. Along with the tea, she'd set out a generous plate of biscuits.

"Oh, no, it was just the tea I wanted," Esther said.

"Nonsense. I know a hungry look when I see one. The biscuits are on the house."

"Well then…thank you," Esther said, taking one from the pile.

Moira nodded, smiling again, and retreated to the kitchen. Esther poured a cup of tea, and sipped it gratefully. Then she took out her map. She found the forest where she'd spent the night, and followed the shore of the loch until she came to the place the woman had just mentioned, Bridge of Gaur. It looked like she'd covered about five miles that morning. Fort William was still twenty miles away on a straight line, and Esther doubted that the route would be anything like straight. She sighed, folding the map back up.

"One of the farmers might be going into town," Moira spoke from behind Esther's shoulder, making her jump. "Sorry – didn't mean to startle you. But one of them might. Would you like me to ask around?"

Esther looked at her plate, uncertain how to answer. She knew that Moira was right – she couldn't walk to Fort William, never mind the whole way to Mallaig. But nor did she want to be at the mercy of an unknown driver. She was still deliberating when she looked up from the plate of biscuits; then she forgot all of it.

A young man stood on the pavement outside the tearoom, a cigarette between his lips and his bright blue eyes fixed on her. He had a face to which it was hard to pin an age, though his smooth skin suggested he wasn't beyond his early twenties. His hair, pushed back under a worn tweed cap, was straight and black and unevenly cut, as if it had been done quickly and carelessly. He wore the baggy, threadbare trousers and weather-beaten waxed jacket of a local farmer, but there was no mistaking him. He was the angel who had held her in her dream. He was Theletos, who had saved her from the convent. She smiled, and his own lips twitched upward – and then, abruptly, he frowned and turned away, toward the battered Land Rover parked behind him.

Esther felt it like a slap. Wondering whether her mind was playing tricks on her, she composed herself to ask Moira, "Do you know him?"

Moira looked out the window, and then shook her head. "Can't say I've ever seen him before. He looks a bit foreign, doesn't he? Must be a traveller," she added with distaste. "There've been a slew of them lately, all headed to Edinburgh. Some kind of festivities planned for Midsummer's Eve, I gather."

"Are there?" Esther asked absently, her eyes still following him. Now he was rummaging for something in the canvas-covered back of the truck.

Moira shook her head disapprovingly. "Be careful, lass. No good's ever come to a girl who takes up with a traveller."

Esther barely heard her. Her mind was still far away, lost in a dream of a crumbling city and the blue-eyed angel who had kept her safe within it. A longing had sprung to life within her, deep and insistent. It redoubled when the blue-eyed man turned toward the teashop again with a look of grim determination and a flask in his hands. He glanced at her, hesitating for a moment, and then he flicked his cigarette into the gutter and entered.

"Mornin'," he said. He had a mild Scottish accent, with a touch of something else – like his appearance, distantly foreign.

"Can I help you?" Moira asked coldly.

"I wondered if you'd be so kind as to fill this with tea," he said. "Black, no sugar." He never looked at Esther; in fact, he seemed to be carefully avoiding it. Her certainty faltered further, yet she couldn't take her eyes off of him. It was as if he shone with some invisible aura, making his surroundings fade by comparison.

When Moira took the flask and retreated to the kitchen, Esther mustered her courage and asked, "Do I know you?"

He looked over at her, and her heart skipped a beat as his eyes finally met hers. There was no doubt now that they were the eyes of the dream angel, but there was a sadness in them now, profound enough to shake her. "I don't think so," he answered, his eyes skittering away again, moving restlessly around the room. "I'm not from here – just passing through."

"Oh? Where to?"

"Fort William," he answered, and though it made no sense, there seemed to Esther to be a note of challenge in the words.

"I need a ride to Fort William," Esther said. "I could split the petrol money with you." Though it would no doubt consume what little she had left.

"The truck's temperamental," he said. "It could take a while."

"It's still better than walking," Esther answered.

"Well then," he said, "you're welcome to the lift."

"Thank you," she said, smiling and offering her hand. "I'm Esther."

He hesitated for a moment before he took it. Esther braced herself for the onslaught of energy and images that had come to her in the confessional. Instead, when his fingers closed around hers, she felt nothing. She couldn't help thinking that he looked relieved.

"Rive," he said and dropped her hand abruptly. Moira came back in and handed him the flask. He gave her some coins in return. "Come on, then," he said to Esther.

Moira raised her eyebrows in surprise. "You're going with him?"

"Aye," Esther said, rummaging in her bundle for her money. "He's going to Fort William." She held out a handful of coins to Moira, who waved it aside.

"It's just a cup of tea and a few biscuits, lass. Are you sure you wouldn't rather wait till one of the farmers is going in?"

"I'm late enough as it is," Esther said. "But thank you, for the offer and the tea."

"Look after yourself," Moira answered, sighing, and turned back toward the kitchen.

Esther took up her things and followed Rive to the front door. He swung into the Land Rover's driver's seat, while Esther let herself in the passenger side. When she was settled, Rive put the key in the ignition and said, "Now, pray."

"What for?"

"That it starts," he said with an ironic half-smile that made her heart flip over, despite his curtness. He turned the key in the ignition, and the engine caught on the first try, which clearly surprised him.

"That's a first," he said.

"Luck of the Irish," Esther said.

Another ironic smile, which disappeared abruptly as a fit of coughing shook him. It had a terrible, hollow sound to it.

"Are you all right?" she asked.

"Fine," he said tersely when the spell had passed. As he pulled the car away from the curb, he asked, "So, you're from Ireland?"

"Dublin," Esther answered. When he said nothing to this, she ventured, "Do you know the city?"

"A bit," he said and lapsed back into maddening silence. If he was Theletos – and she was certain that he was – why was he pretending not to know her? Then a chilling thought struck her: maybe coming to Earth in this human-looking body had changed him as the true humans had been changed. Maybe he had forgotten everything.

As Esther's spirits plummeted, Rive rolled down his window, lit another cigarette, and smoked in brooding silence. Esther stared out her own window, watching the forest thin until they were back on the moor. The sunlit landscape was only slightly less bleak than the cloud-ridden one of the previous day: tough, greenish-yellow grass intercut by black water, heather-dark hills scabbed with rock.

At last they turned west onto a larger road, with lanes running in two directions, though theirs was the only car in sight. "How much farther is it to Fort William?" Esther asked.

"About an hour," Rive answered.

Sighing, Esther rested her head against the window, and shut her eyes. She didn't mean to sleep, but the long night caught up with her, and she fell into a doze. She woke to the judder and growl of the engine as Rive shifted into a lower gear. She sat up, immediately alert. Ahead was a tail of traffic – mostly horse carts, a few cars. It backed up behind a long, black car that was parked horizontally across the road. Two policemen were talking to the man driving the carriage at the front of the queue.

"What's going on?" Esther asked, trying to keep the worry out of her voice.

"A road block, apparently. What for…" Rive shrugged, his eyes on the policemen, who had waved the horse and wagon along its way, then stopped to talk to the next in line. As they conversed with the driver, the door of the black car opened. Esther's trepidation blossomed into terror as the grey-coated figure emerged, with several of her floating black retinue. Frost crept out white on the ground where she set her staff. Her veiled face turned toward the Land Rover.

"Rive," Esther said quietly, "is there another road we can take?"

His eyes, too, were fixed on the strange grey figure. "Not if you want to get to Fort William."

"That doesn't matter," she replied, her eyes following the figure, which had begun to walk toward them.

"What's going on?" Rive asked. "Do you know who that is?"

The white veil fluttered as the figure moved faster, her black-gloved hand tight around the walking stick that she didn't seem to need. The shadowy figures followed, their forms drifting and tattering slightly in the wind. Esther remembered Mother Helena's description of the Prophet, the nun who was spearheading the Sword of Justice, and the pieces fell into place.

"We need to get out of here," she said, pressing herself back against the seat, as if that could distance her from the approaching menace. "I'll explain on the way."

"Mallaig or Rannoch Moor – those are your choices."

"Mallaig," Esther answered. The grey-coated woman was almost upon them, and it seemed to Esther that the temperature dropped several degrees. "Go, please!" she said, panic making her voice brittle. Rive's eyes locked on hers, equivocal. Then, for a moment, something eclipsed it – something that reminded her of Theletos as he had looked when he challenged the daeva in the dream. He put the Land Rover into gear, and with a roar of the engine he swung it around, accelerating back the way they had come.

Esther turned to see the Prophet standing in the middle of the road, gesturing to the policemen, who had begun a frenzied attempt to turn the black car around. But the road was narrow, and blocked with the other cars and wagons. In a moment, they were lost from sight.

"Do you want to tell me what that was all about?" Rive asked. His tone was cold, but Esther couldn't help feeling that he was using it to hide another emotion.

"I can't," she said.

"I don't believe you."

Smarting with frustration, she cried, "I'm not lying to you!

I don't know what that woman wants with me." *Although I have a strong suspicion,* she didn't add. After all, for the moment, suspicion was all it was.

"But you know that she wants something."

Esther looked down at her hands, clenched around her bundle.

Rive drove silently for a few moments, and then he said, "You aren't going to visit relatives in Fort William, are you, Esther?"

"Of course not, Theletos," she said evenly. "I'm going to Ardnasheen, like you asked me to."

To her surprise, he laughed at that – until it set off another fit of terrible coughing, this one leaving flecks of blood on his hand. Yet when he'd finally controlled it, he lit another cigarette. Esther watched with appalled fascination as he drew on it.

"You can forget about that," he said as he blew the smoke out again. "Plans have changed."

"Sure," she said, "so the world isn't ending anymore?"

His mouth was bitter, his eyes hard as he answered, "I said plans have changed – not the grand scheme. But in any case, you're no longer required to give Sophie that message."

"Why? You've found another girl to save the world?"

He gave her a strange look then – vaguely sick, vaguely pleading, and still desperately sad. "It's not that," he began, "it's only…" He shook his head, and his look hardened again. "You'll never make it to Ardnasheen, Esther. Your schoolmate talked, and the Sword of Justice is currently sweeping the country for you."

Esther felt like the air was being crushed out of her chest. Her heart began its erratic stuttering as a wave of hurt washed over her. "Cliona talked to the Sword of Justice?" she asked, barely above a whisper.

Rive's look turned puzzled. "She wasn't called Cliona. Deborah? Dinah? No, Dervla. Ginger-haired girl. She was

206

arrested for stealing, and she told the police everything she knew about you in exchange for not being sent back to the convent. Your new hair colour, your clothes, the fact that you were going to Scotland and travelling with another girl. Once they found that body in Glasgow Cathedral…well, I guess we both know why that roadblock was up back there."

Esther couldn't speak, couldn't even look at him. She thought she might be sick. After a few deep breaths, however, she managed to say, "Why didn't you tell me all of this at first?"

Once again, his demeanour lost its certainty. "I wasn't sure…" He stopped, shook his head. "I suppose I hoped you'd already have changed your mind." There were a few long moments' silence, and then he said, "I'm sorry. You're right, I should have told you." His voice was different – gentler. "But I can still help you. I mean, to get somewhere safe."

"Is anywhere safe when the world is ending?" she asked with soft bitterness.

There was a pause – the faintest catch of his breath, before he answered, "Maybe. I guess it depends on how you define 'safe'."

For a mad moment, Esther was tempted to take Rive up on his offer. After all, what were her chances of outrunning the Sword of Justice when the Prophet was only a step behind her? And for that matter, what proof did she have that this whole thing wasn't a wild goose chase? For all she knew, Sophie Creedon was a figment of Rive's clearly erratic imagination, and there was nothing that could stop the daevas carrying out their plans.

That was where her brief fantasy came up short. She thought of the way the daevas' wing-beats had turned the day to consummate night. She knew that that dream had been no fantasy. It had been a premonition. Likewise, the mighty being who had held her as the world crumbled was real, too, even if he had become the man who sat beside her now, broken and equivocal.

"I'm sorry," she said softly. "But I can't run and hide if I have a chance to stop the daevas."

Rive smiled bitterly. "And how do you plan to outrun the thing in the grey coat?"

"Thing?" Esther asked, alarmed. But before Rive could answer her, the car engine thudded twice and died.

"Damn it!" he growled, steering the car onto the shoulder with the last of its momentum. He turned the key several times, to no effect. He sighed, banged his head onto the back of the seat, and then turned to Esther. "And now we get to try to outrun her on foot."

"Can't you fix it?" she asked anxiously.

"Let's hope so," he answered.

Rive got out and began rummaging underneath the bonnet of the truck. After a moment, Esther got out too. The sun that had shone for most of the day had retreated now behind a bank of cloud rising in the west. More dark clouds were gathering over the shadowy peaks to the south, promising rain.

She walked out to the middle of the road and looked around. A hill rose up steeply from the shoulder where the Land Rover was parked. On the far side of the road, the ground tumbled down to a wide, slate-grey loch, its surface ruffled by the rising breeze. The wind wound through the scrubby bracken and heather with a dry rustling that would have been more fitting on the cusp of winter, rather than few days before Midsummer. Esther shivered and turned back to the car, where Rive was standing with the gas cap in one hand and a stick in the other.

"Any luck?" she asked.

He smiled morosely and showed her the stick.

"I don't know anything about cars," she said.

"The stick's dry. We're out of fuel. The gauge must be broken."

"So what now?"

Rive sighed, looking around at the barren country. "The

nearest house I know of is a B&B a good ten miles up the road. I might be able to borrow some diesel there, but what about you?"

"Am I not allowed to come with you?" she asked sharply.

"It's a long walk, and it's too exposed. I don't want you to be recognized."

"Then leave me," Esther said, though it was the last thing she wanted. "My problems aren't yours."

"I'm not leaving you alone out here."

"It seems to me that you don't have much choice."

The sky seemed to darken and the wind to rise while they stared each other down. Finally, he said, "I have an idea." He pulled a mountaineer's pack out of the back of the truck and stepped onto a sheep track running up the hill.

"Where are you going?" Esther asked, scrambling after him.

"There's a place up here where you can wait. I'll go after the diesel, and come back for you when I've got it."

"What kind of a place?" Esther asked dubiously, the spectres of the past night looming large in her mind.

"A safe one," Rive answered, "more or less." And that was all he would say.

They walked for a good half hour over terrain that rippled slowly uphill. Every once in a while Rive would stop to cough or light a cigarette, and Esther wondered but said nothing about the incongruity, being too glad of the chance to regain her own breath and equilibrium. Finally, Rive stopped on a rise and pointed to the one beyond it. At its top was a church, its whitewashed walls showing clear traces of age and wear. But the arched windows had their glass intact, and the slate roof looked solid.

"What is that place?" Esther asked.

"A church," he answered.

"Yes, I realize that. I meant, what church? Why is it way out here in the middle of nowhere?"

"It wasn't always the middle of nowhere. The church is called Our Lady of the Braes, and it used to serve two parishes of crofters, until they all got rounded up and sent to Canada to make way for sheep."

"That's sad," Esther said softly, gazing at the forlorn church on its windswept hill.

"It is," Rive agreed, with a degree of feeling that surprised her. "But the point is, I can't imagine anyone will look for you there. And if they do, there should be plenty of places to hide."

Esther fought down a wave of panic. Rive might be prickly company, but he was better than none at all, and she didn't like to think of him walking away and leaving her in that abandoned church. Still, there was no way she was going to beg him to stay with her, and he was right when he said that she couldn't afford to be recognized. So she followed him up the hill.

The church door was swollen and stuck with damp, but with a good shove, Rive was able to get it open. It was colder inside than out, as if the stone walls had taken winter prisoner. It smelled like age and rock and water. All that Esther could see at first was the large arched window that took up most of the far wall, its panes parsing the grainy landscape beyond. Slowly, though, as her eyes adjusted, she made out wooden pews and crumbling plaster walls and wainscoting with peeling yellow paint.

Rive walked up the aisle and stood for a moment where the altar once must have been, beneath the arched window. There was a reverence to his expression as he looked up, a gravity that reminded her again of the dream angel. Then his lips twitched into a brief, deprecating smile, and he looked over at Esther.

"In here," he said, and turned to a narrow arched doorway beside the recess with the window. It led into a small room cluttered with old paper and bits of wood and books swollen with damp. It, too, had an arched window, though much smaller than the first. Rive set down his pack, pulled out a folded tarp and a few pushpins and covered the window. Then he took out a couple of candles, lit them and stuck them to the floor. The warm yellow light took some of the chill from the room. Wearily, Esther sat down.

"Are you hungry?" Rive asked.

Esther realized then that she'd had nothing to eat since the biscuits in the tearoom that morning. But she was reluctant to admit any weakness to Rive. "I'll be all right."

Rive gave her his dubious half-smile. He reached into the pack again and brought out a flask and something wrapped in a cloth, which turned out to be a small loaf of dark bread, a paper-wrapped wedge of cheese, and a couple of apples. "Eat up," he said. "You'll need your strength if you really mean to outrun the Prophet."

Ignoring the warning, Esther said, "I can't take all of this. There'll be nothing left for you."

Rive picked up an apple and pocketed it. "This'll do me for now. I'll find something more along the way." His eyes rested on her for a moment, and Esther was sure that he was deliberating about saying something else. But in the end he only said, "There's a coat in the pack if you get cold." And then he melted into the shadows.

Reluctantly, Esther closed the door behind him. She sat down, split the bread and cheese in half and ate them, wrapping up the rest. Afterward she untied her bundle, took out the book of poetry, and leaned back against one wall. She opened the book to the beginning, and began to read. She hadn't read much poetry before, and none at all by Byron, but she found the rhythms of it soothing, the dark and troubled imagery easy to relate to in her present mood. This, plus the food and the flickering light, soon lulled her into sleepiness.

She put the book aside and lay down with her head on her bundle, pulling her coat around herself. But the stone floor was hard, and its damp chill seemed to find its way straight through the threadbare tweed. She sat up again, pulled Rive's pack toward her. His coat was at the top. It was an old navy pea coat, softened by age and wear. As she held it, Esther felt warmth and peace seep into her: a faint but undeniable echo of the way she had felt in the dream, and when she had touched his hand in the confessional.

She crushed the coat to herself, wishing that Rive were there with her now, wishing she knew why he had changed. Perhaps, she thought, she was being naïve. Rive had recently escaped from Hell. She couldn't begin to imagine what it had been like for him there, or what he'd had to do to get out. Both, however, must have changed him, maybe even enough to decide that the world wasn't worth saving after all. And that left her with the dilemma of which version of him to trust.

Esther wrapped the coat around herself, wishing that something – anything – about her life could be straightforward and clear. Since it wasn't, though, she would have to seek out the answers herself. So she sat back against the wall, picked up her book, and tried not to wonder what she would do if Rive didn't come back.

*

She stood behind a broken pillar of intricately carved stone. Beyond her, Lilith sat cross-legged in the middle of a ring of similar pillars – some also broken, some rising whole into the shadows like ancient, petrified tree-trunks. Her hands were cupped around something that cast a blue light. It made her eyes into caves, her poison-coloured smile, a curse.

Esther knew that whatever Lilith held was of vital importance, but though it seemed to move, she couldn't make out the details from where she stood. She crept forward, keeping behind the broken half of the pillar lying amidst the other rubble on the ground. Gradually, she was able to make out a figure within the frayed circle of light. A bit closer, and she saw that it was a man, walking along a narrow road. He had the collar of his jacket turned up against the driving rain, hiding his face, but she knew that waxed jacket and tweed hat, and the way that his baggy, battered trousers flapped against his legs. She felt a pang of emotion too complicated to name.

"I can see you, Esther," Lilith said without looking away from the image of Rive in her hands. "At last, thanks to him. Your heart flickers like a candle flame. So easy to snuff out."

Lilith looked up, her eyes glimmering distantly in the faint light, her mouth a gash against her skim-milk skin. "Come out, have a good look at him." She lifted her hands like a priestess with an offering. Reluctantly, Esther approached. Lilith laughed. "Show some backbone! I can't grab you in a dream, can I? Though more's the pity..."

"What do you want, Lilith?" Esther demanded.

Lilith's delicate eyebrows raised. "You know my name, too. I'm flattered."

"I hate you," Esther said, surprising herself with her own vehemence.

Lilith shrugged. "It doesn't much matter what you think of me. Do you want to see your beloved, or not? It might be the last time, you know."

Esther froze on the point of denying the first statement, when she registered the second. "What do you mean, the last time?"

"He's playing a dangerous game. Come see," she repeated, nodding at the bubble of light. "Here, I'll make it easier." She pulled her hands apart slowly, carefully, stretching the light like a baker stretching fragile dough. It diffused to a mere shimmer, but the scene enlarged and broadened, until Esther could make out not just the road and Rive walking along it with a bundle over his shoulder, but the dark hills behind him, silhouetted against a sky greying toward dusk or dawn.

And then her heart began to skip, because Rive wasn't alone. A spectral light seemed to grow from the darkness behind him, slowly taking on a human form. Except that it wasn't quite human: the proportions were wrong, the limbs too thin, the clothes no more than rags that swam around it as if they were underwater. The figure itself looked watery too, as if it had been filmed through a lens running with rain.

"Oh, Jesus," Esther said, recognizing one of the creatures that she'd watched pursue the woman in Glasgow Cathedral. Clearly, Rive wasn't aware of it, though it was now gaining on him.

"Jesus can't hear you, Esther," Lilith sang cheerily.

"Why are you showing me this?" she asked Lilith, her eyes still glued to Rive.

"I want to see what you do when it hurts him."

Though her heart was pounding, erratic, Esther's voice was steady when she asked, "Why would I do anything? You can't kill an aeon."

She had expected Lilith to be surprised that she knew what he was, but she only shrugged and said, "Once that was true... now, who knows?"

"Stop this!"

"Oh, no. He needs to be reminded who's in charge."

"You're insane!"

Lilith only shrugged again, still smiling blandly. Esther scanned the image for anything that might help Rive, and at last she made out a pale shape on a dark hillside. It was the church where she was hiding.

"Let me go," Esther demanded.

"It's your own dream."

"But you're keeping me in it."

Lilith tilted her head, studying Esther with cold eyes. "Will you cry if it kills him? You shouldn't, you know. He'd never have loved you back. He can't, after what we did to him."

A blind rage filled Esther, more powerful than anything she'd ever felt. Oblivious to her own safety, she lunged for Lilith, sweeping aside the image of Rive, reaching for the daeva's neck. For a second, she saw something register in Lilith's eyes that wasn't certainty, something that might even have been fear. Then she crashed through Lilith's image as if it were no more than a shadow.

CHAPTER 8

18 JUNE
OUR LADY OF THE BRAES

Esther scrambled to her feet. Her head was ringing, her limbs stiff, her knuckles white with clutching Rive's coat. Realizing this, she dropped it and snatched up the single stub of candle that was still burning. She had no idea whether Rive was really as close as he had seemed in the dream. She could only hope that she wasn't too late.

Esther ran down the shadowed aisle, flung open the door. As in the dream, it was pouring rain, dousing the candle. There was just enough light in the sky for her to make her way onto the sheep path. She hadn't gone far when she spotted a patch of greyish, spectral light on the hillside ahead, but it wasn't the only one. Moving with it in a kind of intricate dance was another slant of light, the same ethereal blue as Sophie Creedon's aura.

Esther moved closer, and the patches of light resolved into figures. They weren't dancing, but fighting, Rive with a sword that burned the same blue as his aura, the creature with one that was blacker than night. It reminded Esther of the utter absence of light that had been left when the daevas erased the sky over the dream city.

"Rive!" she cried, running toward him.

He turned to her call, and for a moment she was uncertain whether it really was him. While he looked like the young man she'd been travelling with, he was also entirely different: magisterial and pitiless and somehow ancient, despite his unlined face.

Stay back, Esther.

She couldn't tell whether he'd spoken or she'd heard him in some other, deeper way, but there was no question of disobeying him. She crouched among the bracken with the rain streaming over her as Rive fought the creature, watching in horror as first one, then the other took the upper hand.

The fight seemed to go on forever as the light bled gradually into the sky. They moved so quickly that they became a bright blur, impossible to see as separate figures. Then, abruptly, they stilled. Rive was straddling the grey creature, pinning it to the ground with a foot on either arm. He held the black sword hard against its throat, his own poised over its heart.

The creature screeched in anger: a plangent, inhuman sound that made Esther clap her hands to her ears. Rive, however, seemed unfazed by it. He waited until the creature was silent again, and then he asked: "Why did you attack me?"

Esther had to move closer to hear its slow, papery voice, and so she only caught the end of its answer: "…back…what you've…stolen."

Rive's smooth brow furrowed. "I've stolen nothing from you."

"I speak…for those…whose souls…you've taken."

Rive's look turned furious. "I've never taken a human soul!"

There wasn't enough left of the creature's face to form a true expression, but Esther sensed its sudden confusion in the tensing of its remaining muscles, and the rapid movement of its eyes. "Why then…seek refuge…on sacred ground?"

Rive gave a contemptuous laugh. "The church? It's long

since deconsecrated – no refuge at all for the fallen, if that's what you think I am."

"Forgive…me," the creature said, struggling to rise. "I was mistaken – "

Rive smiled coldly. "Oh, no. You're not leaving until you tell me why you would hunt down a fallen angel – and where you got the power to do it, never mind a demon blade." He twitched the point of the black sword against the creature's chin, and it jerked, but didn't scream again.

There was a brief silence, during which the sound of the sheeting rain swelled and receded, tidelike. The creature's answer, when it came, almost disappeared into it, soft as a breath of wind rustling the heather: "It came from the Deep."

This time, Rive's smile was bitter as well as cold. "Yes, well, so did I – quite recently in fact. And I don't recall seeing any of your kind there."

"Didn't…go…there. She comes…to us."

"Who? Lilith?"

A slight shake of its gaunt head. "Cailleach."

Rive was clearly taken aback by this, though Esther had no idea what it meant. "You've seen the Cailleach?" he asked, both apprehension and surprise in his voice. "In what form?"

"White veil…grey coat…"

Rive glanced at Esther. "That was the Cailleach?" he asked, his voice faint and sick sounding. The creature nodded. "But she's been dormant for centuries! And even before that, she'd never have been abroad so close to Midsummer – "

"Daevas…give her…power…and wraiths…to help her."

"Why would she work for them?"

There was a long silence before it answered, "Even the mighty…must choose…a side."

Rive stared off in the direction of the loch, obviously trying to regain his composure. "So the daevas have given you demon powers and a weapon to go with them. And the other Revenants? Have they been co-opted as well?"

"Many…"

"And what is your task?"

The Revenant said nothing. Rive pushed the tip of his sword into the ragged flesh of its chest. It made a sound of despair, but it answered, "Take back… souls…from fallen."

"And do what with them?"

"Deliver…to them…"

Rive shook his head. "Once a fallen takes a soul, its purity is lost. No doubt it's diminished further by passing back through you, and then the hands of the daevas…how is it good for anything, then?"

When the Revenant didn't answer, Rive leaned on his sword until it gasped. "Good enough…to get them…past staves…to Earth."

Rive went very still. "And even if that will really work, why would you, of all creatures, agree to deal in stolen souls?"

The Revenant sighed again; Esther had never heard such a desolate sound. "They pay. One soul…to keep."

Esther thought of the scene she'd witnessed in Glasgow cathedral. It began to make a terrible kind of sense.

But Rive said, "It won't restore you to what you were. You'll all be damned."

There was a fundamental sadness, a tragic acceptance in the Revenant's tone when it answered, "We are damned…already."

"You want to live as slaves to Hell?"

"To live…"

It was only a whisper, barely distinguishable from the wind, but it transformed Rive. The sky was light enough now for Esther to make out every nuance of the disgust and anger that crossed his face and hardened there. He flung the demon sword at the loch with inhuman strength, and the dark waters swallowed it. Then he took his own bright sword with both hands, and drove it through the Revenant's heart. What was left of its body collapsed, leaving nothing but a scatter of bones in the long, wet grass.

Rive stood there for a moment, looking at them with a fury too potent to make sense to Esther. Then he stood up and hurled his own sword into the air, where it disappeared. He turned and regarded Esther.

"Why did you kill it?" she asked in a quivering voice.

"Why did you watch?" he replied, his eyes pitiless.

"Because I needed to know," she said.

"Know what?"

"The woman in Glasgow Cathedral – "

"Wasn't a woman. That should have been obvious."

"Well, it wasn't!" Esther cried, sick to death of his cynicism. "You don't know what it was like, watching it. They hunted her, and killed her, and left her there like those others, with her eyes and mouth burned out." There were tears on Esther's face, though she didn't remember beginning to cry. "They're the reason I'm running! They did the thing I've been accused of! Wouldn't you want to know why?"

Rive shrugged. "Well, now you know why, and you can let go of whatever guilt you've carried about it. The thing in the cathedral deserved her fate."

"Because she was a fallen angel?"

"No. Because she used her power as a fallen angel to suck the souls out of humans."

Esther paused, and then said, "Why would she do that?"

He shrugged, nudged a stray bone with his toe. "The same reason the Revenants are doing it now. To gain salvation."

"That doesn't make sense."

He smiled, his eyes ruthless. "Don't pretend to be naïve, Esther."

"What does that mean?"

"It means that nothing makes sense anymore, as you know

damn well. In fact, you appear to be the last person on Earth who does know it."

"The last except you."

"I'm not a person, Esther!" he said harshly. "Don't make the mistake of thinking that I'll act like one."

"No, I suppose you're not," she said bitterly. "The man who spoke to me in the confessional was a person. So was the angel who saved me in the city. But you...I don't know what they did to you in Hell, but clearly, it destroyed you."

Rive gazed at her for a moment in surprise, and then he began to laugh – a hollow, broken sound. "You know, since I met you, I've been thinking that you're a poor copy of Sophia. You're as pretty as she is, but you don't have her backbone. Her fire. I guess I was wrong. Too bad it doesn't matter."

"What do you mean by that?" Esther demanded.

"I mean that this journey I sent you on – you can forget about it. The daevas have already won."

"Funny, because I don't see them here," she snapped.

"Not yet," he conceded, "but they're coming, and Sophie can't save us."

"That's not what you said before."

"I know more now than I did then."

"Like what?"

"Like they've roused and turned the Cailleach. She's an ancient pagan deity, as old as the human world, and at one time she was nearly as powerful as the aeons and daevas. She's never given allegiance to anyone but herself. If they turned her, they can turn anyone."

"They won't turn me."

"How can you be so sure?"

"Because I don't want them to win."

"And how do you plan to fight them?" he asked, his voice mocking. "By reciting your Catechism? Dousing them with holy water?"

"If that's what works," she said, refusing to be offended.

He threw up his hands in exasperation. "Don't you understand that everything you've been taught to believe is a lie? Good doesn't triumph over evil! Good and evil don't even exist. There's just one force and another, scrabbling for the most they can get – "

"You're wrong," she interrupted. "Good and evil do exist, especially now. But if you've stopped believing it, you might as well go back to Hell." She turned and began to walk back toward the church.

"Where are you going?" he cried, his voice bitter and breaking. "To pray?"

She gave him a withering look. "I'm going to collect my things, and then I'm going to Ardnasheen to give Sophie Creedon your message."

"There isn't any point!" Rive cried, a mad light in his eyes now.

"Why not?" Esther demanded. "Tell me what's changed your mind, and I'll consider taking your advice." Rive looked away. "Right," Esther sighed, and she turned again, toward the church. She was glad that he couldn't see the sobs wracking her. She felt like her heart was being torn in two. How, she wondered, had she come to care about him so much, so fast?

Or had it been fast? A part of her felt like she'd always known Rive, like he'd always been there on the margins of her life, a listening ghost, waiting for substance. And now, having found it, he was breaking her heart.

She reached for the latch on the church door, but Rive's hand came down and closed over hers. She whirled on him, too furious with him and with herself to care whether he saw her tears. His face, deathly pale, streamed with rain, and there was something in its complicated expression that made her pause – something that reminded her of the way the angel had looked at her.

"What are you doing?" she asked.

"Attempting to reason with you."

She swiped at the tears on her face. "Well?"

There was another flicker of the angel in his countenance as he answered, "Please don't go to Ardnasheen, Esther, because if you do, you'll probably die."

She drew a breath, and then said, "That would be unfortunate. But it doesn't really matter, does it? Not if it saves everyone else."

His hand tightened on hers. He seemed to be weighing his words before he said, "It matters to me."

The sudden, raw plea in his voice made her ache. "I don't understand."

"Don't you?" he asked, his eyes intent on hers. And then, before she could answer, he leaned down and kissed her.

It was barely a kiss, the slightest brush of his lips against hers, but the surge of feeling it called up in her almost brought her to her knees. He drew back, looking as shocked as she felt. "I'm sorry," he said.

"Why?" she asked.

A twitch of a smile turned his lips. Then he dropped her hand and pulled her against him, his hands hot through the cold, wet fabric of her dress. This time there was nothing gentle about his kiss, or her response. He parted her lips with his own, and she knotted her hands in his wet hair, drawing him closer. Esther knew that it was mad, but she couldn't stop, her body responding to his faster than she could think. They sank to the sodden ground, oblivious to the rain, and she gasped as his lips moved to her neck, tracing a fiery line along her collarbone to her shoulder, where her dress had slipped back. Her hands slipped under his shirt, running up the smooth skin of his belly and chest, and he shuddered, curling around her. But when she hooked a finger into his waistband, he froze.

"Stop," he said, catching her hand and pulling it back.

"But – but you – "

"I know. But we can't do this." He disentangled his limbs from hers, and it felt to Esther as if he'd torn her in half. Her eyes filled with tears. "Esther, don't…" he began, but she shook her head, stood up, ran for the church.

Half way up the aisle, Rive caught her hand. The surge of desire – how had she not realized before that it was desire? – shook her. Rive looked human, and young, and immeasurably tired. She'd begun to forgive him when he said: "That was a mistake."

"I'm sorry you think so," she answered coldly. She tried to pull her hand away, but he held on.

"Don't be angry, Esther," he said. "I didn't mean that I regret it – only that I shouldn't have taken advantage of you."

"Don't worry: you didn't."

A smile ghosted across his features. "There's that backbone." The smile was gone as fleetingly. "Please don't go to Ardnasheen," he entreated.

"And what will I do instead?" she asked.

"Come with me."

"Where?"

"I can't tell you that. Not yet."

Esther shut her eyes, shook her head. "How can I agree to that? How do I know that the daevas haven't brainwashed you to say all of this? To keep me from getting to Sophie?"

"I suppose you'd just have to trust me."

"When you won't even trust me with a proper explanation?"

Rive said nothing, though his eyes were imploring. The words of the strange man on the train rang in her head: *You're soon to be tried. Stay true to yourself.* Esther turned away, though it was with a pain that was almost physical. She walked the rest of the way up the aisle, into the room where she'd slept. She stacked her things onto her kerchief, tied the corners with vicious knots. When she looked up again he was standing in the doorway, nothing left in his eyes but defeat.

"All right," he said. "If you're determined, then I won't try to stop you. But you can't go like that."

"Like what?"

"I've told you, everyone knows what you look like now. You've got to change." He held out a worn carpetbag – the bundle he'd been carrying on the road. Hesitantly, she took it, and opened it. Inside were clothes, shoes, and a brown bottle. She pulled it out.

"What is this?"

"Hair dye."

She wanted to argue with him, but she knew that he was right. "Thank you," she said softly.

"You know what to do with it?"

"More or less. I'll need water though."

"I'll get you some." He ducked out of the doorway, as if he couldn't wait to be away from her.

Heartsick, Esther doused her hair with the dye, and then she sat down to wait.

*

An hour later, looking into the back of a collection plate, she was stunned. She'd borne a resemblance to Sophie Creedon before; now, with her hair dark, no one would have doubted they were sisters. It was strange, too, to be wearing different clothing after so long. The dress Rive had brought her was lavender with tiny white flowers and fitted her perfectly. He'd also brought tights, shoes far prettier than those she'd brought from the convent, and a shawl-collared tartan coat in fawns and greys. None of it seemed worn, and she wondered where he'd come by it all in the middle of the night, in the middle of nowhere, but she couldn't bear to ask. She couldn't even bear to think of his choosing these things for her.

"Are you ready?" Rive asked from the other side of the door.

Esther put down the makeshift mirror and opened the door. For a moment, Rive just stared at her, apparently as stunned as she had been by her changed appearance. Then he said, "You'll pass. We'd better be going."

"Going?" she asked. "Where?"

"Mallaig, since I've failed to convince you of the insanity of the idea."

"You're coming with me to Ardnasheen?" she asked, wishing that she didn't sound so hopeful.

"That...wouldn't be a good idea," he answered, his eyes flickering away from hers.

The words were like a slap. "Then why take me there?"

"Because even if the Cailleach weren't tracking you, you could never walk to Mallaig with only four tablets of digoxin. And before you ask, yes, I did try to find more."

Esther had no idea what to say to that. She stood watching dumbly as Rive shouldered his pack, and then picked up the clothes she'd shed and strode out the door. "What are you doing with those?" she asked.

"Burning them. We can't leave any trace. Come on."

She gathered her remaining possessions and followed, watching as he doused her old clothes with the rest of the diesel, and flicked a match into the pile. Then she climbed into the passenger seat of the Land Rover. Neither of them spoke during the drive to Mallaig, but Esther thought. In fact, her mind wouldn't stop turning over all that had happened, all that she'd learned, and most of all, the conundrum of Rive. Because, for all he preached despair, and for all he seemed to be the opposite of the aeon who had first spoken to her, she couldn't quite believe it. Not when he'd kissed her like that...

Don't, she told herself, as another wave of longing crashed through her.

Gradually, they wound down out of the hills to the shore. Though the road followed the coast, the rain was so hard that the

Inner Hebrides, which should have provided a spectacular view, were invisible. Esther could make out rims of white beach, and the low grey forms of the houses in the tiny villages they passed through, but otherwise the world might as well have ended already for all she could see.

At last, though, the shapes of larger buildings loomed out of the rain and mist, and Rive slowed the car. He guided it into a boatyard that seemed to make up the majority of the village. There were a couple of large ferries tied up to the westernmost docks, nearest the open sea. There were fishing boats of various sizes, some already unloading their morning's catch. The docks were strewn with nets and crab pots and various other marine paraphernalia, but Rive drove past them all, finally pulling up beside the easternmost dock.

A boat was tied up there, roughly the size and shape of many of the fishing boats, but there were no nets or boxes of fish on its deck, only wooden crates full of food and liquor bottles. A small terrier with a wiry brown coat was sniffing around them hopefully, and a few passengers milled on the deck, along with two water sprites who were apparently working as deck-hands.

"There you are," Rive said, nodding to the boat. "The Ardnasheen ferry." Esther couldn't help looking at him in surprise. He gave her a small, wry smile. "You didn't think I'd really bring you here, did you?"

"I knew you'd keep your word," she said. "I just don't understand why you gave it in the first place, when you don't want me to go to Ardnasheen."

"It's like I said before: I don't want you to die."

"Seeing as you found my pills, you should know that that's more or less a foregone conclusion."

"Don't say that." His voice was so wistful that her certainty wavered, more so when he reached out and traced a finger down her cheek. She shut her eyes. "Are you sure about this?"

"I'm sure," she said, turning away so that he couldn't see

her trembling lip. Below, the ferry was filling with passengers. "It's only, I wasn't expecting all those people…"

"You'll have no trouble from them. All they're thinking of is the wedding."

She turned to him sharply. "Wedding?"

He sighed. "Yes. Sophie and Lucas are about to get married."

She stared at him, stunned. She'd thought that her task couldn't get any harder, but it just had. "Did you keep that from me on purpose?" she asked, her voice low.

"No," he sighed. "To tell you the truth, I'd forgotten about it until now."

She gazed at him a moment longer. Then she opened the car door, and stepped out into the rain. Behind her, she thought she heard Rive sigh, and she turned back.

"Thank you for the lift," she said, "and the clothes, and… and everything. I hope that you…" Except she didn't know what she hoped for him. She didn't know what she hoped for herself, walking away from him. "Good-bye, Rive," she said, low and shaky.

"Good-bye," she heard him say, his voice soft. It was enough to make her turn to look at him once again, but he had his head down, lighting another cigarette. She shut the door and walked toward the ferry without looking back.

THE DOMINION OF SURIEL

Suri took off her sunglasses and blinked at the dim shapes around her, wondering if the door she'd summoned in the Garden had let them out in some other realm. But slowly, her dazzled eyes adjusted to the dimmer light of Heaven, and she realized that she and Michael were standing in the cemetery, in between the tree (currently a fig) and Lucifer's grave. The hole in the earth was still there, the coffin with its ruined armour just as Sophie had left it when she exhumed it. Suri hadn't been able to bring herself to fill the grave back in.

Now, though, Sam was sitting with his legs dangling into the hole, tossing overripe figs at the sad-eyed statue of Lucifer, apparently trying to hit it in the face. "Azazel," Suri said, coming up beside him and slapping a hand on his shoulder. "Just the angel I was looking for."

Sam turned to her with a rakish half-smile, pushing his white-blonde hair away from his deep-set blue eyes. "Suri – charmed. But I prefer Sam. So much less dramatic."

"Fine – Sam, I need to talk to you about something."

"Let me guess: you've reconsidered my offer."

Suri shuddered. "As if!"

"What was his offer?" Michael asked.

"A far more interesting way to spend eternity than cataloguing the souls of the dead," Sam answered, winking at Suri.

"One more word," Suri said tightly, "and I'll throw you back in the dungeon."

"Since when do you have a dungeon?" Michael asked.

"Since he came back," Suri said, gesturing to Sam.

Sam rolled his eyes, dumped his handful of figs into Lucifer's grave, and stood up. "If it's not me, Suri, then what do you want?"

"Suriel," Michael began, "I'm not sure this is – "

"We need you to help us get back to Earth," Suri interrupted.

Sam looked from Suri to Michael and then burst out laughing.

"What, exactly, about that is funny?" she demanded.

Sam stopped laughing, but he still regarded her with a quizzical smile. "What isn't?" Seeing Suri's look darken, however, he relented. "Oh, very well. What makes you think that I can get you there?"

"You know sorcery," Suri answered.

"Have you forgotten what happened last time I dabbled with that?"

"Believe me, we wouldn't be asking if it weren't a dire emergency."

Sam gave them both a keen once-over, then said, "The thing is, my staves prevent me from making a cup of coffee, never mind bending space and time and who knows what else I'd have to do to get back to Earth."

"You tell us how," Suri said, "and we'll do it."

Sam looked at her incredulously. "You want me to do you a favour?"

"Sam," Suri sighed, "if someone doesn't do something fast, we're all going to Hell."

Sam shrugged. "They say a change is as good as a rest."

"Fine! What do you want?"

"Take away my staves," Sam answered without missing a beat. No doubt, Suri thought, he'd been waiting for an opportunity to demand this since he landed back in Heaven.

"That's impossible," Michael said immediately.

"You did it for Sartael."

"How do you know that?" Suri demanded.

Sam smiled. "I have my sources."

"Yes, well, Sartael isn't a dangerous rogue angel," Michael told him. "And he's currently nursing a killer hangover as a result of that experiment."

"Figure out how to get to Earth on your own, then." Sam began to walk away.

"Michael – " Suri began.

"Absolutely not!" Michael snapped. "Do you have any idea what kind of havoc he could wreak if he's freed of his staves?"

Suri gave Michael a desperate look. "It's like you said – we're at war with the Deep. What does it matter if one fallen angel stirs the pot? Honestly, what harm is he going to do that the daevas can't do tenfold?"

"Surely there's someone else who knows sorcery."

"Yeah – the other fallen Watchers, who are all stuck on Earth."

Michael looked at Sam's retreating form. "I know I'm going to regret this," he said at last.

"Thank you, Michael," Suri said, and then she called after Sam. "Wait!"

He stopped, turned, and in a moment he was back beside them, smiling his knowing, infuriating smile. "You've reconsidered?"

"I'll take off the staves," Michael said, "once you tell us what we need to know."

"Do you think I'm an idiot?"

"Fine," Michael sighed. "I'll take one off now. That will give you your powers back. I'll remove the stave keeping you in the Cemetery when you've lived up to your part of the bargain."

Sam considered it for a moment, and then nodded. "Deal," he said. He held out his hands, showing the two silver bands on his wrists. Michael put his hand around one of them. As with Sartael's, the band glowed brightly for a moment before disappearing.

Sam rubbed his free wrist. "Well, that's an improvement. So, where on Earth do you want to go?"

"Ardnasheen," Suri said with as much conviction as she could muster.

Sam's face hardened. "This is about her?"

"It's about saving the world, Sam," Michael said.

"Forget it," Sam answered bluntly. "I'm not helping anyone who ran me through with a sword."

"You'd just killed her boyfriend!" Suri said.

"He started it."

"None of that matters," Michael interrupted as Suri made to answer. "Sophie doesn't remember you. She doesn't remember anything."

"She doesn't remember me?" he asked speculatively, with the beginnings of a smile.

"Don't even think about it!" Michael snapped.

"You're not really in a position to call the shots. But as it happens, I believe I've decided I want to come along for the ride."

They all glared at each other. Finally, Michael said, "Very well! But remember, you won't have the powers on Earth that you used to."

"Oh, I'm aware of that," Sam said with a slight smile.

"Why doesn't that make me feel any better?" Michael muttered.

"Well, if that's settled," Sam said, "let's get started."

Suri reached into the air and pulled out her scrying glass. "First we'd better see what's going on down there."

The three of them leaned in over the mirror. At first she thought that there was something wrong with it, because it showed nothing but a grey, shifting murk, possibly streaming with water. When she shook it, and nothing changed, panic overtook her.

"Oh my god!" she cried. "We're too late! The daevas have wiped out Earth!"

"Get a grip, Suri," Sam said. "You're looking at Earth."

"But there's nothing there!"

"Sure there is. You just can't see it. Welcome to Scotland in the summertime."

And sure enough, a moment later, the greyness parted long enough for them to make out the form of a car – a Land Rover at least five decades out of date. There was a pale face visible through the passenger side window, but the rain and fog blurred it too much to make out whose it was. Then the fog closed down again, and they were back to staring at the swirling greyness.

"Well, that was informative," Sam said dryly.

"Oh, shut up," Suri retorted. "Unless you have a better plan."

"As a matter of fact, I do."

"Well?"

"Rewind till you get to a spot where you can see something."

"You can't rewind a scrying-glass," Suri argued.

"Give it to me." When she hesitated, he said, "Come on, how can I possibly wreak havoc with a stupid mirror?"

Reluctantly, Suri handed it to him. He took it and ran his finger across it from left to right, and then did it again. "It isn't a smart-phone, Sam," Suri told him.

"No," he agreed, "but it'll work by the same principles if you know what you're doing."

"And how do you know what you're doing?"

"Scrying falls under the category of 'witchcraft.' There."

He held out the mirror, and Suri took it. It was dark now, all except for one small spot of greyish light, which moved across the surface of the mirror in slow, lurching increments. As they watched, the top of the mirror brightened gradually until they could make out the silhouette of hills, and the indistinct grey ribbon of a road running at their foot. As the light improved, the bright spot resolved into a figure – misshapen, but recognizably human – and also illuminated another, dark and solid, walking a few paces ahead of it.

"That's a Revenant," Suri said, pointing to the glowing figure. "But what's the other one?"

"An unfortunate late-night traveller, about to be mugged by the Undead?" Sam suggested.

"A Revenant can't hurt a human."

"You sure about that?"

Suri looked down again, and saw that the Revenant was holding what looked like a sword, though it was blacker than black. Worse, the traveller had turned off the road and started up into the hills. The Revenant gained on him, lifted his sword to attack – and then the dark figure whirled, pulling a bright blue sword out of the air and parrying the Revenant's blow, all in one smooth movement.

"Holy Hell!" Suri said. "That's Rive!"

"Who's Rive?" Sam asked.

"It's what Theletos calls himself when he's pretending to be human."

"I like it," Sam said. "It sounds evil."

Suri rolled her eyes. Michael asked, "But how did he get out of the Deep?"

"Theletos was in the Deep?" Sam asked, with interest.

"Who knows?" Suri said, ignoring Sam. "I mean, we don't even know how long we were in the Garden. It might have been weeks of Earth time."

"It can't have been too long," Michael answered, "if Earth still exists."

"Not for much longer," Sam said laconically, "if Revenants with demonic weapons are picking fights with aeons."

They all settled wordlessly back to watch the fight. They also watched with interest as a girl appeared in the scene, and crouched in the bracken to watch, too. "I think that's Esther Madden," Michael said.

"What's she doing with Rive?"

"Hush," Michael said. "They're talking."

They all fell silent to listen to the conversation between the Revenant and Rive. Suri's and Michael's faces turned grave as they listened, while Sam's expression edged toward gleeful. Likewise they paid careful attention to the argument between Rive and Esther. When he kissed her, though, Sam whistled.

"I did not see that coming!" he laughed. "And I didn't know an aeon could be a lady's man."

"He's not," Michael said shortly.

"Really? Because he sure seems to know what he's doing."

"Will you shut up so we can hear what they're saying?" Suri snapped, once Esther and Rive broke apart. But there wasn't

233

much to hear: just their tense truce as he helped her change her appearance. Finally, they watched them depart for Mallaig.

"This is not good," Michael said, when the two in the car had lapsed into silence, and the car dissolved into the coastal fog.

"But it's bloody entertaining," Sam said. "This will be almost as fun to watch as Lucifer and Sophia. Or maybe better – more fighting, less melodrama."

Michael gave him a dark look and then said, "What's he up to, with the girl?"

Sam smirked. "Want me to draw you a diagram?"

"Shut up, Sam," Suri told him. Then, to Michael, "What do you think it means?"

"Obviously, the daevas have corrupted him."

"He does seem screwed up, but I'm not sure I'd go as far as 'corrupted.' I mean, he is taking Esther to the boat."

"By the way," Sam said, "has anyone else noticed that Esther's hot? In a very Sophie Creedon-like way, but still – "

"Don't even go there," Suri interrupted.

"I'll go wherever I like," Sam retorted.

"No, you won't," Michael stated flatly. "Not until you show us how to get to Earth."

"Guys, stop. Look." Suri tapped the mirror, which now showed what appeared to be a boatyard. They watched as Esther got onto a boat, and it pulled away from the dock. "That's the Ardnasheen ferry."

"Wow," Sam said. "I didn't think Rive would really let her go. He must be battling inner demons. Or maybe even outer ones – this gets better and better – "

"Let's see what he does next before we call it demons."

Suri tipped and tilted the mirror until it showed the Land Rover, which Rive parked behind a warehouse. Then he got out, turned up his collar against the sheeting rain, and went back to the docks. He watched until Esther's ferry had rounded the point into Loch Nevis, and then he approached a fishing boat and called to the captain: "Would you be willing to take a passenger?"

The man looked him up and down, squinting against the rain. "Depends where you're going."

"Ardnasheen," Rive said definitively.

"What?" Suri cried, and Sam smiled to himself.

"Watch," Michael said grimly.

The man shook his head. "Ferry just left for Ardnasheen."

"Which is why I'm asking you to take me there."

The man sighed. "It's a bad sea for it, and it's not the way I was heading. It'll cost you."

"I can pay," Rive said, and pulled a wad of bills from his pocket.

The man's eyes widened. "Aye, then. Come on."

"No," Rive said. "I've got something to do first. I'll be back in two hours."

"And I'll lose two hours fishing," the boat captain grumbled.

"I'll pay you for that, too," Rive said and pushed money into the man's hand. "Two hours." And with that, he strode away.

Suri tipped the mirror to follow him, wondering what he could possibly have to do in a remote port town for two hours. He stopped at his car, climbed into the back, pulled the canvas shut and opened his pack. He took out a scrap of blue fabric – after a puzzled moment, Suri recognized it as a piece of Esther's old dress, which he'd burned. Rive leaned back against his pack, staring at the cloth as if trying to memorize it.

Sam's smirk was back. "Looks like Theletos is whipped."

"While it does offer an explanation for the strangeness of his behaviour," Michael said reluctantly, "does he really need two hours to contemplate a bit of her old dress?"

"No," Sam said. "He wants to make sure Esther is out of the way before he follows her."

"But why follow her?" Michael asked.

"I don't know, yet," Sam said, gazing speculatively into the mirror. "But I'm really looking forward to finding out."

Loch Nevis

Esther stood on the pitching deck of the boat, feeling sicker by the moment. It wasn't the rough sea that was affecting her, but the little white village at the foot of the cloud-ridden mountains, growing inexorably closer. All through her long, strange journey, she'd managed to avoid thinking too hard about its ultimate purpose. Now it stared her starkly in the face: she had to convince a girl she'd never met before that her accepted reality was a lie. Her own family hadn't believed her; why would Sophie?

And then there was the fact that if she did manage to convince Sophie of the truth, it would ruin her life. The ferry was full of her friends and family, coming up for her wedding. Was it kinder to let her go through with it and speak to her afterward? Or better that she know the truth beforehand? There was so little time, and it might take more than one conversation to convince her, if she managed to convince her at all…and yet Esther found it hard to stomach ruining a girl's wedding, especially when she had so little time left with the man she loved.

"Feeling seasick?"

Esther turned. A young man with a pleasant, handsome face and warm brown eyes had come out of the cabin to stand with her at the railing. She realized then that the rain had stopped.

"A bit," she said.

"Watch the shoreline," he said. "It helps."

"Thank you," she said.

"Angus Forsythe," he said, offering her his hand.

"E – Elizabeth O'Connell," Esther stumbled, wishing she'd thought of a false name earlier.

"Pleasure to meet you, Miss O'Connell," he said, smiling. "I didn't know Sophie had Irish relations."

"What?" Esther asked, startled.

"Sorry if I presumed," he said. "You look so much alike, I thought that you must be related to Sophie Creedon."

"Ah…" Esther said, wondering how she could have failed to think of this. Of course, given the resemblance, people would make that assumption. "Well, actually, yes. We're – we're distant cousins. I've never actually met Sophie – Miss Creedon – but when my mother heard she was getting married, she thought that someone should go, to represent the family I mean, and since she's at home with the little ones…"

It sounded ridiculous to Esther, but Angus didn't seem to think so. "Well, I'm sure Sophie will be glad you've come."

Sophie will rue the day she set eyes on me, Esther thought. "Are you a relation as well?"

Angus's smile faltered slightly. "No. An old friend."

"So you've come up for the wedding too?"

"Actually, I live here. I'm the schoolteacher. Anyway, it's been a pleasure to meet you, Miss O'Connell. But I'd better collect my things – we're about to land."

Esther looked up: the pier was only yards away. She retreated behind the cabin as the other passengers streamed out of it with their bags and boxes, waving to the knot of people waiting on the pier. Five minutes later, they were pulling up alongside it. Esther looked up at the people gathered there, her heart beginning to skip.

At first she didn't see her, but then she stepped out from between a tall, redheaded girl and a middle-aged blonde woman, and there was no mistaking her: this was Sophie Creedon. She was prettier than Esther remembered from the brief vision in the confessional, far prettier than Esther considered herself. There was no doubt that they looked very similar, but Sophie seemed to radiate a kind of light, as Rive had – not quite visible, but drawing all the eyes around her nonetheless.

Esther watched as the other passengers disembarked, as Sophie and the blonde woman hugged and exclaimed. Then Sophie turned, with a smile like a flashbulb, and reached for the hand of a man who had been hanging back. She drew him forward to introduce him to the new arrivals. He had dark hair and eyes, darker skin than was usual for Scotland, and a pensive air despite his smile. This must be Lucas – or Lucifer. Esther had no trouble believing that he had once been an angel. It wasn't just that he was handsome – and he was, as handsome as any man she'd seen – but that he had a similar charisma to Sophie's and Rive's, though his was less light-like, more inward-turning. Still, it was evident that he adored Sophie. Esther could have wept for what she was about to do to them.

"Still feeling sick?"

She turned to find Angus at her side again, holding a cardboard box. "A bit."

"Come on," he said, "I'll introduce you to your cousin."

"Oh no, I don't really think – "

"I promise you, Miss O'Connell, she'll welcome you with open arms. No doubt Lucas will, too."

There was a shade of something in his face and voice as he said this – a slight loss of warmth. Esther noticed, but had no time to consider it, as Angus was helping her up the ladder, guiding her forward. And then she was standing face-to-face with Sophie, who looked at her with frank grey eyes and a questioning smile. For a moment her light was almost blinding, the energy coming off of Lucas nearly palpable. Esther couldn't believe that the others didn't notice. The world swam around her; she barely heard Angus introducing her.

Sophie was holding out her hand. "I'm so very glad to meet you, Elizabeth," she said.

Esther reached out, their hands met – and abruptly, the world stopped swimming. Her faintness left her. Even her heartbeat steadied, and for the first time in a long time – maybe the first time ever – she felt fully solid. Anchored. Whole, in a way that she hadn't known she hadn't been before.

But Sophie was looking at her in shock. Abruptly, she dropped her hand, took a step back toward Lucas, whose arm came protectively around her. "I – I'm pleased to meet you," Sophie repeated, though now her voice sounded distant. She attempted a smile, and failed miserably. "We've got to go now, but I'm sure we'll have a chance to get better acquainted later on…" And taking Lucas's hand, she hurried away with the new arrivals, leaving Esther staring bewilderedly after her.

"That was odd," Angus said. Esther turned to him. He was the only one left on the dock.

"Maybe she wasn't delighted to discover she has poor Irish relations," Esther said, but Angus shook his head.

"Sophie isn't like that. Her family isn't wealthy or standoffish. Besides, you're hardly a poor relation." Esther was too rattled to acknowledge the subtle compliment. "Perhaps she's not well, or it could be the stress of the wedding getting to her."

Again, the strange shade had crept into his tone. This time, Esther understood: it was jealousy. It didn't surprise her. Any man with eyes would fall in love with Sophie Creedon. "No doubt," she said, watching Angus watch Sophie's retreating form.

After a moment he shook his head, smiled at her. "Anyway, where are you staying?"

"I…actually, I don't know. I assumed that there would be an inn or something up here…"

Angus gave her a quizzical look. She didn't blame him. Who would arrive for a wedding in a place like this without having booked somewhere to stay? "I'm afraid there's not much choice, and what there is is all booked up with wedding guests."

"Oh…"

"But I'm sure we can sort something out. Come with me to the pub – we'll see if Ailsa has any ideas. She usually does."

"Who's Ailsa?"

"Sophie's best friend. She more or less runs the pub, too. She knows everything there is to know about what's happening in the village. Coming?"

All Esther wanted at that moment was to give up. She felt sick when she thought of Rive, and how she'd turned him down. But at the same time, there was a vein of conviction running underneath her doubt, telling her that she had to see this through. After that…*best not to think about it.*

"All right," she said, and followed Angus up the pier and into one of the low, white buildings.

The pub was busy with lunch patrons, and others sitting over pints of ale or cups of tea. The red-headed girl from the pier was busy filling glasses behind the bar. Angus pushed in among the men and faeries ranged along it, pulling Esther with him. "Ailsa!" he called.

"With you in a tick!" she answered, flashing him a smile before she turned to deliver filled glasses to waiting customers. A moment later she was back.

"Well, Angus, and what'll it be?" Then her eyes fell on Esther. "God, you're the image of Sophie! I thought she didn't have brothers or sisters."

Esther smiled wearily, deeply regretting Rive's choice of hair dye, as Angus explained, "She doesn't. This is Elizabeth O'Connell, a cousin of Sophie's over from Ireland for the wedding. She's needing a place to stay. I thought you might have some ideas."

Ailsa frowned. "Sophie's mum booked everything going months back. Didn't she get you a room?"

Esther answered, "It was a bit of a last-minute decision to come."

Ailsa considered her and then said, "If you're a relation, I'm sure we can find you a room at the house."

"Oh, no," Esther said, "I've only just met Sophie for the first time. I couldn't intrude like that."

Ailsa waved her protests aside. "No one will even notice, the place is in such an upheaval. I'm off in half an hour. I can take you up then, and we'll see what we can do. You're welcome to wait here in the meantime. Like something to eat or drink?"

"No, thank you."

"Nonsense," Angus said. "It's lunch time, and you'll never get a better fish pie than at World's End."

"What?" Esther asked, shocked.

"Sorry," Angus smiled, "that must have sounded odd. It's the name of the pub."

"Of course," Esther said, still rattled.

"So? Join me for lunch, my treat? That is, if you don't find it too presumptuous, and you aren't allergic to fish."

"No, I'm not, and it's not presumptuous – it's very kind." She followed him to a seat near a window. He pulled out a chair for her, and she stowed her bag underneath. He put down the cardboard box he'd carried from the boat on the chair next to him. Anxious that the silence was about to become awkward, Esther asked, "What's in the box? I mean…sorry, that's a rude question."

"Not at all," he said, brightening, and opened the flaps. He pulled out a black canvas bag. The style and the label clearly belonged to the time before the Change.

Esther willed herself to sound calm, even disinterested when she asked, "What is it?"

"Well, that's just it – I don't know." He began pulling other things out of the box. Esther's breath grew shorter and shorter as he laid them out in front of her. There was a purple hairbrush made of modern plastic, a small leather purse, a mobile phone, an iPod and earphones. There were also two older-looking items

241

– a small, corked jar made of cobalt glass, and a silver knife with a knot-work handle, which he unwrapped carefully from a square of velvet.

"How strange," Esther said faintly. "Where did you get these things?"

"I'm an amateur archaeologist," he answered with a self-effacing smile, "you know, on free weekends and such. I found the bag buried in the sand in a sea-cave under the headland. All of these things were in it. I sent them off to a friend at the University of Edinburgh to see if he could make any sense of them. I mean, obviously they aren't antiques – aside perhaps from the jar and the knife – but they aren't like anything I've seen before. He's just sent them all back. That's why I went over to Mallaig this morning – to fetch the delivery."

"And did he have any theories?" Esther asked, racking her brain for what this could possibly mean.

"Well, the dagger is definitely ancient. He wanted it for the museum, but since it was found on Belial's land, it's up to him what to do with it. He was more vague about the jar. He thought perhaps it was Egyptian in origin. Apparently the symbol on the top is a hieroglyph that relates to ancient Egyptian mythology about the soul." He indicated a symbol pressed into the wax sealing the cork lid. "But he didn't think the glasswork was very old, so it's hard to tell. He wanted to open it and examine the contents."

"Really? It looks empty to me."

"Looks can be deceiving. At any rate, I asked him not to. It's probably no more than a silly fancy, but I couldn't help feeling that opening it would somehow destroy it…" He shook his head. "At least, I'd like to find out a bit more about it first."

"And the other things?" Esther prompted.

"The brush is obvious in its purpose – apparently it still had a few hairs in it – but the material it's made of is one he couldn't identify. The purse had a few coins in it that seemed to have been made in Britain, but were unlike any that have ever been in circulation. He kept those back to study further. As for these other two things," he indicated the phone and the iPod, "the jury is out. The best suggestion so far is that they're some kind of prototype communication devices used during the Irish War, which were lost with the bag and washed up here."

"Oh no, not all of that rubbish again!" Ailsa said, approaching with the fish pie.

"Rubbish!" Angus objected.

"Well, you still don't know what it is, do you?"

"Not aside from the obvious bits, no," Angus admitted, collecting the items carefully and putting them back in the box, as Ailsa laid the table.

Ailsa shrugged. "Don't take it to heart. It'll all look lovely in a display case in Lucas's library."

"Thank you, Ailsa, that'll do," Angus said gloomily, and with a wink at Esther, Ailsa swept away again.

"It's all very interesting," Esther said, trying to revive his good humour. "What will you do with it?"

Angus shrugged, serving Esther a portion of the pie. "Hand it over to Lucas, as Ailsa said. It's all his in the end."

"Maybe he'll let you keep it," Esther suggested.

"Maybe he will," Angus agreed, brightening a bit. "After all, none of it seems to be of much more than conversational value, aside from the dagger."

Esther took a bite of pie. Maybe the pub's recipe really was superior, or maybe it was just that she'd had such bland food for so long, but it truly was the best fish pie she'd ever tasted. She tried to eat slowly, not wanting to make herself ill after days with so little food, but it was difficult.

"Sorry," she said, as Angus helped her to another serving, "I suppose I was hungrier than I thought."

"Nothing to be sorry about. Ruadhri would be insulted if we didn't finish it."

Gradually, Esther relaxed as they ate and chatted. Angus told her about his history with Sophie, and how it had led her here, and to Lucas. To his credit, he mostly managed to keep the jealousy hidden. Esther answered his questions about her own past and family as best she could.

"So are you working? Studying?"

"Neither," Esther answered, wondering how to fill in the gaps in her story. Her months in the convent had left her with little idea of what girls her age actually did with their time, post-Change. "Mostly I help my mam with the younger kids. Maybe someday…"

Except that she didn't know how to finish the sentence. Since the Change, she'd thought of little beyond the misery of her day-to-day existence, and before that, though she'd been a good student, she'd never really given much thought to what she would do after high school. University was as unreachable as the stars to poor girls from Ballymun, and she couldn't imagine how the other children would survive if she left. She'd fought against the Change for so long, but now she wondered whether she'd really been any better off before.

"Elizabeth?"

"Sorry," she said, returning to the present, where Angus was smiling at her uncertainly. "I was in a dream. I'm tired, I guess. It's been a long journey."

"Well there you go – that's Ailsa off now. You can have an afternoon nap."

Esther stood, picking up her bag. "Thank you, Angus. Truly. If not for you, I'd still be working up the courage to get off the boat."

He smiled, standing as well. "I don't believe it. But either way, I'm glad that we met. Perhaps later I can show you around the village. It looks like the weather's clearing."

Esther glanced out the window, where watery sunlight was

indeed breaking through the clouds. "That would be lovely. Thanks again."

Then she turned and joined Ailsa.

CHAPTER 9

ARDNASHEEN

"You're in luck," said Ailsa as she led Esther out of the pub. "I phoned the house, and one of the maids left this morning, so there's a free room. It's not much, but it's better than sleeping rough."

"Whatever it is, it'll be fine," Esther said. "Honestly. Thank you for sorting it out."

"You're welcome." Ailsa's smile turned knowing. "So, you seemed to hit it off with Angus."

Esther blushed and turned her eyes away from Ailsa's. "He's a nice lad," she said, carefully neutral.

"Aye, he is," Ailsa sighed, and Esther couldn't help glancing over at her curiously. Apparently that was all the prompting Ailsa needed. "I really shouldn't be telling you this, but he's mad for your cousin Sophie."

"He said they're old friends."

"Aye, they knew each other in Edinburgh. Met at a concert – Sophie's a prodigy on the harp, did you know?" Esther shook her head, though it didn't surprise her. She imagined Sophie Creedon was the kind of girl to excel at anything she turned her hand to. "He asked her up here to do a music segment with the bairns at the school, and no doubt to try to win her over. But once she set eyes on Lucas – well, there was no hope for anyone else, then."

"No, I suppose not," Esther said, trying not to think about how much more there really was to the story.

"He's lovely in every way," Ailsa said, rather wistfully. "Sophie's one lucky lady. Though he's lucky to have her, too."

"They do seem quite devoted to each other," Esther said, wishing Ailsa would shut up, or at least change the topic.

Ailsa smiled. "They are. But that's enough about the happy couple. Tell me about yourself, Elizabeth. Sophie never mentioned she had Irish family – never mind a cousin who looks so like her."

"She wouldn't have – we've never met before. But it was important to my mam that one of us came to the wedding. She couldn't very well leave the smaller kids, so she sent me." Rapidly running out of lies, Esther asked, "What about you? Are you from the village?"

As Esther had hoped, Ailsa launched happily into her own life story. As she chatted, Esther looked around her. The road they followed ran through a forest of old oaks and tangled rhododendron. The strengthening sunlight sparked on rainwater still dripping from the foliage, making everything shimmer. To the right was the sea, and the clearing clouds revealed the mountainous islands she had missed that morning on the drive to Mallaig.

"What are those mountains?" she asked, when Ailsa paused for breath.

"Oh, those'll be the Cuillins of Skye and Rhum. Two of the inner isles."

The mention of Skye made Esther think of Rive, and despite herself, her heart squeezed painfully. She wondered whether he was there yet, on Skye – if he was near those mountains she was looking at. *Stop it,* she told herself firmly.

"It's beautiful here," Esther said.

"It is," Ailsa agreed. "But I'd trade it for the city in a moment."

"The city isn't all that wonderful," Esther told her. "Not if you don't have money, anyway. I mean, not to say that you don't –"

But Ailsa cut her off with a mellow laugh. "If I had money, do you think I'd be minding the bar at the World's End?"

Though she knew now that it was the name of the pub, the words still made Esther pause. "Well, maybe you'll get there one day."

"Here's hoping," Ailsa agreed, "and there's the house."

The woods opened up, and the road became a drive leading to the biggest house Esther had ever seen. It seemed to sprawl on forever, from the ancient tower nearest to them, to a Victorian wing at the far end, meandering through centuries of architectural styles on the way. In the middle there was a crenelated porte-cochere, and this was where Ailsa seemed to be headed.

"Lucas lives in the tower," she told Esther as they passed it. "So does Sophie, if you want to know the truth," she grinned, "but she still keeps a bedroom in the new wing, for propriety's sake. She even pretends to sleep in it, since her mother's been up."

"Does she," Esther said, mortified to know these details.

Ailsa just laughed. "Normally, the house is more or less a museum," Ailsa continued, "as you can imagine a pile like this would be, with only three people living in it. But since we went into wedding mode, it's all been a bit mad." She pushed through a pair of double doors, into an entry hall that was indeed heaving with activity. Guests milled about while harried-looking servants rushed around, dodging them, in last-minute preparations.

"So you live here too?" Esther asked, as Ailsa squeezed between knots of people toward one half of a curving double-stairway.

"Aye," Ailsa said. "Lucas let me a room when I first came to

248

work here, same as he let one to Sophie. It's how she and I got to be friends. They say that I'm welcome to stay on after they're married, but I don't know. It seems odd, somehow."

Esther followed Ailsa up another flight of stairs, and then along several corridors, wondering how she would ever find her way out of this maze again. She caught fleeting glimpses of paintings, carvings, ornate light fixtures and doors both open and shut. Sometimes they passed people – servants or guests – until, finally, they came into a narrow, whitewashed corridor with plain wooden doors, none of which seemed to hang quite right in their frames.

"It's the maids' quarters," Ailsa said apologetically, walking all the way to the end of the hallway before opening a door. "Usually it's empty, but with all of the staff we've had to take on for the wedding, even this bit is packed to the rafters. I wish I could offer you something better."

Esther had to suppress a smile, thinking how far superior this clean, bright little room was to anywhere she'd slept in her life, let alone the last couple of weeks. There was a white iron bedstead with crisp sheets and a tartan blanket, a washbasin on a stand, a chest of drawers and a spindly wooden chair set beside a nine-paned window. Esther set her bag down on the bed.

"It was made up for a girl from the mainland hired as a scullery maid, but she took one look at the house and said it gave her the creeps, then turned around and went home."

"It's lovely."

Ailsa gave her a dubious smile. "There's a shared bathroom across the hall. The hot water takes absolute ages to make it up here, but if you let it run, you'll get it eventually. I've got to go now – sorry I don't have more time to show you around, but they've got me working flat out."

"It's fine, really – you've been more than kind already. And I had an early start. I could use a rest."

"Well, if you need anything, just ask someone where to find

me. There's a buffet supper for the guests at seven in the dining room. That's on the ground floor, near, well – "

"Don't worry. I'll find it," Esther reassured her.

"Okay," Ailsa said. "See you later, then."

When Ailsa was gone, Esther ran a bath. It was so long since she'd had such a luxury, she didn't even mind that the water never got beyond tepid. As she lay back against the tub, though, it seemed that the days of effort to get here caught up with her at once. The sudden exhaustion felt heavy enough to crush her, yet the hardest part of her task was still before her. She wanted to cry, but she was too tired even for that. For a time she just lay there, thinking of nothing.

Minutes or hours could have passed before something roused her from her exhausted trance: music, faint but sweet. She got out of the bath, dried herself and pulled her clothes back on. She followed the music to her room, where it was louder, apparently coming from beyond the window. Esther looked out. Directly below her was a small, walled garden, full of moss and rosebushes that looked like they hadn't been pruned in years. A girl sat on a stool in a patch of sunlight, her dark head bent over a chestnut-brown harp. Her hands flew over the strings, pulling out the intricate music.

Esther's heart began to stutter. She knew that she was unlikely to have an opportunity like this one again. With shaking hands, she opened her bag, swallowed one of her remaining tablets, and picked up the book that Morag had given her for Sophie. She looked out the window again, taking note of where the little garden lay in relation to the rest of the house. Then she let herself out of her room, and made her way downward.

THE ROSE GARDEN

Sophie put the levers down on her harp, and then laid it in its case. She was just zipping it shut when she heard the door in the garden wall creak open. Playing always left her drifting and dreamy, and at first she thought the dark shape in a nimbus of late afternoon sunlight was Lucas.

Then the figure took a step forward, into the shadow of the garden wall, and the halo fell away, revealing Elizabeth O'Connell, her cousin. She looked to Sophie like a pastel version of herself: creamy skin and dainty features and wide grey eyes like a smudged and softened drawing of her own. Even her short, dark bob looked airy rather than angular.

"You!" Sophie exclaimed sharply, drawing back from the other girl. Then, mortified by her reaction and Elizabeth's stricken look, she said, "I – I didn't mean it to sound like that. You startled me. I didn't know that anyone else even knew about this place, aside from Lucas, of course..."

Elizabeth took another step forward, her hand half-raised, as if in supplication, before she realized it and let it drop back to her side. "You don't need to apologize," she said, her accent making her retiring voice sound even softer. "It's your house, and I'm intruding."

She paused, and Sophie could see her mustering her courage for whatever she was going to say next. It both raised her suspicion and made her ashamed of it.

"I heard you playing from my bedroom window," Elizabeth said at last, "and I came down because...well, because I need to talk with you, and I didn't know if I'd have another chance."

Sophie forced herself to smile. Elizabeth couldn't mean her any harm. Her own mistrust must be a symptom of wedding stress. "Of course. Why don't we go inside, we can have a cup of tea – "

"No," Elizabeth said quickly. "It's better here. What I have to tell you..." She faltered, trailed off, closed her eyes for a moment.

"Are you all right?" Sophie asked.

Elizabeth gave her a smile that looked as forced as Sophie's own. Then, taking a deep breath, she said, "Yes, I'm fine – only tired from the journey."

"Well then, what is it you need to talk with me about?"

Elizabeth considered her for a moment, and then she said, "First, let me ask you something. When you shook my hand earlier on the pier, what happened?"

Even thinking of it made Sophie's heart pound and her head swim. Swallowing her sudden nausea, she answered, "I…I don't really know…" She shook her head, willing the world to steady around her. "I'm sorry," she said, her voice wavering, "it must have seemed so rude. I just had…I suppose you'd call it a turn. I felt faint for a moment."

"Is that all?" Elizabeth persisted.

The vertiginous disorientation redoubled as she tried to consider Elizabeth's question. "Yes…no…oh, I don't know!" She put her hand to her head, wondering if this was the beginning of another migraine. "Let's sit," she said, dropping onto the low, stone wall around a nearby flowerbed. Elizabeth sat too, several careful feet away.

"I can't explain it," Sophie told her, "but in that moment when our hands touched, I remembered a dream. At least I think it was a dream…I've forgotten most of it again…" She trailed off, shaking her head. "I'm sorry. I don't know why I'm telling you this; it doesn't make any sense, and it can't possibly be your fault."

"It does make sense, actually," Elizabeth sighed, "and it's the reason I'm here. What was the dream about?"

Sophie didn't even want to think about it, let alone describe it to Elizabeth. But the other girl's wide, patient eyes rested on her like a conscience. Reluctantly, she said, "I was standing on the ramparts of Edinburgh castle. Someone was with me – a man, I suppose, except that one of his arms was made of metal, all cog-wheels and dials, like the inside of a clock. And he was trying to make me do something – something terrible. Only I can't remember what it was…and now you must think I'm mad."

"No," Elizabeth said. "I don't think you're mad at all. Because I've had those dreams, too. And that man is real, except that he isn't a man. He's something else, something evil, and his name is Abaddon." A chill went down Sophie's spine at the sound of the name. "You see? It's familiar, isn't it?"

"Why should it be familiar?" Sophie asked.

Elizabeth sighed. "Because once, you knew all about him. But you've been made to forget."

Sophie knew with utter, inexplicable conviction that Elizabeth was telling the truth. And yet the words she heard coming out of her mouth were a denial: "That makes no sense!"

"I know. But I promise you, it's the truth." Elizabeth caught her eyes with her own, so very like them, and full of supplication. Much as she wanted to, Sophie couldn't look away. "Sophie," she said, in a tone that told Sophie the question was costing her dearly, "do you remember Theletos?"

A bright flash of memory: white skin webbed with black writing, paint-stained fingers, a pit full of impenetrable darkness. Her own voice shrieking the name Elizabeth had just spoken, and the wrenching pain of irredeemable loss.

"That was only a nightmare," she whispered.

"No, it wasn't."

"How do you know?"

"Because I've met him – Theletos." Elizabeth paused, a haunted look crossing her face. Clenching her fingers around the lip of the stone wall, she continued, "I know that he went to Hell so that you wouldn't have to. You saw him do it, but you've forgotten. You've been made to forget. Everyone has…"

"Everyone but you?" Sophie asked, the bitter accusation in her own tone shocking her.

"I know how this sounds, Sophie. But it's all real, and you need to remember. So much depends on it…" She trailed off, shaking her head, and smiled sadly. "*Everything* depends on it. It's why Theletos sent me to find you."

"If it's so important, why didn't he come himself?"

"He couldn't," she said, the pain clear in her voice.

"This is insane," Sophie said, but it lacked conviction even in her own ears.

Sighing again, Elizabeth reached into her pocket and took out a small, leather-bound notebook. She opened it and read, "'When the Morningstar regains the Heavens, the Balance will be restored.'"

On the heels of the words came another spill of confusing images: a hail of sparks from clashing swords, a knight kneeling in the rain, herself weeping into a well of tears. Sophie could only shake her head against the inexplicable, tacit truth of them.

"Take my hands," Elizabeth said.

"What?" Sophie asked.

Elizabeth's offered her hands, palms up. "It worked once," she said. "Take my hands again, and see what you remember."

For a moment Sophie hesitated, remembering the gut-wrenching agony of the last time she'd touched Elizabeth. But then, as if pulled by some force beyond herself, she reached out. Her hands were shaking as they hovered over Elizabeth's, but she didn't flinch as the other girl grasped them.

It was as if she'd been sucked into a whirlpool. She was helpless against the onslaught, the memories ripping through her as if she were insubstantial as a ghost. They came at her so fast that she couldn't make sense of them, but she felt them – an eternity of love and loss crammed into the few moments before she snatched her hands away. And then she was back in the garden, on hands and knees, shaking and retching. Elizabeth was beside her, calling her name, her eyes wide and horrified.

"Who are you?" she whispered. "What are you?"

"Sophie, I'm so sorry – "

"Sophie!"

Sophie turned, her two realities colliding with a sickening jolt. Lucas standing in the garden doorway, calling her name; Lucas calling her name as he fell through a hole rent in Heaven. Then his arms were around her, and he was venting his fury on the girl beside her: "What did you say to her? What did you do?"

Elizabeth, her eyes full of tears, pleaded, "I don't know...I don't know..."

"Stay away from her," he said, pulling Sophie to her feet. "She has enough to worry about right now."

"Lucas," Sophie began, "it isn't her fault – "

"Let's talk about this inside," he said shortly and bent to pick up her harp case.

The moment his back was turned, Elizabeth pressed the little book into Sophie's hand. "Read it," she whispered, and before Sophie could answer, she turned and fled.

ESTHER'S ROOM

Esther sat in the chair by the window, watching the twilight turn the sea to pewter, the mountains to jet. She had sat like that since her talk with Sophie, her mind blank, her heart leaden. She knew that she had to try again. She hadn't managed to explain to Sophie what needed to be done; she didn't even know if she'd convinced her that her "dreams" were true. But she couldn't muster the energy even to leave the chair, never mind try to find a way back to Sophie, past the vigilant Lucas.

There was a knock at the door. Esther waited until it came again, and then she pushed herself heavily out of the chair and went to open it. She didn't know whom she'd expected to find on the other side, but it wasn't the woman who was standing there now: the pretty, blonde, middle-aged woman who had been with Sophie on the dock. She held a covered plate and offered Esther an apologetic smile.

"Hello, Elizabeth," she said. "I'm Anna Creedon – Sophie's mother."

"Oh…I'm…pleased to meet you."

"I've brought you some dinner, since you never came down."

"That was kind of you. I didn't think I should…I mean, under the circumstances…"

"Yes – I understand." *I very much doubt that,* Esther thought, but she said nothing. "Sophie would have brought this to you herself, but she has one of her headaches."

"I'm sorry to hear that," Esther said, wondering what Anna meant by "one of her headaches."

Anna studied her and then said, "Would you mind if I come in for a moment?"

"Of course not," Esther said, wishing she had never answered the knock in the first place. But since she really had no choice, she stepped away from the door. Anna Creedon came in, set the plate on the dresser, then clasped her hands together, as if uncertain what to do with them.

"Sophie told me what happened," she said. Esther almost stopped breathing, until she continued, "I mean, that Lucas saw you speaking to her and assumed that you had said something to upset her. Of course, it was only the headache coming on, but Lucas is so protective of her. Sometimes overly so…" A slight frown crossed her face.

"Is Sophie all right?"

"Oh, she will be. She's always had migraines, though they've been more frequent lately. The pressure of the wedding, no doubt. Anyhow, she's gone to bed early. But she wanted to apologise for acting strangely earlier, and for Lucas's rudeness. And I wanted to apologise as well, for not welcoming you before now. Unfortunately, your mother's letter was delayed – we only received it today."

"Of…of course," Esther said, wondering frantically what the woman was talking about.

Anna was smiling fondly. "I don't know how I could have forgotten your mum. I suppose because it's been so long…but when I read the letter it all came back to me. We holidayed in Cornwall together as children once, before her family moved to Ireland. We were second cousins. I'm so sorry that she couldn't make it herself – and that we sent the invitation to the wrong address. But I'm so glad that you were able to come anyway."

Esther was reeling and trying desperately not to look it. Who could possibly have sent such a letter, verifying the lies she'd made up on the spot that morning?

"Thank you for saying so," she said, trying to smile evenly.

"Please, join us for breakfast tomorrow?"

"If you think no one will mind."

"We'd be delighted," Anna smiled. "Now, I'll let you be. You must be tired."

Esther nodded and shut the door behind Anna. Then she sank to the bed, head in her hands. Unless there had been some wild coincidence, Sophie's mother had not only believed the false letter, she had also "remembered" events that hadn't happened. The only beings Esther knew of that could alter human memories were the daevas – but why would they be helping her?

She looked at the plate on the dresser, but though she hadn't eaten since the early lunch in the pub, her stomach churned now at the thought of food. All she wanted was to forget everything for a little while. She shut off the light, shucked her dress, and got under the covers. In moments, sleep closed over her.

19 JUNE

Esther woke from confused dreams of shadowy stone ruins and an endless corridor of closed doors. She lay blinking at the rippling leaf-shadows on the whitewashed ceiling, thinking over all that had happened the day before. She didn't exactly feel hopeful about the situation, but the exhaustion that had weighed her down the previous night was gone. She was ready to face breakfast, and maybe Sophie would have read the book. Maybe it would have convinced her that Esther was telling the truth…

Sighing, she got out of bed and got dressed. Then she made her way down the corridor, and after a few wrong turns, to the main staircase. In the entry hall, she asked a harried-looking maid for directions to the dining room and followed several other guests inside. There was a buffet laid out on the long table and people milling about. She couldn't see Sophie among the crowd, but after a moment she saw Anna Creedon approaching her with yet another reticent smile. A man walked behind her, whom Esther guessed must be Sophie's father.

Esther was wondering, distractedly, how Sophie could look so little like either of her parents when Anna caught up to her. "Good morning Elizabeth, I'm so glad you could join us. This is my husband, Andrew Creedon."

"Lovely to meet you," Esther said, shaking his hand.

Anna's smile faltered. "I'm afraid Sophie won't be joining us this morning. She's still down with the headache."

Something in Anna Creedon's expression told her that there was more to Sophie's absence than a headache. "That's too bad," Esther said, her heart sinking.

"Never mind," Sophie's father said. "It'll give us the chance to get better acquainted."

Esther forced a smile, wondering how she was going to manage so many more lies, but in the end, Anna Creedon did most of the talking. Peculiarly, she seemed to have remembered even more about the childhood holidays she hadn't actually shared with Esther's mother. Though she was glad to be off the hook for the moment, the detail of Anna's returning "memories" made her uneasy.

When breakfast was finally finished, Esther excused herself

and fled to the front door. She didn't know where she meant to go, only that she needed to get away from the house. The day was beautiful: the sky nearly cloudless, the morning coolness already giving way to mellow warmth. Esther took off her cardigan, made her way down to the shore, and then began walking in the direction of the village.

She hadn't gone far when she noticed someone coming toward her along the road. A few more steps, and she recognized Angus. She was about to greet him when she saw the grim set of his face.

"I'm so glad I found you," he said.

"Has something happened?" she asked, her heart beginning to trip.

"I'm afraid something has," he said, glancing behind him, toward the village. "Ah – would you mind coming up here?" He gestured to the trees separating the shore from the road.

"Why?" Esther asked, suddenly wary.

"Because it would be better if we weren't seen speaking to each other."

It was a strange request, but Esther was exhausted with the effort of second guessing everyone and everything. She very much doubted that he meant to knock her over the head, but if he did, at least she wouldn't have to think about any of it anymore.

"You're in trouble, Elizabeth," he said without prevarication, once they were hidden within the copse of trees. "Lucas has taken it into his head that you mean to harm Sophie."

"Oh, that," she sighed. "He saw us talking when Sophie had the beginnings of a migraine, and he somehow decided that I'd done something to her. He's uninvited me to the wedding."

Angus looked over his shoulder again. "I'm afraid it's worse than that. I know that this will sound mad to you – but have you heard about that Dublin schoolgirl, Esther Madden? The one accused of murdering a priest?"

Esther froze. "Of course," she said after a moment. "It was all over the papers back home."

"Well it's been in the papers here, too, and somehow Lucas has got it into his head that you're Esther Madden, and Sophie is your next target."

"Sweet Jesus," Esther said faintly.

Angus gave her a look somewhere between pity and embarrassment. "I know. He's always been irrational over Sophie, but this takes the prize." He shook his head. "And I'm afraid even that's not the worst of it. Apparently yesterday he called the local chapter of the Sword of Justice and told them about you. Some of their agents have just arrived on the ferry, and they're looking for you."

"What?" she cried.

"Obviously, it's absurd," he said quickly. "I mean, yes, you bear a slight resemblance to that girl, but clearly you aren't her." Esther couldn't make herself answer. She put out a hand to lean on the nearest tree as her heart hammered and her head spun. "The thing is, they have one of their big guns with them – they call her the Prophet. That's got everyone thinking it must be true."

"What am I going to do?"

Esther wasn't aware she'd spoken the words aloud until Angus answered, "You're going to come with me. You can stay at my house until I've had a chance to explain everything."

"I don't know if that's a good idea," Esther said. When Angus looked surprised, she added, "I mean, the Sword of Justice – I've heard that they're quite powerful. They might not believe you, and I really wouldn't want to cause you any trouble."

"You're not the one causing the trouble," Angus said grimly, and then, recalling himself, he added, "Anyway, I don't know that you have much choice."

"I could leave."

He shook his head. "They're already watching the ferry."

Once again, a wave of hopeless exhaustion sideswiped her, making her want to turn herself in just so it all would end. But then she would be at the mercy of the daevas, and that, she couldn't bear to consider.

"All right," she said. "But how will we make it to your house without them seeing me?"

"We'll go through the woods."

Angus stepped out into the road, took a good look in both directions, and then hurried Esther into the thicker woods at the other side. They pushed through the rhododendrons, into the deeper conifer forest behind them. It was shadowy there, the thick fir branches blocking out most of the sun, and also much cooler. Esther shivered, and pulled her cardi back on, wishing she had Arthur's mantle.

Arthur's Mantle. "Wait!" she said, and Angus stopped. "I left all my things at the house. I'll need to go back and get them – "

"Once you're settled at my place, I'll go collect them."

"*All right*," she said unhappily and followed him on the winding path through the forest. At last they emerged into a small clearing above the village, with a little whitewashed cottage at the centre. "It's not much – " Angus began apologetically.

"It's lovely," Esther interrupted. "And more to the point, it's so kind of you to do all of this for me."

He shook his head. "I'm just sorry that it's necessary. Lucas Belial – " But he seemed to decide against voicing whatever he was thinking. "Anyway, come inside."

Esther followed him into a small sitting room and kitchen area. There were a few comfortable chairs arcing around a fireplace, and a table too big for the room, pushed up against the window and cluttered with papers and other objects. Among them Esther saw the bag that Angus had shown her in the pub, with its contents, minus the dagger, spread nearby.

"I'll go now," he said. "Hopefully I won't be long. Help yourself to tea – I'm afraid there's not much else."

"It's fine," Esther said. "I'll be fine."

Angus gave her an appraising look. At last he said, "All right then. Back soon." He gave her what was no doubt meant to be an encouraging smile and then shut the door.

Esther stood in the sudden silence, looking around. She walked to the table and looked down at the objects from the canvas bag. She hadn't seen anything as modern as the mobile phone and the iPod since the Change. She picked up the phone. Despite its time in a sea cave, there didn't appear to be any water damage or corrosion. If only she had a way to charge it, she could use it to help convince Sophie of the truth of her story.

She put the phone down, picked up the bag. It seemed to be empty, and no doubt it had been thoroughly checked at the university, but still, she felt around in the inner pockets. And then her hand closed over something. She pulled it out: a black charging cord. She couldn't help an incredulous laugh.

She attached it to the phone and plugged it in. The screen lit up, showing a charging bar. She had never had a mobile phone of her own, but it didn't take her long to figure out how to open the menu. There were so many icons she didn't know where to begin. At last she chose "messages." There were reams of texts, several of the most recent ones from Ailsa, but they didn't address the phone's owner by name.

Next, Esther chose the "phone" icon, and found a list of contacts. She also found three voice mails, the most recent from the past December. Esther played it, recognising Ailsa's voice: "Hey Sophie, we're coming to the café to meet you if that's okay?"

Esther unhooked the phone and plugged in Sophie's iPod. She was still scrolling through the playlists when Angus returned. "What are you doing?" he cried in horror, which changed to wonder when Esther turned the iPod toward him. "How did you do that?" he demanded, dumping her carpetbag unceremoniously on the floor as he sat beside her, taking the iPod that she offered him. She showed him how it worked, and he spent a few minutes fiddling with it before he looked up at her and said, "How did you know what it was? And where on earth did you get the cord?"

"Angus," Esther said, "I need to tell you something. In fact, a lot of things. You're probably going to think I'm mad, but whenever you start thinking that, look at these." She indicated the iPod, and pushed the phone toward him as well. His eyes widened further. She sighed. "So – I knew what they were because everyone used to have them. Up until a few months ago, you probably had ones of your own."

He looked up at her with a mixture of fear and curiosity and somewhere, though deeply buried, a spark of recollection. "Your name isn't Elizabeth O'Connell, is it?"

Esther smiled dismally. "No, it's not."

*

A couple of hours later, Angus was still struggling to take in all that Esther had told him, although she'd kept it as simple as she could. He sat with the phone in one hand and a glass of whisky in the other. He'd poured one for Esther, too, though she'd only taken a few sips.

"This is just completely mad," he said, taking a sip as he pressed buttons on the phone.

"I know it seems that way," Esther said gently. "For a while I thought *I* was mad – I mean, when everything changed, and no one else seemed to remember. But whenever I start to believe it, something comes along and convinces me again that I'm not. Like the old woman, Morag. Or the strange man on the train."

"I still can't see how we could have overlooked this – this charger contraption." He indicated the cord.

Esther shrugged. "I don't think you did. I don't believe it was there before now."

He looked at her, his eyes full of curiosity and scepticism. "How is that possible?"

"I don't know, but it's not the first time something has appeared like that, out of the blue, when I needed it." She tried not to think about Theletos's key, and whether the phone charger and the letter to Sophie's mother might share its provenance.

"Which seems to suggest that someone very much wants you to succeed in your mission to return Sophie's memories to her," he said speculatively.

Esther wondered if this was true, or if she was walking into an elaborate trap. At last, she said, "So, does any of what I've told you make you remember anything from before the Change?"

Angus put the phone and the glass down and met her eyes. "It's hard to say. I mean, when you were telling me your story, there were parts of it I almost recognized. That woman, Morag, for instance. I feel I could have met her, once. And the '*Book of Sorrows*,' that was familiar. Even that word, daeva, sounds like something I've heard before." He shook his head. "But it's like remembering a story someone read to you as a child – you can't tell what's real from what your mind has supplied to fill in the gaps. There are these flickers, but nothing to connect them to."

Esther's despair must have shown on her face, because he took one of her hands and squeezed it, saying earnestly, "But I do believe you, and more to the point, I think we need to make Sophie believe you. I want to help you, if I can – if you tell me how."

"To be honest, I have no idea. Now that Lucas has it in for me, I really don't see how I'll manage to speak to Sophie. And if he convinces everyone else that I'm evil – well then, I'm finished." She shrugged listlessly.

Angus drummed his fingers on the table and sipped his whisky, looking out the window, where a sliver of sea and far-off mountains were just visible. Finally, he said, "If Sophie *has* begun to remember, then maybe seeing these things will be just what she needs to believe it."

"It might be," Esther agreed. "I mean, I hope to God it will. But how will I get them to her?"

Once again Angus sat considering this. Finally, he said, "Let me talk to her."

"When? She's always surrounded by people, and now Lucas will be more protective than ever."

"I'll go speak to her right now. I'll insist. As an old friend, I don't think she'll deny me that."

Esther gave him a hard look. "Do you really believe me, or are you just trying to get at Lucas?"

He grinned. "I really believe you. But getting at Lucas is definitely a bonus."

*

Angus left soon after that, with the mobile phone in his pocket. For a while afterward, Esther paced anxiously around the room, picking things up and then putting them down again without really seeing them. Trying to calm herself, she pulled a book at random from a shelf and settled on the settee to try to read. But she kept reaching the end of a page with no recollection of what had been on it. In the end she put it aside, downed her glass of whisky, plugged in the earphones of Sophie's iPod and settled back into the settee to wait.

She was finally beginning to relax when something caught her eye: a movement at the edge of the clearing. She stood, expecting Angus, but instead a dog emerged from the trees. A dog that was far too big, with a greenish-black coat and a tail formed of many plaits, its eyes like cold yellow gems. It had its nose to the ground, panting with a forked red tongue, marking a scent. And beside it walked the Cailleach.

Esther dove to the floor. For a moment she was too panicked to think what to do next; then instinct took over, and she crawled for the table, pushing herself up against the wall beneath it. There was a scrabbling on the window glass above her, a breath of frigid air, and then the rake of nails on the glass. She waited for the window to shatter, but instead she heard the dog drop back onto all four feet. She was just beginning to wonder if it had actually left, when there was a sharp rapping against the door.

Open it, Esther Madden. We know you are there.

The words sounded in her head rather than her ears, with chilling, sickening intimacy. She'd thrown the bolt on the door after Angus left, but she doubted it would do much to hold the Cailleach back. There was another rapping, this time so forceful that the door shuddered. The next moment it whitened, glittering with frost, cracks radiating out from the place where it had been struck.

Esther looked around for anything with which to defend herself. She saw a block of knives on the kitchen worktop, at the same time she remembered Arthur's Mantle. Taking a deep breath, she grabbed the mantle from her carpetbag, flung it on, and then ran for the knives. She drew one just as the door splintered. Hiding the knife under the mantle, she crouched in a corner of the kitchen.

The dog walked across the ruined planks, its snout down and its tongue dripping as it peered around with unblinking, slit-pupil eyes. The Cailleach followed, the planks of the door splintering under her feet. The two of them moved toward Esther, who gripped the knife with both hands, willing away the greyness that was starting at the corners of her vision as her heart skipped wildly. The dog stopped in front of her, gazing straight into her eyes.

Greetings, Esther, the Cailleach said, approaching behind it. She reached out with long, gloved fingers, and whipped the mantle off of her, dropping it disdainfully on the floor.

Esther let out a strangled sob, steeling herself for the Cailleach to strike. Instead, the suspended moment was rent by a wild cry. Somebody was flying through the door towards them. Esther caught a flash of blue light and thought of Rive. But the

figure was too small to be Rive, and the cry had been a girl's –
and then Sophie Creedon was standing in between Esther and
the Cailleach, levelling an ice-blue knife at the Cailleach's heart.
A bright blue aura shone around her.

"You don't touch her," Sophie said through gritted teeth.

The Cailleach trilled chilly laughter. *Do I take this to mean
you've recalled your place in the grand scheme, Sophia?*

Sophie looked momentarily confused, but then she recovered
her resolve. "Take it to mean that you are not welcome in this
village, and that I won't stand for anyone threatening my friends.
And if you cross me, you'll feel this knife!"

The words were barely out of her mouth when the dog sprang
at her. There was a flash of blue, and then the dog was lying
still at their feet, black blood spreading across the floor from its
slashed throat. Sophie straddled its body, her face flushed, her
hair wild, her dagger dripping. She held the Cailleach's eyes as
she wiped the dagger on her skirt.

"Get out," Sophie commanded.

For a moment, the Cailleach remained still as the stone
she'd once turned to in the summers of her mythical past. Then,
without another word, she turned on her heel and walked out
the door. Sophie looked up at Esther and Angus, a sickly, shaky
smile turning her lips. It was as terrible as anything Esther
had ever seen. Then she smoothed her bloodstained skirt in a
peculiarly calm, ordinary gesture.

Angus finally broke the silence. "Sophie…Esther…we'd
better get out of here."

"No," Sophie said with the same odd detachment. "The
demon is dead, and as for the Prophet, I've given her plenty to
think about. We're as safe here as anywhere in Ardnasheen."
She turned to Esther, her eyes steely and certain. "And I think
I'm ready now to hear what you have to say."

*

Sophie had downed her first glass of whisky in one gulp,

267

and then sat sipping another as Esther told her all that she knew. Afterwards they sat in silence as Sophie carefully inspected all of the things from the bag, and read the messages on the phone. Finally, she set it down and looked up at Esther and Angus, who were gazing back at her anxiously.

"Well, I can't very well refuse to believe you, with all of this evidence and – that." She waved a hand at the kitchen, where the demon dog was still lying in its pool of viscous blood, though it had begun to dissolve.

"About that," Angus ventured, "I didn't know you were versed in, ah…hunting."

Sophie shrugged and gave him a wry smile. "Neither did I."

"And the dagger? How did you know that it could kill a demon?"

"I didn't. Ever since I saw it, though, I've felt a kind of pull toward it. When you gave it to me to give to Lucas, I didn't. I kept it. I know it sounds mad, but I've carried it with me ever since."

"But you fought the demon dog like you knew exactly what you were doing," Esther said.

Sophie shrugged. "When we got here and saw that you were in danger, something just took over me, and I knew exactly what to do to stop it. I can't explain it."

"I think maybe I can," Esther ventured. "When Rive fought the Revenant, something similar happened. He had a sword that glowed blue, like that knife, and an aura of the same colour. I think that knowledge is a part of the things you've forgotten, but sometimes bits of it break through."

Sophie's gaze was frank. "And there's the snag. It's only bits, nothing concrete."

"I think I can help you with that, if you're willing."

Sophie visibly paled, and Esther knew that she'd taken her meaning. But when she offered Esther her hands, it was with remarkable calm.

"Are you sure?" Esther asked, her palms hovering just above Sophie's.

"Not at all," Sophie answered with a wry smile and closed her hands around Esther's.

This time, although she looked as terrible as she had during the others, Sophie didn't let go. She held onto Esther for several long minutes, her face whitening further, beads of sweat coming out on her brow, and her mouth set in the hard line of someone deeply resolved to bear pain. Esther, meanwhile, tried not to show how much better the contact made her feel, when it was clear that it came at Sophie's expense.

At last, Sophie's limp hands slipped from Esther's. In her face, Esther saw all of the hurt and betrayal she'd felt when she first learned about the Change. Only for Sophie, it must be worse. She had so much more to lose.

As if confirming it, Sophie burst into tears. Angus was instantly at her side. "Sophie, what's happened? What can I get you – water? Tea? More whisky?" Sophie waved him away, and Angus looked helplessly at Esther.

She didn't know what to say to him. She felt like crying, too, though for her, it was out of guilt. She couldn't know exactly what Sophie had seen when they linked hands, but she could guess the worst of it. She had no idea how to comfort a girl whose world had just been torn to pieces. She wondered again if she should have listened to Rive. But no: she couldn't have lived with herself knowing that she had a chance to stop what was coming and chose not to take it.

"I'm so sorry," she whispered.

Sophie smiled bitterly through her tears. "It's not your fault."

"I could have spared you."

"And doomed us all?" She shook her head. "No, you couldn't, and I wouldn't have wanted you to."

"I hate to ask," Angus said uncomfortably, "but I don't know quite what we're talking about."

Sophie swiped at the tears on her face. "I saw what Esther told us I would see: a different world. I also saw the evil creatures that have changed it to this one. And I think – " here she glanced, questioning, at Esther " – some visions of the world that's going to come, if they get their way."

"Did you see the city where they erased the sky?" Esther asked.

"Yes," Sophie said. "That's Edinburgh. But the strangest things is, I've seen that scene before. My mother painted it in the time before the Change."

"I'm sorry," Angus said, "but I still don't understand. I mean, I realize that something terrible has happened to the world, and it's the fault of the daevas, and if someone doesn't stop it, we're all in for it. But why does it have to be Sophie?"

"Because it's my fault that it's happening in the first place," Sophie said, standing up.

"Sophie?" Angus asked anxiously. "Where are you going?"

She looked at them with grim, grey eyes. "To tell Lucas."

"Maybe you shouldn't, yet," Esther said.

"It's almost Midsummer. We don't have time to waste.

"Theletos could have been wrong...he didn't want me to come here, after all."

But Sophie shook her head with a sad smile. "He wasn't wrong. I remember it all now. I remember the things Theletos – Rive – told me. I remember what I promised him. I also remember that I won't live past Midsummer anyway – so in the end, what does any of it matter?"

"Sophie – " Angus began, but she said, "Don't." She embraced him and then took Esther's hands in hers. This time, there was no reaction. "I want you to know, Esther, that I don't blame you for any of this," she said. "And if I can't quite thank you for giving back my memories, I know you'll understand."

And then she walked out the broken front door and disappeared into the woods.

Esther and Angus paused only long enough to collect the carpetbag and the items from Sophie's old satchel before they followed her. Along the way, Esther filled Angus in on all that she knew about what Sophie had remembered. An hour later, they sat in the woods just behind Madainneag, in the sudden twilight that had fallen when a roil of charcoal storm cloud had eclipsed the setting sun. Through the shaded windows of the tower, they watched the silhouettes of Sophie and Lucas in heated conversation.

"Shouldn't we go in and help her?" Angus asked, not for the first time.

"I doubt we'd be helping," Esther answered.

"But he'll think she's gone mad."

"And if we go in there, he'll think we're mad, too."

"Maybe holding your hands would work on him, like it did on Sophie."

"I doubt he'd let me try."

"Well then, maybe we could – " He stopped abruptly, as they heard a rustling in the underbrush nearby. They drew the kitchen knives they'd brought from the cottage, Esther picturing a grey-coated figure spreading frost in its wake. Instead, a dim glow emerged from the trees, and then Ailsa was looking down at them, her questioning look illuminated by the light of a paraffin lantern.

"What on earth are you two doing out here?" Then she smiled and raised an eyebrow. "Or shouldn't I ask?"

Angus coloured. "It's nothing like that. And anyway, what are *you* doing out here?"

"Looking for Sophie's Great Aunt Mary's horrible little terrier. It ran off earlier this afternoon. I'm hoping a spriggan got it." Then her gaze turned keen again. She looked from Esther and Angus to the window of the tower, and frowned. "I don't suppose you know anything about that?" She pointed to the window.

They all looked up. Sophie was leaning against it, her shoulders shaking. A moment later, they heard the tower door slam and footsteps moving away hurriedly.

Ailsa's look turned to one of alarm. "I'd better go see what's happened."

"Really, I don't think you should – "

"Wait, Ailsa, don't – "

Ailsa glared at them. "All right, what *do* you two know about this?" Angus and Esther looked helplessly at each other. "Right, then," Ailsa said. "I'm going upstairs. *I'm* not one to leave a friend crying alone!"

"Ah, crap," Angus said, and then he and Esther hurried after her. Ailsa flung open the tower door, clearly prepared to go rushing up the stairs, and almost ran into Sophie. She took one look at her, dishevelled and tearstained, and then flung her arms around her. "Oh honey, what has he done?"

Sophie shut her eyes for a moment, and then she gently pushed Ailsa away. "Why don't you all come upstairs. I'll make a pot of tea, and we can talk."

Esther was about to excuse herself, but then Sophie gave her a desperate look over Ailsa's shoulder. "Ah – all right," she said.

Sophie led them up a spiral stair and into a comfortable combined sitting room and kitchen. Esther saw books scattered around, a victrola on a stand, a violin on the dining table. "Sit," Ailsa said to Sophie. "I'll make the tea."

Reluctantly, Sophie sat down in an armchair by the coffee table, and Esther and Angus took places on the settee. As Ailsa rattled around, Angus whispered to Sophie, "What did you tell him?"

"Everything," she said grimly.

"And?"

"He doesn't believe me. He thinks the stress of the wedding has driven me mad."

"And Ailsa?" Esther asked. "What will you say to her?"

There was no time to answer, as Ailsa approached with the tea tray. She looked from one to the other of them suspiciously, and then dropped the tray on the table with a clatter. "All right," she said, crossing her arms, "which one of you's going to tell me what's going on here?" They looked guiltily at each other. "Or shall I go hunt down Lucas and ask him?"

Sophie's eyes flew to Ailsa's face in alarm. "No – no, please, don't do that!" Then she turned to Esther and Angus, her eyes troubled but frank. "She deserves to know," she said. "But you'll have to help me."

"Of course," Esther said.

"Anything you need," Angus added.

Sophie reached into her pocket and brought out the mobile phone. Ailsa raised her eyebrows. "Isn't that the strange contraption from the bag Angus found?"

"Yes," Sophie answered. "Push the button on top."

Clearly dubious, Ailsa pushed it – and then, as the screen lit, she shrieked and dropped it. Sophie smiled humourlessly. She retrieved the phone from the floor, and handed it back to Ailsa, who took it reluctantly.

"What is this?" she asked, her voice shaky.

"It's a telephone," Sophie answered.

"It doesn't look like any phone I've ever seen."

"That's because you've forgotten. But you used to have one like it." Sophie took the phone back, pulled up Ailsa's text message, and showed them to her. "You wrote this message."

"Ah, no, I didn't."

"You did," Sophie persisted, "I promise."

Ailsa looked up and around at them, her face white, her eyes wide. She lowered herself into a chair and said, "I think you'd better start at the beginning."

Ailsa listened to the story with little comment, until they reached the part about Sophie returning to the Garden. By that point Sophie was looking out the window, presumably for Lucas.

"But you can't go to any Garden," Ailsa cried. "You're getting married in three days!"

"Apparently not," Sophie said tonelessly.

Ailsa shook her head. "This is mad! Even if it's all true – and I'm not calling you liars, only it's a lot to swallow – well, you and Lucas are still mad for each other. There's no way you aren't meant to be together!"

Sophie turned back to the window, though not before Esther saw her bitter smile. "It seems it isn't that simple." And then she stilled, and put a hand to the glass. "Oh, god – he's coming."

Esther looked at Angus in alarm, but there was nowhere to go, even if Esther hadn't been thoroughly sick of running. They sat and waited as Lucas burst in, flushed and windblown. His anger seemed to fill the room.

"What are you doing here?" he demanded of Esther.

Esther shrank back, but Angus put himself in front of her, his fists clenched at his sides and his eyes furious. "This isn't her fault, Belial," he said.

"Do you have any idea what she's done?" Lucas spat back.

"She's done nothing but speak the truth," Sophie said, putting a hand on his shoulder.

He turned to her, his anger clear. "And I've heard nothing but lies she's been feeding you!"

"They aren't lies, Belial," Angus said. "Only a truth you don't want to accept."

Lucas gave him an incredulous look. "So she's bewitched you, too? And Ailsa, I suppose?"

"Lucas, please," Sophie said. "All of them were willing to listen – why won't you?"

274

He looked down at her, and the love and pain in his eyes turned Esther cold. "Because they want to tear us apart."

"Lucas, these are our friends!" Sophie pleaded. "Why would they want to hurt us?"

He looked at them all, his eyes settling on Angus. "He's been determined to split us up since the day we met. And she's a murderer," he indicated Esther.

"And Ailsa?" Sophie demanded. "Is she somehow plotting against us, too? Lucas, listen to yourself. This is madness!"

"The only madness is what they've made you believe." He turned toward the door again.

"Where are you going?"

"To get the Prophet," he said, "and put an end to this."

"No!" Sophie cried. "You can't do that!"

Lucas turned from her and then stopped abruptly in the doorway. Three people were standing there who hadn't been a moment ago: a young woman with long, platinum dreadlocks, a young man with close-cropped red hair and green eyes, and another with messy blond hair and a supercilious smile. All of them had the faint, incandescent aura Esther was learning marked out Heaven's denizens.

The redheaded man put a hand on Lucas's chest, and all of the fight seemed to leave him at once. With a sad smile, the man said, "I'm afraid she's right, Lucifer. If you want to survive the night, you'd best stay here."

Sophie had been staring at the people in the doorway, stunned. Now she cried, "Suri!" and flung herself into the arms of the platinum-haired girl. "Oh my god, Suri, something terrible has happened – "

Suri kissed her on the temple and held her tightly. "I know. And it's going to be okay. But we've got to find somewhere else to talk, because there's this really creepy woman in a grey coat on her way here now, with what looks like a lynch mob made out of shadows."

"Where can we go that she won't find us?" Esther asked in despair.

Nobody seemed to have an answer to that, until Lucas said, in a voice dull with defeat, "Come with me."

CHAPTER 10

THE WINE CELLAR NIGHT

An hour later, they'd gathered in a forgotten vault in the wine cellar, lit by a wrought-iron candelabra. They'd filled one another in on their recent histories, and those who the Change had affected had taken turns holding Esther's hands, to see whether it would jog their memories as it had Sophie's. It had had no effect. Now they sat silently, considering it all, passing around a bottle of red so old that the label had disintegrated.

When it came to him, Sam drained half of it. "Honestly, Belial, to think you've been hoarding a vintage like this for all of this time! I should have broken in here centuries ago."

Sophie glared at him. "Tell me again what you're doing here?"

"I'm the necessary evil." He offered her the bottle, grinning, his eyes sinkholes in the bad light.

"No, thank you," she said coldly.

"Believe me," he answered, his voice low and his smile gone, "I'm less than thrilled to see you, too."

Sophie snatched the bottle and passed it on to Lucas, who accepted it without comment and then sat staring at it, as if he had no idea what it was for.

"So you're actually, honestly angels?" Ailsa said, taking the bottle out of Lucas's hands and drinking deeply.

"Yes," Suri answered patiently, "though we don't have much in the way of angelic powers at the moment."

"And we were all friends, before the Change?" Angus asked.

"Yes – with the exception of Esther. We didn't know her, before." Suri trailed off, glancing at Esther with a mixture of curiosity and pity that Esther didn't like at all.

"It's all well and good to sit here talking about what went on before our collective amnesia," Sophie said, "but it's not the same as knowing it. Is there any way to make the others remember, like I did?"

"Maybe," Suri answered. "I mean, assuming everything still works like it used to down here."

"But?" Sophie prompted.

"But even if we could do it, it would take time, and we don't have much. Do we really want to waste any on something that probably won't work?"

Lucas looked up at her with haunted eyes, and then he spoke for the first time since he'd led them to the wine cellar: "I'm not going to believe anything until I see it."

Michael smiled wryly. "I see the Change hasn't changed your stubbornness." Lucas rewarded him with a cold smile, and Michael turned to the others. "Angus? Ailsa? Do you also feel you need to see it to believe it?"

"Aye," Ailsa said. "I was with you until the angel bit."

Angus shrugged. "It would make things easier."

"I suppose there's nothing for it, then," Michael sighed. "Suri, do you have your truth concoction? And then we'll need a basin, but nothing made with reactive metal – "

"Ahem," Sam said, from the wine rack he was perusing, "isn't anyone going to ask my opinion?"

"Do we really want to hear it?" Suri snapped.

"Probably – if you want to have any hope of this little project working."

"Well?"

Sam turned from the rack, holding a bottle. It wasn't a dark, dusty wine bottle like the last – it was clear, and filled with a transparent liquid swirling with faint iridescence. "Why go the long way around when you can take a shortcut?"

"What is that?" Michael asked dubiously.

"It's a bottle of excellent red that I've turned into a bottle of distilled memories." He gestured to the others. "Theirs, to be specific."

"Yeah, right," Suri said. "We can't do half of what we used to do down here, but you can change matter into memory?"

"Maybe the daevas like me," Sam suggested.

"In which case, that's probably a bottle of poison."

"Maybe it is," he agreed amiably. "There's only one way to find out. Lucifer? Would you like to go first?" He proffered the bottle.

"No!" Sophie cried. "It must be poison or something just as bad. Sam would never help us."

Sam's smile became a challenge. "Help you? Who said I was helping you?"

"You said it would bring back their memories."

"Yes, and I imagine that remembering will be rather uncomfortable – especially for him." He looked pointedly at Lucas. "That is, if he's brave enough to go through with it."

Sam dangled the bottle in front of Lucas. With burning eyes, Lucas snatched the bottle and downed half of it before anyone could stop him.

"Lucas, are you mad?" Sophie cried, pulling the bottle from him. But Lucas didn't answer. He was staring at her, his eyes wide and glassy, as if he'd never seen her before.

Sophie whirled on Sam. "What have you done to him?"

279

Sam smiled wryly. "I think even you'll agree that he did it to himself."

Sophie shoved the bottle back at him as Lucas sank to his knees. She knelt with him, her hands on either side of his face, looking anxiously into it. "Lucas? Can you hear me?" His lips moved, but nothing came out. Sophie looked around at the others, who stared back at her mutely. This went on for several more long minutes, and then, with a harsh cry, Lucas leapt to his feet. He looked around the room, his eyes wild and unfocused, but gradually he seemed to recall where he was. His eyes settled on Sophie and welled with tears.

"Sophie?" he said in a low, broken voice, reaching for her with shaking hands. "It's all true, isn't it?"

She nodded, meeting his eyes with clear effort. A ragged cry escaped from Lucas, and then he ran. Sophie flung a desperate look at her friends before following him.

"I guess it worked, then," Sam said, holding the bottle up to the candlelight to peer through it.

"You are a complete arse!" Angus said.

"You're not the first to say so," Sam answered nonchalantly, "and no doubt you won't be the last."

"I really don't like him," Ailsa said to Suri.

"You liked me quite a lot, once," Sam said with a smirk.

"What do you mean?" she asked warily. In answer, he offered her the bottle. Ailsa eyed him balefully for a moment, and then she took it.

"Ailsa, perhaps you shouldn't do that," Michael said. "Lucifer is an angel, and you saw what it did to him."

"Aye – it worked, by all appearances," she answered, her face white but her tone resolved. "And we're probably going to Hell anyway, right?"

No one answered that. Ailsa took a deep breath, drank half of what was left in the bottle, and then handed it to Angus, who drained it. "Feel anything yet?" he asked her.

"No…yes…maybe…" Abruptly, Ailsa's eyes rolled back and she slumped to the floor. Within moments, Angus, too was unconscious.

"Are they going to be all right?" Esther asked anxiously, touching their hands.

"Of course not," Sam said, looking down scornfully at the two of them. "They're going to remember everything. It'll very likely drive them mad."

To Esther's alarm, neither of the other angels contradicted him. "Is their past really that bad?"

Suri and Michael exchanged a glance. "They may be out for a while," Michael said at last. "We might as well bring Esther up to speed in the meantime."

"Fine," Suri said, "but I'm telling it."

Michael shrugged. "As you like."

So Suri began, "I guess it started when Sophie applied for a job in the pub…"

*

Lucas was nowhere to be seen by the time Sophie reached the stairs to the wine cellar. Wearily, she climbed them and then stood in the shadows of the doorway, searching the corridor beyond. Though there were many people hurrying around, there was no sign of Lucas. Not wanting to run into anybody who would demand an explanation for their absence at dinner – which meant just about anybody she might encounter – she slipped out a back door and began to make her way around to the tower. Looking up, though, she saw a dim light in the window of her bedroom. It might be her mother putting finishing touches on the dress, but something told her that it wasn't.

Sophie went back inside and managed to sneak up to the bedroom without anyone catching her. She stood for a moment outside the door, trying to make her thoughts slow and her mind work; trying to make reason subdue her aching heart. She wasn't especially successful, but at least her eyes were dry when she finally opened the door.

The light came from the small reading lamp on the bedside table. In the deep shadows, the wedding dress on its form looked like a ghost. Sophie couldn't bear to look at it, but Lucas straddled the desk chair, his chin on his arms crossed on its back, gazing at it as if he might compel it to speak.

Sophie stepped in front of him. He looked up at her, his eyes defeated. "Can you ever forgive me?"

"What for?" Sophie asked.

"I've put you through hell."

Sophie shook her head. "It's all right, I understand. You didn't trust Esther, and you were trying to protect me – "

"No, not that...or not just that. I meant everything you've been through since the day we met."

"I was right there with you, through all of it."

"Yes, you were. And you've saved me how many times, now?"

"As many times as you've saved me. Lucas – what is this about?"

He gave her a wretched smile. "I've remembered *everything*, Sophie. Including the fact that you promised to go back to Theletos, before...before everything changed. And I understand why you did it."

"I don't think you do," she began, but he interrupted.

"It's okay, Sophie. I don't know how you could love me after everything that happened with the sea witch."

She felt as if the wind had been knocked out of her. "Not love you, Lucas?" she said when she'd gathered herself again. "Because of some stupid enchantment?" She took his hands. "Don't you know by now that nothing could make me stop loving you?"

There was confusion in his eyes along with the pain. "Then why did you agree to go back to Theletos?"

"I didn't agree to go back to him. I agreed to go back to the Garden with him – because it's the only way to repair the Balance."

"You only have his word for that, though, right?"

"Well, his word and Michael's pet theory. But Rive has always dealt honestly with me. He helped me rescue you from Dahud, and he went to the Deep in my place – so why would I doubt him?"

He shrugged listlessly. "I don't know. But equally, I don't know why you should believe him. Everything else is turned upside down, why not that?"

"We have to believe something, don't we?" Sophie asked helplessly. "To try whatever might stop what the daevas are planning?"

"Maybe. But I don't see why you alone should have to bear the burden of that."

She sighed. "I wouldn't bear it alone. Rive would have to bear it, too."

Lucas looked puzzled. "But he'd have you back."

Sophie smiled ruefully. "He doesn't want me back, Lucas."

"What?"

"He doesn't love me."

"He told you that?"

"Quite specifically. I think if he had the choice, he wouldn't have asked me to go with him at all. But the Keeper told him to bring me back, so that's what he means to do."

"The Keeper..." Lucas repeated speculatively. "So going back to the Garden with Theletos is strictly an obligation."

"How could you think it would be anything else?"

For the first time since he'd drunk from the bottle, there was a spark of hope in his eyes. "And after you've gone there and done whatever it is you're meant to do, you'll be free to do what you like?" Sophie couldn't bear his tremulous hope. She looked away, but not before she saw the light go out of his face. "Right. So there were terms."

"Yes," she said softly.

"You had to promise to leave me."

"He never asked me to leave you," Sophie said with quiet misery.

"Well then, what did he ask?" Sophie bit her lip, trying not to cry. Lucas took her arms and looked at her intently. "Sophie, what did you promise?"

"To stay there."

"In the Garden."

"Yes."

"Where angels are forbidden to go," he said softly, his eyes burning into hers.

"Yes."

"And you had to promise to stay forever, I suppose." His own voice trembled now.

Sophie looked up at him through a blur of tears. "How else could it possibly work?"

"All right," he sighed. "So he came to get you on the Keeper's orders. But since then, the rules have been tossed out. More to the point, Theletos isn't here now. I'd say that nullifies any promise you made him."

"I wish it did," Sophie faltered, "but from what Esther showed me, I think it's up to me now, to find a way for both of us to keep it. Lucas, I know that it's not what you want to hear, but what's happening to us all is my fault. And if there's something I can do to change it…well, then I'm going to do it. I have to do it."

He studied her, his dark eyes suddenly, alarmingly remote. "Tell me one thing, Sophie," he said softly. "These past months – have *they* been real? I mean…did you really want to marry me, or was that the daevas working on us, too?"

"How can you ask me that?" Sophie asked, and then she

burst into tears. Stricken, Lucas caught her up, gathered her against him fiercely as she clung to his neck. "I've only ever wanted *you!*" she wept. "I would do anything to make all of this go away and marry you like I meant to."

"Then that's what we'll do," he said.

"We can't. Not now, with everything coming to pieces –"

"No, not now," he interrupted gently. "But someday. I refuse to believe that this is the end – that it's impossible for us to save the Balance and also be together. I can't. I've loved you far too long, through too many impossibilities. We're meant to be together."

"How?" Sophie asked brokenly.

"I don't know yet," he answered, "but we're going to find out."

*

Their friends were onto a third bottle of wine by the time Sophie and Lucas returned to the cellar. Ailsa looked ill, Angus sombre, but they shifted without comment to make room for Sophie and Lucas in the circle.

"Are you guys okay?" Suri asked cautiously.

"Not really," Lucas said, "but we're here, with memories intact. You two?" He looked at Ailsa and Angus.

"Likewise," Ailsa said. Angus only smiled grimly.

"So you remember everything," Lucas prodded.

"Aye," Angus answered, "and I think I preferred being a schoolteacher."

Suri smiled at him sympathetically, then asked Sophie, "What about you? How much do *you* remember?"

"I remembered everything when Esther and I linked hands," Sophie answered.

"Even your life as an aeon?" Suri asked, scrutinizing her.

"Well, no, not that. Or not all of it. I only remember what I knew before the Change, I guess…why?"

Suri glanced at Michael. He sighed and then said, "Sophia,

we've learned some things about your past since the last time we met."

Sophie's heart began to beat quickly. She gripped Lucas's hand. "Tell me," she demanded.

"I will," Michael answered, "but you need to know that not all of it is…well…pleasant."

"Because the rest of this is a sunny summer holiday," Ailsa muttered.

"Just tell us, Michael," Sophie said.

"Very well. A few days ago, Suri and I went to the Garden."

"I thought angels couldn't go to the Garden?" Lucas said, his eyes lighting again with hope.

"We can't, when everything's as it should be," Michael answered. "But obviously, it isn't."

"So you went to ask the other aeons about Sophie? Whether they really need her back or not?"

"Actually, no. We went to ask them about Esther."

"About me?" Esther said, clearly startled. "Why?"

"Because you'd been brought to our attention," Suri told her.

"Who by?"

"Actually, we still don't quite know. We'd been watching what was happening down here, through Sophie's old scrying-glass." She pulled the mirror out of her pocket and handed it to Esther. It showed nothing at the moment but billows of charcoal cloud. "And then one day it showed you to us. We saw Theletos contact you through that priest in the confessional, and realized that you'd come through the Change with your memories intact. We wanted to know why. We got the idea that you might be connected to Sophie – I mean, there is a resemblance, and Theletos was able to bypass the staves to speak to you. Anyway, we thought the other aeons might know something about it."

"Did they?" Sophie asked impatiently.

"We don't know. They weren't there."

Sophie took a moment to absorb this. "Where have they gone?"

"We don't know that either. But no doubt, it has something to do with the Change."

"So then how did you manage to learn anything, then?" Lucas asked.

"We went to Sophia's Dominion," Suri answered, her eyes on Sophie's, "and tore time."

"Eh, what?" Ailsa asked.

"It's a way of looking in to the past," Michael explained.

The blood had drained from Sophie's face. "You saw how I did it," she said in a low, wavering voice. "How I made myself human."

"More or less," Suri answered, looking uncomfortably from Sophie to Esther and back again. "Okay, look, there's no easy way to say this, so I'll just say it: you copied Esther's soul, and used the copy as your own."

"What!" Sophie cried, looking wildly at Esther, who was equally shocked. "How is that possible?"

"How is any of this possible?" Michael answered tiredly. "Sophia, there's no question about it: we watched you take a soul from the Well, copy it, put one version back, and then go off with the other. The only logical conclusion is that you used it to become human."

"But where did I get my body?"

"That's still anyone's guess."

"And how do you know the soul was Esther's?" Angus asked.

"Because we have the same aura," Esther said quietly, before anyone else could argue. "And the same birthday. And we look similar. And as for the body – " she drew a deep breath, kept her eyes firmly on her hands " – I think maybe I can explain that, too. I had a twin, who died when we were born."

"But you're from Dublin, and I was found in London," Sophie said plaintively, after a moment of stunned silence.

"Aye," Esther answered, "but I was born in London. My mam had me before she met my dad – not my real dad, but the one I grew up with. She was in London, trying for an actress. Well, she was before my sister and I came along. We were born fast. There was no time to get to a doctor or anyone else, not till afterward. Then, when she knew my sister was gone, she left her at a church door."

"St. Patrick's, in Soho," Sophie said bleakly.

"She hoped they'd give her a proper Catholic burial," Esther replied.

"Jesus H. Christ!" Ailsa said.

In the ensuing, leaden silence, Lucas wrapped a protective arm around Sophie and gave Esther a murderous look. Finally, Angus said, "Please tell me that's the end of the Earth-shattering revelations."

Suri and Michael exchanged an uncomfortable look. "What else?" Sophie asked grimly.

"Well," Suri said reluctantly, "there was one other thing we saw when we tore time. When you turned human, it did something to Theletos."

"What kind of something?"

"It's hard to say. You went off with the soul, and a while later we saw him looking for you, and he looked bad. Sick."

"I don't understand," Sophie said.

"How can you not understand?" Michael snapped. "Haven't you seen him cough blood?"

"Yes," Sophie said softly.

"You and he are fundamentally joined, Sophia," Michael continued harshly. "When you made yourself human, you changed him, too. So if you're doomed to die after eighteen years, it looks like he is, too."

"I never meant to hurt him," Sophie wavered.

288

"But you did," Michael said, his eyes merciless. "And now he's missing."

"Don't you blame her for that!" Ailsa said angrily. "A couple of weeks ago Rive still wanted to get Sophie back to the Garden. Obviously it's the daevas who've screwed him up, not whatever Sophie did sixteen lifetimes ago."

"Unless he didn't know about it until the daevas told him."

"It's been thousands of years since it happened," Angus said. "And he knew Sophie disappeared around the time he got sick. Surely he'd have worked it out long ago."

"Why, when he trusted her implicitly?" Michael asked. "I'd bet he was ignorant until the daevas told him the truth."

Sophie lowered her head, her shoulders shaking. Lucas held her tighter, and Suri laid a gentle hand on her back, saying, "That's enough, Michael." After a long, fraught silence, she continued, "There's something wrong with all of this. Or at least, there has to be more to it than Theletos suddenly learning the truth. I mean, even if the reason he's sick is because she messed with their soul, I can't see why he'd send us all to Hell in a hand-basket over it. He'd know that she did it for a good reason."

"Whether he did or not," Lucas said, "the one sure thing is that he didn't want Esther to come here and deliver his message."

"So clearly, the daevas corrupted him," Angus said. "I mean, why else would he try to stop Esther coming here?" Michael and Suri exchanged a look. "What? *Is* there another reason?"

"Go on," Sam said, his eyes bright with glee. "Enlighten them."

"It's not for us to tell," Michael said, glancing at Esther, whose face burned.

"To tell what?" Ailsa asked, giving her a pointed look.

"I – I can't…" Esther said, turning her face to the shadows.

Rolling his eyes, Sam said, "Well I can. Before he took her to the ferry, we saw Theletos snogging our good little Catholic girl. Only after seeing that, I'm not sure how good she really is. I mean, that was *seriously* sexy when you – "

"Enough!" Michael growled, as Esther dropped her face into her hands.

"Don't be embarrassed, honey," Ailsa said, patting Esther's shoulder consolingly. "I mean, like any of us wouldn't have jumped at the chance to make out with *that!*"

"Thank you, Ailsa," Michael said irritably. "The point is, Rive's lack of enthusiasm for Esther coming here and delivering his message might have a personal, rather than a cosmic explanation. Thoughts, Esther?"

"I really have no idea," Esther said, still flushed and miserable.

"All right," Suri said, "let's stop torturing the poor girl, since this is all conjecture at the moment. Anyway, you still need to hear the rest."

"There's more?" Sophie asked.

"Yep. We were still watching in the scrying-glass when Theletos took Esther to the ferry. Turns out, he didn't leave after he'd dropped her off."

"Where did he go?" Esther asked anxiously.

"He paid a fisherman to bring him here."

"What!" Lucas cried. "He's in Ardnasheen?"

"We don't actually know that," Michael answered. "After we saw him make the deal with the fisherman, we came here as fast as we could."

"But why would he come here secretly?" Esther asked.

"We don't know that he did," Ailsa pointed out. "No one's seen him – or so I assume." She directed this at Esther.

"I haven't seen him since Mallaig," Esther informed her.

"Right. So maybe he didn't make it here after all."

"Maybe the Sword of Justice caught up with him," Lucas said.

"We should look for him," Angus said.

Michael shook his head. "We'd never find him. He'll find us when he wants to talk. If he wants to talk."

There was another fraught silence, which Sam finally broke. "So none of you are going to point out the elephant in the room?"

"I'm guessing you are," Ailsa said coldly.

Sam smiled blandly. "Without Theletos, how are we going to send Sophie back to the Garden?"

Lucas bristled. "Why should she go back at all? Theletos isn't exactly making a case for it, and from what Suri and Michael say, everything in the Garden has changed anyway."

"Why shouldn't Sophia be the one to remedy that?" Michael said.

"Why are you so determined to get rid of her?"

"This is hardly about getting rid of her," Michael retorted. "It's about restoring her to her rightful place."

"Theletos made Sophie promise to go back with *him*. He's not here. End of story."

"Midsummer is only a few days away! We don't have time to sit around debating this. We need to find a way to get Sophia and Theletos back to the Garden, and do it quickly!"

As Michael and Lucas glared at each other, Sophie said in a thin, hard voice, "Isn't anybody going to ask what I think?" They all looked at her rather sheepishly, and she produced a small book from her pocket – the leather-bound notebook that Esther had given her. "*The Book of Sorrows,*" she said, tossing it into the centre of the circle. "My testimony to the prophet Enoch, just before I left the Garden to come to Earth."

The angels looked stunned – even Sam. "Where did you get that?" Suri asked.

"From Esther," Sophie answered.

"And where on Earth did Esther get it?" Michael demanded, giving her an accusatory look.

"Belfast," Esther told him. "Morag – the Morrigan – gave it

to me. I didn't say so earlier because...well, because it's Sophie's book. I thought it should be up to her."

Michael frowned, but his voice was even when he asked, "Did the Morrigan tell you why she wanted Sophie to have it?"

"She only said to heed the prophecy."

"Which is what, exactly?" Angus asked.

Sophie picked up the book and flipped to a marked page near the end. "'When the Morningstar regains the Heavens, the Balance will be restored.'" She looked up at the others. "'Lucifer' means 'Morningstar.' This prophecy is the reason I copied the soul, and came to Earth, and all the rest."

"Not to get into Lucifer's pants, you understand," Sam muttered.

"You are vile," Ailsa told him.

"Only vile? I should work harder."

"The thing is, Sophie," Angus said, looking uncomfortable, "even as an aeon, pardoning and reinstating Lucifer wouldn't really have been in your jurisdiction, would it? Especially since you were involved in his...ah...downfall."

"That's why I had to put it right."

"But how were you planning to do it?" Ailsa asked.

"Tell us!" Sam said. "The suspense is killing me."

Sophie glared at him, and then she turned to Lucas. She drew a deep breath and said, "By giving him my soul."

"Sweet, isn't it?" Sam smirked in the shocked silence. "Though one could argue that it isn't actually Sophie's soul to give, seeing as it's actually Esther's...although I suppose it's irrelevant, since Lucifer didn't want it anyway."

"Everything has changed, Sam," Sophie snapped.

"I'm willing to bet that that hasn't." He looked pointedly at Lucas, who glowered back.

"Sophie, I don't want to argue with you," Suri said, "but isn't it possible that you were mistaken about Lucifer restoring the Balance? Especially since Theletos was specifically sent here to bring you back to the Garden?"

"Anything's possible," Sophie conceded. "But I know that I wouldn't have done the things I did to get here if I wasn't sure that they were absolutely necessary."

"You can't be meant to give away your soul and go back to the Garden," Lucas said.

"Unless the Garden has some previously unknown use for Revenants," Sam suggested.

"Will you shut up!" Suri snapped.

"Lucas is right, though," Angus said. "It can't go both ways."

"Precisely," Michael answered, "and the *Book of Sorrows* is hearsay, while Theletos had his orders straight from the Keeper."

"Michael, you do know that you're a sanctimonious arse?" Ailsa said, prompting a chortle from Sam. "And even with all your books and prophecies and secret meetings with God, I still don't get why it's all up to Sophie to save the world. I mean – and don't take this the wrong way, Sophie – what's so great about her? It wasn't like she was head aeon or anything, right? And we've already agreed that she wasn't the only one to mess up, so why does she have to take the fall for everyone?"

"Maybe we've been looking at this the wrong way," Sophie said in the ensuing silence. "Maybe it isn't about transgressions and punishment at all." She looked up, her eyes clear but sad. "I'm the one who made the world. So maybe that makes me the only one who can save it."

"But by going to the Garden?" Lucas pleaded. "The other aeons have deserted it, Theletos has changed his story – it's all wrong. It could be a trap – "

"Or it could just be too late," Sam interrupted. "What say we make the most of our last few days on Earth. Eat, drink, be merry, get married – if you last long enough." He smiled at Sophie, who glared back.

"All hilarity aside," Angus said dryly, "we do need a plan. I mean for the immediate future. We can't very well stay here. After what happened with the Prophet at my place this afternoon, Ardnasheen isn't safe."

"But where will we go?" Ailsa asked. "We don't even know what we're meant to do next."

"Yes, we do," Sophie said, looking at Esther. "We're meant to go to Edinburgh. My mother painted it, Esther keeps dreaming about it...whatever's going to happen, it's going to happen there."

"How can you know that?" Michael argued.

"Wait," Esther said. She opened her bag, took out the map, and spread it on the floor in front of them. "Morag gave me this as well as the book. She told me to use it if I was in need of direction. At first I didn't think much of it – I mean, it doesn't even show any roads. But as I've travelled, I've realized that the places where these blue lines intersect have all been important in some way." She pointed out Troon and Glasgow and Blackwood and Ardnasheen. There was another large convergence on Edinburgh.

"But what do they mean?" Ailsa asked.

Angus's eyes lit with excitement. "They're ley-lines!"

"What?"

He sat back and explained, "In the twenties, an amateur archaeologist called Alfred Watkins discovered that a number of places of historical and geographical interest in Britain were aligned. You know, monuments and standing stones and river fords and things. He thought they were ancient roadways, and their alignment had to do with Neolithic navigation and..." He trailed off, taking in the others' glazed looks. "Ah, sorry – that's all a bit tangential. The point is, later on people added to his theory, with the idea that the ley-lines marked spiritual and mystical alignments as well. And Edinburgh is a hotspot, as far as ley-lines go."

"I wonder if we can find the Morrigan there," Sophie said. "In the coffee shop, or maybe the cavern under the Hermitage…"

"There's only one way to know."

"Yes," Michael said gloomily, "if we can figure out how to get there without alerting that Prophet and her spies."

"I told you," Sam said, "I can get you there. For a price, of course…"

"Actually," Suri said, "I have a better idea. I don't suppose any of you know what happened to Freyja's falcon cloak?"

The Wine Cellar

From the shadows of the next vault, Rive watched them leave.

You are stalling, Abaddon's voice sounded in his mind.

I don't know how I'm meant to do this when I can't lie, Rive answered.

I grant you a dispensation, Abaddon said. *Though of course, you'll still be unable to lie to* me.

Wonderful.

Get going, Theletos. Or I'll tell the Cailleach exactly where to find Esther.

Rive shut his eyes for a moment, wishing that he could shut out Abaddon's voice as easily. *All right,* he said. *I'm going.*

The Tower

"This is a bloody nightmare," Sophie said from Lucas's writing desk, where she was attempting to compose a letter to her parents explaining why they would find her bed empty in the morning. Lucas had offered to do it, but she'd insisted that it had to come from her, and so he'd borrowed Esther's invisibility mantle and gone looking for Freyja's cloak, while she wrote.

"I'd be worried about you if it wasn't," Ailsa answered from the settee. She and Esther were sorting through a pile of Sophie's clothes to find something for Suri to wear that wouldn't stand out in the changed Edinburgh – no easy task, as Suri seemed determined to veto everything. "Still, I don't envy you," she said, taking a couple of items to the bathroom, where Suri was changing, and handing them in. On the way back she called upstairs, where Sam and Michael were trying on clothes of Lucas's. "How's it going, gentlemen?"

"Everything's too big," Michael complained.

"And it smells like Lucifer," Sam added.

"At least you don't look like a nineteen-forties housewife," Suri said, emerging from the bathroom in a tailored skirt and blouse, her dreadlocks wilder than ever.

"Nor do you," Ailsa said, "with that hairdo. Maybe if you wore a hat?"

"Just cut it off," Michael said, coming downstairs in a neat grey suit. It was slightly too big, but he still pulled it off. "It was tremendously liberating when I did it."

"No freakin' way!" Suri said, throwing herself into an armchair.

"I think you look lovely," Angus said, looking up from the *Book of Sorrows*. Suri glared at him, and he shrugged, returning to the book.

A few moments later, the upstairs door opened. Even though the angels had charmed the doors and windows to appear dark and empty, and to open only for one of their group, they all froze, looking up at the sleeping loft. But it was Lucas who appeared on the stairs, carrying what looked like an enormous bird.

"I'm guessing this is it," he said, shaking it out as he reached the ground floor. It unfurled into a long, feathered mantle. He laid it on the settee, and it shook itself, fluffing up like an angry bird.

"Yep, that's it," Suri said distastefully. "And you'd better be polite to it, or it'll dump us in the ocean or something."

"No," Lucas said, "it owes me one for rescuing it from a wardrobe full of mink stoles and moth balls."

"It's not big on gratitude," Suri told him. "I guess it's a Viking thing."

"Viking or not, it gives me the creeps," Ailsa commented.

"As well it should," Angus said. "From my recollection, it has a distinct mind of its own."

"It's also our best bet for getting out of here under the radar," Suri said, smoothing the cloak's feathers. "What else do we need?"

"Weapons," Michael said. "Preferably Sacred ones."

"Don't angels have swords?" Angus asked.

"Not for us. For you."

"Well I've still got the dagger," Sophie said from the desk.

"That's a start," Michael said. "Anything else?"

Lucas crossed to the painting of the angel slaying the sea monster and opened the compartment hidden behind it. He took out a short sword and a couple of timeworn daggers. "I'm afraid this is it," he said.

Michael sighed. "Hopefully we'll be able to liberate a few more from the museums in Edinburgh. So, are we ready?"

"I guess we are," Sophie said, propping her letter on the dining table. She didn't look ready at all. Lucas put his arms around her, and she leaned into him.

"Better go get Sam," Ailsa said to Michael. "He's probably still looking for an outfit that compliments his colouring."

Michael called for Sam, and when he didn't answer, he went upstairs. When he appeared again at the top of the stairs, his face was white. "He's gone!"

"Where would he go?" Lucas asked. And then he, too went white. "Oh no – " he said and bounded up the stairs. The next moment, they heard him cursing.

"What is it?" Esther asked anxiously.

Lucas came back down the stairs, with Michael behind him.

"That mantle you lent me," he said tiredly. "I put it down when I came in the door, and now it's gone."

"You mean Sam is out there now, somewhere, invisible?" Ailsa asked anxiously.

"That appears to be the case," Michael said.

"That really isn't good," Suri said.

"No, it isn't. So I suggest we get out of here before he has a chance to – "

The downstairs door rattled violently, interrupting him. Lucas looked out the window and then turned back, grim-faced. "It's the Prophet, and a number of her followers."

"Then we have to go. Now." Michael snatched up the feathered cloak, which puffed again in annoyance.

The downstairs door crashed open, and heavy footfalls sounded on the stairs. "Come on," Lucas said, taking the stairs to the sleeping loft two at a time.

"Where?" Suri asked, tying the doorknobs together with a belt she'd rejected earlier.

"The roof," he answered tersely, and they all followed. Sophie snatched up her old satchel from the bed as they passed through the room, hoping that all of her belongings were still in it.

Lucas locked the bedroom door behind them, and then led them on a twisting path through the upstairs corridors. Once or twice they spotted maids or guests, but no one who knew them well enough to question them. Finally, they climbed a narrow flight of stone steps, and Lucas pushed open the door at the top. They emerged in a rush onto a crenelated square of roof and then stopped short. The Prophet was standing there, with Sam by her side and an entourage of drifting black wraiths flanking them.

"Really, Lucifer, that was far too easy," Sam said with a feral grin.

"It didn't take long for you to show your colours, did it?" Lucas commented.

"It took long enough. If I'd had to listen to one more moment of your angst-ridden revelations, I'd have gouged my eyes out."

"No one asked you to stay," Sophie pointed out.

"Mouthing off as usual, when you should be begging for your life."

"If you wanted to kill me, you'd have done it already."

His smile flattened. "No one wants to kill you. In fact, we've all been most carefully instructed not to harm a hair on your head. But your friends – well, I can't really speak to their security. If you agree to come with us now, though, I'm sure I can convince the powers that be to spare them." His eyes fell on Esther, and she shrank back. "Even the little murderess."

"And this, Suriel, is why I wanted to leave him in the cemetery," Michael muttered.

"Too late now," Sam answered cheerfully. "Sophia? Shall we?" He offered her his hand, which she regarded with disgust.

"Don't even think about it, Sophia," Michael said.

Sam's smile twisted into a scoff. "Do you actually think you can fight us and win?" The Cailleach moved closer to him, and her floating minions seemed to grow in stature.

Michael's gaze remained steady and calm. "I don't intend to fight you," he said. Sam's smile faltered for a moment in confusion, then Michael called, "Skanda!"

There was a raucous squawk in reply, and then, in a flurry of brilliant feathers, Michael's peacock alighted on the wall beside them.

"Seriously?" Ailsa groaned. "That's your plan?"

"I believe your skills might be of service here, Skanda," Michael said to the bird, ignoring Ailsa. It cocked its head, fixing him with one beady eye, and then, in the space of a blink, it was no longer a bird but a young Asian man dressed in bright red trousers and a golden crown, his bare chest crossed with golden straps threaded with knives. In one hand he held a bright spear, in the other, a mace.

"Michael," he said, his voice deep and rippling and musical. "How may I be of service?"

"Hold them off," Michael said, pointing at the Prophet and her wraiths, "until we can get away."

"Gladly," Skanda said with an anticipatory grin. He took a step toward the Prophet, whirling his mace and his spear until they were blurs of gilded light.

"Our cue," Michael said and flung the cloak wide. Miraculously, it encompassed them all. "Please take us to Edinburgh. The Hermitage." They clung together as the cloak lifted them with a sickening lurch. Then they were in the air, the rooftop they'd left a swarm of battling figures.

From a shadowed corner of the roof, Rive watched them go.

CHAPTER 11

20 JUNE
EDINBURGH

They landed in the middle of a wet stand of shrubbery. The night sky was overcast, and it was difficult to see anything at all. They struggled free of the waterlogged feathers and then Michael said, "Is everyone all right?"

"I think I'm seasick," Ailsa groaned. "And probably hypothermic – "

"Everyone's conscious and no one's broken anything?" Michael interrupted impatiently. When they'd all accounted for themselves, he said, "Then we're doing well enough. Sophie and Angus, do you think you can locate the Morrigan's cavern?"

"It's easy enough if we can find the Tollhouse," Angus said. "But with no light, I don't know how we're going to do that."

"That's easy to fix," Suri said. She bent and picked up something off the ground. The next moment she was holding an electric torch, which illuminated her smile. "Glad to see we can still manipulate matter."

"We still don't know which way to go," Ailsa pointed out.

"The water," Sophie said. "If we can find the burn, then we only have to follow it upstream to get to the Tollhouse. Listen for it." They all fell silent, straining to hear the running water amidst the rush of rain in the trees.

At last, Michael said, "This way. Follow me." He wadded up the falcon cloak under his arm and walked off briskly.

The others huddled close to him, following him through the underbrush and stands of rhododendron, until the light of Suri's torch fell on the path. By then, the sound of the burn was clear. They followed the path upstream until at last, a light showed through the trees. Drawing closer, they saw that it was a light over the back door of the Tollhouse.

"I thought you said the house was deserted," Esther said.

"It was," Angus answered, "before the Change."

"It doesn't matter," Suri said. "Anyone living there will be asleep this time of night – or rather, morning. So where is this cavern?"

"It was under the well, which was near the foot of the cloutie tree," Sophie told her, peering into the overgrown yard. The gate with the triskelion on the stone posts was still there, as was the cloutie tree, its branches laden with scraps of fabric as they had been before the Change. Sophie pushed through the gate, and the others followed her to the tree. She knelt on the ground, cleared the long grass away from a small ring of stones. She remembered the sweet, wild smell of the water in the well below, like crushed fern and mint. Now, though, she smelled nothing but stone and dust.

"It's dry," she said worriedly.

"I think I'd rather climb into a dry well than a wet one," Ailsa observed.

"But the water was sacred. This is all wrong. Suri, can you shine the light down here?"

Suri angled the beam of the torch into the well. It showed a flight of cracked and flaking stone steps littered with dust and dry leaves, descending into darkness.

"I don't much like the look of that," Angus said.

"If something's happened to the Morrigan, we need to know," Sophie said resolutely. "I'm going down."

"No," Lucas said, "let me go first. In case there's something… unexpected."

"We'll both go," she said, pulling Carnwennan out of her waistband.

"Here," Suri said, "take the torch."

She gave it to Lucas, who stepped into the hole first and started down the staircase, with Sophie close behind. Their footsteps echoed eerily in the silence as they wound down and down, with no end in sight. At last, though, they reached the bottom. Lucas offered a hand to Sophie, and she took it gratefully as they walked into cavern.

It was still recognisable as the place where she and Angus had spoken to the Morrigan, but it was as if it had been empty for decades. The table and shelves and stone dresser were still there, but they were covered in a thick layer of dust, the bottles and pots that the shelves had held toppled and broken, as if someone had swept a violent hand across them. The hearth held only a scatter of ashes and a swag of cobwebs. The stream that had run through the middle of the room was no more than a dry, stony bed.

"It's like she was never here," Sophie said.

"I suppose it makes sense, though," Lucas answered. "None of the other sacred places have escaped the daevas' influence."

"But this place is different. It seemed like it was her home base. We know she's alive and well, so why would she leave it?"

Lucas shook his head. "At any rate, it's a dry place to spend the night. Let's get the others."

They called up the stairwell, and a few minutes later their friends joined them. "What now?" Angus asked, pushing a broken pot with his toe.

"Now," Michael said, "you humans need to sleep. Suri and I will go see what we can find out about the state of things here and whether the Morrigan is around. If she isn't, we'll deal with it tomorrow. Lucas, you keep watch."

"I'd rather look for the Morrigan," Lucas said.

"I'm aware of that. But Sophia needs to rest, and she would never let you go without her. Right, Sophia?"

"You know me too well," Sophie answered.

"Very well," Lucas said.

Michael nodded. "We'll see you in the morning."

*

Esther lay staring at the ceiling of the cavern, as she had for hours. Angus had managed to coax a fire from the ashes in the fireplace, and it had warmed the room, but still, Esther felt cold, as if her blood couldn't reach her limbs. Her pulse had been sluggish and jagged since they'd left Ardnasheen, but there was nothing to be done about it: the digoxin she thought she'd pocketed before their hurried departure wasn't anywhere to be found. They surely would have helped now, but she tried not to dwell on it. She would find Rive and bring him to the others if it was the last thing she did.

She sat up and looked around. The other humans were long since asleep, and even Lucas had sunk into a still, trancelike state, tucked into a corner with Sophie's head in his lap. Esther stood up, pulling her coat around her. She picked her way among the sleeping bodies, finally reaching the staircase. She tiptoed up the stairs and emerged into the garden, still and ethereal in the light of the swelling dawn. Esther stood for a moment breathing in the sweet, cool air, willing her heart to be strong enough for her task. She didn't know where to look for Rive, but she felt deep down that he wasn't far away.

Nevertheless, she let out a yelp of surprise when she turned from closing the garden gate to find him standing there, gazing at her steadily with his sea-blue eyes. She knew that she should yell, or drag him down into the cavern, or demand that he tell her what he could possibly mean by surprising her like this, or maybe all three.

Instead she asked, "What are you doing here?"

"Bringing you this," he said. On the palm of his extended hand was a small, brown glass bottle.

"What is it?"

"What do you think? Now take them, and swallow two right now – your lips are purple."

With a trembling hand, Esther reached out and took the bottle. She shook out two of the tablets and swallowed them. Though they couldn't possibly have had time to work, just knowing that they would made her feel steadier. She offered him the bottle back, but he shook his head, with a sad, ironic smile.

"What would I want with those?"

"I don't know," she said. "I just…it seems strange you'd give them to me, after everything…"

His look took on a shade of exasperation. "Do you think a philosophical disagreement would make me withhold medicine you need so desperately?"

"No. But I do find it strange that you'd follow me all the way to Edinburgh just to give me a bottle of tablets."

"You think I followed you?"

"I *know* you followed me, at least as far as Ardnasheen. So why not to Edinburgh? Look, Rive, everyone's here: all of your old friends." She gestured to the ring of stones that marked the entrance to the cavern. "You need to come talk to them. Especially to Sophie."

Rive passed a hand across his face, and for a moment, when he dropped it, he looked immeasurably old. His eyes rested on her, heavy as river-stones. "I do need to talk to Sophie. But first I want to talk to you. Walk with me?"

Esther knew that she should refuse – that she should insist that he come and speak to the others. Instead, she nodded. Rive turned toward the road, and she fell into step beside him.

They came out of the park and turned right. Now she could see sandstone houses and tenements rising up against the brightening sky. It wasn't the skyline she remembered from her dreams, but then, she doubted they were in the same part of the city. It was a peaceful, beautiful morning, but all Esther could feel was trepidation.

Rive chewed his lip, looking at the ground. At last, he took a deep breath and said, "Esther, I'm sorry."

Her cheeks flamed. "You've said that already."

"No – I mean I'm sorry for trying to stop you giving Sophie the message."

Esther stopped in her tracks. "*What?*"

"You heard me. And it still stands, what I told you in the confessional. I need to get Sophie to come with me."

"You lied to me?" she asked incredulously.

"No," he answered. "I believed what I was saying when I said it, but I've since come to see that I was wrong. I was wrong to send you off alone to Ardnasheen, too. I should have gone with you, even if I thought you were misguided. I know there's no way that I can make it up to you, but I needed you to know that I'm sorry."

She waved the words aside. "You're honestly telling me that you and Sophie are going back to the Garden?"

"Yes," he said, so low that she barely heard it.

Esther's eyes filled with furious tears. "Then why did you kiss me?"

"Because what I want is very different from what I can have."

Esther waited for him to say something more, but he only looked at her, silent and miserable. She turned and began to walk back the way she had come.

"Esther, wait!" he cried, the anguish of it plangent, almost palpable. She stopped, hating herself for it, and equally unable to resist him. He caught up to her. "You have to know that this isn't what I would choose, if the choice were mine."

Esther turned to face him. "Does it matter?"

"It matters to me."

"All right, Rive," Esther said, sighing. "For what it's worth, I accept your apology. Now go talk to Sophie."

"I would," he said, "if I thought I'd get within ten feet of her. But I very much doubt Lucifer will allow that."

"That really isn't my problem."

"I know it's not," he replied. "And if I thought there was any way around it, I wouldn't ask you."

"Ask me what?" Esther asked warily.

"To help me see her – on her own."

"I don't think she'll agree to that."

"Which is why she can't know that's what's happening."

"You want me to lie to her?" Esther asked incredulously. "How can you ask me that?"

"Because we're out of time. Sophie and I need to go back to the Garden now, if there's to be any hope of stopping the daevas."

Esther felt sick, and if she were honest with herself, it wasn't really at the thought of lying to Sophie. It was because Rive was asking her to be the instrument of his leaving her. She wanted to scream, to cry, to beat her hands against him, but she didn't. What point was there, when they would only have a few days together even if they both left their responsibilities and ran? What was at stake dwarfed her pain, and his.

Stay true to yourself – the old man's words echoed like a refrain, and there had only ever been one purpose to this journey. From what seemed very far away, Esther heard her own voice asking, "What's the plan?"

Rive let out a long breath and then handed her a scrap of paper. There was an address written on it. "Bring her here. I'll be waiting."

Esther looked at the brightening sky and then at Rive, whose eyes were brighter still. "I can't promise anything," she said at last. "But I'll try."

THE MORRIGAN'S CAVERN

The others had awakened by the time Esther returned to the cavern, and they sat around the Morrigan's table, eating rolls with jam. "Where were you?" Suri demanded. "We were worried!"

"I couldn't sleep," Esther said, swallowing the looming tears. "I went for a walk."

"With all of your things?" Lucas asked, eyeing the carpetbag in her hands.

"I…thought I might find breakfast. That I might need money."

"Michael brought breakfast," Ailsa said, pushing the bag of rolls and jar of jam toward her.

"Thanks," Esther said, sitting down beside her, though she still felt sick. Then, to deflect attention from the fact that she wasn't eating: "What about the Morrigan? Did you find her?"

Michael sighed. "No. Matrika's coffee shop is currently a drinking den for trolls. There was no sign of the Morrigan at all, though there seem to be an unusually high number of faeries about."

"Maybe she's still in Belfast."

"Maybe," Michael said. "We'll carry on without her, if we have to. But first, we'll try to contact her."

"I'm guessing you don't mean on a telephone," Ailsa said, spreading jam on a roll and putting it in Esther's hand.

"No," Michael answered. "When I didn't find her on Victoria Street, I stopped in at the central library to refresh my memory on her parameters. I'd forgotten this, but being a goddess of life and death, she frequents battlefields."

"Terrific," Ailsa grumbled. "Where are we going to find a battlefield in the middle of a city?"

"Actually," Angus said, "most of this city has been a battlefield at one time or another."

"Exactly," Michael replied. "But the area around the castle has seen more than its fair share of strife. It would be a good place to begin."

"You still haven't told us *how* we're meant to call her," Lucas said.

"We bring her offerings," Michael told him.

"What kind of offerings?" Sophie asked dubiously.

"Well, she's fond of ale, crows' feathers, wine, raw meat and blood – "

"Blood!" Ailsa cried. "Whose blood? And how much?"

"I couldn't find anything specific about that," Michael admitted. "But I imagine a pricked finger would do."

"We didn't have to do weird spells last time we needed her help."

"The world wasn't ending last time we needed her help."

"So where are we going to get all of that stuff?" Angus asked.

"Once everyone's eaten, we're going to split up into groups and go looking for it," Michael said.

"And then?" Lucas asked.

"Then we reconvene at the castle and call her."

"The castle is huge," Angus said, "and generally full of tourists. Where can we go that no one will notice us doing strange things with beer and raw meat?"

"Here," Michael said, taking a folded page from his pocket. It looked like it had been torn from a book. He opened it, revealing a plan of the castle and grounds, and pointed to a small rectangle. "St. Margaret's chapel. It's small, so it should be easy to secure."

"Do you really think there's ever been a battle in a chapel?" Ailsa asked.

"Actually," Angus answered, "when the Earl of Moray captured the castle in 1314, the chapel was the only building that wasn't completely destroyed. When Robert the Bruce was on his deathbed he insisted that it be repaired because…" He trailed off, realizing that everyone was staring at him with various degrees of incredulity. "Anyway, the point is, I think it'll be all right," he said. "Who's bringing what?"

"I'll take ale and wine," Ailsa said. "I am a barmaid, after all."

"I'll go with you," Angus said.

"And me," Suri added. "Best to have an angel in each group."

"I can buy meat," Sophie offered.

"I'll join you," Lucas said.

"Crows' feathers it is," Michael sighed. "Esther, will you accompany me? Or do you prefer to go shopping?"

"Feathers are fine," she said distractedly.

"Very well, then," Michael said, "let's go."

*

Sophie and Lucas were the first to arrive at the chapel. Sophie had bought a cheap handbag along with two pounds of beef, so that she could carry it inconspicuously. They waited for a while outside of the building, trying to look interested in its architecture, but in the end it was only a stone rectangle with a few windows and a door.

"Let's look inside," Lucas said.

They stepped into the little church. While it didn't look like much from the outside, the inside was quite pretty. Simple wooden benches formed two lines in front of the altar, which stood in an apse surrounded by a decorative arch. Five small, arched, stained-glass windows cast jewel tones on the walls and floor.

There was another young couple standing under the arch, talking. As Sophie listened, it became clear that they were discussing their upcoming wedding. "I just don't think it's big enough," the man said, gesturing to the room.

"But I've wanted to be married in this chapel since I was a little girl," the woman argued. "It's only your mother who wants a big wedding, anyway!"

The man gave Sophie and Lucas an embarrassed glance before guiding his still-disputing fiancée out the door. Lucas watched them go, and then he said to Sophie, "That should be us."

Sophie laughed ruefully. "What, fighting about the future in-laws?" She walked to one of the windows and looked through the coloured chips of glass at a distorted world. She knew that if she looked at Lucas, the laugh would turn to tears.

"I meant that that should be us planning our lives – not the end of the world."

"I know what you meant. I just don't know what to do about it."

"Maybe the Morrigan can help."

"I hope so…"

Before Lucas could reply, Ailsa, Angus and Suri came in with a rattling satchel. "I hope the Morrigan likes rot-gut red," Suri said, putting the bag down on one of the benches, "because that's all we could afford with the money Michael gave us."

"I'm sure it doesn't matter," Sophie said distractedly.

"At least the ale should be decent," Angus said. "No sign of Michael and Esther?"

"Right here," Michael said, coming in with Esther at his heels. He stuck a sign to the door that read "Closed For Repairs", and then shut it, pulled a padlock from the air, and locked it.

"Won't somebody catch on?" Ailsa asked.

"Hopefully we won't need very long."

"Okay," Angus said, "so what do we do with all of this stuff?"

"Burning generally does the trick when it comes to pagan offerings," Suri said.

"Are you serious?" Ailsa demanded. "Have you ever smelled burning feathers?"

"A necessary evil."

"Never mind getting beer to burn…"

"We can but try," Michael said, taking an armful of sticks out of the knapsack he'd acquired. He arranged them on the stone floor, then snapped his fingers and a flame sprang up in their midst. "Esther?" he said. She reached into her coat pockets and brought out two handfuls of black feathers, then dropped them onto the fire. The smoke that rose from them did indeed smell awful.

"Now, the meat," Michael said, unperturbed by the others' gasping and coughing. Sophie dropped the beef onto the smoking mass, where it hissed for a moment and then, improbably, sprang into flame. "Suriel?"

Suri opened the bottles of wine and ale, and poured a little of each onto the meat. The smell rising from the pyre was now all but intolerable, but Michael remained stoic, saying, "And now, the blood."

"I'll do it," Lucas said.

"I believe it should be human blood."

Before Lucas could protest, Sophie pulled Carnwennan from her waistband, nicked her finger, and let it drip onto the fire. Black smoke began to pour from it, so thick that within moments, none of them could see a foot in front of them. And then they heard a loud, croaking call. Abruptly, the smoke coalesced, condensing until it became a large black bird. A raven. It stood on the floor where the fire had been, eyeing them curiously, and then let out another raucous croak.

"Ahh…I'm guessing that's not what we were aiming for?" Ailsa said, inching away from the bird.

"Actually, it may well be," Angus said. "Traditionally, the Morrigan could take the form of a raven. I guess that's what the black feathers were for."

"Couldn't you have told us this before we used the black feathers?"

"Doing my best, Ailsa."

"The Morrigan's the Morrigan," Michael said in a placatory tone. Then, crouching down to meet the raven's eyes, he asked, "Morrigan, could you perhaps take human form?"

The raven only stared back at him.

"Hang on," Sophie said as the others began to exchange hopeless looks, "belief is what gives deities their power, right? So why not their shape?"

"We already believe in the Morrigan," Suri said.

"I know, but right now we're all thinking 'bird.' Maybe we should try picturing her as a human…or as close to human as she gets."

"Anything's worth a try," Michael said. "Which form of her should we picture?"

"Matrika's is the one we knew best," Sophie answered. "So…go."

They all fell silent, concentrating on the black bird, and their memories of Matrika, if they had them. Gradually the raven's shape began to change, stretching and heaving until it was no longer a bird, but a middle-aged woman with dark skin and green eyes and long, black hair threaded with white. She wore an emerald sari, with a faded denim jacket on top.

"Matrika!" Sophie cried, throwing her arms around the woman, who hugged her back. Angus embraced her after Sophie let go, and then Matrika turned to Esther, and with a smile, folded her into her arms.

"You see? I told you you could do it," she said in her soft Irish lilt.

"You're really the same person as Morag?" Esther asked. In response, Matrika smiled, and for a moment, her face shrivelled, creased with lines. "Aye, hen," the old woman quavered, and then she was the middle-aged Indian woman again, smiling serenely at them.

"Whatever form," Michael said, "we're glad you're here. We need your help."

Matrika's smile faded. "I'm not sure how much help I can offer at present…but try me."

"The prophecy from the *Book of Sorrows*," Sophie said. "We can't see a way to follow it, while also keeping my promise to Theletos to return to the Garden."

Matrika sat down on one of the benches. "I have guesses," she said, looking suddenly tired, "but no concrete answers, I'm afraid. Either way, you'll need to ask the right questions. So – who would like to begin?" She looked around at them, pausing for a moment on Esther. Esther's eyes flickered away.

Sophie said, "All right, I'll start. Did my copying a soul and coming to Earth make Theletos sick?"

"Quite probably, though I can't say for certain." Matrika sighed, as if she regretted what she was going to say next. "An aeon's soul isn't like a human's. For one thing, it's made of a different essence. For another, it's intrinsically shared between both members of a syzygy. So, when you incorporated Esther's soul – an alien essence – into yours, you also affected Theletos'."

"But why would it make him ill?" Angus asked. "I mean rather than, say, giving him extra powers?"

Matrika opened her mouth to answer, but Esther spoke first: "Because I'm dying."

The others exchanged shocked glances. Finally, Angus said, "Surely that's not true!"

"Aye, it's true," Esther answered with calm certainty. "I have

314

a heart condition. I always have. The doctors said I probably wouldn't live to be twenty."

"You're telling us this now?" Ailsa cried.

"When was I meant to tell you?" Esther demanded, her voice breaking. "And in the end, what does it matter? I came to you for a purpose. I've fulfilled that purpose."

Esther shrugged, but her eyes caught briefly on Sophie before she looked away. Sophie thought she knew why. Into the queasy silence, she said, "Right, so, Esther's heart condition. Rive's cough. And me? I can't have escaped. I suppose it has to do with the headaches." Lucas put an arm around her, but she didn't relax against him; if anything, she curled further into herself.

"Yes," Matrika said softly.

"What is it? A brain tumour?"

Matrika shook her head. "An aneurysm."

"Which ruptures right around my eighteenth birthday – the same time as Esther's heart gives out, and Rive chokes on his own blood." She raked her hair with her hands. "I suppose I knew the limit of Esther's soul when I copied it?"

"The span that a human soul will cleave to its body is ordained at its inception," Matrika said sadly. "As the mother of souls, you'd have known that. You couldn't have been ignorant of what lay in store for Esther's."

"So that's how I knew to put my time limit into the *Book of Sorrows*."

"Sophie – " Lucas began.

"Did I know that it would doom Rive as well?" Sophie interrupted.

"You wouldn't have wilfully done that!" Suri insisted.

"Wouldn't I?" Sophie asked brokenly. "Not even to save the world?"

"None of this makes sense!" Lucas cried. "Why would Sophie choose a sick soul?"

"Because it was the only one that matched," Sophie answered, "and I was running out of time."

"So you chose to kill yourself to save me? I would never have agreed to that!"

"Which is clearly why I didn't tell you. Reinstating you is the key to restoring the Balance, and since I was the one who messed it up in the fist place...well I guess that's poetic justice."

"And what about Esther?" Angus asked, looking at the girl's drawn, downcast face. "Is anybody thinking about how this effects her?"

"I've told you, it doesn't matter now," Esther replied. "I've done what I was meant to do."

"You can't know that," Michael said. "None of us can. And before any of you write her off," he gave them a hard look, "remember that it was Esther who heard Theletos' call from Hell, Esther whom the daevas speak to in dreams, and Esther who's brought you all back to your senses. She's given us a chance to save the world."

"Exactly," Suri said. "We have a day left. We can't waste it bickering."

"So, what should we do?" Lucas asked.

"I don't know, but it all seems to come down to one basic conundrum: Sophie can't give up her soul to Lucas and also return to the Garden. It's one or the other – unless we're missing something, Matrika?"

"I'm sorry," she said. "If you are, it's beyond me."

After that, they sat in gloomy silence for a long time. Then, abruptly, Michael leapt to his feet. "Wait," he said. "Wait!"

"Don't you keep telling us we don't have time to wait?" Lucas asked bitterly.

Michael gave him an exasperated look. "I meant, wait, we've got it all wrong. The prophecy says, 'When the Morningstar regains the Heavens, the Balance will be restored,' right?"

"Right..."

"And we've all been operating under the assumption that Lucas is the Morningstar in question."

"Of course he is," Sophie said. "It's the meaning of his name."

Michael's eyes were bright with inspiration. "But not his alone. Esther, has anyone ever told you the meaning of your name?"

"No," she answered.

"It comes from the Persian word for star."

Esther looked up at Michael, suddenly wary. "That can't be so unusual."

"And your surname is Madden – awfully like the Irish word *maidin*, which, if I recall my Irish, means morning."

Sophie blanched, Lucas looked stricken, and the others gazed at Esther in shock. "You can't be serious," she said, feeling like the world, once again, was spinning out of control.

"Why not?"

"Well, to begin with," Esther said, "because Lucas is an angel, and I'm a human. If one of us is the Morningstar, it must be him."

"But Lucifer is a fallen angel," Michael corrected, as Lucas glared at him, "and from what I've seen, you're an exemplary human."

"This can't be right," Sophie said. "The whole reason why I came to Earth in the first place was to find Lucas."

"No," Michael argued, "you came to Earth to find the Morningstar. The prophecy says nothing about Lucifer specifically. As far as the *Book of Sorrows* is concerned, Sophia's meeting him a few months ago could as easily have been by coincidence as by design."

"But I wrote that prophecy long before Esther existed," Sophie argued.

"No," Michael said. "The prophecy came through you, but that doesn't mean you were its author – only its vessel.

And as I said to you not long ago, prophecies are slippery fish. Likewise, aeons aren't infallible. You might have thought that you understood the prophecy, and come flying down here to save Lucifer, when it never had anything to do with him at all."

"This is mad," Esther said shakily, and nobody contradicted her. Nobody said anything at all. A long, leaden silence stretched out, as a cloud covered the sun, and the jewelled light from the windows turned to shadow.

"So if Esther is the Morningstar..." Angus began and then trailed off.

"Then there's no conundrum," Michael finished for him. "The prophecy and Theletos request can both be fulfilled."

"Theoretically," Lucas countered. "If Theletos were here, and in his right mind. Which he isn't."

"And so we come back around to the beginning," Michael said. "We've got to find him."

"But how do we do that?" Ailsa asked. "He could be anywhere!"

"Morrigan?"

Matrika shook her head. "That, too, is beyond me," she said, though she glanced at Esther, who looked pointedly away.

"Well, he's bound to come out of the woodwork sooner or later," Michael said. "In the meantime, we need to arm ourselves to the teeth."

"What with?" Angus asked.

"I'd be willing to bet there's a sacred weapon or two in the castle armoury. Then there's the museum. Shall we?"

*

In the museum, wandering among the exhibits of ancient Celtic artefacts, Esther finally had her chance to speak to Sophie alone. Matrika had left them at the castle. Lucas was with the other angels, browsing antique swords. Angus and Ailsa had gone on to a different level. Esther found Sophie leaning her forehead against a glass case containing an ancient-looking harp. Her eyes were closed.

"Sophie?" Esther asked uncertainly.

Sophie opened her eyes, stepped away from the case, and gave Esther a weary smile. "Hello, Esther. Just taking a break."

"Are you all right? You aren't getting a migraine, are you?"

"I don't think so. Just an ordinary, bone-weary, stressed out headache."

She knew that she wouldn't have a better chance of getting Sophie to Rive than this, but she still hated the duplicity when she said, "Do you want to go for a walk? Get some air?"

"Actually, yes, that would be lovely."

Earlier, Esther had studied a map of Edinburgh and located the address that Rive had given her. It wasn't far from where they were now. They left the museum by the main doors, which let them out onto George IV Bridge. It was nearly eight o'clock, but it was so near midsummer that the sun was still high in the sky. Sophie stood for a moment, gazing at the traffic on the bridge. It seemed to Esther to be overly populated by faeries, but she didn't have much time to consider it before Sophie was saying, "Sorry if I'm in a daze. I feel a bit like my head is going to explode."

"I know what you mean," Esther said, beginning to walk up the street.

"I imagine you do. No, actually, I can't imagine. To have kept your memories through the Change, and then face those horrible accusations, the journey here, and now all that's been thrust onto you since you met us – honestly, I don't know how you bear it."

Esther shrugged. "No choice, I guess."

"What do *you* think, Esther? I mean about the prophecy, and the message from Theletos, and what Michael said about the meaning of your name?"

"I don't know what to think," Esther answered, pausing

to let a stately group of trouping faeries, mounted on graceful white horses, pass in front of them. "Except that I very much doubt that I'm the answer to anything. You?"

Sophie shook her head, smiling ruefully. "I don't know. I'm so tired of thinking and thinking and never knowing what's right. Honestly, I just wish that somebody would tell me what to do."

They had reached the junction with the Royal Mile. Sophie stopped on the street corner. "So where is he, Esther?"

"What?" Esther asked, looking as if she'd seen a ghost.

"I know you're taking me to Rive. Listen, it's all right – I know why you didn't tell me. But I also know he's nearby."

"How?"

Sophie shrugged. "A syzygy thing? I really don't know. It's just like that. So where is he?"

"Near here. He gave me an address." She took the paper from her pocket and handed it to Sophie.

"I know where this is. We're almost there." She folded it into her hand, looking up at Esther thoughtfully. "And do you trust him?"

Esther sighed. "I don't believe that he's working for the daevas, if that's what you mean. He says he intends to try to save us, and he needs your help, and aeons can't lie, right?"

"Right. But you don't sound convinced."

Esther shrugged. "In the end, what do I know?"

"Much more than you think you do, I suspect. Okay, I'll see him – but only if you come with me."

"Of course," Esther said and followed her up the street. Sophie stopped in front of a lit doorway. It was a restaurant with an elaborately lettered sign over the door reading "The Witchery." "A restaurant?" she asked.

"Not just a restaurant – the best restaurant in Edinburgh, or so I've heard. It says 'Heriot' under the address." She pointed it out on the scrap of paper. "Do you know what it means?"

"He didn't say anything about it – he just gave me the paper."

"Well, let's find out," Sophie said and opened the door.

The room in front of them was like a dining hall from a fairy-tale castle. The walls, where they weren't hung with tapestries, were covered in elaborately carved panelling. The seats were upholstered in red leather, and gilded leather screens separated the tables. A bronze bust of Bacchus grinned out at the diners. The entire place was lit by candles in church candlesticks.

Esther wanted nothing so much as to run back out onto the street, but Sophie walked right up to the maître d' and smiled. Despite Sophie's travel-worn clothing, the man returned it. "May I help you, Miss?" he asked.

"I hope so," Sophie answered, slipping her arm through Esther's, as if she'd picked up on Esther's wish to bolt. "My sister and I are meant to be meeting a friend here. I'm afraid we lost the directions, but I believe the reservation may be under the name 'Heriot?'"

"Ah, yes!" the maître d' said, smiling. "The young man told me to expect you. It's the Heriot suite he meant. It's just upstairs. I'll have Roxy take you."

Roxy turned out to be a very large man, who beamed at Sophie and Esther when the maître d' introduced them. Esther didn't deceive herself that it had anything to do with her. She doubted that there was anyone on earth whom Sophie couldn't charm. Roxy led them up a narrow turret staircase, into a hallway elaborately decorated in red and gold. The hallway led into another fairy-tale room, this one done in dark, rich colours. The walls were panelled in oak wainscoting, with jewel-toned floral wallpaper above it. A grandfather clock ticked in the corner, its brass pendulum shaped like a sun.

But Esther didn't see any of it. Her eyes had locked immediately on Rive, who was sitting in a leather armchair, gazing into a glass of whisky that he held in both hands, a black wedge of hair falling across his face. His shabby shepherd's clothes were gone, replaced by an immaculate suit and a long, black coat. He was shining, stunning, even before he raised his brilliant eyes. They flickered over Esther and came to rest on Sophie, with a look of pain so profound Esther caught her breath.

Sophie didn't seem to notice. With a cry, she ran to Rive and flung her arms around him. Esther watched as they embraced, long enough to know that it didn't matter what everybody said. It didn't matter what Sophie herself felt. They were two halves of a whole, and nothing would ever be able to change that.

Blinded by tears, Esther backed away – straight into a pair of arms that closed around her, flooding her with a cold so profound it took her breath away. Blearily, she took in the bell sleeves of grey wool, the black velvet gloves. The voice sounded inside her head, as it had in Angus's cottage: *And so, finally, we meet, little star.*

CHAPTER 12

THE WITCHERY

Esther screamed. Rive leapt to his feet, pushing Sophie behind him. "Let go of her!" he demanded, his face dark with anger, but not surprise. Esther knew that something about this was very wrong, but the Cailleach's wrenching cold had made her mind sluggish, and she couldn't think what.

Behind Rive, Sophie was white and wide-eyed. She fumbled at her waist, reaching for Carnwennan, but before she could draw it, five of the Cailleach's wraith attendants had surrounded her, pinning her arms.

"Rive!" she cried.

Rive stopped, looking from one girl to the other, his blazing eyes settling at last on the Cailleach. "This was not what we agreed," he said, his voice low and menacing, but again, unsurprised. And so Esther began to understand.

"Rive?" Sophie said, her voice fragile now, uncertain.

"One should be careful when consorting with the enemy," the Cailleach said to Rive, her spoken voice driving fresh needles of cold into Esther.

"What does she mean?" Sophie asked, barely above a whisper.

"Would you like to tell her, or should I?" the Cailleach asked.

"I had no choice," Rive said, his voice leaden, and it seemed to Esther that he was speaking to himself, rather than any of them. "This has grown bigger than all of us." He looked back at the Cailleach. "Let Esther go. She isn't the one you came for."

"Rive!" Sophie cried, hurt surfacing in her eyes.

"I'm afraid I can't do that, Theletos," the Cailleach said. "Abaddon's orders were precise: bring him both Sophia and Esther."

Rive's expression turned cold, furious. "That is not what he said to me! It's not what I agreed to!"

There was a supercilious smile in her voice when she answered, "You should know better than to make a deal with the devil. Come, Sophia," she said, holding Esther with one hand while she reached out the other toward Sophie.

Sophie recoiled. Rive demanded, "What could he possibly want with Esther?"

"To be rid of her, of course."

"What?"

The Cailleach smiled and ran a hand down Esther's hair. Esther wanted to scream, but the Cailleach's bitter cold had paralyzed her. "She's a pretty thing…sweet, too. Unfortunately, she's also deadly – like a cancer, eating at the heart of your syzygy. You've never worked properly since Sophia incorporated her. It's time to cut her out."

"If you lay a hand on her, I'll kill you!"

"Now Theletos, don't be rash. You're outnumbered, and if you try to fight us, you might be damaged. We need you and Sophia operating at full capacity."

"Me?" he asked.

"Of course, you," the Cailleach answered. "Sophia won't work properly on her own."

"Tell your master that the deal is off!" Rive said, and reaching into the air, he pulled out his blue sword. The Cailleach shoved Esther into the arms of one of her attendants and then faced off with Rive, holding her staff horizontally with both hands. Rive's sword flashed out, but the Cailleach parried with her staff. The weapons screeched together in a shower of sparks and frost.

As the warmth slowly returned to Esther's body, her mind thawed too, and she realized that there was another struggle going on beside her. As when she had fought the demon dog in Ardnasheen, Sophie had begun to glow, her bright blue aura standing out around her like a halo. Struggling against the restraining arms of the Cailleach's retinue, she finally managed to free one arm of her own. When she drew Carnwennan from her waistband, it glowed as brightly as her aura. She slashed at the wraith holding her, and it let go, screeching in pain. She turned on the one holding Esther, driving the knife into its back. Its black robe fluttered to the floor, empty.

The remaining wraiths swarmed around Sophie, locking her arms against her once more. The Cailleach, distracted by the commotion, took a slash across the arm from Rive's sword, and then, faltering, another to the shoulder. Rive turned wild-eyed to Esther and yelled, "Run!"

Esther stumbled toward the hallway, but her heartbeat lurched brokenly. She couldn't even pull enough air into her lungs to make it through the door. The room swam in front of her eyes, and darkness began to close in. Then, as she fell, someone caught her. She looked up into Michael's blazing green eyes.

He tried to smile at her. "Don't worry, Esther," he said, and then passed her to Angus. "Take her to the other room," Michael told him. "Give her her medicine – it's in the bag."

Esther caught a glimpse of Ailsa holding her carpetbag. She followed as Angus carried Esther into the adjoining room – a bedroom even more elaborately decorated than the sitting room. He shut the door.

"Sophie – " Esther began, but Angus stopped her.

"Sophie will be all right. The angels will look after her." He set her on a bed hung with green and gold curtains.

"But Rive – he's dangerous – "

"We know," Ailsa said grimly, taking the bottle of tablets from Esther's bag and handing her two of them.

"We saw it in Suri's mirror," Angus added.

"What?" Esther asked.

"When we couldn't find you and Sophie in the museum, we looked for you in it and saw you coming here. What were you thinking, coming by yourselves?"

"Don't pester the girl, Angus!" Ailsa scolded. "Look at her, she's barely conscious."

A moment later the door opened, and the angels entered, pushing Rive in front of them. His hands were tied behind his back, and Suri held his sword. Sophie, pale and haggard, clutched Lucas's hand. Esther thought it was for support, until she realized that Sophie was holding him back from Rive.

"Where is the Cailleach?" Esther asked, shuddering with the memory of her aching cold.

"Gone," Michael said. "We couldn't kill her. She's wearing some kind of armour. But we drove her off."

"Shouldn't someone follow her?" Angus asked.

"We can't. She froze the door shut on her way out."

"So we're stuck here?" Ailsa asked.

"Until it thaws," Michael answered. "Hopefully that won't be too long. At any rate, it gives us time for Theletos to explain himself." He steered Rive into a carved wooden chair that reminded Esther of the seats in the chapel at the convent. Michael pushed him into it, and Rive slumped there, listless and pale.

"What needs explaining?" Lucas asked. "He tried to turn Sophie and Esther over to the daevas. He's a traitor, plain and simple."

"I don't work for the daevas," Rive said quietly.

"Then why did you bring the girls to the Cailleach?" Michael asked.

Rive was silent, staring at his feet. Esther thought that he wouldn't answer, but at last, he looked up. "In the Deep," he said, "they tried to turn me. They chipped away at me every day for six months, in every way that they could think of."

"And apparently, they succeeded," Lucas said.

"No, they didn't."

"You just tried to turn Sophie over to them!"

"Because I realized that there was no other choice."

"You chose to give me to them?" Sophie cried.

Rive shut his eyes, sighed. "I chose to save Esther's life," he said ponderously. "Giving you to them was the only way to do it."

Lucas swung his sword faster than Esther's eyes could follow. Nearly as quickly, Michael's hand shot out, stopping the ember-red blade an inch from Rive's throat. "So you're a traitor too!" Lucas spat at him.

"Contain yourself, Lucifer," Michael said. "We need to hear what Theletos has to say."

Lucas's look was murderous, but in the end, he lowered his sword. "Let's hear it, then."

Rive looked up at Sophie. "It's simple, really. In trying to wear me down, the daevas let me know more than they should have. But it only started to come together when I tried to contact Sophie and reached Esther instead."

He turned to Esther, his eyes pleading – for what, she wondered? "I reached you, and I didn't understand why. So I watched you after I sent you to find Sophie. I needed to know how you fit into all of this, because clearly, you did. Otherwise, the Change wouldn't have passed over you. You wouldn't have been be dreaming of daevas or their plans for taking Earth. And they wouldn't have been trying to turn you to their side."

"You saw my dreams?" Esther asked.

His eyes didn't move from hers. "Yes."

"And the one with Lilith, and the stone steps," she said softly. "Were you really there?"

"I was there in spirit," he answered and continued to hold her gaze until she flushed, and looked at her hands. He turned back to Michael. "So Esther was dreaming of the daevas, long before she knew what they were. The only way that could have happened was if the daevas themselves were sending those dreams. But why would they send prescient dreams to an ordinary schoolgirl?"

"Ah," Michael said, with a sigh.

"Ah?" Ailsa repeated. "As in, you get it? Because I sure don't."

"The dreams weren't meant for Esther," Rive explained, "at least not originally. They were meant for Sophie, and Esther was somehow picking up on them. But I still didn't know why." He glanced again at Sophie. "Not until the daevas showed me what you'd done. In the Garden, with the soul."

"I had no idea that it would hurt you," Sophie said. "If I had – "

"I know," he interrupted, "and I understand why you did it, though I have to admit, I still hated you for it." Sophie flinched, and Lucas's eyes flared as he tightened his arms around her. "For a little while, anyway. But then I realized that I'd been as mistaken as you had."

"Meaning?" Sophie asked warily.

"Your prophecy, Sophie. Didn't you ever wonder where it came from?"

"I assumed I'd made it myself, but I know not everyone agrees with me about that – or about what it means." She glanced at Michael.

Rive gave her a joyless smile. "And as usual, Michael is right on both counts. It didn't come from you, Sophie: it came to you."

328

"From where?"

"From the Keeper."

"But the Keeper hasn't spoken to us in centuries!"

"Nevertheless, it spoke to you, then."

"How do you know?"

"Because it gave me the same message, more or less. And I got it just as wrong as you did."

"Okay, is anybody else really still not getting it?" Ailsa asked.

"Sorry," Rive said, "but I've been living in my head with this for so long, it's hard to know how to explain it all – "

"Why don't you just cut to the chase?" Lucifer said.

Rive sighed. "Very well. Sophie and I are both guilty of hearing what we wanted to hear. The Keeper's exact words to me were to find my consort on Earth and return to the Garden with her. But it never named Sophie. Likewise, you, Sophie, were sent to find the Morningstar, and return it to Heaven. I understand why you thought it was Lucifer. 'Morningstar' was one of his titles, and he was on Earth, and you cared so much about him. But you were wrong."

"How?" Sophie whispered.

He met her eyes frankly, though he clearly didn't like what he was about to say. "You stopped being my consort on the day you became human. And Lucifer isn't the only Morningstar on Earth – or the one you should have been looking for." He turned again to Esther, a plea in his eyes. "Esther is. And our only hope of stopping the daevas is for her to come back with me – to the Garden, to our Dominion – as my consort. That's why I was willing to give you to the Cailleach, Sophie. It wasn't a choice between you and her, but a choice between fulfilling the prophecy or not. And we all know that fulfilling the prophecy is the only thing standing between us and Armageddon. What would you have done?"

There was a moment of stunned, perfect silence. Then,

"One question," Sophie said in small, hard voice, her eyes fixed on Rive. "What were they planning to do with me, after you handed me over?"

"Use you to bring their army to life," he said wearily. "The daevas have fabricated legions of demons. The bodies are perfect, deadly – but inert. The daevas don't have the power to make souls for them." He looked at Sophie. "You do."

"And you were willing to let them do this?" Lucas cried.

"It was the lesser of two evils," Rive answered. "And I thought that once the Balance was restored, we could rescue her."

"Sure – if there was anything left to rescue!"

And then everyone was arguing. It went on for a few grim moments, until Michael roared, "Enough!"

Silence settled again, but it was an uneasy one. At last, Suri said, "Wow, I definitely didn't see that coming. Are you sure about the consort thing? I mean, Esther is lovely, but she's human."

"Is she?" Rive asked, his eyes on Esther. She didn't know where to look. "Her soul is mixed up with mine and Sophie's. I'd say that makes her something else."

When no one responded to this, Lucas said, "Really? You're all just going to buy this story and send Esther off to god knows where?"

"I'm not going to kidnap her," Rive snapped. "It's her decision."

"Theletos, a little delicacy?" Michael chastised. "I mean, consider what you're asking the poor girl – "

"I'll do it," Esther interrupted, her voice soft, but steady and clear.

"What?"

"I'll do it. I'll go with Rive to the Garden – just as long as one of you will look in on my mam and brothers and sisters. Make sure they're *all right*."

"Yes, of course," Michael said, "but Esther, are you sure? Because you can't possibly understand what you're agreeing to. None of us could."

"I don't mean to contradict you," Esther answered, though her eyes remained steady on Rive's, "but I think I do know. All of my life, it's seemed to me that something was missing. That I wasn't quite whole. That the life I was living properly belonged to somebody else. But when I met you, Rive...well, it began to makes sense. Not in a way I can explain. But still, I know it. I know that this is what I've always been meant to do."

There was a silence, and then, once again, everyone seemed to be talking at once – everyone except Rive and Esther. Their eyes were caught in a long look. "Are you sure, Esther?" he asked her.

Her eyes were clear and direct. "Do you love me?" she asked.

"More than anything," he said, and then he cupped her face in his hands and kissed her, and warmth, and peace, and wholeness flooded her. In that moment anything seemed possible, and everything else faded: her bickering companions, her imperfect heart, the months of misery and weeks of terrible anxiety.

When he finally pulled back, she smiled. "I'm sure."

Rive smiled back, offered her his hand. "Come on then."

"How does it work?" she asked.

"If all is as it should be," he answered, drawing her with him into the sitting room, "then I open a doorway between this world and the Garden, and we step through. Do you have a preference?"

"Of what?"

"Of what the door looks like."

She thought for a moment. "I want it to look like home. Not the flat in Ballymun – a real home."

"And what does that look like?"

"Can you see what I imagine?"

He smiled. "Only if you want me to."

"I want you to." She pictured a panelled wooden door, with the golden patina of age, a knocker in the shape of a crescent moon, a doorknob twined with Art Nouveau leaves.

"Got it," Rive said, and then it was there in front of them. He reached out, turned the knob – and nothing happened. He rattled the handle, turning it back and forth, but the door stayed resolutely shut.

"What's wrong?" Esther asked.

"I don't know," Rive answered, distraught. "This has never happened before."

"Let me try," Esther said, but she could no more make the door move than Rive could. She turned to him, stricken. "Maybe you were wrong about me being the Morningstar."

"You have to be," Rive said. "It all adds up."

"Well then…could it be the wrong kind of door?"

"No – a portal is a portal. What it looks like is down to glamour."

"Actually, it kind of makes sense," Suri said. Esther turned to see the others gathered in the bedroom doorway. "I mean, the daevas made it impossible for us to get to Earth from Heaven. I guess they don't want anyone going the other way, either."

"But you got here," Ailsa pointed out.

"Aye – with the help of Sam's sorcery," Michael said.

"So, then, do it backwards or whatever. It can't be that hard."

"We don't know what he did," Suri said. "He wouldn't let us watch."

"Great," Lucas sighed. "So now what?"

Before anyone could answer, the grandfather clock began to toll. Twelve sonorous chimes rang out, and then echoed away into a silence so perfect that it felt, for a moment, unbreakable. And then something clattered against the window. They all ran to look out, and Esther's breath caught in her throat. Creatures thronged the street below: faeries, fallen angels, ancient deities,

332

Revenants – even a few who looked human – plus myriad more that she couldn't classify.

"Who are they?" she asked.

"Our army, I'm thinking," Suri said with a glint in her eye.

Directly beneath them stood a dark-haired girl in a threadbare coat, looking up – looking, it seemed, for someone specific.

"Sweet Jesus," Esther said, "that's Cliona!"

"Who?" Sophie asked.

But Esther didn't answer. She pushed the window open, leaned out and called, "Cliona!"

Cliona burst into a grin. "Mad Girl!" she cried. "You're here!"

"I am," Esther called back, smiling. "But what are you doing here? Didn't you find your mam?"

Cliona's smile faded. "Oh aye, I found her. Turns out she really is doolally. Ranting and raving, the whole bit. She kept telling me to go to Edinburgh and join the Morningstar's army. I wouldn't have listened, except when I left the hospital it seemed like every faerie in Britain was on the move, and guess where they were headed?"

"Here, apparently," Esther said.

Cliona nodded. "Turns out they had the same message as Mam gave me."

"But how did you know where to find me?"

"I didn't. I fell in with a couple of werewolves back in the shanty town, said they were tracking angels. I thought that sounded interesting. And then they brought us here, and there you were, standing in the window, only I almost didn't recognize you with that hair...anyway, I don't suppose you have any idea what all this is about?"

"Unfortunately, yes," Esther said. "Listen, Cliona, you'd better come upstairs."

CHAPTER 13

21 JUNE
00:45 A.M.

"So you're honestly, truly angels?" Cliona asked for the fifth time, studying Michael, Suri and Lucas. Then, without giving them a chance to answer, she said, "But I suppose if the demons are real – sorry, daevas – then angels must be too… So anyway, how is this army bit meant to work?"

"I suppose they could be an army," Michael said thoughtfully, "if they were organized into regiments and such… if we had time."

"Seeing as we don't," Suri replied, "let's just hope they got the 'Hey, the world's ending!' memo and they're on our side."

"Assuming they are on our side, we'll need a bigger base."

"St. Giles Cathedral," Suri said. "It's just around the corner."

"Not a bad suggestion," Michael said. "It's large, it's central, and it's consecrated ground…though I don't know that that even matters anymore."

"It can't hurt."

"Well then, let's go."

They gathered up their possessions and the cache of weapons they'd taken from the museum, and then made their way down the narrow stairs, past the darkened restaurant and into the street. Lucas took Sophie's hand as they pushed through the crowd, moving back toward the Royal Mile, across George IV Bridge, and then into the cathedral courtyard. The church was a brooding black hulk, the vast crown steeple thrusting into a sky already purpling as the short night tipped toward dawn.

Michael plucked his sword from the darkness, illuminating the entryway with his fire-coloured aura. Many of the faeries dropped to their knees at the sight, but Michael paid no attention. He climbed the steps that spread from the arched doorway, pushed the door open, and disappeared into the church.

Inside it was pitch dark. Suri, Lucas and Rive drew their swords as well, pushing the shadows back. Suri touched her sword to a candelabra, and the candles came to life, burning with her pure, silvery light. Lucas, Michael and Rive did the same, and soon the vast space was lit softly with banks of flickering candles burning silver, red, gold and blue.

Michael had barely lit the last of the candles when the main door opened again, and a group of figures came in. Rive and the angels rushed toward them, swords drawn, the humans following more slowly. Michael's expression turned thunderous, and few steps closer, Sophie saw why. The three figures who'd entered looked like beautiful humans with metal cuffs on their wrists. The woman's strappy vest revealed the edges of an intricate black tattoo that ran across her upper back, leaving no doubt that she was a fallen Watcher. And though her face looked tired now, her clothes shabby and dirty, Sophie recognized her.

"How dare you come here!" she cried, furious now as Michael, who turned to her in surprise.

"You know her?" he asked.

"I know her," Sophie answered, glaring at the woman, who shrank back against one of the men. "I almost killed her in a club last winter. She was trying to steal Angus's soul. She's called Berith."

"Didn't I send you back to your territory?" Suri demanded.

Berith offered her a wan smile. "You did. But the staves failed again, and a good thing, too. If they hadn't, I'd never have been able to run when those things came after me."

"Things?" Sophie asked. "You mean the Revenants?"

"If that's what you want to call them," one of the men answered.

"I can't say that I blame them," Suri said, "given that you made them what they are."

"No – nor can I," Berith answered, surprising Sophie with her frankness. "But we've found something out – something you need to know. They aren't killing us for revenge. They're killing us for the souls we keep, and they're giving them – "

"To the daevas," Michael said. "Who else? Thank you for the information, and consider yourselves absolved of your duty."

Berith looked back at her companions. The one who'd spoken earlier gave her a slight nod. "No," she said, turning back to Michael. "We also came to help fight the daevas."

"Why would you do that?" Suri asked.

"Because they're killing us. We don't imagine that will end if they win."

Michael gave her an appraising look. At last, he said, "How many of you are there?"

"All of us who are still alive," the fallen man answered. "Our estimate is about one hundred and fifty."

Michael and the other angels exchanged looks. At last, sighing, Michael said, "Very well. Are you armed?"

"We left our swords with the others," Berith said, "to speak to you. Many of them have weapons, but not all of them."

"Send those that need them to us," Michael said. Berith nodded and then retreated with her companions.

"Do we really mean to trust them?" Suri asked.

"Do we really have a choice?" Michael asked. "We need all the soldiers we can find."

Before he could say more, another rag-tag group of fallen

arrived at the top of the steps. "We were told to come for weapons?" asked the one at the front.

"Angus, will you oversee the dispersal of the weapons for the time being? You others can help him."

"Aye," Angus said. "But where are you going?"

"To see if I can find more. Suri, coming?"

"Do you have to ask?" she answered.

"I'm coming too," Cliona said.

"I'm not sure that's a good idea," Michael said. "It's dangerous out there."

"I came from out there – remember?" Cliona answered, her chin jutting in challenge.

"Oh, very well…" Michael sighed.

"I'll stay here," Rive said, "and make sure that whoever comes in is meant to."

"And I'll help," Lucas told him. "It's a lot to do on your own, right?" he asked, smiling wryly. Rive looked like he wanted to object, but he kept his mouth shut and took his place on the opposite side of the door from Lucas.

"Right, then," Michael said. "Let's go."

*

It wasn't long before other creatures began to join the trickle of fallen angels into the cathedral, looking for weapons, and not long after that that the supply ran out. Angus kept back only enough for himself and his friends. Rive and Lucas had been turning people away empty-handed for a half hour when Angus said, "Wait a minute! We're being complete idiots."

Ailsa cocked an eyebrow. "Speak for yourself, love."

Ignoring her, he said, "We have an endless source of weapons right here."

"Where?" Ailsa asked, looking around doubtfully.

"Sophie! I mean, she made Carnwennan, right? And Lucas's sword, when we were in Dahud's palace." He beamed with inspiration in spite of his friends' dubious faces.

"I don't think it works that way," Sophie said. "Lucas's sword didn't come out of thin air: I had the remains of it to work from. And I made Carnwennan completely unconsciously, and under extreme duress. I've never been able to summon weapons under normal circumstances."

"Right, and the impending Apocalypse is normal circumstances? Come on, Sophie. As my grandmother loved to tell me, you can but try."

"Okay, I'll try. Any requests?"

"You know Carnwennan best," Lucas suggested.

"Yes, we've had a deep connection since the night I skewered the cat demon," Sophie said dryly, but she pulled the dagger from her waistband nevertheless. She laid it in her lap and concentrated on it. But the eager eyes of her friends, fixed intently on her, were distracting. Her thoughts scattered every which way.

Sophie shut her eyes, took a deep breath, and tried again. She pictured Carnwennan, the feel of it in her hand, the bluish sheen of its metal. At first nothing happened, but then the odd, familiar tingling began in her fingers. It condensed, took on form, became a cold weight in her hands. Sophie's eyes flew open. She was holding an exact replica of the dagger lying in her lap.

"You did it!" Ailsa cried, and reached to hug her friend.

"I did," Sophie said, staring at the two knives in partial disbelief.

"And, ah, you're glowing."

Sophie's eyes moved from the knife to her hands, which did in fact exude a subtle blue glow.

"See?" Angus said. "I told you it would work."

Looking at his bright face, at his clear faith in her, she recalled the beginning of the understanding she'd had months ago, when he offered her a soul in a blue glass jar, and a life that had nothing to do with monsters and angels and the fate of the world. She couldn't call up her aeon power at will, but she could do it if a human life was in danger. No one needed to tell her that it was time to go into production.

02:13 A.M.

It got easier. After some trial and error, she'd found that it worked best if she touched the creature who was to wield the weapon. Most already had an idea of what would best suit them, and their belief seemed to boost her own creative ability. Nevertheless, by the time Suri, Michael and Cliona returned, Sophie was ready for a break.

She finished making a bow and a quiver of arrows for a centaur, and then looked up at them. They'd changed clothes – Michael into plain, dark garments covered by a long, black coat, Cliona into jeans and a T-shirt, and Suri into a deep pink cat suit. Sophie had to smile. The world might be ending, but there was no way her friend was going to be anything less than fashionable.

The smile died, though, when Michael dropped his clanging collection of weapons and demanded, "What are you doing?"

"Making weapons," Sophie said. "There weren't nearly enough to go around."

"If you're going to yell at someone, yell at me," Angus told him. "It was my idea."

"I'm not going to yell at you," Michael said. "I think it's brilliant – *if* Sophie can cope with it. Creation takes a toll."

"Sophie isn't a child," Lucas said. "She knows her limits, and I'm sure we can trust her to tell us when she's reached them."

"Right. And I'm fine," Sophie told Michael, hoping that he didn't see through her smile to her growing exhaustion.

"Do you think we can help?" Suri asked. "I mean us other angels and Rive?"

"I thought only Sophie could create things," Angus said.

"Only Sophie can create things from nothing," Lucas explained. "But the rest of us can transmute objects – well, usually. Suri says it's harder now, but if Sam could do it…" He picked up a hymnal from a bench, shut his eyes in concentration, and a moment later it had become a short-sword. He smiled. "Then it can be done."

"Terrific," Suri said, setting two bundles on the ground. "But I imagine you're all hungry," she opened one of the bundles, revealing a stash of food. "And tired of dressing like the cast of a BBC historical drama."

"Definitely," Ailsa said. Suri grinned, and tossed her a heap of fabric that turned out to be a navy-blue military style jacket and black trousers, though they looked far too fashionable to have been a real uniform, and then a pair of knee-high boots.

"So change," Suri told them, "then eat. Then we'll start up the munitions factory."

A half hour later, they had devoured all of the food and dressed in what Suri apparently considered appropriate battlefield attire, though most of it bore designer labels. Suri and Michael had also filled them in on conditions outside.

"The city is packed with faeries and the like," he said. "But very few humans are to be seen."

"It was the same in my dream," Esther said. "They're hiding."

"But how do they know to hide?" Angus asked. "And for that matter, how did all these faeries know to come here?"

"I don't know," Michael said.

"Cliona? Did you ask any of them?"

"I asked, but I never got a straight answer," she said. "To be honest, I don't think they know themselves. But they were all quite certain there was a battle coming."

After that they re-opened the doors of the cathedral and went back into production. Esther, Ailsa and Angus gathered piles of objects to turn into weapons, while the angels took turns transmuting them and guarding the door.

Though she was tired, the repetitive work was soothing in its way, and Sophie lapsed into a dreamlike state. She no longer took much note of the appearance of the creatures whose hands she grasped; the weapons she conjured for them were more real to her. She was aware of the light seeping slowly into the windows' coloured panes, and the ebb and flow of the collected murmurs of the crowd outside. Still, time seemed to slow, and she could almost believe that the calm would last, that what they feared would fail to come.

In a brief pause in the endless line of creatures waiting to be armed, she glanced up to find Lucas's eyes resting on her. *We should have been married today,* she thought, but the thought was surreal, belonging to an enchanted time that was already a distant memory. Some of this must have showed on her face, because Lucas came to her, touched her cheek. "It will be all right," he said.

And then Hell broke loose.

05:37 A.M.

At first Sophie thought it was thunder, but it shook the ground beneath their feet. Or an earthquake, except that earthquakes, as far as she knew, eventually shuddered themselves out, and this one seemed to be gaining in intensity as the moments passed. Too late, Sophie remembered where she'd felt this before: it was the same ground-rending roar that had heralded the approach of the daevas in Dahud's palace.

On the heels of the thought, the floor in front of them wrenched open, shattering marble and sending tiles flying. The floor heaved, and she skidded toward the dark cleft until Lucas caught her hand, dragged her back from the precipice as new cracks spidered outward. They all fell back from the path of the destruction, toward the far end of the cathedral where bright shards of glass were falling from the great, arched window. Pillars began to shudder and crack, and for a moment, looking up, Sophie wondered if the stone roof was about to come down on them.

Then she forgot about the roof as something emerged from the rift in the floor. She shrank back against Lucas, picturing vividly the daevas' beautiful, terrible forms, but it wasn't the daevas the Deep disgorged. It was monsters: a Gothic church's litany of gargoyles brought to life. They clawed their way through the ruined floor and then took wing, wheeling and diving, their tined tails whipping through the clouds of dust rising from the shattered masonry. They screeched at Sophie and her friends, their eyes bright with fire. Ailsa cried out as a tail-spine whipped across her cheek, leaving a gash that filled with blood.

"This way!" Suri cried, and then, pausing only long enough to skewer an attacking gryphon, she stumbled toward the back right corner of the cathedral.

The others followed as best they could, fighting off anything that came after them. Now other monstrosities were emerging from the Deep: boar-tusked demons, horrific dogs like the one Sophie had slain in Angus's cottage, creatures that slithered like huge, armoured serpents, great black cats that stalked with a fluid grace that froze Sophie's blood, and myriad others. They poured out of the brutal entrance they'd opened and through gaping doors and shattered windows, to engage, judging by the shrieks and cries, with the army gathered in the streets.

At last, Suri reached her destination: a door at the far corner of the church, hidden in shadow. They passed through a medieval arch into an ante-chapel with the names of kings inscribed on the walls and carved stone roses on the ceiling. Suri paused to slam the iron grate into its place within the arch and turned a bit of crumbled masonry into a crowbar, with which she pinned the gate shut. Two gargoyles crashed into it, screaming and spewing stone feathers that shattered as they fell, but the gate held.

The chapel itself was small but elaborately decorated. Wooden stalls with tall, carved pinnacles lined each side, bearing coats-of-arms and topped by painted models, presumably of various noble families' emblems. Above these were narrow, arched, stained-glass windows portraying various martyrs and saints. Michael slammed the great door shut behind them and then shoved the heavy wooden altar table up against it.

"So I guess consecrated ground didn't do much good," Ailsa said in a shaky voice.

"It could have been worse," Michael pointed out. "They could have been daevas instead of demons."

"Which doesn't actually matter much, when the demons are built to kill and aimed at us," Angus answered.

"It's not just us," Esther said, looking toward the windows, which dulled the clash of battle beyond but couldn't drown it out.

"No," Michael agreed. "It looks as if we have our work cut out. I take it the demons coming out of the floor are the army you told us about?" He aimed this question at Rive.

"Yes," Rive said, turning from the door where he'd been listening to see if anything was trying to break through. His blue eyes were shadowed; he looked exhausted. "But only a fraction of it."

"I don't get it," Ailsa said. "I thought they needed Sophie to bring them to life."

"They do," Rive sighed, sitting down in one of the intricately carved stalls. "The main body of it, anyway. But they have enough souls to get them started."

"Where did they get them?" Cliona asked.

"From the fallen. They're all those souls the Revenants stole."

"What's a Revenant?"

"Long story," Lucas told her, "which is really rather pointless now. However they did it, their army has arrived. We can't just sit in here waiting for the world to end."

"Indeed," Michael said. "We need to find a way to get Rive and Esther back to the Garden."

"How, when we can't open a portal?" Rive asked.

"The daevas opened a door from the Deep," Suri pointed out. "Maybe something's changed. Try again."

Sighing, Rive got up and concentrated on once of the wooden stalls opposite him. It rippled, shivered, and then took on the appearance of a plain wooden door. He pressed the latch, pulled – and nothing happened. Each of the angels tried, then the humans, but no one could make the door open.

"Maybe it's you," Lucas said, and smiled blandly at the glare with which Rive answered.

"Let me try," Suri said, and she pulled a door of her own from another one of the stalls: battered and covered in graffiti, with a row of locks running down one side.

"That's the door to Lux Aeterna!" Ailsa said.

Suri shrugged. "First thing that came to mind." She pulled on the handle, jiggled it, shook it and finally kicked it with one half-laced boot, but it didn't move any more than the other doors had. With a growl of frustration, Suri wiped a hand across the door, and it disappeared. She slumped, dejected, in the stall where it had been. "I don't suppose any of you ever learned any sorcery?"

No one answered.

"Do you think the end of the world will hurt?" Ailsa asked.

No one answered that, either. Sophie shut her eyes, trying to concentrate, to make herself come up with some kind of plan. She knew that they couldn't give up, but it was so difficult under the weight of her leaden weariness and the familiar pain beginning to corkscrew into her skull.

And then Suri sat up straight, the light kindling again in

her eyes. "Wait wait wait! Of course there's someone else who knows sorcery. There are lots of them: all of the fallen Watchers!"

"Right," said Michael, "and just now, they're all out there ripping the throats out of demons – I hope."

"Lucas was a Watcher, wasn't he?" Angus asked.

"Aye," Lucas answered, "I was the Watcher who ratted out the other ones for divulging the secrets of Heaven. The others weren't exactly keen to let me in on them after that."

"Then we need to get one of the ripping-demon-throat ones," Suri said resolutely.

"Right," Sophie said, trying to push her exhaustion aside. She tottered to her feet, trying not to think what the greying edges of her vision might mean. "Let's do that."

"No – not you," Lucas said.

"Why not me?" she demanded. "What else matters now but this?"

"Keeping you out of the daevas' hands," Lucas said. "You're far too valuable to them to risk putting you in their path."

"So you want to leave me here, alone?"

"Not alone." He looked up at the others. "The humans should stay here until we get back."

"I'm not staying here," Cliona said. "I can find a fallen angel as well as you."

"Cliona, it's far too dangerous for humans out there."

"Well, according to my mam, I'm half demon."

Michael stared at her, speechless. With a smirk, Suri said, "I think that means you win." Cliona grinned, while Michael shook his head in exasperation. "But you'll need a weapon. Is there any you have experience with?"

"Knives," Cliona said definitively.

"Really?" Esther asked. Cliona just shrugged.

"Here," Sophie said, pressing the copy of Carnwennan into Cliona's hands. The other girl looked delighted.

Michael turned to Rive, who was strapping his sword to his back. "No. You've got to stay here, too."

"What?" Rive asked. "Why?"

"Because you and Esther are the key to winning the Balance back," he said. "You need to stay alive, and you need to stay with her."

Rive was poised to argue, when the weak light from the windows dimmed abruptly, as if storm clouds had rolled across the sky. But Sophie knew, with a sick, sinking certainty, that they weren't storm clouds. She looked over at Esther and saw the same certainty in her eyes. And then they were clambering up the sides of the stalls to balance on the peaked tops and try to see through the narrow windows.

The glass saints made a kaleidoscope of the sky, but Sophie could see them anyway: white, winged creatures pitching toward earth, leaving blackness in their wake. "Daevas," she said.

"All right," Michael said after another bleak silence. "It's time to go do our bit."

"And what is that?" Suri asked. "Don't you remember Ker-Ys? How can angels fight daevas – daevas with wings no less."

It was the first time Sophie had ever heard Suri sound daunted, and she was right to be, given those odds. But her words gave Sophie an idea. It wasn't much, but it was something, and at the moment, they needed any advantage that they could get.

"I think I can do wings," she said.

"What?" Suri asked.

"Wings – you know, feathery things that stick out of your back? Then you'd be on equal footing with the daevas…well, sort of…"

"Sophie, even if it's possible, you must be exhausted after making all of those weapons," Michael said. "We couldn't possibly ask you to do something like this."

"You didn't ask me," Sophie said, "I offered. Now take off your shirt."

"What!"

"Tops off, Michael – the wings come out of your back, remember?" When he continued to stare at her dubiously, she said, "Consider this payback for making me strip after the grindylow attacked."

"Oh, very well!" Michael shed his coat and then the sweater underneath.

"T-shirt too."

With a sigh, Michael took off the T-shirt. Underneath it he was beautiful as a classical sculpture. Esther blushed, Ailsa was openly gaping, and Michael looked utterly mortified. "Turn around," Sophie said, and he turned his back on her, revealing his sigil. It swept outward from his spine to his shoulders like curls of flame.

Sophie studied it, memorizing it. Then she laid her hands on his shoulder blades, and shut her eyes. She felt the hard ridges of muscle beneath the skin, the harder bone beneath. She reached deeper, feeling for the energy that made Michael what he was, and her hands filled with his fiery essence. She concentrated on it, pulling it up and out of him, stretching it, shaping it, until she felt it take form.

She opened her eyes and stepped back, watching, riveted, as Michael's wings grew and spread. They weren't made of feathers, but thousands of tiny flames, flickering with fire colours from the cobalt blue of a candle-wick's base, to a bonfire's roaring gold, to the deep red of dying embers. The dips and curls of his sigil ran along their surface, scribed in the searing white of a sword smith's furnace. Michael flexed them, his eyes wide with awe.

"Well?" Sophie asked. "Do they work?"

Michael spread them wide again and beat them once, then twice. On the third beat, he lifted off of the floor. The downdraft was enough to send everyone sprawling, but Michael didn't apologize. Instead, his face broke into a grin. It was the first time Sophie had seen him look anything but anxious since he'd returned to Earth, and it made her forget, for a moment, the mounting pain in her head, the dizzying clouds at the edges of her vision, her utter exhaustion.

Michael settled back onto the ground and folded the wings behind him. Then he wrapped his arms around Sophie and hugged her tightly. "Thank you," he said to her. "They're beautiful."

Suri cried, "Me next! But I am not getting naked in front of you all. If you can make wings, I'm sure you can make holes in my clothes to accommodate them."

Sophie smiled and willed her head to clear. She laid her hands on Suri's back, on top of her clothes, hoping that she had the stamina to work another miracle. But it was easier this time. A few minutes' concentration, and Suri was spreading a pair of iridescent double wings like a dragonfly's, her sigil embroidered across them in silver lacework. Suri squealed and clapped, and immediately launched herself toward the carved stone ceiling, turning somersaults in the air.

Sophie turned to Lucas. "Are you sure, Sophie?" he asked. "You don't look very well – "

"I'm giving you wings, Lucas," Sophie said, forcing a smile, "if I have to knock you down and tie you up to do it."

"That would be a bit dramatic, don't you think?" he answered, pulling his shirt over his head. "But honestly – promise me you'll stop if it's too much."

"I promise," Sophie said, and though she knew him so well that she could have pulled his wings out of thin air, nevertheless, she laid her hands on his back for the familiar, comforting warmth of his skin.

She'd known the moment she suggested it what Lucas's wings would look like. She barely had to think about it to call up the image that he'd shown her in the grey light of his library what seemed ages ago, though it hadn't yet been a year. It was a Persian miniature painting of Lucifer, his hands bound but his crimson and gold wings free and spreading above him.

She remembered how Lucas had gazed at the painting. She imagined him diving into the flames of Alexandria's burning library to save it, along with a handful of others. She thought of him poring over those bright images, alone in his cold, Earthly prison, for years beyond measure. She wondered how many times he'd wished for those crimson wings to lift him up and away from his solitary grief. And then she felt them flex beneath her hands.

Sophie opened her eyes, and Lucas turned to face her, stretching first one, then the other wing above him in wonder. They were more beautiful even than she'd imagined, glowing a rich, sunset red, his sigil spreading out across them in gold, from shoulder-blade to wing tip. Sparks of gold flickered around the symbols, making them seem to pulse with life.

"Sophie," he said, and then he was folding her into those wings, their deep red warmth making a living curtain around them as he kissed her. She clung to him as if she could make that moment last forever.

"Ah, I hate to interrupt," Angus said, "but I don't think things are getting any better out there."

Reluctantly, Lucas dropped his wings, and Sophie looked up at the windows. It had grown darker still – so dark that they wouldn't have been able to see if it hadn't been for the light of the angels' wings. Despite telling herself to be brave, Sophie found that she was clutching Lucas's hand. She made herself let go.

"He's right," she said. "You need to go."

Lucas looked down at her, his brow furrowed. "Please don't do anything daft, Sophie."

"Daft? Me?" She kissed him once more, trying not to wonder if she would ever kiss him again; and then went to help the others pull the table away from the door. Michael opened it carefully, his sword raised and ready, but the ante-chapel was empty. They picked their way to the iron grate through piles of broken masonry. It was still pinned shut with Suri's crowbar.

The church beyond lay in ruins, splintered pews interspersed with shattered stone, the great pillars supporting the ceiling riven with cracks. The banners that had lined the central aisle were in tatters, the candelabra toppled and candles extinguished, the atmosphere cloudy with dust thrown up by the rending stone. But there were no demons to be seen anywhere.

"Does it not seem strange to you that they'd leave," Angus asked, "knowing we were still in here?"

"Is anything about this not strange?" Ailsa replied.

"Maybe they figured the demons were more useful out there fighting than trying to break down the door in here," Suri suggested.

"Or maybe they just knew that we'd have to come out sooner or later," Cliona answered.

They'd reached the entrance, its double doors splintered into matchsticks and strewn over the steps. Beyond them the battle raged: demons and fairies, angels and Revenants and creatures Sophie couldn't begin to classify all roiling together. The cobbles were slick with blood, red and countless other colours. Carcasses littered the ground, but it was impossible to count them, let alone tell from their tally whom might be winning.

Sophie looked up at the sky. The daevas were still too far up for her to make out any details other than their vast white wings. The darkness they trailed dripped and widened as they wheeled, yet they didn't seem to be descending. Maybe, she thought with a chill, they were waiting until the sky's erasure was complete.

"Let's go," Michael said and launched himself into the air, causing a momentary lull in the battle as creatures gazed in wonder at his bright wings. Suri followed him, and they hovered two storeys up, swatting at gargoyles as if they were flies as they waited for Lucas. Cliona had already slipped away into the crowd.

"Promise me you'll stay in the chapel until we get back," Lucas said to Sophie.

"Promise me you'll get back," she answered. She held his eyes for a moment, hoping that he could read in them all of the things that she didn't know how to say. He nodded, kissed her, and then followed Suri and Michael into the air. She watched as they ascended, graceful and certain as if they'd worn wings all their lives. She watched until she felt Esther's hand on her arm.

"It's time we went back inside," Esther said. "We're beginning to draw attention."

Even as she spoke, a trio of boar-headed demons climbed the steps toward them, maces swinging in their thick, hairy arms. Sophie pulled Carnwennan from her belt, glad that the others had had the sense to pick up weapons of their own. Angus raised his claymore and severed the arm of the nearest demon as it swung its mace at his head. Rive, his blue sword shining, took the heads off the other two in one stroke.

They didn't wait around to see what might follow in search of revenge, but retreated into the church, stumbling down the cluttered aisle to the chapel. Sophie expected a horde of demons to chase them, but when she turned to pull the iron grate shut behind her, she saw no one. Once again, this felt all wrong, but she didn't know what to do other than bar themselves in the chapel. They shut the door, pushed the table back up against it, and then slumped in the stalls.

For a long time they were lost in their own thoughts. Then Ailsa said, "What are the daevas actually planning?"

"World domination, last I checked," Angus said.

"Don't be condescending!" she snapped. "I know they want to take over the world. But, I mean, does anyone actually know what that would look like? Will they harvest our organs, or hook us up to electrodes and stick us in aquariums, or brainwash us into worshipping at their feet 24-7 until we starve to death?"

"Of course not," a deep, sarcastic voice answered. "You'd be of no use to us if you starved to death."

She'd heard that voice only once, six months earlier, but she'd have recognized it after as many decades: smooth and rich, it gave the impression of warmth while turning her veins to ice. Rive was on his feet in an instant, sword raised, aura bright and face livid as his eyes fixed on a point above Sophie's head. Slowly, her skin crawling and her mind screaming at her to run, Sophie rose from the stall where she'd been sitting and walked to Rive's side, Carnwennan clutched in her hand.

Steeling herself, she turned to face Abaddon. He sat on the pinnacle of the chair she had just left. It was the tallest in the room, opposite the altar, in the place where, earlier, there had been a statue of a saint. He glowed with his own diabolical light, stark and colourless as his eyes, picking out the metalwork on his clockwork arm and the hilt of the sword strapped to his back: a twining snake in black and silver. The shadows around him were black as the trails the daevas had left behind them in the sky.

Except, of course, they hadn't been daevas. They'd been nothing more than decoys. "How long have you been here?" Sophie asked.

"As long as you have. We arrived with our army, but waited to show ourselves until the angels left."

"We?" Rive asked.

Abaddon smiled, and all around the chapel, the statues and carvings grew and twisted into their true forms, forming a ring around Sophie and her friends. There were thirty of them in all. The last to change was a carved swan whose plumage morphed into a white gown, its face into a woman's, with glittering black eyes and a smile dark as blood. Abaddon reached out a hand to her, and the two of them alighted gracefully from their perches.

"Rive – " Esther whispered, but Abaddon cut her off.

"Theletos won't help you. He has an understanding with us."

"Not anymore," Rive said through gritted teeth.

"If you raise that sword to me," Abaddon told him, "you'll be cut to shreds in seconds."

"Try us," Sophie said, stepping forward with Carnwennan held high.

"I don't think so, Sophia. We have plans for you." He reached out and plucked the knife from her hand, then flicked it into oblivion. Angus raised his sword, but another daeva – the one with dark skin and tree roots encasing half of her face – disarmed him as easily as Abaddon had Sophie. She tossed his sword aside and lashed his hands with a spiked chain she pulled from the air.

"Shall I kill him?" she asked.

Abaddon cocked his head and then said, "No – not yet. He may still come in handy – if she refuses to cooperate." His unblinking eyes turned back to Rive. "Theletos," he said, "sheath your weapon." For a moment, Sophie thought that Rive would defy him. Then, with a shudder, he shoved the sword into the shadows where it disappeared, as if he really had sheathed it. "Thank you. Now, come."

Abaddon put a hand on the back of Sophie's neck, sending a shudder down her spine, and steered her toward the doorway. Her friends followed, flanked by the other daevas. The body of the church was dark now, only the faintest charcoal light showing in the ruined doorway. Lilith picked up a candelabra that had fallen, and it burst into sulphurous, blood-red flame. Its light sent chiaroscuros streaming along the stone walls and pillars, so that it seemed a host of demons leapt and flickered around them.

In their midst, though, two remained still: great, hulking shapes, twice as tall as a man and several times as wide. It was to these shapes that Abaddon led them. Lilith danced ahead, her candles gradually illuminating the massive forms. They were demons, identical, shaped like coiled snakes with scales in patterns of red and black. They had hoods like cobras and slitted yellow eyes, but here, Sophie saw a slight difference. While the pupils of one of the demons followed her movements, the other was still, as if waiting for the spark that would animate it.

And that, Sophie realized, was the point. She looked up at Abaddon. Though he had taken his hand from her neck, she still felt it there, ready to circle her throat if need be. A wave of dizziness sideswiped her, and she swayed on her feet. She shut her eyes, willed herself to be strong, and said, "You want me to bring that thing to life."

"Clever girl," Abaddon answered. "But it isn't a thing. It's Apep, the Egyptian deity of darkness and chaos."

"Then it seems there should be only one of them."

"Why, when one hundred would be so much more useful? Please copy the living one's soul, and put it into the other one."

"No," she said, too tired even to sound defiant.

"Very well," Abaddon replied, calm and steely. "Euryale, kill the boy."

A female daeva stepped forward, a long, cruel knife in her hands. She had the face and body of a beautiful woman, but hands made of brass, smaller versions of Abaddon's arm, and a mass of writhing snakes where her hair should have been.

"Don't do it, Sophie," Angus said. "I'm not worth it."

Sophie didn't answer him. Instead she stepped forward, circled the living version of Apep, trying to feel its spirit, but all she got was a vague sensation of dense darkness, trying to push her back. She tried to remember her aeon self, what it had felt like to hold Esther's soul in her hands, but she couldn't. Hard as she racked her brain, that part of her history remained hidden from her.

When she'd come around again to the front of the demon, she looked up at Abaddon.

"I can't do it," she said.

"You haven't yet tried," he answered.

"I *was* trying."

"You've done it before," he argued, his voice taking on a hint of irritation.

"But I can't remember that."

"Then it's lucky we have your other components to hand to help you."

"Pardon?"

The daevas holding Esther and Rive shoved them forward, so that they stood with Sophie. Esther's face was white, her eyes huge, and she clung to Rive's hand. He, in turn, looked furious.

"In some blasphemous way," Abaddon explained, impatience buried in his tone like a coiled spring, "the three of you equal a syzygy. But then, they do say that three is a magical number. Let's put you together and see if we can't resurrect a memory."

"Put us together how?" Rive asked.

"I imagine it would be as simple as touching each other."

Abaddon's eyes were dangerous. Sophie glanced at Angus, still held at knifepoint by the serpent-haired woman. Reluctantly, she offered her right hand to Rive. He took it, and despite everything, she felt peace settle over her, as it always did when she touched him. Rive was still holding Esther's right hand with his left, so Sophie took Esther's free one. She shut her eyes, tried to concentrate on Esther and Rive, tried to feel their energies. But it was impossible with the daevas staring at her.

Sophie closed her eyes, pictured the Well of Souls, as she'd seen it in dreams. She focused on the image, made herself remember the feel of the water and the surrounding grass. Then, to her astonishment, she felt something else: something beating against her cupped hands like a netted butterfly. She looked down, saw a blue brightness pulsing between her fingers, and she knew: this was a soul. She remembered the feeling of teasing it apart, like unspun wool, until she knew it intimately. And she remembered pulling out a tuft of the fibre of Creation, and making from it another soul to match the first.

Sophie's eyes flew open to find Abaddon's fixed on her. His look told her that there was no point in denying that she'd remembered. She let go of Esther's and Rive's hands, and turned to the living demon. Its eyes followed her pointedly as she approached. Fighting her revulsion, and trying not to hear her friends pleading with her to stop, she reached out a hand and laid it on the demon's head, between its eyes.

Her aura, which had been growing ever brighter, suddenly dimmed, but she didn't remove her hand. Instead she concentrated on Apep's energy, shoving past the turgid darkness until she could feel the contours of his innermost self. It was slimy, scarred, difficult to hold onto, but she had enough of an idea of it to try to make another.

Sophie took her hand from the serpent's head, and cupped it with her other one. She put all of herself into feeling the shape of Apep's soul again, and gradually, it began to materialize. She heard the daevas' gleeful muttering. Then, while it was still a viscous ooze, the soul suddenly lost its cohesion and trickled through her fingers. She opened her eyes to see the last of it slipping away, a fetid slime that clung to itself like mercury.

"What happened?" Abaddon demanded from behind her shoulder, making her jump. He no longer tried to hide the impatience in his voice.

"I couldn't make it hold together," Sophie answered.

"Try again."

"I don't think – "

"Try again!"

Taking a deep breath, Sophie conjured the monster's soul in her hands once again. Once again, it fell apart just as it began to take shape.

"You are purposely sabotaging it!" Abaddon roared.

"I'm not," Sophie said, and despite her fear, her voice was clear and steady, because she understood now that there was no way that Abaddon could make her do what he wanted. No one could. "I can't do it, and I'll never be able to do it. Do you see my aura?"

Abaddon frowned. "No."

"Exactly. It shows whenever I access some of my old aeon power. But I've never been able to control when that happens. For a while, I thought that it was random, but then I started to notice something. It only happens when a human is in danger."

"Aren't your human friends in danger now?"

"Yes. But it's not just that. It comes when a human is in danger, and I'm trying to protect them. Copying this thing's soul...well, it's not exactly going to help the human race, is it?"

Abaddon's eyes narrowed. "You're sure about this? You can't do it?"

"Yes, I'm sure," Sophie said, thinking that he sounded far too calm.

He nodded. "Very well. Then we have no further use for you." He pulled the sword from the sheath on his back.

CHAPTER 14

EDINBURGH CASTLE
8:15 A.M.

Lucas stood on the castle's highest rooftop, scanning the battling swarm below him. So far he had located only two fallen Watchers, and both were fighting for the daevas' side – or had been, before he killed them. He was gazing at the sky, considering where to look next when the white forms of the daevas, still hovering high above, paused abruptly in their movement. Then, as a body, they dove toward the ground.

Lucas gripped his sword, preparing to fight the one that was heading straight toward him. But as it drew closer, he realized that something was wrong. It didn't resolve into a solid form; in fact, it seemed to be dissolving. He leapt into the sky to meet it, but when it finally came level with him, there was hardly anything left of it. For a moment its white wispiness took on the shape of a sardonic, laughing face. Then it dispersed in a swirl of smoke.

The next moment, Suri and Michael caught up to him. "They aren't daevas!" he gasped.

"We know," Michael said, his face dour. "Let's go."

Lucas didn't need to ask where.

8:18 A.M.

Sophie was vaguely aware of someone screaming and crying, and the commotion as the daevas subdued her friends. She felt someone binding her hands, though she'd made no attempt at a struggle, but that, too, seemed distant. Only the blade of Abaddon's sword was real, black as the void, yet somehow shining. It was mesmerizing – or maybe it only seemed that way because she was so bitterly weary, her head so full of pain that had crashed over her without warning, when the second, failed soul ran through her fingers.

"You're certain you don't want to try again?" Abaddon asked, his unblinking gaze holding hers captive.

"There's no point."

"Pity," he said and raised the sword.

Sophie shut her eyes and waited for the bite of the blade, but though she heard the whistle as it fell, the thud as it connected with flesh, the pain didn't follow. She was still breathing. There was a moment when this – her own ragged breath – was all that she could hear. And then she was falling, pushed to the ground by a dead weight, and something hot and sticky was flowing over her arms, pooling around her. She'd felt this before: a heart's blood pouring itself out while she was helpless to stop it. And something more: the silky brush of a limb not made of flesh and bone. A limb made for flight. No – oh please no, not again –

She didn't know whether or not she spoke the words out loud. The moment when she opened her eyes seemed to last an eternity. But it couldn't last forever. She seemed to see him from many miles away, lying in her arms, his bright wings fading and draggled with the blood that poured from the wound in his neck, painting them a darker crimson, extinguishing the sparks of gold. Somewhere nearby a fight was raging – she saw the flash of swords and the sweep of brilliant wings – but those things, too were distant. The only things that were real to her were Lucas's dark, dimming eyes gazing up at her.

"Lucas," she said at last, choking on a sob, "what have you done?"

"What I was created to do," he whispered.

"You weren't made to die for me!" she cried.

"Yes, I think I was," he said, his eyes soft.

"No! You were made to be with me – to love me – "

"And I have loved you. It's been the meaning of my life. I'll love you as long as there is breath in my body. But now, you have to go. Run while you can. Save them all."

"I can't!" she wept. "I can't leave you. The soul – maybe there's enough left to – "

He smiled a little. "Send me back to Heaven? What good would that do? No – it's time for me to stop dragging you down. You can save them, Sophie." His voice was so faint now she could barely hear it. "Only you can."

"Lucas, please!" she said, clutching his hands, which were already cold.

"Kiss me, Sophie. Then let me go."

On her lips, the taste of salt – she didn't know whether it was blood, or tears, or both. But she kissed him as he'd asked. And for the moment that he kissed her back, she was in Heaven again, lying twined with him in the long blue grass, nothing between them but joy. The next moment, his lips slipped away from hers. His chest rose, and fell, and didn't rise again. And before Sophie could even begin to register this, his wings flared, and then exploded into particles of red-gold light, illuminating the ruined church like a glorious sunset.

The moment stretched and lingered. It must have, because a moment wasn't long enough for Sophie to take in the reactions of her friends, ranged around her, pinioned by the daevas. But she saw them all: Suri's face streaming with tears, Esther and Rive clinging to each other like lost children, Ailsa shocked and terrified, Angus's kind face full of despair. Michael, though, was looking right at her, his eyes pleading. And when she met them, he looked down.

Sophie followed his gaze to Lucas's sword, lying in front of her in a pool of his blood. It no longer ran with the colours of his aura, but it looked sharp enough. Calm descended on her, then. The pain in her head was gone, along with the fogged vision, the dizziness. She knew exactly what she had to do. She picked up the sword as Abaddon lunged toward her. With a skill she didn't know she had, she brought the sword up and parried his thrust. She felt a dull victory when she saw rage on his face instead of the preternatural calm. She raised the sword as he swung again, and again she blocked it, though the clash of the blades shuddered through her to the bone.

She was raising the sword again when Michael cried, "Sophie!"

It disintegrated into an agonized scream that came again and again, like the shriek of tearing metal. She didn't understand until she felt the sharp, cold pain beneath her shoulder blade, and saw the ice-blue tip of Carnwennan, bright against the dark blood that was running down her chest. She clawed at it in shock until she realized that it was the wrong way around, it's hilt at her back. It had driven straight through her. She turned to see Lilith, her dark lips curved cruelly upward, her eyes glittering and feral.

"Lilith, what have you done?" Abaddon roared.

Lilith's glee turned to petulance. "She was a bad dolly. She didn't do as she was told."

Sophie waited for Abaddon's answer. But the room was darkening around her, the red candles dimming, and his words, when they came, seemed to come to her through water – padded, indistinguishable. She looked up at her friends, wondering blearily why Ailsa was screaming, why Suri's face ran with blood and tears. She looked at Esther and Rive, who slumped now against their captors, apparently unconscious. But before she could make sense of these things, the church exploded again with light. For a moment it hovered, bright and blue as a summer dawn. And then there was nothing but darkness.

THE HOLLOWS

For a time, the darkness was all there was. She couldn't hear anything. She couldn't feel anything. Her corporeal body seemed to have dissolved, leaving her consciousness to drift, unbound, in the void.

It wasn't unpleasant. It wasn't anything, and she could quite happily have resigned herself to it, if it weren't for a flicker of memory, a tiny crimson flame blinking in and out on the periphery of her consciousness. She didn't know what it was, but she knew that it was important.

She drifted, and she thought. The thinking rolled in like waves on a shingle, spinning half-formed images like stones and then pulling them back as it retreated. She began to anticipate it – to wait for it. She pictured seizing it, imagining a hand, perhaps the one that had once been hers. She didn't know when imagining became reality; only that at some point, the hand was there, white and transparent, but hers.

The next time the memory flickered to life, she was ready. She reached out with her hand and caught it, closing her ghost fingers around the burning red. For a moment it beat against her hand. Then it stilled, and she remembered warm black eyes, a reticent smile, a galvanizing kiss. And once again, her world exploded.

*

When awareness returned to her, the drifting had stopped. The black had been replaced by a toneless grey that wisped around her like cloud. Her body was whole again, though it wasn't what it had been. The form was the same, but it was transparent, with no shade or colour to it, as if she were made of some pliant kind of glass.

Yet she remembered everything: not just Lucas, and not just her human life, but all the way back to the beginning, when she'd first opened her eyes in the Garden, curled into Theletos like twins in a womb. Theletos, whom she loved dearly, but never the way she was meant to. She remembered the restlessness that had made her push the boundaries of her existence. She remembered the Keeper's voice, coloured with disappointment, and she knew where she was, and why. It was called the Hollows, and it was a waiting room for human souls whose fate was in the balance. A last resort before damnation.

They were everywhere, all around her, wandering, lost. They looked like she did, clear and colourless, but where she was able to see them, they didn't seem able to see her. They didn't seem to see each other, either. Their expressions were blank as they walked in aimless circles, drifting through one another when they met, with no sign that they'd felt it.

Sophie had a good enough idea why she was here, but she didn't intend to stay. She searched the void for a portal, finding nothing but endless drifting souls. Finding nothing until she found him.

He was like the others, his black hair and eyes and golden skin leached to grey. He still had his wings, though those had greyed too, and they dragged behind him now like an unravelling shroud. She called out to him, certain that he would know her, that seeing her, he would remember. But he only brushed past her as if she weren't there.

"Lucas!" she cried, anguished as he retreated from her, but he didn't turn. "Lucas!" she called again and reached to catch him, to make him see her, but her hand passed through him, insubstantial as mist.

She watched him retreat, weeping with great, gasping sobs. When he disappeared, she began to scream. It was too much:

she'd lost him too many times, she couldn't bear another. Then the screams took form, as if something beyond herself controlled them, and she realized that she was screaming for the Keeper, shrieking into the Hollows' nothingness, demanding that it answer her. But there was no answer. She wondered if that was because there was no one left to give one.

No. There had to be. She dropped to her knees, spent and despairing. "Please," she whispered. "Keeper, if you ever loved me, please…"

There was still no answer. After a moment, though, something began to materialize out of the grey nothingness. Sophie stared, hardly daring to believe it even when its form was finally solid: a plain wooden door. Drawing a deep breath, she pushed it open.

THE DOMINION OF THE KEEPER

As soon as Sophie was past the threshold, the grey mist cleared, revealing a room so long that she couldn't see its ends, only a pastel smudge of distance. The walls were white, as was the marble floor. Sunlight streamed through high windows, illuminating the framed pictures that hung evenly spaced on the walls. Looking behind her, Sophie saw that the door that had brought her here was gone.

She stepped forward to look at one of the paintings and found that it wasn't a painting. It was a kind of screen, like her scrying-glass, showing a moving, living scene. A battle. At first she thought that it was the battle she'd just left on Earth, but the battlefield was ochre and yellow, the sky a dry, blazing blue, the background scored by the dark green slashes of cypress trees. The men who fought wore the short kilts and sandals of the Roman legions. As she stared at it, her head filled with the shriek of clashing weapons, the smell of blood and rage.

Sophie stumbled away, toward the next frame, where a vast

building burned at the edge of an azure sea. She smelled burning paper and despair. Alexandria, some long-forgotten memory told her. The picture beside it showed dark-haired labourers laying stone on a green hillside, an unfinished wall stretching away into the distance. The next showed a market scene in medieval Europe, and then Viking ships landing on a pebbled strand, and so on, she imagined, into eternity.

Sophie turned away from the pictures. "Keeper, where are you?" she called. "Why won't you speak to me?"

For a moment there was only empty silence; the next, she felt a presence. She turned, and found a man standing beside her. He wore a neat suit and a tag that said "Curator." His appearance was entirely ordinary, even dull, but looking at him, Sophie felt a profound sense of recognition that made her wonder how she could ever have forgotten him. Because once, this man – or more specifically, the spirit his form contained – had been a constant part of her. A beloved part.

What could I possibly say? he asked her, though he never opened his mouth. The words formed instead as a resonance within her.

"You could begin by explaining why I'm still alive, when I was meant to be obliterated on my eighteenth birthday."

Because your eighteenth birthday isn't over yet. This vestige of you will remain until it is.

"So what am I? A ghost?"

There has never been anything like what you are now. You are a wisp of spirit, held together by the force of your tremendous will.

"Terrific," Sophie muttered. "No rulebook." Then: "And Lucas? Why is he in limbo? And why doesn't he know me?"

He is in limbo for the same reason that those other souls are: his fate hangs in the balance.

"Why?" Sophie demanded. "Because he loved me?"

No. Because he died in exile, unpardoned.

"Unpardoned?" Sophie spat, sudden fury burning in her breast. "Who was there to pardon him? His fellow angels chose his fate, and you didn't even send an aeon to intervene. How dare you judge him, when you abandoned us all!"

There was a long pause before the answer came, and when it did, the abject despair in the voice made Sophie regret her anger. *I would have come for him, Sophia, if I could have. The distancing was not my choice. I was pushed away.*

"By whom?"

By you. By my aeons and daevas, my angels and demons, but most of all, by the humans whom you serve.

"I don't understand."

Don't you? Their faith is the key to your power, and that, in turn, is the source of mine.

"But how could your power be subject to us, when you created us all?"

Sophie felt a shivering within her, and understood it as wry laughter. *Because I am the Keeper of the Balance, and since the human race was born – or more to the point, since Heaven and the Deep took an interest in it – there has been no Balance for me to keep. Your beloved humans are so fragile, yet so powerful; capable of creating so much beauty, yet equal horror. Of late, they have made the latter their god, and now they are reaping that harvest.*

"So that's it? You're just going to let the daevas destroy them, without even trying to help?"

Before her eyes, the nondescript curator became a beautiful, auburn-haired woman in a deep green Renaissance gown, but the voice, when she spoke, was the same. *Sophia,* she said, with infinite patience and infinite sadness, *I did try to help. I tried, and I failed. Or more to the point, you failed.*

"I don't know what you mean," Sophie said, but a part of her was beginning to. Another memory was nudging at her, trying to materialize. She felt the Keeper sigh, and then it began to speak again, walking along the gallery as Sophie hurried to follow. With each word the memory took shape, along with the incipient despair:

Humans had not walked Earth long before they began to give their ear to the Deep more readily than they gave it to Heaven. Long before I sent the Flood, it was clear that they were being corrupted, and that because of the power of their faith, this corruption would skew the Balance.

I wanted to end it then. Do away with them and their Earth as well. After all, it had caused nothing but grief since you made it. But you pleaded for them. You begged me on your knees. And so I spared a few good ones, and sent the Flood for the rest, and hoped that that would be enough.

You know the story. The corruption grew back as fast as the human race. It spread like a blight across the Earth, and as it grew, so did the stature of the creatures of the Deep. Such horrors those humans spawned...the Inquisition, the Witch Trials, two brutal World Wars, to cap a million more mundane cruelties. And so, at the turning of the most terrible century since their inception, I prepared once again to end the human race. And once again, you intervened. There was so much goodness in them, you said; only it was so easy for the evil to overshadow it. It would be a sin, you said, to destroy the good for the sake of the bad.

The mist was peeling back from this last, hidden memory. Sophie remembered kneeling, weeping before this god who wore a million faces, who was her only and beloved parent. She remembered this gallery, its brightness blurred by tears. She remembered her anguish at the thought that the Keeper would destroy the creatures whose souls each held a spark of her own; whom she'd guarded as lovingly as any mother guards her child.

"'I'll grant you one more chance to save them,'" she said softly. "That's what you said to me. 'But if you mean to prove to me that this race is worthy of salvation, you must show me that though weak, breakable and corruptible, they can act with nobility and grace. You must become one of them and transcend yourself.' I agreed – and then you took my memories." The words came out with a rancour Sophie hadn't known she felt.

Of course I took your memories! The Keeper answered, the Renaissance lady fading into a black-clad nun. *For one thing, keeping them would have made you easy prey to the daevas. For another, it would have given you an unfair advantage in your test. But mostly, you could not be the frailest of beings and retain an aeon's consciousness. It would have driven you insane.*

"You think you spared me that? Those missing memories have tormented me all of my human life! And the Revenants – "

Were an unfortunate corollary. It couldn't be perfect, Sophia – I was manipulating the very fabric of Creation. What matters is that I never thought you would agree to it. You are Wisdom, after all, and the chances of success were so slim. But I had forgotten about Lucifer.

At the mention of his name, the pain of loss that Sophie was holding back broke through. She clenched her hands until her nails dug into her palms, to keep from shrieking at the Keeper, but still, her voice was full of torment when she demanded, "How could you forget him, when he had been your favourite?"

Once again, there was the shuddering sensation of a sigh. *It was a conscious forgetting. The memory was too painful.*

"Did you know that they meant to exile him?"

The affairs of angels are their own.

"Their own, and humans'."

We stray from the point.

"Fine. You sent me to Earth as an ignorant human, to try to save the rest."

My aim wasn't to thwart you, Sophia. Remember, I am the Keeper of the Balance. Letting you keep your memories would have been favouring Heaven, and I couldn't do that. But in recompense for what you were giving up, I allowed you a clue.

"The *Book of Sorrows*."

Yes. I brought Enoch to Heaven and let you dictate to him what you would.

"But Rive – Theletos – says that the prophecy in the book wasn't mine. It was yours, just like the one you gave to him before you sent him to Earth."

He is correct.

"And is he also correct that Esther is the Morningstar, not Lucas?"

As an aeon, you would not have had to ask me that.

"Well I'm not an aeon anymore, am I?"

There was a long pause. At last, the Keeper said, *The future is a cypher, Sophia – even now, and even to me. Certain things are set in stone, but the path that leads to them never is.*

"Then the fight isn't over yet?" she asked, hope kindling for the first time since she'd awakened in the Hollows. "There's still a chance to save Earth?"

Yes, they're still fighting. But Earth is beyond salvation.

"Are my friends still alive?" she demanded.

More or less.

"Then it's not beyond salvation. Let me see them."

The Keeper paused while the nun's habit changed into rough brown robes, the plain, female face into an elderly man's, with a long, white beard and a yarmulke on his thinning hair. *It will only upset you*, it said at last.

"Please!"

Very well... the Keeper said reluctantly.

The framed scenes went dark: all except the one nearest to them, which showed a play of murky colours. Sophie stepped toward it. Slowly, shapes shimmered up from the darkness, becoming a ring of daevas, dressed in carnival colours that blared against an austere ruin of St. Giles. She counted ten of them, ringed around her friends.

"Can I see them more closely?" she asked.

369

The Keeper didn't answer, but the focus zoomed in on them. Angus and Ailsa were huddled together, terrified. Suri cupped her wings around Rive and Esther, who lay together, unmoving. Esther's eyes were shadowed, her lips purple, while Rive had blood trickling from the corner of his mouth. Though she couldn't see enough to tell whether they breathed, Sophie guessed from Suri's protective stance that they were still alive. She hoped that they were still alive.

At last, she turned to the ones she'd been avoiding. Her body and Lucas's lay together, still and blood-soaked. But what broke her heart was Michael, who sat clutching them, one in each arm, his fire-gold wings dark and draggled with their blood, his face blank.

"Has Michael gone mad?" she asked.

Michael blames himself for your death and Lucifer's. As for mad, I really can't say.

"And Rive and Esther? Are they dead?"

Not yet.

"What's happened to them has happened because of what I did with their souls, hasn't it?"

They, too, are in limbo, the Keeper agreed.

Sophie's eyes snapped angrily to the rabbi's. "Esther is my fault, I accept that. But Rive – you sent him down there! How can you just abandon him?"

Like you, it was his choice to go. And like you, it's beyond me, now, to influence what happens to him.

"Then send the other aeons to Earth to help him."

I cannot send them to Earth.

"You did it for Rive."

Sophia, you aren't listening to me. It's not that I'm unwilling to let your brethren go to Earth and fight the daevas: it's that they physically can't.

"Why not?"

The corruption of humans, and the resulting fault in the

Balance, hasn't just given the daevas power; it has also leached power from Heaven. It's why the aeons haven't come to help you, and why they can't now.

Her heart beating with sudden trepidation, Sophie said, "Can I see them?"

I believe it will only upset you further.

"And what does that matter, now?"

Very well...

Once again, the scene in the frame faded to darkness, and a new scene began to form in the mist. But it didn't resolve into focus like the last one, only continued in drifting shades of grey.

"Is that the Hollows?"

Yes.

As she watched, a figure surfaced from the mist. His movements weren't like those of the wandering spirits she'd seen in her brief time in the Hollows. He drifted like a corpse in a river, at the mercy of the currents. Slowly he turned, revealing his face. It was blank, his eyes open but unseeing. And Sophie recognized him.

"That's Logos!" she cried.

Yes, the Keeper answered, its voice thrumming with sadness.

"What is he doing in limbo? And what's wrong with him?" When she looked back at the Keeper, it had become a small girl in an ancient Egyptian headdress.

It's the only place left where he can exist, the child told her. *The daevas' mounting power has sapped him until only this is left. Soon enough, I imagine, this scrap of spirit will be gone, too.*

"And the others?"

The same. All except you and Theletos.

Sophie felt like her knees were about to give way. "There must be a way to give them their strength back."

The only thing that could save them now is the faith of humans; but what little human faith in us remained has been lost

371

with the invasion of the daevas' army. They see Hell marching to destroy them, and nothing to challenge it but a few more monsters.

"Then we need to change that. Give them something to hope for."

How? the Keeper asked, and Sophie knew by its simple despair that the question wasn't rhetorical, that it really did hope she might have an alternative to offer.

She thought for a moment, and then she said, "What about the angels? Are they still functioning?"

To an extent. But they don't have the strength to leave Heaven, let alone get to Earth.

Sophie turned back to the frame and watched the aeons fade in and out on their long, slow drift to nowhere. She thought of the human souls that wandered with them through those mists, befuddled and alone, their own despair destroying them, like the humans still on Earth. Except that they weren't on Earth. They were in limbo, awaiting consignment to Heaven or Hell...

"What if we could give them the strength?" Sophie said, looking down at the child beside her.

How? the Keeper asked again.

"Angels mean Heaven to humans. If we could get them to Earth, then that would restore the humans' faith in Heaven, wouldn't it? And maybe that faith would be enough to restore the aeons?"

Perhaps...but it's a conundrum, since to have the strength to get to Earth, they need the faith of humans.

"There are hordes of humans in the Hollows."

Sinners awaiting final judgment. Few, if any of them have any faith left to speak of.

Sophie tried not to show how that smarted, given that Lucas was among them. "Don't you think that might change if they could see an angel? Wouldn't that make them believe in the power of Heaven? And it might just be enough to free the other angels."

It's an interesting idea, but I'm not sure they would recognize an angel as such. Angels look very different from the humans' myths.

Sophie smiled. "I can fix that."

How?

"Bring me an angel, and I'll show you."

Any one in particular? the Keeper asked flippantly. Clearly, it thought she was mad.

Sophie considered this, and then she said, "Arithiel. She looks like she belongs on top of a Christmas tree."

Very well, the Keeper said.

Sophie drew a deep breath, and meeting the Keeper's long, dark eyes, she said, "There's one other thing."

You want me to pardon Lucifer. Send him back to Heaven.

"Am I so obvious?" Sophie asked.

The Keeper laughed. *No, you are tenacious. It's been a great source of frustration to me, since the moment I made you. At any rate, I've been waiting for you to ask for that since you stepped through the door.*

"Well then? Will you?"

There was a long silence. At last, it said, *A fallen angel is a different thing entirely from a human in limbo. I will try, but I can't promise that it will work.*

"It will work. It has to."

Very well. But the humans come first.

The door materialized in front of them – a double door covered with golden panels, showing scenes from the Annunciation. Sophie recognized it from a trip to Florence several years back – it was called the Gates of Paradise, which was fitting for Arithiel, angel of the sun, who was as beautiful and golden as her Dominion.

In fact, Sophie had forgotten quite how beautiful she was

until the doors opened and she stood before them in all her glory. Her skin, her hair, her gown were all varying shades of gold. Even her eyes were a deep golden brown. A sun-like warmth radiated from her; when she smiled, it was blinding.

But she didn't smile now. Instead, she looked confusedly from Sophie's glasslike form to the Keeper, who had changed again, this time into a young man in a black leather biker's jacket and boots. However, the mundane figure didn't fool Arithiel any more than it had Sophie. She fell to her knees, mist-fine golden skirts billowing around her, and said, "My blessings, Keeper!" which surprised Sophie, since none of the angels, as far as she knew, had ever laid eyes on it.

But Arithiel was in no doubt. "To what do I owe the honour?" she asked.

It is Sophia who has requested your presence here. Rise, Arithiel, and enter.

Arithiel stepped into the gallery and the door disappeared behind her. "Greetings, Sophia," she said, and to her credit, there was no sign that she found Sophie's new form strange. Or maybe, Sophie, thought, in this universe gone mad, nothing was strange anymore.

"We need your help, Arithiel," Sophie said. "The battle for Earth is not going in our favour, and we need a way to win some human faith, quickly."

"I don't understand," Arithiel said.

A smile crept across Sophie's face. "Have you ever wanted to have wings?"

*

That is beautiful work, the Keeper said, looking up at Arithiel, who hovered above them now, her wide, golden wings shimmering in the sunlight from the windows. *I have no doubt that she will at least give the lost souls pause...but there is another problem. Even if they repent, and I pardon them, without the aeons, there is no one to transmute their souls. You know that they cannot exist in the Garden unless they are properly prepared, and if they don't reach the Garden, then their energy cannot help the aeons.*

"I was an aeon, once," Sophie said.

But not anymore, as you yourself pointed out.

"No – not entirely. But sometimes, under the right circumstances, the aeon part wakes up. Please let me try."

The Keeper didn't reply to that, but a few moments later, a doorway appeared in one of the hedges: a sliding door of iron bars, like the kind in a jail cell. Beyond it, Sophie saw the grey of the Hollows. The door slid back, and the first of the supplicants came through the doorway: an old woman, looking dazedly around her. When her eyes fell on Arithiel, though, her expression turned to one of wonder, and she fell to her knees, gazing up at the angel. She didn't even notice when the Keeper, now in the scrubs and sensible haircut of a hospital nurse, laid a hand on her shoulder.

At first, it seemed that nothing was happening. But then, the old woman's shoulder began to shimmer under the Keeper's hand. The light spread and brightened until the kneeling woman's frail form was subsumed in white fire. The next moment she was gone, reduced to ash so fine that it dispersed before it reached the marble floor. All that was left was a small, flickering light of a deep burnt-orange, hovering in the air beneath Arithiel.

That light called to Sophie, stirring a sensibility deep within her. She stepped forward and cupped her hands around it. It fluttered against her fingers like a minnow, dredging memories she thought she'd forgotten. Her hands began to glow, her transparent skin housing a crackling light the colour of a gas flame. It spread, filling her with a heady incandescence. The soul in her hands burned brighter in response. She opened her hands. The soul rose up, blazed for a moment, and then disappeared.

Sophie turned to the Keeper. "Did it work?"

For the first time since she'd come out of the Hollows, there was a smile in its voice. It worked.

"Then we'd better call the next one."

There's no need. Look.

Sophie turned. The doorway to the Hollows was crowded now with grey souls, all of them with their faces clocked to the golden angel. "Come," Arithiel said to them, and they poured in.

CHAPTER 15

EDINBURGH
14:37 P.M.

Normally, Suri would have been acutely aware of the passage of Earthly time. However, the absolute darkness of the sky had obliterated that sense. She could have been sitting for months among the broken stone and splintered wood of St. Giles. Only the stickiness of the blood on the floor told her that it really hadn't been long since their plans had turned to disaster.

She looked up and around at their captors. She knew their names and descriptions from books and rumours, and she had seen them once before, in Dahud's palace, but the reality of them was still shocking. Their brightness, their beauty, seemed impossible. Such evil beings shouldn't have claim to either one, and yet they were the epitome of both, ringed around herself and her friends, impassive as pillars.

She didn't know their names, aside from Abaddon and Lilith, who had left with the better part of their cohorts once they were certain that Sophie and Lucas were dead. And so Suri was surprised to see Abaddon now, striding up the aisle toward them with a purposefulness that was almost a hurry, Lilith trailing behind him, glowering, with a retinue of demons and Unseelie fae.

Suri wondered what could have brought them back. Then, as Abaddon whispered to one of their captors, she saw a flash of light beyond the great round window at the far end of the aisle. The daevas looked up at it, and then fell back to their whispered consultation with added energy. Suri was watched the windows now, and she saw Michael looking too: the first sign since Sophie had died that he saw anything at all. As they watched, another blaze of light flashed past the windows, then another. The coloured glass distorted their hues, but Suri recognized them despite it. Nothing but a Heavenly aura shone with quite that luminous clarity.

"Angels," Michael said dazedly as the sound of the fighting outside took on a different quality: a note of elation added to the grim clash of war.

"But how did they get here?" Suri asked.

"Sorcery?" Michael suggested, with a sick-looking smile.

"There's no one left in Heaven who knows sorcery."

"Except the Keeper."

"You think the Keeper would decide to help us *now?*"

"I think that anything is possible."

Suri didn't answer. She had a different theory, but the possibility that she was wrong was so painful that she didn't want to speak it.

"Come," Abaddon said to the daevas, who moved after him, while the demons that had flanked Lilith took their places.

"Where are you going?" Suri called after the retreating daevas.

They didn't answer. When they were gone, however, one of their new guards, some type of goblin, nudged the faerie next to him – a creature with the body of a lizard but the torso and head of a man. The goblin said, "Look. Them angels have wings, too."

His companion glared at him. Suri summoned her best

angelic charm and smiled at him. "Wings too? Who else has wings?"

"Angels," the goblin said, despite a whack from his friend. "I never seen angels with wings before today."

"You've seen other angels today?"

This time, when his companion punched him in the arm, he got the message. "Ah – no," he said. "Nothing like that."

"Oh, really? Then what are the lights falling from the sky?"

The goblin shrugged, and another, bigger one growled, "Shut up!"

But Suri had learned what she needed to know. The Keeper might have freed the angels to come to Earth, but if those angels now had wings, it wasn't the Keeper's doing, and she'd have bet her life that she knew who was responsible. She caught Michael's eye. When he smiled, she knew that his guess was the same. For the first time since the Witchery clock had struck midnight, she began to wonder if they might not have a chance, after all.

THE DOMINION OF THE KEEPER

Sophie watched in a large, gilt picture frame as the last of the angels – Quan Yin, her wings the softly melting colours of a summer dawn – glided out of her Dominion and into the sky over Edinburgh. The focus pulled back until Sophie could see them in the thousands, little blinks of coloured light streaming toward the darkened city. She tried not to think about the fact that Lucas wasn't with them and hadn't come to the door with the supplicating humans. He would come. He had to come.

"Is it working?" Sophie asked, shoving the dark thoughts aside.

It's too early to tell, the Keeper answered, now in the form of an ancient Chinese nobleman, with a silk tunic and cap. *But they're certainly giving the daevas' army a headache.*

The Keeper pointed to another frame, further along the wall. Sophie saw little Ambriel, framed by wings the colour of spring leaves, alight on George IV Bridge. Drawing her sword, she slew two Cyclops three times her size, then flitted into the air to avoid a third seeking retaliation. Moving to another frame, Sophie saw Arithiel and Dumah fighting back-to-back, cutting down trows as fast as they could. In every frame she looked at, angels were fighting and winning.

There's something else you should see. The Keeper led her to a small frame on the opposite side of the room. At first, Sophie couldn't see how it differed from the others. It showed an Edinburgh street, packed like the rest with desperately fighting creatures. *Look at the windows,* the Keeper said.

Sophie peered into the picture, and at last, she saw them: faces in the darkened windows. Human faces. The light from the angels' wings illuminated them, showing expressions ranging from terror to curiosity to outright wonder. Something in Sophie loosened, then, and a flicker of hope sprang to life.

"It's the angels, isn't it?" she said. "They're coming to watch the angels."

And not just watch.

The Keeper led her to another frame, where people, armed apparently with whatever they had to hand, were trickling out of a tenement. There weren't many, but there were enough to fan her spark of hope into a flame.

"Are they going to join the fight?"

It appears that way.

"Then it has to be helping! Please, let's check on the aeons… and Lucas."

Very well.

The Keeper had left the door to the Hollows where it was when the last of the now-exculpated souls had come through. They stood for a time, watching the empty, swirling greyness. Every once in a while Sophie thought that she saw a limb or a face or the tip of a wing begin to materialize out of it, but then they would fade away again: no more, perhaps, than wishful thinking.

They haven't wakened, said the Keeper, now wrapped in the voluminous robes of a Bedouin sheikh.

"Then I'll wake them," she said, stepping toward the doorway.

If you go back into the Hollows, I can't promise that the door to my Dominion will admit you a second time.

She gave the sheikh a sad smile. "It doesn't matter, does it? I have only a few hours left, anyway."

Sophia...

"I'll bring them to you, and you can reverse their staves, and send them to Earth. And then you can help Lucas." Without waiting for the Keeper to reply, Sophie stepped back into the mist.

THE HOLLOWS

For a time she stood still, peering wide-eyed into the mist for any sign of her brothers and sisters. But the swirling grey remained empty.

"Lucas!" she called, and then, "Logos! Zoe!" She called them all by name, but it produced no response.

The mist was so dense she could easily believe that they couldn't hear her. She thought of the humans who had so recently been trapped here, of the way that they had wandered, oblivious to all the others wandering with them. It could be the same with the aeons. She needed to give them something to gather around, to follow out of this place.

Sophie looked down at her transparent hands. Since she became human, she had never been able to force her aura to show, to pick up her aeon power by choice rather than by chance.

But she'd only ever tried it on Earth. Maybe here, it would be different.

She stared at her hands, trying to regain the feeling that had been in them when she'd transformed the pardoned humans' souls for their flight to the Garden. It had been different from the times on Earth when her aeon part came forth and her aura shone out from her. The aura had turned inward, filling her with a light that seemed to hum with energy. She remembered the first, faint tingle in her fingers, and the way that it had suddenly magnified, poured through her.

And then it was real, though brighter this time. Stronger. Her light turned the grey to blue, and a moment later, they came: not drifting, not shuffling, but running toward her as if she were an oasis in a desert they'd wandered to the brink of death.

The first to reach her were Logos and Zoe. They were still grey, but otherwise as she remembered them.

"Sophia!" Logos cried. "What are you doing here? What happened to you?"

"I died," she answered. "But never mind that. Have you seen Lucas – ah, Lucifer?"

"No. I didn't know that he was in limbo."

"Yes," she sighed, peering into the mist, willing him to emerge. "He died, too, and he's in here somewhere..." But the mist kept its secrets. Shaking her head, Sophie said, "Follow me," promising herself that she'd come back and look for Lucas once the aeons were safe.

"Where?" Logos asked.

"To the Dominion of the Keeper. And from there, I hope, to Earth, to fight the daevas."

"They've invaded?" Logos asked, at the same time Zoe said, "You've seen the Keeper?" in a hushed tone, her eyes wide with wonder.

"Yes and yes," Sophie answered. "The daevas haven't won yet, but they will if you don't stop them."

"And the Keeper can get us to Earth?" Zoe asked.

"I hope so," Sophie sighed. They'd arrived at the door to the Keeper's Dominion. "Are you ready?" she asked. The aeons murmured their affirmation. "Go on, then. I'll follow you."

Zoe and Logos exchanged a glance. Then, joining hands, they stepped through the doorway together. For a moment Sophie saw them clearly on the other side. The thin veneer of grey fell away from them like scales, and they were the brilliant, living aeons she remembered. Then they moved away, and Sophie knew that it had worked.

"Who's next?" she asked.

EDINBURGH
17:26 P.M.

Suri was deep in meditation when a sudden commotion roused her. She heard voices arguing nearby. Opening her eyes, she saw that it was the goblin and the lizard-centaur.

"He told us not to leave the prisoners under any circumstances," the lizard-centaur said.

"Aye, well, he never thought this would happen, did he?" the goblin retorted grimly.

What's happened? Suri wanted to scream, but she kept her mouth and eyes shut, feigning unconsciousness.

"We got to get out while we still can," the goblin said.

"He be right," said the bigger goblin. "They'll know their kin be here. When they come, we have no chance."

Who? Suri's mind screeched at her. *Who could possibly be coming that would make their guards consider betraying a master as cruel as Abaddon?*

"Then kill them," the first goblin said eagerly. "Two is dead already, two more good as. We can take two angels and two humans."

The centaur never had a chance to reply. Something burst

through one of the windows, showering them all with coloured glass, and alighted in their midst. The figure drew an emerald-green sword, and before Suri could process what she was seeing, the heads of their captors were rolling away into the shadows.

Suri was on her feet, her own sword drawn and blazing, when she realized who she was looking at. She flicked the sword away, and then fell to her knees, along with Michael, who cried, "Logos – you're here!"

"Yes," he said, reaching out a blue-black hand to pull Suri to her feet, "thanks to Sophia."

"Sophia is dead," Michael said coldly.

Logos and Zoe exchanged a look, and then Zoe gave Logos a slight nod. He said, "Her human body is dead, but her spirit hasn't yet dispersed. As such, she brought us out of the Hollows."

"The Hollows!" Suri exclaimed. "What were you doing in limbo?"

"Dying," Zoe said, her voice as soft as her brown eyes, "for lack of human faith."

"And Sophia redeemed you?" Michael asked, his narrowed eyes keen. "How?"

"She convinced the Keeper to pardon the humans in limbo –"

"Haaang on a minute," Suri said, holding up a hand. "Sophie is with the *Keeper?*"

"Where else would she be?"

"So she isn't really gone," Michael said softly.

"Not yet," Zoe said gently. "But she won't last much longer. Her power was already fading when we left…"

There was a moment of dense silence. Then Logos roused himself and said, "We can't forget our duty, which is to restore Theletos and his consort, and return them to the Garden."

"So you know about that," Michael said.

"Yes. Sophia filled us in."

"Do you know how to cure them?" Ailsa asked.

Zoe shook her head. "We don't even really know what's wrong with them. Our guess is that it's to do with their joined souls – that when Sophia died, she took part of them with her, and now, like hers, their existence is tenuous."

"Couldn't she just give it back?" Angus asked. "I mean, whatever she took from them?"

"Maybe," Zoe answered. "If we could get them to her."

"You're aeons," Michael said. "Can't you make a portal to the Keeper's dominion?"

Logos shook his head. "Only the Keeper can do that."

"Then why doesn't he?" Angus asked.

"By the laws of its nature, the Keeper cannot favour one side in this war."

"That's crap!" Ailsa said.

"It is," Zoe agreed. "But it's also the law."

"Then what do we do?"

"Keep fighting," Logos answered. "If we can gain enough ground, maybe we'll find a way to reach Sophia…" But he didn't sound particularly hopeful about this. "Right now, though, we need to get them out of here: Abaddon is on his way back."

"Where is there to go that they'd be safe?" Ailsa asked.

"I know a place," Logos said.

"Okay," Ailsa said, "but we have to bring Sophie and Lucas, too. We can't just leave them here for the daevas to…" She stopped as her voice wavered toward tears.

"Of course we won't leave them here," Logos said, and he picked up Sophie's body. Zoe lifted Esther, and then two more aeons appeared at their side to lift Lucas and Rive. "Come," Logos said.

"But won't someone see us?" Angus asked.

Logos smiled in reply, and abruptly, he disappeared before Angus's eyes. A moment later, he returned. "Don't look so horrified," Logos told him. "It's only a glamour."

"Right," Angus said, trying not to sound shaken, "of course."

Pressing close together and glamoured invisible, they made their way to the front door of the cathedral. Looking out, Suri was appalled at the carnage. The dead were everywhere, in places piled layers deep, yet the sight of other angels fighting with all they had gave her hope. Her hand ached to hold her sword, her heart to jump into the battle alongside them. But she remembered Logos' words: "We're all here, thanks to Sophia." If Sophie still existed in some form, somewhere, then their first duty was to help her. That meant finding a way to wake Esther and Rive, and get them back to the Garden before the day was over.

Logos led them up the High Street, toward the castle. The crowd thickened as they moved, as if the castle were the epicentre of the battle. "Are you sure this is a good idea?" Suri asked. "The fighting seems worse, here."

"Trust me," Logos said, starting up the sloped path toward the caste gate.

When they reached them, they found the great arched doors closed and locked. But Logos laid his hand over the latch, and the doors creaked open. They pushed through, and then Logos locked the doors again from the other side. Suri was surprised to find the castle grounds nearly empty. There were a few clumps of angels fighting winged demons and faeries, but apparently the castle was still secure against any who couldn't fly over the walls.

Logos strode ahead, and the others followed silently, past stone buildings silent and circumspect, their windows dark; through courtyards full of shadows thrown by the aeons' glowing swords. At last, Logos stopped by the door to one of the buildings. The sign by the door read "The Great Hall." He coaxed the locked door open as he had the castle gate and then stepped through the door.

As soon as Suri followed him, she knew why he had chosen this place. It was a long, vaulted room, late medieval, Suri guessed, by the heavy beams of the roof. At one end of the room was a vast stone fireplace. The walls were half panelled in dark wood, the rest painted a deep red, and bristling with every kind of medieval weapon she could think of. It had to be as safe a place as anywhere left in the city.

Logos laid Sophie on the carpet by the fireplace, pulling off his coat to cover her. Zoe laid Esther next to her, and the other aeons spread their coat and cloak respectively for Rive and Lucas.

"So what now?" Suri asked, gazing down at the four of them.

"Now, we go and fight." He gestured to the corridor from which they'd come. "I'd suggest that you and Michael stay here and guard Theletos and Esther. We will come to you if we learn anything."

"That's it?" Suri asked. "We just sit here, waiting?"

"If you like," Logos said, sighing, "you can pray."

THE DOMINION OF THE KEEPER

Sophie stood by the doorway to the Hollows, watching Lucas pace. She had long since given up trying to get his attention. She'd even tried to drag him through the door, but her hands passed through him as if he were made of smoke. She'd begged the Keeper then to try to bring him through, but one try had been enough to make it shake its head – now wearing the body and elaborate headdress of a Thai princess – and tell her it was impossible.

"How can anything be impossible for you?" Sophie had demanded.

Nobody can be saved who doesn't want to be.

"Why wouldn't he want to be?"

Perhaps he knows, deep down, that if I were to restore him, he would have to face the reality of losing you. Perhaps he's chosen oblivion as the kinder fate. Or perhaps there simply isn't enough of him there to save. I've never seen an angel land in the Hollows before – not even a fallen one.

"Why not? Where do they normally go when they die?"

They disperse into particles of energy, and are incorporated into the body of Creation.

"That's…cryptic."

Put simply, they don't leave anything visible behind.

"Then why is he still here?"

No doubt it's a symptom of the broken Balance, but as for why, or how, or where it will lead – well, that's beyond me now.

Part of Sophie wanted to argue, to beat her hands against the Keeper, to throw herself to the marble floor and rant and rage, but the rational part of her knew that it would be pointless. Hopeless. Forcing herself to turn away from Lucas, she said, "Have you thought of anything that will help get Esther and Rive to the Garden?"

The Keeper sighed and turned into a Dust Bowl era hobo. *Unless someone on Earth can open a portal to the Garden, then nothing will help them.*

"*You* could do it."

Sophia, you know that I can't.

"You mean that you won't," she said bitterly.

I know that you are suffering, the Keeper said sadly, *and I wish that I could change that. But I cannot interfere in this fight.*

Once again, Sophie had to bite back all of the angry words she wanted to say. They wouldn't help; the Keeper's will was absolute. And yet she couldn't accept the alternative, either, because the alternative was to give up, give in to the fate that had nearly overtaken her. She could already feel herself growing weaker. She didn't think that she'd be able to summon the blue fire again, even to save her friends.

She moved back to the picture frame that showed them. The aeons had joined them in the church, and now they were speaking in hushed tones. Sophie was only half-listening, her mind still running over and over the reasons why Lucas couldn't be brought out of limbo, when Ailsa asked, "Do you know how to cure them?" and Zoe answered, "We don't even really know what's wrong with them. Our guess is that it's to do with their joined souls – that when Sophia died, she took part of them with her, and now, like hers, their existence is tenuous."

She listened carefully to the rest of the conversation, until Logos said, "By the laws of its nature, the Keeper cannot favour one side in this war." The words rang in Sophie's head. The Keeper might not be able to favour on side, but maybe she could convince him to do her one last, little kindness.

"Keeper!" she called.

Yes, Sophia?

"Do you think you'd be able to send me back to Earth?"

You are only spirit now. I don't believe you could manifest on Earth.

"Could I manifest if I had a body?"

The Keeper was silent for a few long moments. *It is possible,* it said at last. *But the body you left is ruined. With a pierced heart, you'd only last moments.*

"I only need moments," Sophie said. "Just long enough to give Rive and Esther the missing part of their souls – the part I still have."

There is no guarantee that it will work. There's no guarantee that you'll even survive the journey.

"It doesn't matter. I'm going to die anyway. If there's even a chance that this could get them to the Garden, then I have to do it." She could see the uncertainty on the Keeper's lined face. "Please. *Please.* You won't be interfering – not really. All I need you to do is open a portal. I can do the rest – or if I can't, well then, so be it."

The Keeper wavered for another moment. Then it shut its eyes, raised its hands, and a stone doorway appeared in front of them. The sign beside it read "The Great Hall." As she watched, the door opened a crack.

"Thank you," Sophie said to the Keeper, and then she slipped through the doors.

EDINBURGH
21:41 P.M.

Sophie drifted down the long room to the huddled group at the far end, her body drawing her like a beacon. Still, it was strange to actually see it, pale and blood-stained and inert. Until that moment, she hadn't thought about how she would actually enter it, or whether it would even be possible.

No time for that. She let herself drift downward until she lay on her body.

For a few moments, she thought that it wasn't going to work. Then, like a wave pulling the sand from beneath her feet, her body reached and enveloped her spirit, and they were one. She felt the sudden, solid weight of flesh, the flow of blood. She felt it seeping from the wound in her chest, and she knew that she had only moments before her body would give out again. She gasped in a breath, and rolled over, looking around dizzily at her friends' horrified faces.

"What is this? What's happening?" Aisla cried, a hysterical edge to her voice as she backed away from Sophie.

"No time," Sophie gasped. She didn't know what was making her riven heart beat, but she knew that she didn't have the strength to move her body. "Bring them…to me…" She gestured to Esther and Rive.

"What are you going to do to them?" Ailsa wailed.

"Save them," Sophie whispered. "Bring them *now.*"

Suri and Michael scrambled to lift Rive and Esther, and lay them on either side of Sophie. She took a hand in each of hers, and Suri, understanding, joined their free hands to each other, so that they formed a circle. At first, nothing happened. But then Sophie's aura began to glow, and with it, Esther's and Rive's. Esther's lips turned from purple to pink, and the bruised grooves beneath her eyes disappeared. The trickle of blood from Rive's mouth faded as the colour came back into his face. And then their eyes fluttered open.

"Where are we?" Esther asked faintly.

"That was what I was going to ask," Rive said, sitting up gingerly. Sophie's hand slipped from his, limp and white. He blinked and then realized what he was seeing. His face blanched again.

"Oh my God, Sophie!" He touched the stain on her chest and looked wildly around at the others. "Why doesn't somebody help her? She's bleeding!"

"She's beyond help, Theletos," Suri said through her tears.

"I don't understand," Esther said, pushing up against Rive, who wrapped his arms around her. Both of them, Sophie saw through her hazed vision, still had a slight blue luminescence and the serene remoteness of Heavenly beings.

"She was dead," Michael said, his voice shaking. "The daevas killed her, back in the church. You both lost consciousness then, so you won't remember…we thought she was gone. She *was* gone, until a moment ago. I think…I think that she returned to give you your souls back…"

He stopped as Sophie choked on a mouthful of blood. Spitting it out, she turned her eyes to Michael. "Get them to the Garden," she whispered. "Promise."

"Sophie, I can't – "

But she reached out a trembling hand, laid it over his mouth. "You can," she said, and then her hand dropped, and her chest didn't rise again.

There was a moment of perfect stillness, all of them paralyzed by grief. And then Michael's face took on a look of stony determination, and he said, "No." He took hold of one of Sophie's hands, and one of Lucas's, gripping them so that it seemed he would crush them. His hands began to glow with his fiery light, and slowly, the light transferred to Sophie and Lucas.

"Michael," Suri said uneasily, "you aren't strong enough to bring them back."

"How do you know?" he gasped as light filled Sophie's and Lucas's veins, drawing a fiery lacework on their skins. "No angel has ever tried – "

He cut off with a muffled cry, and Suri leapt to his side. There was a flash, a push of energy that knocked her backward, and then the light in Michael's hands died. But it continued to spread across Sophie and Lucas's bodies, shining brighter by the moment. The wound in Sophie's chest closed over, then the one in Lucas's neck. As Michael's eyes glazed, Sophie's blinked open. She lifted a hand, held it above her. For a moment she stared at it, puzzled, and then she turned and saw Michael's grey face. With a cry, she sat up.

"Michael! What have you done?"

"Saved you," he whispered, with the ghost of a smile. "Lucifer too, I hope."

Sophie glanced at Lucas. His colour had come back, and his chest rose and fell with breath. The slash in his neck had become a ropey scar. Sophie's heart leapt at this, but then she remembered Michael. She knew what he had done. She had seen Suri do the same for him in Ardnasheen, in December, when he'd needed more energy to control the storm on their way to the sea cave. But Suri hadn't given her energy to the point of depletion.

Sophie reached for Michael's hand and squeezed it. "You've got to take some of it back," she said.

"Doesn't work that way," he murmured.

Sophie felt tears slipping down her cheeks. "This is mad! You can't kill yourself for me!"

"Apparently I can," he said, his voice barely more than a

whisper. "Haven't I told you all along that we can't afford to lose you?"

"It's Rive and Esther you need – not me."

He smiled faintly. "Yes, you. Now more than ever."

"Why, when I've messed everything up, done everything wrong – "

"Sophie," he interrupted, "you've been brave and true. You've only ever followed your heart, and I've tried to thwart you at every turn."

"Because you're sensible."

"No. Because I was jealous."

The words knocked the wind out of her. "You were…what?"

"You heard me."

"You can't mean that…"

He smiled again, and there was a rare glint of humour in his green eyes. "But I do mean it. Comes as a shock, I imagine, but it's true: I've always loved you, from the moment you set foot in Heaven. And I've tried – God knows I've tried – not to let it colour the way I treated you, or Lucifer. But it has." He paused, drew a laboured breath. "I should never have exiled him."

"Michael – "

"I shouldn't have. Not for loving you. It was wrong, Sophie, and this is the best I can do by way of making amends. Your bodies are healed. I hope it's enough…"

"Michael?" Sophie called. "Michael!"

But he was gone. His body remained for a moment, still and grey as ash. And then it collapsed into golden dust, so light that it dispersed even on the stagnant air of the hall.

Sophie looked up and around. Everyone was staring at the place where Michael had been, stunned into silence. Everyone but Lucas, who still lay on the floor, breathing but unconscious. She bent over him, took his face in her hands.

"Lucas," she said. There was no response. "Lucas!" she

said sharply, and when he didn't stir, she took his shoulders and shook them. "Lucas, wake up! Wake up!"

She was still shaking him when firm hands closed around her, and lifted her away from him. "Let me go!" she wailed. "He has to wake up! Michael healed him, he has to wake up, he has to!"

"Sophie," Rive said, setting her down and turning her to face him. "He will or he won't, but you can't force it."

"But Michael...what he did, it can't be for nothing!"

"It wasn't for nothing," Esther said softly. "He saved you."

"What for?" she wept. "If I'm human, I can't help you, and what else is my life worth, without Lucas?"

"How can you ask that?" Suri cried, on her feet now and shaking. It took Sophie a moment to realize that she was shaking with rage. "Michael just died for you! You'd damn well better make it worth something!"

Sophie stared at her, stunned. She'd never seen Suri angry before. "Suri – " Angus began, but Sophie interrupted.

"No. She's right." She took a deep breath and looked around. "What time is it?"

"I don't know," Rive answered, "but I'm guessing it's close to midnight."

"Then we'd better move," Suri said. "We have to find a fallen Watcher to help us."

"Let's go, then," Rive said.

"I think you and Esther had better stay – "

"No," Esther interrupted with quiet finality. "No more of that. We're in this together."

"What about Lucas?" Ailsa asked.

"I'll stay with him," Sophie said. "I'm not leaving him here if he might still..." She couldn't make herself say it. She couldn't stand to have another hope ripped to shreds.

Rive nodded and then turned and led the others toward the door. As he reached for the latch, though, the door swung inward.

Sophie was wondering how someone had managed to unlock it when she saw the light: a brilliant gold, glowing with the clarity of a Heavenly aura. Two figures were silhouetted against it. By the colour of the light, she knew that the larger one was Sam. Yet it was the smaller one who held the sword, driving him with its tip to his back. And then Esther cried, "Cliona!"

EDINBURGH CASTLE
23:17 P.M.

Cliona? Sophie ran to the doorway in disbelief, but it was true: a smug-looking Cliona held Sam in front of them with his own sword. He grinned at them superciliously from behind a fall of pale hair. "So, we meet again," he said.

"What are you doing here?" Sophie demanded.

Sam glanced over his shoulder at his sword. "I'd have thought it would be obvious; I'm not exactly here by choice."

"What's the matter?" Cliona asked. "You said you wanted a fallen Watcher, and I brought you one. I'm guessing you still need him, since Esther and Rive are still here."

"Yes," Esther said, "but he's not exactly the most trustworthy of fallen angels."

Cliona shrugged. "Hence the sword."

"How did you get that off him, anyway?" Suri asked.

Cliona smiled. "Let's just say he has a weakness for the ladies. I distracted him, took the sword when he was…ah… otherwise engaged, and here we are."

"That's all well and good," Rive said, "but how will we get him to open a portal?"

"You can ask me, you know," Sam said. "I'm standing right here."

Rive gave him a cold look. "Well then? Will you open a door to the Garden for Esther and me?"

Sam gave them a shrewd look. "Maybe. What's in it for me?"

"How about not getting skewered on your own sword?" Cliona asked, jabbing him with it.

"That would certainly be a perk," he answered. "But I don't think you really mean to kill me. Even if you have it in you, you don't have time to find another Watcher."

"Would you consider it a 'perk' not to be subsumed by Hell in half an hour?" Suri demanded.

Sam shrugged. "I don't know. I think the daevas and I might reach a nice understanding."

But Sophie saw something beneath the irony on his face. Uncertainty. "I don't think you believe that," she said.

"How would you know what I believe?" Sam growled.

"Because I know you," she retorted. "You like things to be interesting, and interesting to you is creating havoc – particularly among humans. Pander to the daevas all you want, but deep down you know that if they win this fight, humans will be off-limits to you. In fact, I can't really see what use they'd have for a traitorous fallen angel."

"And remember, I've got your sword," Cliona added, prodding him again with the tip.

"Not anymore," he said, whirling and plucking the sword from Cliona's hands. He slashed it through the air inches from her face, and she scuttled back toward the others. "Did you honestly think you'd got the better of me? I let you take this because I wanted you to bring me here." He turned to Sophie, the laconic humour gone and his eyes hard. "I wanted to hear you beg."

"What for?" Sophie asked.

"For salvation." His smile was gleeful and too wide.

"Fine. I'm begging," Sophie said.

"On your knees."

Glaring her hatred at him, Sophie dropped to her knees.

"Please, Azazel. I'm begging you to open a door to the Garden for Rive and Esther."

Sam smirked. "What will you do in return?"

Hating him even more, she said, "Anything."

"*All right* then. Kiss me."

"Azazel, you are such an ass!" Suri snapped.

"Maybe. But I hold the cards here. So?" he asked Sophie, with a taunting smile.

Taking a deep breath, she stood up and stepped toward him, fighting her revulsion. He leaned down, until his face was inches from hers. She shut her eyes and waited – and nothing happened. She opened them again, in time to see Sam smirk as he stepped away.

"Well?" she demanded.

"Well nothing. I just wanted to see if you'd do it."

"Open the door, Sam!" Sophie snapped.

"Very well. To begin with, I need the blood of a virgin." His eyes scanned them all, settling on Esther. "You look the likeliest bet."

Esther flushed scarlet, and Rive leapt forward, twisting Sam's collar in his fist. "Leave her alone!" he growled, his eyes dark with fury. "You can have mine." He shoved Sam away and pushed his sleeve back, offering one black-latticed arm.

"Touching," Sam smirked, "particularly the fact that you qualify. Honestly, what have you been doing all of these millennia if you haven't been – "

"Enough!" The roar came from the doorway like a blast of winter wind, and for a moment everyone froze, staring at Abaddon, silhouetted against the doorway's murky light, a sword in his clockwork arm. Then Rive and Suri drew their swords in response, backing up to each other by instinct, putting themselves between their friends and the door. But the daevas were everywhere, swarming out of the shadows, surrounding them in seconds.

"What – ?" Cliona cried.

"As your friend said, I'm not the most trustworthy of fallen angels." Sam smirked at her. But it died when he saw Abaddon bearing down on him, his face white and furious. Sophie could see now that the sword was a part of his arm, and she shuddered.

"Indeed!" Abaddon said. "I told you to open a portal to the Deep and send the consorts through. Instead I find you here toying with them!"

"I was only having a little fun – " Sam began.

"We have no time for games! Now do what I sent you to do!"

"All right," Sam sighed, "but I really do need the blood of a virgin. A human virgin," he added, with a pointed look at Rive, who glared back at him with palpable hatred.

Faster than her friends could react, Abaddon reached out, grabbed Esther's arm and jerked the blade of his sword across her inner wrist. Esther gasped, staring down in horror as the gash filled with blood. Rive lunged for Abaddon, but four pairs of daeva arms shot out to restrain him. Abaddon never even looked up from the blood on Esther's arm.

"Now what?" he asked with cold calm.

"Now," Sam said, finally serious, "you let the blood make a pool on the floor."

Abaddon turned Esther's arm so that the welling blood dripped onto the flagstones, as she wept quietly. Sam watched as the dark pool grew until it was several inches in diameter. "That's enough," he said, and Abaddon closed his hand around her wounded wrist. When he let go, it had healed, smooth and scarless. Esther retreated to Rive's arms, where she stood weeping and shuddering.

"And now?" Abaddon asked.

"All of you, make a circle around us." The daevas shuffled into position, restraining the prisoners' arms. Sam knelt beside the pool of blood, and began chanting over it, in a language both familiar and foreign to Sophie.

"Is that what you call speaking in tongues?" she asked.

"No," Suri answered. "That's the language of angels." Then the daeva holding her shook her hard, and she fell silent again, watching Sam in despair.

A point of white light appeared in the centre of the pool of blood. As Sam continued to chant, the point grew larger, until it enveloped the dark liquid. Sam stood, spoke one more word in a commanding tone, and then drove his sword into its centre. A blaze of unearthly light shot up from the planted sword. As Sophie watched, it swam and twisted, gradually changing into an arched doorway, through which she could see a city made of dark stone, its buildings connected by a tangle of elevated walkways.

"What is that place?" Esther asked tremulously.

"That's Pandæmonium," Rive answered, wrapping his arms more securely around her. "The daevas' city – capitol of the Deep."

"And your new home," Abaddon added, his voice almost bland in its assurance, "for eternity. Say good bye to your friends. It's time to go."

Esther uttered a gut-wrenching sob and turned her face to Rive's chest. "It's all right," he told her, "it's going to be all right. We'll be together." She looked up at him, and he touched his lips to hers.

"Oh, for the love of God!" Sam said. "Do you want to make me vomit all over my lovely doorway?"

"Indeed," Abaddon said. "It's time." Esther and Rive broke apart, though their hands remained laced together. They turned and faced the doorway, then hesitated. "Go through that doorway," Abaddon said, beginning to sound impatient, "or I will kill your friends, one by one, until you do."

Sophie saw Esther take a deep breath. She braced herself

for the wrenching pain she'd felt the last time Rive went into the Deep, and for whatever would come after the daevas' triumph. She looked down at Lucas's still, beautiful face, and she needed to hold him, even if he couldn't comfort her, even if he'd never know it. She pulled free of the daeva who was holding her, and he let her go, entranced now by the scene in the portal. She laid her head on Lucas's chest, breathing to the rhythm of his heart as Rive and Esther stepped into the doorway, and it blinked out of existence.

The daevas erupted into cheers. Sophie shut her eyes, curled her fingers in Lucas's hair, and tried to think of nothing. After a few moments, though, she realized that she could feel something: a shivering of the floor beneath her free hand. A few more moments and she could hear it, too: a roar similar to the one that had sounded when the cathedral floor split open to release the army of the Deep.

But this was louder, more visceral than that had been. Her teeth rattled, and plaster began to fall from the ceiling, weapons clattering down from their mounts on the walls. The windows, wrenched out of alignment, rained shattered glass down on them. And beneath it all was a keening that seemed to be made of thousands of voices, from the deep and guttural all the way up to the shrillest screech. This, Sophie thought, is how the world ends.

And then she heard something else: the daevas, no longer cheering, but screaming. She opened her eyes to see them running every which way, screeching and clawing at themselves as if in agony. In the chaotic light of their drawn swords Sophie found her remaining friends. They looked as stunned and befuddled as she felt, but they didn't appear to be in pain. She began to understand.

There was no time now to think about it, though: the building was coming down around them, masonry and roof slates adding now to the raining plaster. She gestured to the others, and they gathered around Lucas, dodging the flailing daevas as best they could. "We have to get out of here!" she cried.

Angus reached down, dragging Lucas over his shoulder. He staggered, and Sophie knew that he could never run with him. Then, as she looked around for an option, Sam emerged from the shadows and took Lucas from Angus, holding him as if he weighed nothing. Sophie wanted to scream, to snatch him away, to do anything but let Sam touch him. But there was no time.

Holding onto each other, they fled the great hall, Sam and Lucas bringing up the rear. They reached the courtyard a moment before the building collapsed, and then they stopped short. The cobbled yard in front of them had cracked down the middle, leaving a dark, gaping fissure in the ground like the one that had opened in the cathedral. This time, though, it was taking Hell back, sucking in demons and Unseelie fae and every other manner of being who had fought on the side of the Deep, as if it were a black hole.

They screamed as they went – the source of the keening – and scrabbled for purchase on anything they could find, but the black hole pulled them relentlessly onward until it swallowed them. The same thing seemed to be happening on the streets below. Given the volume of the screeching, it must be happening all over the city. And as the creatures of Hell disappeared into the ground, the sky above began to clear, star-studded cobalt eclipsing the black that the daevas had brought with them.

"What the hell is happening now?" Ailsa cried.

"This, sweet Ailsa, is Hell not happening," Sam said, dropping Lucas unceremoniously on the ground.

"What?" Cliona asked.

Sophie was gazing at Sam in disbelief. "That portal you opened – it didn't go to the Deep at all, did it?"

"Keep your voice down!" he said. "You'll ruin my credibility."

"Where did it go, then?" Ailsa asked.

"The Garden," Suri answered, her voice full of wonder. "Esther and Rive made it! They made it!" And she began to cheer, a cheer that was taken up by everyone around them who had fought on their side. It spread and spread until it drowned out the screaming of Hell's creatures.

Sophie turned away from the rejoicing and knelt beside Lucas. Esther and Rive's ascension hadn't revived him; it hadn't changed him at all. And then, as she leaned over him, the world lurched around her. For a moment she thought that it was some further cataclysm, but then she saw that the others hadn't noticed it. They were still watching the sky, wild with joy as the angels turned and wheeled against the stars.

Understanding hit as the pain drove into her skull. Sophie gasped, holding her head as the world spun and wheeled around her and blood began to stream from her nose. Suri was the first to notice, her smile turning to dismay at the sight of the blood. She flung herself at Sophie, catching her before she collapsed beside Lucas. And then the others were there too, a whirling ring of horrified faces hovering above her. Their conversation came to her in disjointed segments:

"Happening to her…thought she was cured…Lucas…Rive leaving…" and then, suddenly, Suri's voice, clear as a bell. "We've been fools," she said bitterly. "Michael healed her body, but she's still lacking a soul of her own. It must be midnight. She's dying, just like the book said she would."

"There must be something you can do?" Ailsa pleaded.

"If there were, don't you think that I'd be doing it?" Suri snapped. "I can't make her a soul, and that's the only thing that will save her!"

Can't make her a soul. The words spun in Sophie's mind, prodding her with a memory: a gift. Blue glass, a symbol pressed into wax. She couldn't speak for the blood filling her throat, but she forced her fingers to move, plucking at the flap of her messenger bag lying beside her.

"Sophie?" Ailsa said. "What is it?"

Angus said, "I know what she wants." He took the bag from her, opened it, and removed the blue glass bottle.

"What is that?" Cliona asked dubiously.

"A soul," Angus said, his voice strange and tight, "if you believe the witch-doctor I bought it from."

"That's absurd!"

"And the rest of this isn't?"

"Fine. How does it work?"

"I don't know," he admitted.

"Oh, for God's sake!" Suri cried, and taking the bottle from Angus's hand, she bit through the wax seal and then pulled out the cork. A wisp of iridescence curled up from the top.

Suri lifted Sophie's head, causing the pain to stab through it fiercer than ever. It obliterated everything – or almost everything. Sophie felt the cool glass touch her lips. She breathed in, and the coolness spread. It was slow at first, but as she continued to breathe, it moved faster, unfurling through her body, erasing the pain as it went. Gradually, her vision steadied and the bleeding stopped. She moved her fingers, and they felt whole again, strong, but also subtly different. Weightier.

"Sophie?" Suri asked anxiously. "Is it working?"

"It's working," Sophie said, and pushed herself to sitting. She was still weak, and not entirely convinced that another wave of vertigo wouldn't knock her flat. But she reached out her hand and said, "Let me have the bottle."

"I'm not sure it's finished," Suri said.

"That's what I'm hoping." She took the bottle from Suri and then turned to Lucas. She held it to his lips, as Suri had done for her. Sophie could see the wisps of shimmering mist moving into him, but though she waited and watched for any sign that he was waking, his eyes remained stubbornly shut, his body inert.

"Sophie," Angus said gently. Sophie ignored him, clutching the bottle, willing Lucas to move. "Sophie, it's gone."

For a moment Sophie didn't acknowledge him. Then she sat back, the bottle slipping through her fingers to shatter on the cobbles, just another piece of discarded glass.

"Oh, Sophie," Ailsa said, and Sophie didn't realize that she was crying until Ailsa put her arms around her. Then she let go, allowed the sobs to wrack her battered body.

"I don't want it!" she cried. "I don't want a life, if he can't be in it."

Nobody said anything. There was nothing to say.

Sophie pushed away from Ailsa, wiping blood and tears from her face. "No," she said with resolution.

"No what, honey?" Suri asked.

"No, I don't accept this. Not now. Not after everything we've been through. Not when we've won." She looked up at the starry sky, still flickering with rejoicing angels. "Keeper!" she shouted. And then she screamed, calling on the Keeper over and over again, pushing off her friends' hands when they tried to stop her, to sooth her.

And then, abruptly, their hands fell away, as a doorway materialized behind them, full of light. It was bright and pure, seemingly made up of every colour and none of them. As if it were a beacon, the courtyard flooded with angels. In moments it was filled, but the angels kept coming, alighting on rooftops and battlements, filling every vacant space as far as Sophie could see. And despite her fury, despite her grief, she had never seen anything so beautiful. She clutched Lucas's hand, though he couldn't clutch back.

Deep within the door's lustrous nimbus, Sophie could make out the Keeper's current form, that of a small child, though boy or girl, she couldn't tell. *You called me,* it said to her. *Why?*

"I wanted you to bring Lucas back." She stared unflinchingly into the Keeper's brightness. She knew that it was an outrageous request. She didn't care.

The Keeper studied Lucas for a few moments. Then it said, *I cannot give you what you want.*

"Of course you can! You're the Keeper, in charge of all Creation!"

That isn't what I meant. Yes, I could restore Lucifer's angelic form. I could return him to Heaven. But you are human now. He would be just as lost to you.

The fight went out of Sophie then. She bent her head and began, quietly, to cry.

Sophia – will you give up so easily?

She looked up at the Keeper, hollow with despair. "What else can I do? I'm human now. I'm powerless."

Humans, powerless? The Keeper repeated. *When they brought the Balance of Creation to its knees?*

"That isn't the kind of power I need."

And it isn't the only kind of power you possess. Do you remember what you said to me, long ago, about humans? It would be wrong to destroy the good in them, for the sake of the bad. What made you see that good, Sophia, when I couldn't? What made you willing to sacrifice yourself to save them?

Sophie looked up at her friends, watching her with anxious misery. She looked out at the scores of kneeling angels, and realized, for the first time, that there were scores of humans kneeling with them. And she knew the answer, as simple as it was undeniable. "It was because I loved them."

And you were right to. What's best in humans, what makes them divine, is their capacity to love. That was your gift to them. You gave it to all of them in the tears you shed for them. You gave them their souls, and I think you can do it one more time.

"I don't understand," Sophie said.

"My soul and his soul were but one soul in two bodies." One of your better prophets wrote that, and is it not the meaning of love?

"I suppose it is…" Sophie looked down at Lucas's face,

alight with his aura, even now. She looked at his red and gold wings, the bits of his sigil that showed through his tattered shirt, the useless staves around his wrists – all the things that had marked him as angelic. But she didn't care about them. She never had, in the thousands of years that they'd loved each other. The only thing that mattered was his hand in hers. So, taking both of them, she leaned down and kissed him. When her lips touched his, all of those years seemed to spin through her mind at once, in a blinding stream. For a moment she felt shaken loose, as if she were barely clinging to the earth. And then his arms came around her, pulling her back, anchoring her.

"Sophie," Lucas murmured into her neck. "I thought you died."

Sophie choked on a sob, but she smiled. "It's a long story."

"I feel different," he said. Before Sophie could reply, she felt a tingling in her hands, which rested now near the roots of his wings. As she watched, the wings began to disintegrate, scraps detaching and blowing away like dry leaves, until they were gone, and his sigil with them. His back was smooth and blank. He sat up, and the bands of his staves opened and clattered to the pavement.

"Am I human, now?" he asked, looking at his hand.

"I don't know," Sophie said. "Try to do something angelic."

Lucas picked up one of the metal cuffs, and glared at it as he did when he was trying to shift something's form. But no aura lit around him, and the cuff remained a battered piece of metal. After a moment, he dropped it. His face was difficult to read.

"The Keeper could probably still make you an angel again," she said, the words like glass in her throat, "if that's what you want – "

He looked at her incredulously. "Sophie, all I ever wanted was a life with you."

"So this is all right?" she asked.

"This is perfect," he smiled and he kissed her again.

"And it couldn't be more revolting," Sam muttered.

"If you don't like it, you can probably still find a hole in the ground to jump into," Suri retorted.

Sam grinned at her. "And miss spending eternity tormenting you?"

"Are Esther and Theletos all right?" Sophie asked the Keeper.

Very much so.

"And the other aeons?"

They are back in their rightful place, as are the daevas. As all of us must be. The Keeper turned to the angels and said, *Come.*

"They're leaving?" Sophie asked, stricken.

Earth is the domain of humans now, as it was always meant to be.

The Keeper hadn't really answered her question, but Sophie understood. She turned to Suri. They looked at each other for a long moment, and then they wrapped their arms around each other.

"I don't know what I'll do without you," Sophie said, her eyes wet again.

"Oh, please," Suri said. "You'll have *him*," she patted Lucas on the shoulder, "while I've got, what? An endless parade of dead people, and Sam to brighten things up?"

"Who said I was going back to Heaven?" Sam demanded.

"Well you can't stay here, and like Hell would take you, now you've helped out the good guys?" Sam scowled, but Suri took his arm, grinning. "You can hang with me in the cemetery. It'll be fun."

Despite herself, Sophie had to laugh at the look on Sam's face while wiping tears at the same time.

"Take care of her," Suri said to Lucas. "I'll be watching you."

"You know you don't need to say it," Lucas told her, and then they were hugging, too.

It's time, the Keeper said, and there was a rustling as thousands of angels shook out their wings and prepared to take to the sky. *Good-bye, Sophia. May we meet again – but not for a long, long time.*

The Keeper reached out a hand, and Sophie stretched hers to meet it. For a moment, their fingers touched. Then the Keeper dispersed in a cloud of sparks, and the angels took flight, lifting into the air like bright birds, circling up and up until they were no more than specks of coloured light. In a moment those were gone, too, leaving the sky empty, except for a single, bright star hovering on the golden dawn horizon.

Sophie moved to the battlements to gaze at it. She felt her friends follow her, felt Lucas's hand, warm and alive, on her shoulder. They watched in silence as the sky brightened and the star faded and the people who had come to kneel before the Keeper wandered dazedly away. Then the sun crested the buildings of Princes Street, spreading buttery light across the city. Everywhere its rays fell, the signs of the battle and the six past, strange months melted away. Modern cars lined the streets again, gas lamps changed back to electric, broken stone repaired itself, even the rubble of the castle's great hall pulled back together until it was whole. The hum of a living, modern city returned, as if someone had flicked a switch.

"So," Angus said at last, "what happens now?"

"I don't know," Lucas answered. "What do normal people do on an average morning?"

"Curse the alarm clock?" Ailsa suggested. "Pour coffee down their throats until they can function?"

"Coffee sounds like a great idea, actually," Cliona said.

"I wonder if Brewed Awakening is back?" Angus asked.

"Only one way to find out," Ailsa answered. "Coming?" she

asked Sophie and Lucas with a quirk of a smile. "Or would you rather find somewhere to make out?"

"Coffee first," Lucas said. He slipped an arm around Sophie's waist, and she smiled up at him. And then they set off into the brightening morning.

ACKNOWLEDGEMENTS

There are many thanks due here, especially having moved continent half way through the writing! First of all my Scottish writing group, Carol Christie and Clare Whittaker, who have been with me on this trilogy, encouraging and criticizing, from the beginning. Colin, as always, for his willingness to help me through the times when I want to throw the laptop out the window and stick my head in the sofa cushions. My new and wonderful American wine…I mean book group, who kindly double as critics when needed: Shawna Brantner (who should have been an editor!), Shasta Bell and Lorraine Robinson. My Snowbooks editors, Emma Barnes and Anna Torborg, for being here every step of the way. And last but not least, every one of you readers who's loved this story as much as I have – you are the reason I do it!